KING OF THE
MOUNTAIN

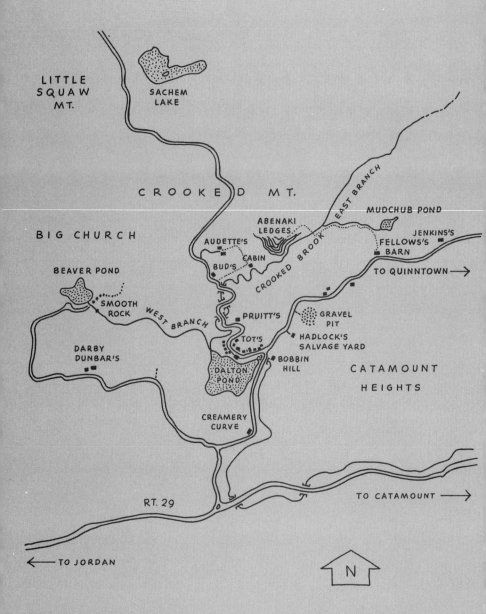

LITTLE
SQUAW
MT.

SACHEM
LAKE

C R O O K E D   M T.

BIG CHURCH

ABENAKI
LEDGES

MUDCHUB POND

JENKINS'S

AUDETTE'S

FELLOWS'S
BARN

CABIN

EAST BRANCH

BUD'S

CROOKED BROOK

TO QUINNTOWN →

BEAVER POND

SMOOTH
ROCK

WEST BRANCH

PRUITT'S

GRAVEL
PIT

DARBY
DUNBAR'S

TOT'S

HADLOCK'S
SALVAGE YARD

DALTON
POND

BOBBIN
HILL

CATAMOUNT

HEIGHTS

CREAMERY
CURVE

RT. 29

TO CATAMOUNT →

← TO JORDAN

N

DALTON   POND,   VERMONT

KING OF THE MOUNTAIN

A Novel

DON METZ

1817

HARPER & ROW, PUBLISHERS, New York

Grand Rapids, Philadelphia, St. Louis, San Francisco

London, Singapore, Sydney, Tokyo, Toronto

FIRST EDITION

Designed by Alma Orenstein

Library of Congress Cataloging-in-Publication Data

Metz, Don.
    King of the mountain / Don Metz
        p. cm
    ISBN 0-06-016377-1
    I. Title
    PS3563.E849P6   1990   89-46108
    813'.54—dc20

90 91 92 93 94 CC/HC 10 9 8 7 6 5 4 3 2 1

To my mother and father

I would like to acknowledge my gratitude to the New Hampshire State Council on the Arts, and to my friends at the Vermont College Writing Program, and to Buz Wyeth and Sallie Gouverneur for their support and encouragement.

The falsehood that exalts we cherish more
Than meaner truths that are a thousand strong.

—PUSHKIN

KING OF THE
MOUNTAIN

PROLOGUE

THERE ARE other places like it; our ancestors divined them.
They applied the ancient science of geomancy, surveyed the
lay lines, harmonies, and confluence of energies, the water
sources, mountains, trees—stone, stars, and moon—the
points of the compass, the elements of earth and sun and fire.
They found a power vested in the carefully observed phenom-
ena of nature, and certain sites were marked as sacred, re-
vered for their exceptional concentrations of spiritual presence.

These places exist all over the world. Most are crowded
with pilgrims and priests, magnificent temples, instruments of
astronomy, and the tombs of kings and holy men. Others may
yet be discovered, hidden away beyond the few remaining
frontiers undisturbed by humankind.

And some have been abandoned. One such place, deep
in the north Vermont woods above the village of Dalton Pond,
is the palisade on Crooked Mountain, the Abenaki Ledges.

Approach it on a summer night: like a great white fortress wall, it rises straight and taut and smooth above the dark
treetops, a moonlit beacon to the lakes and mountain forests
to the south, earthbound companion to the bright arrays of
Sagittarius and Scorpio on the far horizon. Survivor of the
aeons, unmoved through hoarfrost, quake, and blowing dust

1

and sun, this living palisade of metamorphic gneiss was upended when the continents collided three hundred million years ago.

For most of the last thousand years, the Abenaki Indians have known the site's power. They called the place Pompasook, curtain of secrets, Tooth of the Earth. They held councils and prayer ceremonies at the crest of the Ledges, and they buried their shamans in unmarked graves in the deep, rich soil below. Charcoal embers from their ritual fires were carried back to their villages, ashes were offered to the cleansing wind, nothing was allowed to desecrate the sacred ground, and, as always, signs were observed. Ravens perched above these solemn occasions were believed to signal the coming of death; the sighting of an eagle soaring in the wind promised strength and endurance; a dun weasel seen in the light of a planter's moon predicated a seven-year drought.

Others saw the Ledges too, surveyors, trappers, hunters, farmers, loggers—they saw a great white cliff above a meandering brook, and they thought of it as an obstacle, an inconvenience to their needs. They mapped out boundaries across it, cut blazes into tree bark, and marked their corners with piles of stones. They were interested in ownership. They traded land for goods and money, value measured in the quantities of lumber, potatoes, milk, and wool a certain parcel might provide. And when those owners' provisions could no longer be met—or they died, or declined, or became disillusioned or eager to buy another enterprise—they sold the parcel and all the rights they claimed accrued to it, and the land became the private possession of yet another owner.

The scattering of the Abenaki people left the Ledges all but forgotten, although the unique matrix of astronomy and elemental forces continued to exist, still flowing intact around and through the megalith. And even now, the Ledges are not ignored; one full-blooded Abenaki is left who knows the power of Pompasook, and occasionally he visits there.

Away from the Tooth, in the state of Maine, where he lives alone in the woods, his name is Horton Flint. He is an older man, creased, dark, and small, but sinewy and quick

enough to move through the forest on a shadow's wing. When he returns, he approaches the site from the south, up through the alder maze and berry thorns along the brook, along the pathway of the ancients. Or he comes to the Tooth of the Earth from the north, as the shamans did, through the tumble of spruce-thicketed hills above the boulders at the top. Either way, the route he chooses is open and accessible to him, unhindered, as it is to no other.

He brings a necklace with him on his visits, an amulet inherited from his grandfather, the last great Abenaki shaman, Eagle-in-the-Wind.

At the top of the Ledges, Horton Flint sits astride the topmost boulder, high above the forest floor. When he puts the necklace on and looks out at the world unfolding far below, he feels a pulse of life and harmony in everything he sees. In this place, at these times, he is at home. On the tip of Pompasook's Tooth, he is Horton Eagle-in-the-Wind.

1

POLE STAR NORTH

WALKER OWEN drove into a cold November rain, speeding northward on the smooth macadam interstate. He traveled over cattailed marshlands, sixty miles an hour past raw palisades of dynamited bedrock, fallow cornfields growing fortress garrison colonials and raised ranch houses set on quarter-acre estates, their borders bright with chain-link fence. He saw the empty tenements in the broken heart of downtown Springfield, sped by the sprawling shopping malls and car parks choked around Northampton, the weathered tobacco barns in Hadley, the fertile Agawam bottomland—and always the river, the indomitable rain-swollen Connecticut, majestic, oxbowed, broad or narrow, sweeping down the valley to the sea.

He drove without stopping, fast and sure, into the rugged foothills of Vermont's archaic Appalachia, into pine-scented memories of surrogate parents Snoot and Frouncy—old, pleasurable associations despite his ten-year absence, still pleasurable despite their son, Junior, angry and petulant, coiled like a snake in his chromium wheelchair.

He drove without looking back, and by way of forgetting the woman he was leaving behind, he looked ahead and remembered the unforgettable Claire.

He drove northward past Brattleboro, saw the landmark silo by the dairy barn that was now a motel, watched for the orange wind sock at the grass airstrip by the edge of a cornfield. The little silver plane was still there in its makeshift hangar, the same plane—yes, the same milestones applied in both directions, and he wondered if his journey wasn't inevitable, if everyone didn't need to return someday to the place where they fit, and didn't fit, where they were loved, and unloved—return because they had to if they were ever to feel completed.

His journey began at six-fifteen that morning; glasses on, head back against Nicole's cold pillow, he watched steam tumble out of the bathroom door and spread across the ceiling. The shower was on; she wasn't singing.

And then the telephone rang, a startling sound. He thought of his father, a widower, alone in San Diego. Or, more likely, Nicole's hospital clinic paging service, another emergency for her to rush to—or her parents in St. Augustine, early risers, avid golfers, vigorous Kennedy liberals who never once asked why she and her lawyer boyfriend hadn't married.

He picked up the phone on the second ring, static and clicking, a wheezing rasp mingling with the rumble of traffic from the street below. "Hello?"

"Walker Owen?" It was Snoot. "You know who this is?"

"Grizzly?" Walker was suddenly wide awake, smiling at the sound of Snoot's voice. He swung his feet over the side of the bed and held the phone with both hands. "What's going on?" He hadn't talked to Snoot for years.

"Shit's hit the fan, Walker. All frigged up."

"What?" Snoot wasn't one to complain. "What's happening up there?" Now Walker was standing, pacing, naked, wishing he'd kept in touch with the giant logger from Dalton Pond.

"Frouncy's took sick."

Walker sank to the bed. Snoot's wife was redheaded, ruddy, and big; she wore army boots and baked six pies at a time in a wood-fired cookstove. How could she have changed from the way he remembered her? She could lift pigs.

"She's down to the Home. Can't say her words right."

"I can't believe it." Walker leaned back against the bed-side table and tipped a glass of water over onto the floor. "Shit!" He threw a T-shirt on the spill and pushed at it with his foot. Frouncy had been more of a mother to him than his own. Maybe if he'd stayed in Dalton Pond, if he'd kept an eye on her, he could have seen the signs in time. . . .

Nicole's silhouette blurred through the shower door, blond and leggy, more beautiful than he wanted to admit. He turned away.

"Have you got her a doctor?"

Snoot mumbled "Yas," unconvincingly, then unleashed a vintage set piece about doctors getting paid to touch and look at the naked bodies of other men's wives.

"Make sure she gets a good one." But he knew Snoot wouldn't—not from lack of concern but from an intractable tradition of stubborn independence. "Should I come up for a while?" Why else would Snoot have telephoned?

Snoot grunted. "If you want. . . ."

Walker glanced at the shower door. "I want. I'd like to. I will. I'm glad you called."

The line was silent, distant, hollow. "It's changing, Walker, too damn fast." There was something else on Snoot's mind, something left unsaid.

"Everybody else all right?" Snoot didn't answer. Walker would find out soon enough; he wanted to ask, what about Claire?

˙Nicole turned off the shower and came into the bed-room wrapped in a towel. "Who is it?" she mouthed, water dripping from her hair.

Walker turned his back to her, tried not to imagine the hurt on her face when she heard. "Look, I need to make a few phone calls later this morning, tidy up a few things at work, then I'm free." A little time away was what he needed. "You take it easy until I get there, okay?"

"Your father?" Nicole asked. Nicole the physician, healer of bones and tissue. She touched his arm, miles distant from his heart.

He shook his head no, apologetic but determined. "It's

Snoot," he said, palm over the mouthpiece. "Frouncy's had a stroke."

Nicole sat on the edge of the bed, tightening the towel around her, preparing herself. Walker watched as she arranged her narrow feet parallel to the cracks between the hardwood flooring, symmetrical and tidy against the pull of his messy northwoods past.

"So I guess you're going," she said, half to him, half to herself.

He lifted his hand from the receiver and nodded, northward to Vermont. "I'll be there tonight," he said. "Don't worry, okay?" When he hung up the phone, Nicole was back in the bathroom, behind a locked door.

The hitchhiker appeared to be in his late teens, a little more than half Walker's age and size. He was shivering when he climbed in the car. His thin, imitation-leather shirt and pasteboard suitcase betrayed him as one of those New England natives lost in the shuffle toward prosperity.

"Thanks, man."

"No problem." Walker turned up the heater. "You look cold."

The hitchhiker glanced in the backseat. "Yard sale, huh?"

"Moving some stuff." Nicole had insisted he take everything he could fit in his Wagoneer, and he did, exactly as they knew he would someday—exactly. "Where you headed?"

"White River."

"No problem. I'm going most of the way to Canada. Waaay up." Nicole had never understood his attraction to Dalton Pond; for her, the woods were teeming with poison snakes and bears. She felt safer in a Lower East Side alley than she did in a sugarbush grove. Walker nodded northward, up the interstate. "Just follow the yellow brick road."

"What?" Red gums showed around the tops of rotting teeth. A few more years and the kid would have none left.

"Like Dorothy. You know, in the land of Oz?" Walker saw the hitchhiker staring at him. Nobody home. "Up to Dalton Pond, little town west of Catamount. Near Jordan Center?"

"Oh." He looked into the backseat again. "Building condos?"

What did he see back there to give him that idea? "Not me. I'm going up to see some old, old friends." And Junior.

"Condos is where it's at. All kinds of bucks in it." The kid sucked at his wobbly molars. "My uncle's built seven hundred in the last three years. Running close to fifty guys. Ever hear of Ragazzo?"

Walker shook his head no. He'd brought suit against a few condo entrepreneurs in western Connecticut, seen footings settled two feet into uncompacted fill, seen uninspected septic systems built overnight in swamps, but he'd never heard of Ragazzo.

"Ragazzo Corporation. He owns it, Bobby Ragazzo. Sharp as a tack." The kid was coaching himself, rehearsing his lines. "I get to use one of the company rigs: four-by-four Chevy, Sierra package, deck, quad speakers, air—full boat." Then he said, "Going to put me on the framing crew." It sounded like a question.

Walker glanced at his passenger's hands. The pale, thin fingers too delicate for heavy work; the nails were chewed down to the dirty quick. They were a pair of hands, Walker thought sadly, that looked to be too unformed for anything but disappointment, the hands of a failed adolescent.

The kid was a country cousin of the dozens Walker once defended in New Haven, pro bono, swimming against the tide. Back then he believed in due process, in the notion that justice would be served through a vigorous application of the law. Inevitably, he was assigned to defend a child molester and then a serial rapist, both brutal psychopaths who openly boasted of their exploits, who insisted they would continue doing exactly as they pleased—and suddenly Walker felt dirty. The system had failed him, despite its noble premises, and although he thought it was still the least imperfect of any legal system ever devised, he quit defending clients he couldn't believe in and began defending the environment instead.

But the kid beside him was still just a kid. Walker

9

smiled at him, hoping. "So you're a carpenter? D'you like it?"

"Starting Monday, I might. Hey, why not? Like they say, man, take the money and run." A studded cowboy watchband emphasized the thinness of his wrist; those fingers twisted at the reluctant trace of a mustache. "They got power nailers, precut panels; all the doors are factory-hung. Fuck it, man, any asshole can slam up a condo."

Walker once spent a summer helping to rebuild a curved staircase in a doctor's house in Dalton Pond. It seemed almost magic, the way the pieces fit together, absolute and compelling in the geometry of their design. Somewhere he had a photo of the finished stair, oiled teak treads and burled walnut balusters. He wished he had a way of letting the kid know how it felt to make a thing beautiful, but he knew he didn't, not this time. Any asshole can slam up a condo—and go home empty in a big shiny truck.

He thought of Snoot sitting at his kitchen table sharpening an eight-point handsaw—razor sharp—proud of it, eager to use it well.

They drove along the river. "You married?" the kid asked. Man talk now, another thing they wouldn't have in common.

Walker shook his head no. "Never had the pleasure." He thought of Claire, who had.

"My old lady's expecting in March."

Walker smiled his congratulations, a halfhearted mix of approval and pity. He had no children; he didn't know what to say.

They drove for miles in companionable silence. Across the river, in New Hampshire, Walker saw the giant red billboard advertising BASKETVILLE. The first time he saw it was twenty-some years ago, from the passenger seat of his father's Buick, on their first trip north, a fishing vacation to Dalton Pond. The last time he saw it was ten years ago, on his last trip south. The sign used to offend him, seemed like a blemish on an otherwise beautiful landscape. Now the pasture behind it was dotted with buildings, and the adjacent farmhouse appeared to have been remodeled into apartments, with a paved parking lot where the barn once stood. The billboard seemed suddenly harmless.

When Walker lived in Dalton Pond, there were no condos, no prehung doors, no air-conditioned pickup trucks. Back then, there were more cows than people in Vermont. That Vermont, as everyone knew, had vanished, but now, as he drove back into the Green Mountain State, he wondered how much of it he'd dreamed into existence because he wanted it to be that way—his way—pure and uncomplicated.

Snoot used to tease him about being a nouveau native, and the playful accusation hurt; he'd wanted to fit the paradigm, to be a real Vermonter. Funny, but by the time he realized he wasn't, the real Vermont was gone. The kid beside him—and Junior, and Claire—they were the real Vermonters. Would he ever be able to see it their way?

When he pulled off beside the exit ramp at White River Junction, Walker rummaged through the heap of clothes in the back and found an old green baseball jacket. "Why don't you take this?" he asked. It was an impulsive gesture, but it felt right—not enough, nowhere near enough to bridge the gap, but something. "I don't wear it anymore," he said. "It'll keep your pitching arm warm."

"Hey, thanks, man." The kid smiled as he put it on. "Fucking A. Fits decent." The sleeves covered his hands to the tips of his fingers.

"Good luck with the job," Walker said. "It's a good trade, carpentry." Even building condos. "Get rich quick, huh?"

"Better believe it, man." He gave Walker a thumbs-up sign and slammed the door. "Good luck selling your shit."

By three in the afternoon, Walker had traveled two hours' worth of I-91, which was yet unbuilt when he'd last driven down the valley. He was close to the Canadian border when he finally saw the exit for Quinntown, Kendall Corners, and Dalton Pond. He was pleased to recognize the rolling piedmonts gathering to the west, climbing toward the Catamount Heights, and the pleasure soon mixed with the excitement and dread of returning to a painfully cherished place. Shifting down for the exit, he shifted back in time.

It began when he was fourteen, and every summer, all through school, he'd found an excuse to go back—first with his father, fishing for trout, then, in college, alone, still renting the cabin from Snoot and supporting himself any way he could. After graduating from the University of Connecticut, he packed his psychedelic VW bus and headed north again, long hair blowing in the breeze. Law school could wait. He'd go someday; it would just be a matter of time.

He'd thought of himself as one of the lucky ones. A spinal fusion after a childhood sledding mishap kept him out of the draft, although he was quick to explain to anyone who would listen that he would have refused to serve, if called. He was convinced he would have gone to jail or to Canada, but he was always uneasy about the luxury of never having to prove his conviction. He knew that about himself, and when the first of his friends was listed as missing in action after the Tet offensive, he couldn't eat for days.

It was odd, thinking about it now, how it all had seemed so black and white, so reductively easy to categorize the peaceniks and the hawks as good guys and bad guys. While Junior was ducking mortar fire in Vietnam, Walker went to rock concerts, learned to play the guitar, and fell in love with Junior's former girlfriend, Claire.

She was bright and petite and smelled like lilacs, and she flattered him with her curiosity. They discussed Camus, Buddhism, and Kahlil Gibran, fancying themselves as intellectual exiles. And so it went: books, and dope, and talk, and falling in love. They read Thoreau aloud to each other sitting naked in the middle of a stream; the raven-haired Claire Tatro and the lanky flatlander, Walker "Weed" Owen, Hansel and Gretel, living the good life alongside Crooked Brook.

Walker pulled up to the stop sign at the end of the exit ramp.

The good life: that's how he'd thought of it. He'd had everything he was supposed to have—even made his own hard cider, like his hero and mentor, the giant logger, Snoot.

12

Four years of it, and somehow the good life died. He lost touch with the mountains, stopped taking winter hikes and watching the crows from the tops of the ridges. It came apart. He felt like a tourist. He watched it crumble as he fought with Claire, blamed her for his growing dissatisfactions, stopped talking about ideas, stopped trying. He fled from it—whatever *it* was—traveled around in his decrepit bus, stayed a few nights at a commune in Strafford, at others in Jordan, in Kendall, in Canaan, played the lonesome desperado to a circuit of willing earth mothers while Claire stayed with her mother in town. Their dream turned, and he had been too much inside it to ever know why.

Walker swung left onto the road to Dalton Pond.

The dream ended altogether when Junior came home from Vietnam hunched over in a wheelchair, legs amputated six inches above the knees. Snoot and Frouncy's boy, the daredevil jock, cocky soldier, party animal, ladies' man—the only guy in his high school class to punch out a cheerleader and look like a hero doing it—Junior, everyone's rival, had lost the war.

Walker wept when he saw him; Claire did too. She began spending time with him, drawn to his suffering, dedicated to bringing him back to life.

Walker fought with her and felt her pulling away each time they quarreled. He packed his bus, and on the day he planned to leave, he woke up with the flu. He was suddenly as sick as he'd ever been in his life, too weak to leave the cabin, wondering if he wouldn't rather die anyway. He slept feverishly all afternoon and into the night, hallucinating, frightened, soaked in sweat, then awoke to the touch of a hand on his forehead: Frouncy's, not Claire's.

She'd been sitting with him all day, cooling his fever with a wet towel, watching him, waiting. "Snoot's been out to check on us," she said. "Junior never let us set with him when he was sick."

"Snoot's been here?"

"Every hour, nervous as a cat. He's went for the doctor."

Walker had suddenly found himself weeping—from

shame, from fatigue, from wanting Claire to be there, from feeling alone in the world, from feeling loved, he didn't know exactly why—but when Frouncy held him to her vast bosom and stroked his forehead, he bawled like an aching baby.

"It's not the end," she told him, pressing him tighter to her heart. "It's the start of something new."

"But *Claire!*" he'd bawled, loss overflowing.

"Claire loves you," Frouncy reassured him. "At *least* as much as Snoot and I do."

"Then why . . . ?"

"It's going to take time, that's all. You'll see."

He'd wanted to believe her, but he didn't. Two weeks later and ten pounds lighter, he applied to law school, cut his hair, and moved back to Connecticut.

Walker passed the all-night gas station where he worked one summer when he lived with Claire. There was a deep gully next to the entrance, and he remembered the truck-load of drunken pulp cutters who left the pumps one night without paying. As they sped off, they swerved into the gully, where they stayed for the next twenty minutes arguing about a woman named Jolene, water three feet deep in the cab. One of them told the State Police they were waiting for the light to change. The story made the newspapers, even mentioned Walker's name.

A mile beyond the gas station, he passed a farmhouse on the right, then Fellows's Auction Barn, and a strip of six new houses. Had that been a hayfield before? He couldn't quite place it. Or was that the orchard where he and Snoot saw the cow moose browsing apples?

He drove at twenty miles an hour despite the open road. The dips and swales and curves and flats became increasingly familiar, but different too—narrower? Had the bushes grown in along the banks, above the narrow turns?

Ahead, a plastic sign for a marina pointed down a dirt lane, toward the water. The lane used to end at a wobbly fishing camp, a rumrunner's stop in the old days, they said. Walker bought an old wooden canoe there once, from a man who claimed to have bootlegged booze down from Canada on

Lake Champlain in the dark, in the very same canoe he was anxious to sell for fifty bucks.

Soon, another sign—this one with gold-leaf lettering—REAL ESTATE. Hiram Fogg's house had been gentrified: a real estate office with a gift shop on the second floor. PURPLE THIS-TLE, read the sign in the window. *Gifts from Olde Vermont.*

Dalton Pond village looked cleaner and whiter, more paint on the pickets and shutters. Tot Tatro's General Store loomed large on the right, the only store on Main Street. Claire's stepfather had inherited it from *his* father, a man so penurious he'd once sold water during a summer drought, three cents a gallon, a penny a quart; little wonder they were resented for their money. Darby Dunbar's father once drove a team of oxen up onto the porch and in through the double doors, glass and splinters all over the merchandise. Old man Tatro had apparently cheated him two cents on a hundred-pound keg of nails, and old man Dunbar—the only one in town tighter than the storekeeper—wanted his proper change.

As Walker passed the store, he realized he was slouched down in his seat. Let them talk, if they had to. Walker Owen, peacenik, jilted hippie, had the nerve to come back. So what? It wasn't so one-sided as it used to be. This time, he wasn't trying to be anyone other than himself. He sat up straight.

Merton's Texaco was across the road from the store, still open, still busy, the only gas within ten miles. Before he'd gone to Vietnam, Junior worked at Merton's. When Walker stopped for fuel, he always noticed Junior's hands, the thick, blunt fingers nicked with cuts and scrapes, grease in the scabs—a tribute to honest work, in Walker's mind. He'd en-vied Junior his hands and tried to emulate Junior's persever-ance and mechanical skills—but now, looking at the pumps and lifts, he understood that no matter how much he might have worked and suffered, the grease and cuts on him—an educated flatlander—were in a way gratuitous; there was no parity. Garage work was optional for him, just as going to Vietnam had been optional, even if it was medically out of the question. Living with options was easy compared to living with none. Walker understood that, even then, and in the simple act of counting out change, Junior always made it clear he understood it too.

Walker was surprised at how many trees he remembered as individuals. Some were gone—the great Dutch elms in front of the school, the row of box elders in back of Dodd's—but there, taller than ever, were the twin bull pines by Mrs. Pippin's and, farther on, the scarred yellow birch at the Latham Hill switchback, growing too far into the road for its own good.

They seemed, these branchy old survivors, like loyal friends waiting for him, accepting and familiar. And they were noticeably bigger, too, especially the groves of pine in the abandoned pastures. In a pine tree's life, ten years meant more than a dozen extra feet in height, another half a foot in girth. They'd kept on growing. Walker was pleased. They'd kept on doing exactly what they were meant to do.

The long incline up Crooked Brook Road to Snoot's came all too soon; the five hours' drive from New Haven was finally two minutes short of completion, and Walker still had no idea how he'd explain himself to Junior and Claire. Did Snoot tell them he was coming? Would she be happy to see him?

Beasley Pruitt's little stone house was suddenly there, on the right, then the narrow cut through the ledges and First Bridge over the brook. Another curve, then Second Bridge and a reverse curve to Third Bridge and the roadside turnout. Another minute. Opposite the Staircase Falls, a trail led up to the cabin Walker rented from Snoot. The trail was still open, as it always had been. A good omen.

Next came police chief Bud Benoit's double-wide home. Walker wondered if he was still alive, if the ancient feud between Bud and Snoot had ever been resolved. He slowed for the one-lane S-curve. A cathedral of old-growth pine arched overhead. At the far end, beneath a proscenium of soaring limbs, Snoot's rusty mailbox tipped forward on its welded-chain post like a tired puppet.

He drove up the lane slowly. Most of the climb was

twisting and steep. The grassy hump between the wheel ruts dragged at the Wagoneer's undercarriage. Walker was surprised to see so many saplings crowding into the right-of-way. Alders, chokecherries, and poplars filled in the understory, brushing his fenders as he passed. Snoot always kept them trimmed back, had no use for what he called weed trees.

At the crest of the hill, off to the left side of the road, was the World War Two ambulance, long ago rechristened Frouncy's Dodge Mahal; it was full of poultry.

Walker stopped and went over to it; it looked as if the chickens were driving. They were perched on the steering wheel, concentrating, nesting in the glove compartment, flying in and out of the open windows and cackling the way chickens do when they're excited. He looked in through the windows at the dust and chaff and chicken shit on the seats. On the floor by the brake pedal, two leghorn hens scratched and pecked at a corncob. In the back of the truck, where the bunks and the kitchenette were to have been built, there were stacks of discarded egg cartons and two musty bales of alfalfa.

Around front, a winged angel decorated the hood's dented nose. Walker recalled the day Snoot bought the angel for Frouncy, when the Dodge was still running. Snoot claimed he paid a fortune but insisted she'd lead them safely wherever they wanted to go. The angel still looked willing; even now, she was bright as polished silver, streamlined wings folded back to the wind.

Beneath the angel, the hood was six inches ajar. Walker looked in; the engine was gone. Oil stained the earth black where the crankcase had drained. A startled bird flew out in a rush of feathers, almost touching Walker's head. He pulled away and surveyed the truck that was meant to have been Snoot and Frouncy's home on wheels for a trip across country. Glass clouded, paint faded, tires flattened, it sat like a tombstone surrounded by feathers.

He left his car by the Dodge Mahal and walked toward the house between islands of junk—tires, appliances, car carcasses, lumber, machinery—all of it even rustier, rottener, and more forlorn than he remembered it, even more useless

17

now than before. Some of the piles had trees growing up through them, slippery elm and staghorn sumac, flagpoles, ships' masts, casting broken shadows on the treasures Snoot swore to God he'd use someday.

Eastward, behind the barn, inside the ragged wire fences, three Holstein heifers watched him, chewing intently, black and white against the hillside. Beyond the pasture and the cows, he saw the dark tunnel through the looming hemlocks where the road ran to the cabin. In the distance, high above the treetops, the Abenaki Ledges rose in a great cleft palisade. He'd often climbed the steep side trail to the top, drawn inexplicably to the boulders rimmed along the edge, fearlessly sitting on the highest one and watching the sun bury itself south of Little Squaw Mountain.

Next to the barn, Walker saw the stockpiled firewood Snoot was always working on. In the old days, he'd cut fifty cords a winter in his spare time and sell most of it to the houses in the village. From the looks of the mountain of fresh-split logs, Snoot hadn't slowed a bit.

He stopped at the foot of the ramp in front of the house. He'd known it was there, of course he did—five feet wide, railings on both sides, sloped upward to the kitchen door—but it was the last thing he wanted to see.

He helped Snoot build it, and yet he remembered wishing to destroy it with each cut of his saw, make it disappear with every swing of his hammer. The first time he watched Claire wheel Junior up the raw new ramp, he imagined it collapsing, both of them swallowed deep into a hole in the earth.

He walked up the incline. As he passed a window, he was startled by his own reflection. Who was this slender stranger with the tortoiseshell glasses and the quizzical, clean-shaven face? Those rippled window mirrors were used to the crooked line of his broken nose, the deep cleft in his chin, but where were the ragged Levi's, the bushy beard, the hair tied in a ponytail? The old context, the house, the hills, Snoot's stacks of firewood—they hadn't changed. He had. He stared closer, and lost sight of himself to what he saw inside.

The worn white-enameled wood cupboards were as he remembered them. Frouncy's wood-fired Empire cookstove still sat squat against the far wall. A flyswatter lay on the oilcloth-covered table by the window. Frouncy's chair still had her cushion tied to it, arranged to support her ever-aching back, but it was one of the other two chairs that interested Walker. Unmistakable in its size and grimy patina, Snoot's ladderback was next to Frouncy's, both with their backs to the stove. Across the table, near the window, was an empty place for Junior's wheelchair, and next to that was Claire's chair; he'd seen her sitting there in the weeks before he left. A decade had passed, and yet the arrangement of chairs still seemed wrong, still incongruous.

Walker knocked at the door; no response. He knocked again. When he felt he'd waited long enough, he opened the door and stepped into the kitchen. "Anybody home?" he called. "Snoot? Junior?"

2

JUNIOR'S HOUSE

WALKER CLOSED the door behind him. The smells of chimney creosote and springwater were exactly as they'd always been, impossible to remember but, now renewed, immediately recalled.

The kitchen was cluttered and work-worn, but bright; the last of the afternoon's sunlight patterned trapezoidal shadows across the wide pine floorboards. A hunting rifle—wasn't it Snoot's Remington?—was propped against the wall beside the door to the hall. Snoot and Walker had spent hours in that room: Snoot in his listing La-Z-Boy rocker, Walker propped into the corner of a sagging sofa, drinking Hawaiian Punch and gin.

Walker called again. "Snoot?"

Still no response. A folded red plaid hunting jacket and a box of shells lay on a table by the woodbox.

He walked to the table and sat in Snoot's place, facing the window. The house was quiet except for the creaking of the chair and the dripping of water in the soapstone sink. He picked up the flyswatter and squinted through the mesh at the view beyond the window.

It was all so important in '68. He'd collected junk too, insisting it would be put to good use some day, just like Snoot's. What a game it had been. He aimed the flyswatter at the barn, aimed at a tractor with one missing wheel, a hay baler with none. Claire understood his need to reinvent himself; she grew up wanting some of what he wanted to discard, and vice versa. Symbiosis. Yin and yang. Wasn't that what they called it? The difference was, she never lost herself in the process of reinvention.

Walker aimed at the Dodge Mahal. He tracked a chicken walking across its roof. So why'd she marry him? "Kapow!" Sad-assed hulk of a truck. Frouncy never drove it once.

He aimed at three more chickens, flapping out the driver's side window, and pulled an imaginary trigger. "Bam!" he whispered. "Bam, ka-bam!" A chicken each for Frouncy, Snoot, and Walker. "Bam!" A big fat hen for the beautiful Claire.

A voice behind him stopped him short. "What's going on?"

Walker spun around. It was Junior Audette—in his wheelchair, with the Remington across his lap. He'd wheeled to within three feet of Walker without making a sound. His expression told nothing, although the rifle looked more like an afterthought than a threat. Same square face, but older, worn, with bitter lines around the thin-lipped mouth. Still handsome, too, in a hard, lean way—hair still thick, a touch of gray—and cocky, even sitting in a wheelchair. How did he do it? And the other thing, irrevocable and absolute: Junior's legs were still cut off above the knees. Weren't they? Of course they were. It couldn't have changed. But Walker stole a quick glance anyway—to be sure—then looked up, wary as a thief. "Junior?"

"Last time I checked."

"It's me, Walker Owen." His voice betrayed him. "Hi."

Junior stared at him. In the silence that followed—and in the years of silence that might have justifiably followed after that—Walker realized there would never be a question of Junior's identity. This was his house, his land, his town, his Vermont. His ancestry pressed in from all around; he belonged there, Walker didn't. So he began again: "I used to live out back?"

Junior's lips formed what might have been the beginning of a smile; clearly he remembered everything—much more than where Walker used to live. He stared as though he were rehearsing every past offense. Was he wondering at the change in the hippie who courted Snoot and Frouncy—and Claire—as if he were one of them? Or did he even care?

"I never forgot you," Junior said.

Walker believed him. "Sorry for barging in like this."

"Cut your ponytail, I see."

"Snoot called me, asked me up—"

"Didn't think I'd be here, did you?" Junior laughed the way survivors are entitled to laugh, enjoying himself. "It's my place, now. Dad gave it to me, straight and legal." He swaggered a glance around the room. "Quite a dump, ain't it?"

Walker looked around and shrugged. Maybe it was, but he'd never thought of it that way. What did he mean, it's *his* place now? "Where can I find Snoot?"

"Out in the cabin. Running around. Gone to the village for groceries, maybe."

"And Frouncy?" He wanted to ask about Claire.

"Mother's down to the Home. Lost her fast pitch."

"A stroke?" Snoot had been vague on the phone.

Junior ignored the question. "They feed her good." He made it sound as though she were in a kennel.

"Any progress?"

"She probably wouldn't know you." Junior smirked. "She's had a shock—you know." He made a face, drooped on one side. "Can't talk too good."

"I'll go see her, first thing," Walker mumbled. Then the room was silent. What was there to say? Walker glanced at Junior's shirt pocket; it was full of ballpoint pens and stitched with someone else's name—Randy. Or was that Junior's real name? Walker realized he didn't know.

Junior's arms and torso were thick and muscular. He'd lifted weights while Walker ran in marathons. A ring of keys hung from his belt. His pant legs were folded against his shortened thighs. At the front of the wheelchair, two stainless steel footrests were folded shut and taped to the frame, designed for someone else's feet.

Walker wondered if Junior thought Frouncy needed no sympathy. She still had her feet. She, at least, could stand up, tall enough to look down on someone.

"What'd you come by here for, anyway?" Junior finally asked.

"Here?" Snoot hadn't told him. "Just visiting." The explanation still sounded incomplete. "For a while."

Suspiciously: "What for?"

Walker shrugged and laughed. "Something to do. It's nice around here."

Junior spat the obvious deception from his lips. "I fix radios and TVs," he said, jerking his head toward the back of the house. "Gets busy as hell sometimes. What do you do to stay out of trouble?"

"I'm a lawyer." It was a funny thing to be saying in the Audettes' kitchen. Snoot's contempt for the profession was one of the few things he and his son shared in common. "Environmental law, mostly," he added, a futile gesture toward redemption. "I like it."

"Save the birdies and clams?" Junior asked.

"Something like that," Walker said, ignoring the barb. "It's interesting stuff."

Junior rolled his eyes, then stared at Walker, looking for a soft spot; he took another tack. "Claire got promoted." He was in control now, and he enjoyed it. "Head nurse, runs the kiddie ward." He leaned the rifle barrel against the table's edge, discarded it, as if to make clear his advantage.

Walker felt himself sweating. "Haven't heard much news since I left." Snoot's chair squeaked as he rearranged it under him. The room seemed suddenly stuffy, hot; he wished he could open a window. He wanted to lose himself in something from his past with Claire that Junior couldn't share: the pull of her breath when they'd made love, her poems to him, her brilliant black hair spread across his pillow. He pictured her at Robin's Cove where they skinny-dipped and lay sunbathing, glistening on a golden afternoon. One day he caught Junior watching them—watching *her* from behind the bushes—and Walker said nothing; he wanted Junior to watch and hurt, wanted him sick with desire.

But now it was Junior's turn, Junior's house, Junior's wife. "She makes good money," he said, "for a woman."

"I'm sure she does." Walker's mouth tasted dusty. He wished he'd exposed Junior that day at Robin's Cove.

"With me in rehab, somebody had to bring in the bread."

"Lucky for you," Walker said. He thought of Claire's taut, smooth stomach, her tiny brown nipples, and decided it was time to go.

He stood up, remembering how he'd once felt awkward standing in Junior's presence—apologetic for his own good fortune—and was relieved to find he felt none of that now. When he turned to push back his chair, he bumped the table; the rifle tipped and slid along the edge. Junior grabbed for it and missed. Walker caught it before it fell. He balanced the weapon in his hands, felt better as he placed the barrel deliberately against the wall by the window. "I'd better catch Snoot before it gets dark." Then he saw the open box of ammunition on the table by the woodbox. It reminded him of Junior's tour in 'Nam, and he wondered, if it had been him, what kinds of compensation he would have expected in exchange for *his* legs.

"Don't get lost in the woods," Junior said, as he rolled across the kitchen.

"I'll manage."

" 'Course, you've probably saved enough snakes and bears so they wouldn't dare bother you."

Walker ignored the remark, paused at the open door, and fixed his eyes on a haunting profile across the yard. The question was in the air before he knew what he had asked. He gestured to the Dodge Mahal. "Want to sell that thing?"

"Mother's truck?" Junior laughed and shook his head. "That hunka junk?"

"To you, maybe," Walker said. "I'd buy it, if you're at all inclined."

Junior squinted at it, then at Walker. "You're still a weirdo."

"I get by."

"I imagine you do." Junior inhaled the next few words; they were barely audible. "Any way you can."

"I'll find Snoot," Walker said.

"Not if he finds you first," Junior said, tall in his chair, wheeling himself backwards into his house.

Walker hurried across the hillside pasture, into the gloaming woods, and up the winding road along the brook. He walked quickly, falling into a trot on the level stretches, pursued by the idea of Junior and Claire together. The old Junior was cocky enough; *this* Junior was downright nasty. He wondered if he'd had the whole thing wrong from the beginning. Maybe he'd never understood Claire at all.

The cabin was set in a grove of old-growth hemlock; its narrow porch faced Crooked Brook. The forest floor surrounding it was clear of brush and saplings, soft underfoot with rotted needles and mosses. Even at the summer solstice, no sunlight made it through the dark green canopy above. Now, on a late November afternoon, it was deep in shadows, purples and browns. The cabin walls were sheathed in battened boards, weathered gray and streaked with feathery moss. A bed of hemlock needles blanketed the shingled roof. No smoke appeared above the chimney.

Walker ran the last hundred yards. As he grew close he looked for lights and saw none. He listened for sounds inside as he mounted the wobbly steps. "Snoot?"

No answer. He crossed the narrow porch and pushed the door open. Inside, the smell was cool and woodsy, a damp dark forest. "Snoot, you in here?"

He wasn't. Walker glanced around the room, sucked in the smell of an empty decade, and was overcome with a nostalgia so palpable and precious that it seemed all of his past in Dalton Pond had been compressed into a single inhalation.

26

The day had triggered many memories so far, but one deep breath inside the brookside cabin reverberated deeper than all the other memories combined, and he was convinced he was in the right place, finally, for the second time in his life.

The first time was in 1961: He was fourteen years old, off on a fishing vacation with his father. It rained all the way from Connecticut to Dalton Pond, and he'd decided he hated fishing. They were parked in his father's Buick in Snoot's dooryard, unannounced, waiting to pick up the keys to the cabin they rented out back in the woods by Crooked Brook.

Nobody was home. Walker thought his father was a jerk; he was embarrassed by his shiny car, his neat sports clothes, and perfect cuticles. Walker sat in a slump, stewing, watching iridescent streaks of oil floating on the puddles. He knew he was bad company, but he didn't care. At about the time he thought he couldn't stand it any longer, he heard the growing roar of an approaching vehicle. He turned around to see a huge truck bouncing toward them, splashing through the muddy potholes, steam blowing out from under the fenders. A Diamond Reo. Very big. A man and a woman rode high in the cab. A young boy sat between them, scowling over the dashboard.

"A logging truck," Walker's father said. "Must be Snoot. Some truck, huh, Walker?"

Walker didn't answer. The truck lurched to a stop a foot behind the car with the Connecticut plates, and a huge man in greasy wool pants and a dirty plaid shirt threw open the truck door and jumped to the ground. Most of his face was hidden behind a preposterous black beard. His nose was as big and lumpy as a potato. Walker thought he must have been glad to see them because he appeared to be in such a hurry. But instead of coming to their car, he swung himself up onto a steel ladder behind the truck cab, scrambled to the top, and perched himself on a little seat in front of a half-dozen levers. Raised from its resting place in the bed of the truck, a hydraulic boom suddenly swung in an arc toward the car. At the end of the boom was a huge pair of pincers, which opened wider as Walker watched. They were aimed, he was certain, for the roof of the Buick.

"Dad!" Walker yelled, but before he could say another word, the door was flung open and a husky woman with red, raw skin grabbed his father and dragged him out.

"It ain't him, you dumb shit!" she shouted up into the rain, even louder than the roar of the truck. "Get off'n that rig, you big galoot!"

That was how they first met. Walker smiled at the memory; it was exactly like that. And there was more.

The pincers had clanged shut and dangled a yard above the car, like a warning. Walker watched Snoot climb down from his perch, hands big as baseball mitts reaching in the cab, turning off the motor. The boy still glared through the windshield glass, still as stone. Walker turned away, embarrassed. For a moment, he confused the thumping of his heart with the sound of raindrops on the roof of the car.

"Snoot thought you was somebody else," Frouncy said, smiling widely. She turned to Snoot. "He's from Connecticut, for starters. And that's his boy in there, if I ain't mistaken." Walker froze while Snoot glowered at him through a maze of whiskers and tangled hair. Then Frouncy said, "They come to rent the cabin, asshole."

Walker had never heard a woman talk like that in his life. Would Snoot club her? Would he murder them all and bury them behind the barn? Instead, he saw Snoot open his huge pink mouth and roar with laughter, slap his giant paws against his thighs, and bellow so loud that everyone began to laugh with him—except the boy in the truck, who looked down on them expressionless, solemn and apart.

"Would of swore he was somebody else!" Snoot guffawed at Frouncy, pointing to Walker's wan father. "Wish I'd saw the look on his face when them jaws come a-snapping!"

Walker's father offered an apologetic smile.

"Would of had me some wicked good salvage, you hadn't drug him out so quick." Snoot thought it was all very funny.

"We lost the paper you wrote us," Frouncy said. "Snoot

cashed the check, though. You probably knew that." She seemed so sweet, like somebody's grandma talking to Walker's father, big but gentle, giggling as she smoothed out the dents she'd made in his jacket sleeve.

Then the scary part: Snoot had gestured to Walker to get out of the car. At first Walker hesitated, terrified, but Snoot grinned and winked at him, irresistibly, and before he knew what he'd done, Walker was standing between the towering logger and Frouncy, with both of their arms around his shoulders.

"This boy and us's going to get along good." Snoot grinned down at Walker. The big potato above his mouth seemed to be grinning too. "That's the truth, ain't it, boy?"

Walker looked up at Frouncy, then at Snoot, glanced at his father's thin smile of approval—then looked up again and nodded his allegiance. Something wonderful and frightening and inevitable had begun. Walker felt it happening, and he didn't care what his father thought. Snoot roared and coughed and hugged him so hard Walker thought he heard something crack.

Walker left the cabin, loped down the tote road through the woods, and climbed over the gate to the pasture. Shivering, he began to make his way back to his car through the dusk, past the house and barn, past the woodpiles and islands of junk and the prickly presence of Junior. He looked for a vehicle that might have been Claire's but saw nothing new in the yard or the sheds.

At the crest of the hill, he stopped beside the Dodge Mahal. It looked so big and sad in the failing light. He touched its cold fenders, caressed the doors, and stroked the rusted hood. Before he left, he cupped the winged angel in his hands, held her, warmed her like an injured bird. When he felt a pulse against his own, he let her go.

A few days later, on a rock in a streambed, Claire would trace her finger across the rusty lines on his palm, and he'd find himself wondering. Did it work like a tattoo? Could old memories alter the color of skin?

3

FATHERS AND SONS

WITH A BAG of groceries cradled against his chest, Snoot pawed a prickly branch from his face, stopped still, and listened for Crooked Brook. A thin slice of moon and a bucket of stars spilled over the sky with a promise of light, but he was deep in the woods; he would hear his way through, feel for his footing across the sag and back up to the road by Beasley Pruitt's.

He groped at a fallen tree in his path, pushed down against its girth, and crawled over it, his eyes closed tight against hidden barbs. Damned slash; if the place had ever been logged off right, a man could walk on his own hind legs. Ahead of him, he heard a trickle. He grunted, pleased to be on course. The road lay a hundred yards beyond the second loop of Crooked Brook.

Snoot stopped in a clearing, looked up to the heavens, and found the Big Dipper—the Plough, his daddy called it—the Great Bear. From the plowshare's tip, he followed a course to the Pole Star, then doglegged back, searching for the Seven Sisters, still hidden below the horizon. Clouds permitting, he knew they'd soon emerge, followed by the Great Hunter, Orion, and his Great Dog, Little Dog, Hare, and Lion, bright companions in the eastern sky.

He sniffed at the night: it smelled like early snow was

on its way, cool cotton pressing down between the trees—
maybe before dawn. It would come from the southwest when
it came, lazily, across the still unfrozen pond, then mix and
swirl with the cold air draining down the ridges, silent, clean,
and white. It would stay until April or May—a long time or a
short time, who could say? It all depended, Snoot thought, on
how time was counted—whether it was a good time or a bad
time for Frouncy. She always fancied the smell of snow.

Snoot preferred night-walking in the woods. Roads
tended toward a sameness, and he missed the natural quirks
and disarrays of land left free of human interference. He
preferred the nightbirds' calls and the scurrying sounds of
creatures to the whine of tires on macadam. The woods were
moist and soft as a woman in bed. The trees were always
willing to have him pull their flowing skirts around him as he
eased his way through a jumble of blowdowns, finding his
route by smell and feel and branches silhouetted against the
sky.

With the murmur of running water still in his ears, he
stopped and surveyed his surroundings. Alders, hemlock, yellow birch—spars of dead elm, moosewood. What's this? Balm
of Gilead. He twisted a branch between his fingers, tore open
the bark, and sniffed at the pulp: Frouncy's favorite tree. A few
hours earlier, she'd fallen asleep during his visit, dumped her
supper in her lap, and never knew it.

Through the trees on the bank above him, Snoot saw a
car come up the road from Dalton Pond. He watched the
headlights flicker through the trees like scenes from the movies he saw as a child, five cents to sit in the balcony and watch
the cowboys shoot at the Indians. The headlights passed, and
then he saw the brake lights brighten as the car slowed down
and turned up Beasley Pruitt's driveway. Walker was bound
to be late. Knowing him, he'd probably had a flat. A dog began
to bark and whine, a car door slammed. Snoot heard Beasley
baby-talking to his beagle, singing snatches of a song; the dog
howled in return. Beasley, no doubt, took in a Planning Board
meeting, went out after, and got himself toasted. Snoot
crossed the brook and started up the bank to the road.

Frouncy, Francine, woman, wife. Thirty-three years in the same fourposter bed, and not a single night to regret.

On his way up the slope, he pulled at a sapling to steady himself and yanked it out of the ground, roots and all. He found a bigger tree; it held his bulk and he pulled himself up to the next, then the next, until he was standing by the road.

She was in there someplace, behind the medicine. She'd pick her time to come back to him; she'd do it when she was good and ready.

With Frouncy in the Home and winter on the way, Snoot's nights yawned open like empty caves. Junior wouldn't talk to him—never had; he'd shut himself in his tinkering room soon as he finished supper. Claire liked to visit, sit and talk, but more often than not she came home late and had to argue with Junior, him picking on her for nothing. Snoot's old friends were all off in the woods, or lost, or crazy, or locked up. Or dead.

His driver's license was gone for good, thanks to that sonofabitching town cop, Bud—and who were his neighbors? Bud? Beasley, the gutless little lawyer? The answer was, nobody worth a popcorn fart. So with Frouncy gone, and no one to talk to, he'd started walking. From seven until after midnight, on moon-bright nights, in the darkest dark, and in the foulest weather, Snoot prowled the woods and logging roads from Dalton Pond to Catamount, to Jordan, up to Sachem Lake, and back over the mountain to Mudchub Pond—grunting, wanting, sniffing, wishing, pawing at the dark—hoping with each step he took that Frouncy'd soon come home.

He waited between the roadside trees and caught his breath, then crossed the guardrail cables and stood on the macadam. The next stage of his route would follow the shoulder of the road past Beasley's house. Then at Third Bridge, at the turnout where fishermen angled and tourists admired the Staircase Falls, Snoot would cut north into the woods and follow the path along Crooked Brook's east branch.

He hadn't told Junior he'd cleaned out the cabin for Walker's visit. It was none of Junior's goddamned business, and besides, as long as he hiked up the brook path instead of going in through the dooryard by the house, Junior would never know anyway. There were still some things a man was entitled to after he'd worked a section of land all his life, no matter who said they owned it.

Sometimes Snoot spent the night in the cabin alone, listening to squirrels at work behind the paneling, dreaming of log drives up in northern Quebec on Big Goose River, when he was a boy. But he always felt restless when he woke up in the cabin to a lonesome dawn, so he'd hike down to the Home for a morning visit with Frouncy. Sleepy Thibodeau's widow ran the kitchen there, as generous with her breakfasts as she'd once been with her bed. He'd greet her with mud on his boots and burrs stuck to his damp wool trousers, tease about how her husband was always the last one out of his bunk in the pulp camps. She'd pretend to scold him for dirtying her linoleum, try to act like an old lady instead of the pip she'd been when the twin peaks of her mountainous bosom were every logger's dream of kingdom come.

The sound of a truck, then the glare of its headlights zigzagged down the mountain from Sachem Lake. V-8 Ford motor. Snoot considered a guess at the year—'74 or '75?—and stepped back into the row of maples to listen and wait. The truck rolled by, brakes squeaking as it slowed for the curves at Second Bridge. Snoot sniffed the air. Just as he thought: Truman Fogg had got himself another load of moldy Canadian hay.

Snoot walked out into the middle of the road, looking up at the heavens, craning his neck to find the so-called Seven Sisters.

When he reached the stone house, he glowered up the dark driveway and made a point of noisily clomping by. His footsteps echoed off the pavement, but the dog never made a sound. Beasley had probably sung the hound to death.

Snoot's pace held steady as the road grew steeper. He tucked in his chin and leaned into the incline. A hundred yards short of the waterfall turnout, another pair of headlights—faint at first, then growing brighter—probed the trees

34

along the curves above the falls before coming into full view, beaming straight down the road at him.

His first instinct was to hide himself. He didn't care what people thought about his P.M. rambles, but it was easier to be invisible, avoid explaining himself to the gossip-hungry coffee hounds at Tot's lunch counter every morning.

The road between Snoot and the oncoming lights was cut into a narrow trough, with steep shale cliffs to each side. There was no place to hide, so he stepped off the edge of the macadam and waited for the car to pass. Probably Bud on a wild goose chase.

But it wasn't Bud's Bronco, and it wasn't his International pickup, either. Snoot heard the downshift, heard the car decrease its speed as it approached.

Who in—? Walker would be coming from the other direction. Snoot turned his head to avoid the glare. Bud burped his si-reen when he flew by. The car was about to stop.

Who in hell? Snoot listened as the engine eased and idled. Eight cylinders, American Motors made. Wisps of exhaust vapor streamed across the headlights. He could see the window rolling down.

"Snoot?"

"Says who?" Snoot turned his good ear toward the voice and braced himself, more against impatience than fear. At fifty-seven, most of his bones had been broken at least once, but only a few had been harmed at the hands of another man. Another scuffle would be more of an inconvenience than a danger. Tonight, his only wish was for privacy—and to see his old friend, the flatlander. He watched the car door open. The dome light shone on the head and shoulders of a younger man. "By the Jesus!" Look at him, still a doozy of a boy. "Walker Owen! Hot *damn!*"

Snoot dropped his sack of groceries and took a step closer, eyes blinking, focusing. "Rig and a half!" They met on the double white line. Snoot lifted Walker off the pavement and whirled him around. "Put on some meat since I hefted you last." Snoot swallowed against the lump in his throat. "Son of a hoor, I thought you was never going to get here!"

Walker hung on to Snoot until the spinning stopped. "I've been looking for you, Grizzly, all over. Been here for a couple of hours," he said, catching his breath. "Good to see you."

" 'Bout time, ain't it?" Snoot held Walker at arm's length, then hugged him again, like a long-lost son. "Went to get some grocery food, just lugging it back." He nodded at the tipped-over package on the road. "We'll camp in the cabin. I hoed it out decent this forenoon."

"I went out there, looking for you. Kinda spooky. Junior said you might be—"

"You saw Junior?" Snoot had hoped that part of Walker's visit wouldn't have begun so soon.

"Wasn't exactly the one I was looking for."

"Use you kind of prickly, did he?" There it was again, the ripping sensation across Snoot's chest. How had he drawn Junior in the lottery of fatherhood? Why had his son, from birth, been so unlike the one he'd hoped for, so unlike the boy in front of him, the one he'd called to join him on the dark road of his final years?

"He was okay." Walker shuffled his feet. "Same old stuff."

"Still puts the wood right to you."

"I don't know. Hey, it's good to see you."

Snoot cleared his throat and hawked a gob over his shoulder. "Still an awful little turd when he sets his mind to it. Lot worse now from when you knew him. Blames everybody for every little goddamned thing that ever happened to him."

"He was all right, really. So tell me what's been going on."

"Don't let him get to you, that's all." Snoot put his arm around Walker's shoulder and squeezed. "Let's get off'n this Christly road and make some supper. Hungry?"

Walker backed the Wagoneer up to the turnout, and they began the hike up the hill to the cabin. Snoot led the way, feeling younger than he had in years. Every twenty paces he paused and turned to look back, to make sure Walker was following. "So much to gab about, don't know where to commence." Another few paces: "I wouldn't of barely recognized you, Walker. No disrespect, you just look altogether different. Lawyering can't be treating you too goddamned awful." Wouldn't Frouncy be tickled to see him? "You knew me soon as you saw me, right?"

"I knew it was either you—or Snow White."

Snoot heard himself laughing for the first time in weeks. "Walker's back, no doubt about it!" And he felt like singing:

> *Hinky dinky tong-tong, wooga wooga whoa,*
> *Got me some wimmens down in Mex-i-co!*

Snoot stopped where the path crossed a rise in the land and waited for Walker to reach his side. Ahead of them, a swelling sea of hemlock tops rose to the base of the Abenaki Ledges. The cliff stood silver-black and silent, a spectral palisade bejeweled with giant boulders at its crown. He scanned the curtain wall of rock as he'd done now for six decades, watching it the way a person watches flames in a fire, looking for nothing, seeing it all.

Closer in, he watched the little clouds of exhaled vapor he and Walker made in the chill night air, and he wished the frosty residue of their two lives could meld together, his and Walker's. Like a father and a son, he thought, like every man deserved—just once—to stand on the same piece of ground with his own blood beside him, the weight of them reaching down deep in the ground, like the roots of a tree.

They walked slowly up the trail, then down a dark ravine that split off in two directions at the end—Snoot's daddy called it Polly's Crotch—and then up along the spine of another ridge. Snoot stopped, and in the middle of a hundred and sixty acres of land that had been in his family for four generations, he let it go: "Junior sold the farm."

"Sold *what?*"

"You heard me." Good. Walker was riled, still had some spunk.

"The *farm?*"

"We deeded it to him last July, Frounce and me. Felt sorry for him, handicap crippled and such. He kept pestering us, so we deeded it to him, clear and free. Then he turned around and sold a share each to Bud and Tot, kept a third share for hisself." Snoot dipped into a pouch of Red Man and stuffed a wad under his lip. "Tot's the brains behind it, wouldn't you know. Hired a Boston architat to draw a hotel lodge, then put up a mess of condoms."

"Bullshit. We can't let him do that." Walker sounded like he thought it was funny.

Snoot explained: "A development, is what it is." He wiped the word off his mouth with his cuff. "You see them on the TV station. Gobs of money. 'Course, Tot and Bud's had a bundle in the bank for years—sets there gaining, seven days and nights a week; festers, stews, and churns—a great green wad of it, so they claim. Bud and Tot and Junior boy, they make an awful bunch, now, don't they?"

"Snoot, what about the terms of the deed?"

Sometimes Walker sounded like a goddamned pinhead. "Ha!"

"You put any restrictions on it? Any covenants, lifetime rights, any conservation easements?"

He could sling the bullshit when he got wound up.

"Gayboy Beasley wrote it up the way Junior wanted, and that was that." Snoot wouldn't admit he hadn't read the contract—*couldn't* read the goddamned fancy six-bit words. "Frounce felt sorry for the boy, so we give him the whole nine yards. She paid old weaselly Beasley over two hundred dollars for the legal papers, and look what's took and happened now." He swung his arm in a wide semicircle. "Dumbest goddamned thing I ever did." He didn't know how to begin to explain himself—or his son, or how it ever turned out the way it had between them—and it made him feel like he wanted to break something all to hell. "Let's go," he said. "This kind of talk gives me a pain in the rectus."

They walked. Snoot touched the pocketknife in his pocket, worn smooth as river stone from years of use. Junior had given it to him when he was still a boy—earned the money himself and picked the best knife in the store, a Buck, a beauty. Snoot was never without it. A man needed a good knife—like he needed a son. Year by year, the blade had been honed down to a fraction of its original width, stropped razor sharp, cleaned, oiled, and folded safe into its turquoise eagle handle.

Snoot wrapped his fingers around it now, warm in his pocket after twenty years of cutting, and still as good a knife as ever there was. Each time he touched it, he thought of his son and wondered if his gift of a knife was meant to cut them loose from each other or carve a deeper surgery.

To the west, the forest opened to a pasture that rolled down the hill and flattened out at the rear of the house. There were lights in the windows, Junior's lights, dull yellow blocks in a low blank wall. Next to the house, Snoot made out the shadowy islands of his collections, his pyramidal woodpile, and the outlined shapes of the barn with the sagging ridge line, the four-bay tractor shed, and the caved-in henhouse. Farther on, beyond the dung pile, rows of fruit trees—Bartletts, Pipestone plums, and Winesaps—dotted the piece where his grandfather planted potatoes.

"I'll want to see that deed, for starters, and get a look at a copy of all their permits," Walker said, sneaking up on Snoot's bad ear.

Snoot turned to Walker impatiently. "It's gone, goddammit, *gone.* Tot's greased the skids, knows all the big shots over to Montpelier. Claire's talked herself blue in the face, but none of them'll give an inch."

"What about the Planning Board?"

Snoot wondered if Walker had learned a thing down in Connecticut. "Huh! Beasley and them Christly cowards ought to leave town twice and come back once."

"No objection from Fish and Game?"

"Not since my last citation for jumpmeat venison." What a laugh. "How'n hell should I know? Buncha gobbledegook, you ask me. All I know is, Bud and Tot's took care of it, handed out the money, browned their noses, spread their cheeks—whatever it takes, they've went and done it. And Junior runs the applause machine from the sidelines, pockets full of cash." Snoot felt a pressure building, held it in, then let go a walloping fart. Pleased with his perfect timing, he added, "Thieving Huns are all in it together." Then he spun around and walked quickly up the trail, away from the dimming farmhouse lights, from all the things he didn't understand.

The hill flattened out. They crossed a stone wall, and Snoot slowed his pace. "Meanwhiles, Junior keeps tinkering with his televisions, rolls around on them skinny little wheels." He stopped to wait for Walker. "And here *she's* paying for Frouncy's medical." Walker bumped into him. "Claire don't ever quit."

Walker stood on the dark side of a hemlock four feet through. "I wondered. . . ."

Snoot ignored him. "She always liked you special," he said, moving slowly this time, unsure if Walker was following or not. There would be a better time to talk about Claire, to do it right. "We'll slip by tomorrow and see Frouncy," he shouted, "see how she's doing." How had it ever come to that? " 'Course, she might not recognize you, with your whiskers gone and everything."

Long after they reached the cabin, lit the lamps, and stoked the stove, Snoot still marveled that Walker was really back in Dalton Pond. "Love a duck, never thought we'd see the day." He used any excuse to handle Walker, hug him, punch him, rumple his hair, make sure he wasn't a ghost. They sat at the worn plank table timidly at first—one moment fully synchronized, another moment disjointed. Snoot had so many questions he wanted to ask, they seemed to logjam in his mind, and sometimes all he could do was stare across the table, grinning, or reach across to Walker and whack him. "You wasn't cut out to be a woodchuck—and it's lucky you wasn't." He'd always wondered what made Walker stay around as long as he had, what with his fancy education and reading books.

When he tried to answer Walker's questions about

Frouncy's health, Snoot wanted to make it sound as if she were all right.

"She's biding time. Bound to get better." But when he tried to say more, he found he couldn't, and he couldn't look at Walker either, squinted out the window at the trees instead.

"How long's she going to be there?"

Snoot said he guessed maybe a week or two, but he knew he was lying. "She understands you—if she wants to." He shrugged. "But she don't always want to. And she don't talk right. 'Doxie,' 'cherries,' and 'in the cupboard.' Everything she says, it comes out 'Doxie' and such. And her the one that always jabbered like a poleaxed Frenchman." Now there was nothing to cling to past wanting—hopeful, hollow, painful wanting.

Snoot was reminded how the deep cleft down the middle of Walker's chin flattened out when he got stubborn, his chin out to there, his *lawyer* look, now. Walker always could bulldog a subject to death.

"What happens to you and Frouncy when—*if*—they want to tear down the house?"

"Happens?" Snoot got up, opened the wood stove, and blew on the hissing wood, coaxing the fire. Hiding his face behind the iron door, he said he and Frouncy had a few places in mind, maybe move to the Canadian border, maybe over to New Hampshire—any place, it didn't matter. "We'll make do."

"And Claire'll go with Junior?" Walker asked after a long silence.

Snoot pulled his head out of the smoke. "It's a miracle she ain't already gone. Don't none of us deserve her." He shook his head at the times he'd seen her staring out the window, tempted to be somewhere else. "Been like a daughter to Frounce and me. I told the boy if he ever struck her, I'd geld him." He poked at the fire. "Don't know why she puts up with us dumb Canucks."

He'd asked Frouncy, did she want some pudding? and she acted like she didn't know him.

"Claire's got a head on her shoulders. Stubborn, too." Both qualities Snoot admired.

"Some things never change."

"Still takes night lessons over to Johnson State. Keeps herself busy—and who's to blame her?" Snoot sat down, put his elbows on the table, and cracked his fingers one by one. "Quiet girl, lot on her mind." He studied the dark walls in the lamplight; he built the cabin in '54 with lumber traded for a twelve-gauge bird gun. Junior was three or four years old at the time and full of the devil—switch him ten times a day, and he still wouldn't mind. "I should judge there's a lot on everybody's mind, about now."

Walker held his bottle up to the lantern, turning it slowly as though he were studying something in the murky brown glass.

"Goddammit." Snoot felt the ripping sensation again, felt himself rising and sinking, somewhere between barely floating and drowning. He'd felt it first the day they rushed Frouncy to the hospital, rank strangers in starched white trousers strapping her onto a canvas stretcher, streaks of red light slapping at her blanchy skin—they wouldn't let him ride with her. He'd felt the wave come crashing down, flood over Frouncy's disappearing ambulance, blot out the sky, the woods, the barn—the wave crashed down and smothered him before a drop fell on the sullen son watching it all without a hitch from his roller chair by the kitchen window.

That day marked the first time Snoot had ever thought of himself as getting old, getting sick, without a place and a reason to live. It felt to him like a wave from above, and it felt like sinking down, like a sphagnum bog in an April thaw, bottomless, sucking him in. Why did it have to work that way? He told himself over and over not to dwell on things he couldn't change, but it didn't seem to help. Something had to give.

He stole a glance at Walker. What were his chances with Claire. Maybe? Yes? It was as much for Claire as anything else that he'd called the boy in the first place. Some good might come of all this gloomy business after all. For *them*, he'd swim. He'd stay afloat as long as he could.

Snoot took a deep breath, leaned across the table,

grabbed Walker's arm, and tried on a grin. "Back in the cabin, Walker. We're back in the goddamned hemlock woods!"

As the cabin warmed up, Snoot warmed up with it and returned the conversation often to Claire. " 'Course she knew better"—he watched Walker come to attention—"but she's a girl that don't give up. Same as Frouncy. Except Frounce ain't so young as she used to be." Snoot had seen her carry a hundred-pound bag of potatoes under one arm and a bouquet of meadow violets in the other, never crushing a petal. "Claire marrying him was out of pity, is all it was." He crossed and uncrossed his legs under the table, then groaned as he resettled his bulk. "A few months with Junior, and that's all she wrote."

Walker got up and fiddled with the stove.

"He mouth-abused her something awful. You live in a house with somebody, there's not too much goes on in private." Snoot studied Walker. Was he digging too deep? He focused on an image of Claire and Walker in the old days; he blinked at it, but it wouldn't dissolve. "Frounce and me, we kept our nose out of it." He cleared his throat. "But we'd talk about you in front of her, and mister man, it shined her apples, every time. 'Course, it's none of my beeswax."

Walker looked embarrassed, added his empty bottle to the empties on the windowsill. "I thought she'd probably forgotten me."

Snoot smacked the table. "It's a wonder she didn't, too! You been a stranger too goddamned long." He watched Walker pace up and down the length of the room. "Lucky Frounce likes to jabber your name. Hell's bells, nobody's perfect, that's the goddamned truth, but you've been scarce around here, and you know it." He looked past Walker and saw a glow in the trees. Funny, how the light played in the hemlock boughs on frosty nights. "Feels like snow, don't it?" He wished Walker'd been the mule kicking in Claire's stall, all this time. Snoot pushed away the thought, confused by a nagging trace of allegiance to a son he loved and hated. What would Frouncy think if she knew he felt the way he did? He got up from the table and opened the broken-down refrigerator, his mouse-proof pantry stocked with food and beer. "If you and me had any goddamned common sense a-tall," he said, "we'd open some more of these sudsies before they go bad."

The warm buzz released him. Talking and drinking as the evening wore on, Snoot finally felt himself floating above the wave, sailing free in a fresh gale of words. He found himself laughing again, spilling out an old story about a woman he'd courted and discarded.

"What a mis'able reptile she was, by the Jesus!" Walker's smile encouraged him. "I told you about old Canvasback?"

"No, no. Go on."

"Some valentine she was." Thank the jeez, Walker was pulling in his lawyer chin. "Born on a rainy morning and everything she's touched has been mist." Snoot mimicked a pickpocket's fingers. "She was so mis'able, she'd steal the shit off a lame chicken."

Walker was laughing. What a night it was!

"Reach right up its ass and *snap* it off!"

Snoot heard himself talking like an addlebrained dolt, and he had no intention of stopping.

He told stories about tractor accidents, chain-saw mutilations, Siamese births, and mating moose, and inevitably he held forth on "How to breed a woman." The lecture was brief and utterly serious. "The thing of it is," he whispered, rolling his eyes, "you won't get nowhere without you give 'em plenty of *snoozle.*" He was so pleased with himself! "You got to move comfortable, bide your time. Stir it slow and easy before you bring it to a boil." Then he grinned with an old man's appreciation of knowledge mastered long ago, however little used of late. "You got to let it *soak.*"

From women, the topic swung to engine swapping, hunting partridge, then farming. "Animals? The White House don't know jack shit about animals! They had any idea what you could do with a couple of rabbits, couple of sheep. . . ."

He recited the do's and don'ts of breeding meat rabbits, the economics of ducks, geese, milking goats, and pigs. He'd raised turkeys, a thousand at a time, "dumber than dog dirt," and short-horned Herefords: "wade through a five-strand barbed-wire fence like it was made of cobwebs." He retold the family stories of how he and Frouncy had never gone hungry, always paid their taxes on time, how they grew vegetables in random plots weaved in around their buildings—corn by the henhouse, tomatoes by the back door, squash and cucumber vines running over the junkpiles. Snoot hated straight rows—had he told Walker all this before? Frig it, maybe he had, but he'd tell him again: how he planted his gardens in spirals, triangles, and star patterns. He planted messages for airplanes, four-lettered obscenities in spinach and broccoli. He reminded Walker how he'd logged for years with a team of Belgians—hay was free, gas cost money. When he had to, he worked out, driving for the bobbin mill. He boasted he once drove to Boston and back in ten hours flat in a deuce-and-a-half International. He hated Boston, the noise, the stink. He was convinced Crooked Mountain was the prettiest place in the whole goddamned world, and he couldn't understand why anybody'd live anywhere else. Junior was the one who was willing to travel ten thousand miles to get his ass shot off—"which he might as well of done," he'd added, his enthusiasm suddenly gone, "for all he's been worth to this place." Then Snoot drained his bottle and wiped his mouth on his sleeve. "My mother's milk tasted half that good, I'd still be sucking on her teat. Hungry?"

Walker shrugged. "Sure."

"We'll fix some groceries." He brought out the entire contents of the refrigerator: Spam, sardines, Velveeta, soda crackers, jerked beef, pretzels, peanuts, and beer. He put a pan on the stove and opened a tin. "You ought to taste it, though, Walker, really. Claire's one hell of a cook."

By midnight, the wood stove was roaring and Snoot's union suit was soaked with beer sweat. His conversation was becoming as fuzzy as his teeth tasted, but it was a hell of thing to be talking again. "You can't go back," he said, determined to keep out from under the voice that repeated *Doxie, cherries,* and *in the cupboard.* He picked at a nail head on the tabletop, leaned over, and cuffed Walker's arm. "Thought I'd never see you again."

"I'm awful glad you called. Feels good to be back." Walker smiled like he meant it. "And what you said about Claire—I guess I was worried about how she felt."

"Nothing to worry about, then. She knows what's what, had plenty of time to see it clear." In the light of the lantern, Snoot saw his own face reflected double in Walker's glasses. It seemed all the smart ones wore spectacles. Except Claire. "Jeesum, she learned a lot from you."

"It went both ways. We traded."

Snoot had always wondered about all that, the notion of swapping ideas, people in cities, reading books and working inside all day, making nothing but papers, living in buildings with elevators. Walker was the closest he'd ever come to knowing something of that world, and learning more about it always seemed more trouble than it was worth.

Snoot yawned. "What about your daddy? How is Mr. Flyrod? Still cherchez le mudchub?" Now there was a man who never enjoyed a day of his life.

"He quit fishing and moved to San Diego when Mother died. It's stamps now," Walker said. "I went out to see him last Christmas. Pretty sad. He's living in a little condo, by himself. Pool nobody uses. One scrawny tree in the yard. Stamps all over the house, in his bathroom, in his food."

"Claire had some foreign stamps—from England or someplace over there. Maybe you could send him some." Snoot had always felt sorry for Walker's parents, the nameless mother he'd never seen and couldn't even imagine, the timid father—a machinist, wasn't he, clever with tools?—a man who never raised his voice and seemed to have no firm opinions on anything. Neither seemed right for Walker, or Walker for them. Maybe Junior would have worked out better with a stamp man for a father. "Jesus, Mary, and Joseph, I'm tired."

• • •

Snoot awoke at three in the morning. It was snowing. The only light in the room was a pale orange ring around the stove door, flickering as the last log turned to coals in the firebox. He sat up in his bunk near the window, near the fresh air, wrapped in a bearskin robe. Walker slept in the loft above him, in the place Snoot thought of as upstairs, where a son was meant to sleep—serenely, without malice. In the old house, Junior had slept upstairs, but it always seemed as though the ceiling in the room below would crack with the weight of his anger, the floor joists giving way to his unappeasable dissatisfaction. With Walker above him now, Snoot thought of the loft as weightless, a goosedown quilt stretched over the room.

He got up and pissed off the edge of the porch, resettled himself in his bunk, and soon was dreaming:

He was gathering tools and materials: framing squares, saws, hammers, crow bars and chisels, nails, screws, plumb bobs, mortar, trowels, caulk, and paint, and a mason's four-foot level. When he had it all assembled, he lugged it to the house and began the repairs he'd put off for so many years. The parlor and kitchen were first, all new cupboards and plaster and tight-fitting windows. Then the bathroom and bedrooms: fresh wallpaper and sanded, sealed floors. He and Walker patched the barn roof, rebuilt the el, and repainted the clapboards. Meanwhile, they laid in some venison, made their own home brew. They set out a trapline, skinned and sold the pelts, boiled maple sugar when the sap began to run, and always had a pot of stew simmering on the stove. Together, they worked and laughed and rested and worked some more—always together.

Frouncy was her same old self, speaking freely and often, and appeared in every scene. Claire was married to Walker. They slept in the same bed, a fourposter like Frouncy and Snoot's. Bud, Tot, and Junior were absent.

He awoke again and focused on the night. He listened to frozen grains of snow ticking against the window glass, to the click of the cooling stove, to the steady cadence of Walker's breathing. He smelled the scent of frozen air, of mice and

47

grease and hot cast iron. He considered his dream: most of it was good, was what he wanted, but it blurred at the part he wanted most, the part about Frouncy. The rest, he decided, was going to come true. It *had* to, that's all there was to it, and he fell asleep determined to dream it through again.

4

MAKING CHOICES

CLAIRE HAD BEEN frying eggs for Snoot's breakfast when he made the phone call. "Catch him before he heads out to work," he'd said. It was six o'clock.

"Catch who?" Claire asked. She was still sleepy, thinking about the coming day at work.

"Walker, that's who. He'll be some surprised."

"Walker?" Claire realized she hadn't said his name out loud for years, and suddenly there it was. "Why call Walker?" She was gripping the edge of the stove without feeling the heat, staring at pillowy egg whites without seeing them.

"To talk to him," Snoot said, using the grumpy tone he'd fallen into lately. "What else would I call him for?" he asked, as he dialed the number she knew by heart.

The spatula shook in the pan. From time to time over the years she'd called information to confirm Walker was still living in New Haven. And whenever she did, there was always that anxious pause before the operator found the number, when Claire held her breath against the possibility that he was no longer listed, a missing person.

Snoot finished dialing, clamped the phone to his ear, and looked up at the cracks in the ceiling; he was doing what she'd wanted to do for years. "Hello, goddammit. Walker Owen?" A pause. "You know who this is?" Snoot still didn't

49

understand how telephones worked; he was convinced long-distance calls required extra volume, and since he was calling to Connecticut he shouted into the receiver.

Claire held her breath, hoping to hear Walker's voice—but she couldn't. Snoot's last words were, "Lord love a duck, yes. Stay's long as you like," and he hung up. Just like that. "He's coming." Snoot grinned for the first time in weeks. "Maybe stay for a while." He rubbed his paws together and added, "That okay with you?"

Claire poked at the eggs. The smell of bacon grease was unexpectedly nauseating. "Of course." She put Snoot's eggs and bacon on a plate and added four pieces of toast sliced into triangles. Snoot liked his toast light. She remembered Walker had liked his toast dark, almost burnt. After their first night together, he got up early and made breakfast while she slept, brought it up to the loft on a plywood tray. She remembered waking to the clink of a spoon in a cup; he was stirring honey into her tea. She remembered watching his graceful, tanned fingers as he spread butter, then jelly, on her toast; before he cut the last slice of butter, he wiped the sides of the jellied knife clean on the exposed end of the stick, so that once that slice was made, the leftover butter was perfectly clean. She'd never seen anyone do that before, especially a man. It impressed her, and it made her wonder about their future. Such a little thing, but she'd never forgotten it.

Snoot seemed pleased with himself. "Two eggs side by each, and a double pair of toast!" he joked in his imitation French patois. He waved a knife and fork in each hand, a sure sign of his optimism. "Gran' merci, ma belle." When Claire turned from the table to bring him his coffee, he reached to her. His grip covered most of her forearm, gently pressing her starched uniform sleeve.

"He's coming tonight," he said.

A tinny-sounding "Oh" was all she could afford.

"Nothing to get wrapped up around the axle about."

"I'm *not.*" Her voice squeaked, and she felt like a girl. "Why should I?" She withdrew her arm from Snoot's hand and brushed at her hair. "It'll be nice to see him," she said, turning away, steadying herself against a chair. "It's been a long time."

Snoot paused, then explained his sudden invitation. "Woke up this morning and it come to me like a bolt of a dream, except I was full awake. Maybe Walker can scuttle the development. He's a clever piece of industry, ain't no two ways about it. Jeesum, what I'd give to see him put the wood to weaselly Beasley." Snoot seemed determined to convince Claire the visit was a good idea. "Besides, it'll do Frouncy good to see his face. Me too, I suppose."

"What about J?" She nodded toward the corner of the house where her husband slept in a little room two doors away from hers. For how many years had they slept apart? Did it matter any more? "Will you tell *him* who's coming?"

Snoot shrugged, said nothing. Maybe, maybe not.

"He's not going to like it," she said, imagining the way Junior cocked his head when he was angry. "You know how he is about Walker."

Snoot lowered his head like a bull pawing dirt. "Then he never should have started this Christly business."

"Still. . . ." It felt odd, appearing to defend Junior against Snoot—against anyone. There was a time when she would have battled the world on her husband's behalf—and did. There was a time when she even resented Walker for being what Junior wasn't, but those days were long gone. "I just hope he doesn't . . ."

Snoot promised to keep Walker away from the house. They'd bunk in the cabin and stay out of sight. "Nobody's going to get ugly."

But she would worry, she thought—all day, all night— every moment until she saw him and knew what else his visit meant.

Claire kissed Snoot's forehead, as she left for work, and asked him to give Frouncy a hug for her. Outside the door, she started down the ramp, then paused in the cold and looked back at the house she'd always thought of as Frouncy's. Yet it was undeniably her home too—home for both of them and almost incidentally the men they were married to, home for two women who by some miracle had never once had a difficult moment between them. From the day Claire moved in, they seemed only to grow closer, while they watched their husbands grow farther apart. Now Frouncy was gone and Walker was coming back. Claire knew she was leaving a house that would never look the same again.

The drive to the Jordan hospital was a blur. Familiar landmarks fled by the headlights in disconnected patches, each one mixed with images of Junior—Junior angry, Junior sullen, Junior announcing he was going to sell the farm, Junior consulting no one on anything. She swerved to avoid hitting the guardrail on First Bridge, swung the wheel angrily at the thought of his refusing to discuss even the selling price. He'd said nothing about the future, about where they would live when they moved, and gave no clear answers to anyone's questions except to insist he had it all figured out.

She went through the day in a daze; her work seemed pointless, she was irritated at little things, cross with herself for letting Junior behave the way he had—and thinking too much about Walker. Why on earth should he have forgiven her? Besides, he could be married and the father of six, for all she knew. And he was coming to see Snoot, wasn't he?

Claire's best friend was a redheaded nurse named Jody Jarvis; Jody asked Claire if she was okay. Claire insisted it was nothing, "Just daydreaming—kind of tired," and wished Jody would leave her alone.

She watched the clock all day, didn't eat lunch, and was uniformly impatient with her wards. Even her favorite, a leukemic six-year-old nicknamed Doodlebug, failed to pull her out of her mood. And then, as she was bathing him, Claire realized she was furious, not at him—he'd suffered a lifetime in the last three years—but at the perverse application of fate. Who the hell was in charge anyway? Why did everything have to happen at once?

At five o'clock—it was surely the longest day in nursing history—she realized she dreaded going home. She started her car, drove two blocks, and stopped, as she often did after work, at the Jordan library. In the last few years, she'd rediscovered the pleasure of reading, losing herself in the real world of fiction, finding a way to make sense of other people's lives, at least.

The library smelled good; it was quiet and overly warm. Claire roamed the stacks, picked out a novel at random, and sat in her favorite leather chair. When she opened the book and began to read, the clatter in her brain kept still for a while, and she surrendered to the prose of an exotic place and time. Then, page by page, she found the characters had all somehow become involved with Walker; he'd intruded himself into the narrative and wouldn't leave. She turned back to the beginning and started again, but there he was. She closed the book. She hadn't been reading at all, just going through the motions while she thought about something else. What she'd been doing in the Jordan library for the past two hours was a perfect metaphor for what she'd done with her husband at home, for years.

The temperature in the kitchen was down to fifty degrees when she got home at eight. Junior was in his workroom—she saw a crack of light under his door—and Snoot was gone, out in the cabin with Walker no doubt. Just as well. She snapped on the lights, turned up the thermostat, and busied herself with preparing a quick dinner. Junior kept his door shut, but he knew she was home.

Claire enjoyed cooking for Snoot and Frouncy, but cooking for Junior was a mechanical housekeeping task, nothing more, like taking out the trash. She did it as efficiently as possible, with as little expectation of pleasure as he showed in eating the food, no matter how well prepared it might be. Tonight, as always, she did without his help; she preferred it that way and he expected it. When the chicken, peas, and rice were ready, she called to him. "Dinner."

He rolled into the kitchen slowly, floorboards creaking as he approached the table. When she saw the hard light in his eyes, she knew instantly that Walker had arrived.

Minutes passed without a word between them. "Where've you been, anyway?" Junior finally asked.

"I stopped at the library." She told herself she would be all right if she refused to argue.

"Pick out a book to read—with Walker?"

Claire decided not to act surprised at the mention of Walker's name. Why play games? She passed him his plate and said nothing.

"Snoot invite him up?" He looked up from his food. "Or did you?"

She stood with her back to the stove and stared out the window, over Junior's head. She couldn't talk and she couldn't eat; there wasn't a particle of nourishment for her in the entire room.

He continued eating, noisily, without speaking, packing it in as if he were wadding a cannon.

She took a deep breath; the charade was too absurd to continue, too exhausting. How many more years of turning blank pages? She decided to light the fuse. "Why do you need to hate him so much?"

"Hate him?"

"You seem"—she inhaled again—"to get satisfaction out of hating him."

"Me?"

"Yes, J. You."

"Bullshit." He chewed at another mouthful. "Why should I hate that asshole?"

"You call a lot of people that, but I think you call him that—because you've always been jealous of him."

Junior stared at her with heavy-lidded eyes. He tipped his head the way he did when he was preparing to hurt, a marsh bird about to spear its prey.

"Bullshit," he said. His face changed color, from turnip to beet. "Question is, why should I even *like* him? Should I like him for running out on his country?"

"He had three fused vertebrae, Junior. They wouldn't take him, and you know it!"

"Should I like him for being a college pinhead? For getting between me and my folks?"

"They happened to like him." But Claire knew the argument was already lost.

"*They* happened to like him? What about you?" Junior shoved his wheelchair away from the table, shouting. "Should I like him for fucking you silly?"

So there it was again, she thought, the one and only, inevitable reduction of love to the dirty word *fuck*. Her plate rattled as she put it in the sink. He'd made that accusation a thousand times, and it still made her sick to her stomach. "Just stop it, J."

"You started it," he yelled, spinning his chair around, aiming it at her.

"Okay, then I'll stop it too." Claire surprised herself with the calmness of her voice—or was it weariness, the kind that came of spending too much of a life trying to understand a man who couldn't afford to understand in return? "There's no way to even begin to talk about that kind of thing with you. We've been through it too many times—"

"And you always take his side, so frig it." He wheeled to within inches of her feet. "What'd you ask him up here for?"

"I didn't."

"See? You're taking his side again."

"I'm not taking anybody's side. Except my own."

The footrests of Junior's wheelchair nudged at her ankles, trapping her against the counter. He tipped his head so that his ear almost touched his shoulder. "If you fool around with him—I'm warning you—I'll break your goddamned arms."

Claire looked down at the carotid artery bulging out from the side of Junior's neck. As if from a distance, she saw herself watching him with a nurse's trained eye: shallow breathing, perspiring, pale skin, pulse rapid—that twitching movement under his ear. And then she saw herself pushing past him, floating to her room and closing the door behind her, standing with her forehead pressed against the wall with her eyes squeezed shut. She saw herself standing there, weightless, still, outside of time, until she heard the sound of his fork on his plate, heard him eating, heard him belch. What did he say? The rice was too salty?

She undressed, shivering, and slid into bed. The night suddenly seemed enormous with possibility; the air around her crackled as she wound herself into her blankets. She heard him coughing in his room, off and on all night, until she finally fell asleep.

In her dream, Claire is driving alone, along the Jordan road. Ahead of her, Junior drives a truck with his arm out the window, making a wing with his hand in the wind. In her dream, she is pleased; his hand looks so graceful, soaring and dipping, riding invisible currents, and she follows him closely, nodding her head to the dance of his arm. But at the curve by the creamery, he suddenly changes. In the way only dreams will allow, he is transformed into an injured bird, pinned to the road in the path of her onrushing wheels. She tries to stop, skids, screeches to a halt. The sound of a crowing rooster puts an end to her sleep, but the man-bird dream clings.

Dark outside. Cold, quiet. Five A.M. glowing green on the bedside clock, a quarter of an hour until her alarm. Cotton mouth, the nag of some unspecified dread, followed by the memory of the night before. Awful. Eyes open. The bird was stuck to something in the road. Claire turned toward the window, looking for clues to the weather. Had it snowed all night? In her dream, she couldn't steer her car around the bird. The wheels were aimed straight at it, wouldn't turn. Would she have to walk out to the cabin and bring Snoot back to plow the lane? Too cold. Too dark. Yawning. Snow. She tried to remember more about the dream, but the harder she tried, the more fragmented it became. Alert. Up on her elbows. Wide awake. J said he'd break her goddamned arms.

Claire pushed back her hair, massaging her temples with her fingertips. When she was living with Walker, her hair was so long it fell beyond her waist, long enough for her to sit on. She cut it short when she married Junior, snipping away a history she thought she'd abandoned forever, as if to dedicate all her energies to Junior's recuperation. Lately, she'd let her hair grow long again, wearing it up during the day, letting it fall in against her skin at night, a small but comforting pleasure—for her, alone.

She got up and tiptoed across the freezing floorboards to the window, hugging her nightdress around her. An inch or two of snow had whitened the pasture behind the house. She wouldn't need Snoot to plow the lane. Seeing Walker would have to wait.

She put on her robe and carried her clothes across the hall to the bathroom, where she closed the door, took off her robe, and draped it over the handicap grab bar by the shower. The chrome was yellowed and pitted now, the mounting screws were rusted. Snoot installed it for Junior when he first came home from rehab, paid a hundred dollars for it so that Junior could care for himself. She remembered how she helped him into the shower for the first time, how vulnerable he looked in his bath chair, how he wept into the water cascading over him. And those first long nights when she began to realize the full significance of what had happened, lying beside him, wanting to be held, to make love to a man who needed love so badly he'd never dared speak its name.

Claire stood naked, waiting as the water warmed. For the first time in months, she weighed herself on Frouncy's scale; the needle barely passed the hundred mark. Walker Owen. Steam clouded the mirror above the sink. She looked down at the grab bar, adjusting a fold of fabric so that her robe completely hid the tarnished tubing, and for a peaceful moment its purpose ceased to exist.

After her shower, she stood in front of the dripping mirror with a pair of tweezers. Her near-perfect eyebrows were quickly perfected. Feeling foolish but unable to stop, she rummaged through a makeup kit for lipstick and eye shadow, surprising herself as she made up her face. She stared at herself in the mirror, at her pinned-up hair, then finger-curled a wispy tendril dangling by the curve of her neck. Now she turned her head so that a taut ridge stretched from ear to collarbone, pursed her lips into the shape of a kiss. She knew she was pretty, but the idea of being valued for it made her uncomfortable; it embarrassed her when friends insisted she was beautiful. They raved about her high cheekbones and perfect nose, but they especially envied her eyes—Walker called them obsidian—black and backlit with a deep, dark flame, framed with long thick lashes. Her father's eyes.

Claire spent hours of her childhood staring at the grainy photograph of Horton Flint. He was standing next to a dusty old car, one foot resting on the running board. She knew him well, in snapshot form—the calm intensity of his gaze, the weightless ease of his posture—but she knew him in two dimensions only, and his absence ever since her second birthday made her think of him as a picture rather than a flesh-and-blood father. Horton Flint—the notorious shaman's grandson, Horton Eagle-in-the-Wind—had left a legacy of beauty.

Claire let her hair fall, shook it loose, and felt her breasts sway. Had she changed? Her hands pressed down her rib cage to the indent of her waistline, to the smooth curve of her narrow hips. The mirror was not unkind.

Wrapped in her bathrobe, she opened a jar of cream cleanser and rubbed off her makeup—all but the eye shadow; that much would stay. Within minutes, she was dressed in her uniform, white, starched, and pressed, closing her bedroom door tight behind her.

In the kitchen, she paced back and forth waiting for the kettle to boil. The morning before, Snoot was shouting to Walker, long distance on the phone. Now—a century later— Walker was asleep in the cabin, a half mile away.

The kettle began to blow steam. Claire paused for the last time at the frosty east window, searching for traces of dawn in the woods. This is stupid, she thought. She dropped a tea bag into a cup of water and held it to her lips, blowing across the rim. Her toast popped up and she buttered it. She heard the sound of Junior coughing in his room.

He was sick again, another round of bronchial infections that seemed to plague him every year as soon as the temperature fell. Again he coughed, ragged, angry sounds. She heard him clear his throat, probably still asleep. His bed squeaked. Was he getting up? He must have rolled over. She pictured him punching his pillow, grumbling, stinking. When he was angry, his cough seemed to get worse. She made a mental note to have his prescription refilled at the hospital pharmacy. Later, she'd realize that for the first time ever she'd forgotten all about it.

Outside, the brisk morning air brought tears to her eyes. She wiped a mitten across her cheeks, then swept a handful of snow from the ramp's railing and watched it fall; it was light and fluffy, cold dry snow; the roads would be safe. She walked to her car, still searching the woods to the east for a sign, but dawn dragged down the mountain too slowly; she knew she would be most of the way to Jordan before the timid winter sun was high enough to show a single tree.

She started her car, then got out and scraped at the frost and snow on the windows. The cold felt good, fresh and un-compromising—the way she wished she could feel, just once. Each pass of the scraper left clean, wide stripes across the windshield. She took her time, enjoying the simple task, the hum of the idling motor, the brightness of the headlights against the barn wall. On most other mornings, she scraped only a tiny patch, drove down the dark hill hunched over the steering wheel, peeking through her little scratch of a window until the defroster finally melted the rest of the ice away. But this morning, she would scrape and dust away every crystal of ice, every drop, every flake of snow and rime from every centimeter of glass, as if seeing clearly were a matter of ut-most priority, as if perfect vision would be finally hers.

At the bottom of the lane, she turned left; hers were the first car tracks on the road. She drove down the road past Benoits' and saw lights in the kitchen, saw Pearle look up from her kitchen sink, a lonely woman, a halfhearted wave—a warning of what can happen. Then past Beasley Pruitt's. The little bachelor's house was dark as it always was in the morn-ings. Who knew how late he slept? Next was the long stretch of woods before the village, then the thirty-some households bunching up toward the common, some of them stirring, most still asleep. The lights in her stepfather's store were blazing—

he was open for business as usual at six. She passed the church and the schoolhouse and the Home, the light in Frouncy's window a dim and distant beacon.

Past the Home, Claire turned south onto the Jordan road, crossed the iron bridge, and drove the three miles to Creamery Curve. As she did every day on her way to and from work, she slowed when she came to the bend in the road. This morning, she pulled off at the weathered signpost and turned into the empty parking lot; the boarded-up creamery was behind her when she stopped. Her headlights shone on a row of ancient sugar maples across the road.

When he was sixteen, Junior demolished his first car against those trees. Drove like he didn't care if he lived or died, they said around town, shaking their heads, kind of proud of the boy. He climbed out of the twisted pile with a half-inch scratch on his pinky finger. The next day he took his friends to Hadlock's salvage yard to gawk at the wreckage, take pictures of a crumpled wreck that would have killed anybody else twice.

Two of the old trees still showed scars where the car slammed into them. Bark was bunched up around the wounds like puffy lips. Someone once suggested the trees should be cut down; they could have killed the best athlete Dalton Pond had ever seen. Ran like a deer, threw a football like a bullet. He was two grades ahead of her, but that didn't matter. And he had a reputation: handy with the girls. Claire almost believed him when he told her she was beautiful. She was tired of hearing that worn-out line, but there was something about the way he said he was going to show the army what it took to make a soldier. Junior Audette, everybody's hero—except his father's—king of the mountain, indestructible. A miracle is what he was.

Claire collected stories about him. She gravitated to him the same way she was drawn to the legends about her absent father—except her father was nowhere to be found, and Junior Audette, big as life, came to school five days a week. Did she have a choice back then, she wondered? Could she have predicted he'd leave her after graduation for a painted hussy from Catamount, a peroxided coke addict who moved to California the moment news came back from Vietnam he'd lost his legs?

Claire switched on her high beams for a better look at the trees across the road. For the last ten years, the maples had reminded her twice daily of bad luck and hasty decisions, none of which had ever seemed redeemable. For the last ten years, they reminded her something was wrong but never told her how to fix it. Or maybe they had, she thought, and she wouldn't listen.

A car drove by, a Pontiac, Vera Parker on her way to work at the Superette in Catamount. Vera and Claire were friends in high school. Now they waved through windshields twice a day, when light permitted, but hadn't spoken in years. Was she still married to that creepy guy, Dennis? Did he ever threaten her? Did she drive to work wondering about another man, too?

Claire switched off the headlights, then the ignition, and sat in silence, cozy and warm. Another car drove by, taillights blurred in a plume of exhaust as it disappeared around the bend. Claire closed her eyes for a moment, then opened them wide. The dashboard clock glowed its reminder; she'd be late to work, but it didn't matter. "I'll break your goddamned arms," she whispered to herself.

Hints of daybreak: tops of the maples catching light, faint phosphorescence on the spiky branch tips, skeletal emerging limbs, crooks, massive trunks dry-brushed with the dirty-yellow tint of winter's dawning sky. Walker was awake, no doubt. Claire wiped the vapor from the windshield and watched the color of the sky and snow become the same hue, and when they found that perfect pastel equilibrium, she left the creamery and drove to work—skillfully, fast, and wide awake—on a road she felt she'd never truly driven before.

The hospital droned with the call of its duties. Again, Claire was distracted all morning, but she had an energy she hadn't had the day before, found herself running in the hall, taking stairs two at a time. Around eleven, she was in the midst of changing the sterile dressing on Doodlebug's IV access when she heard shouting at the unit desk; she immediately recognized the grating voice of Dr. Sarnoff—prima-donna surgeon and nurse's pest—an imperious runt whose expensive platform shoes did nothing for his stature.

"Who's in charge here?" He was ranting, as usual.

Claire put aside the dressing, picked up a toy clown, and handed it to Doodlebug. "Isn't Bozo silly?" The boy smiled and nodded, pale, blue-eyed, grateful for her attention.

Down the hall, the yelling subsided as a pair of nurses deflected the doctor's wrath. Claire completed her procedure, then stroked the boy's forehead and repositioned his pillows. When she was satisfied he was as comfortable as possible, she said goodbye and left the room with blood and urine samples—two little plastic vials, still warm, swimming with unforgiving evidence.

She decided to take the samples to the lab herself, hoping her complicity might somehow help to tip the balance in Doodlebug's favor. But first—and only because it was on the way—she would deal with Dr. Sam Sarnoff. She prepared herself by walking slower than she'd walked all day—down the hall and around the corner, white shoes squeaking on the waxed linoleum.

He was stooped over the unit desk with his back to her. Claire tapped his shoulder with the warm container of Doodlebug's urine. "I'm in charge of this unit, doctor," she said. "As I've told you before, we don't raise our voices here." If the stuffed-shirt surgeon didn't like it, he could take her to Administration. "These kids have enough to be upset about. No one needs to shout in the Pediatric Wing."

Sarnoff began to say something, then changed his mind. She stared at him unblinkingly; then, holding Doodlebug's yellow specimen up to the light, she asked, "Think it'll snow again tonight?"

During her lunch period, Claire left the hospital and hurried two doors down the street to the P and C Supermarket. It was Friday, and, as she had for years, she spent her noonday break buying groceries for the weekend. Inside the doors, she grabbed a wire shopping cart and steered its wobbly wheels up and down the narrow aisles. The mental list she'd practiced filling over the years was a matter of rote by now, and as she loaded the cart with sugar and flour, coffee, milk, and vegetables, she tried to remember Walker's favorite foods.

At the end of the last aisle, opposite the meat counter, she stopped unexpectedly in front of the display of peanut butters, jellies, and jams. Wasn't there a funny jam he liked, an imported brand in a ceramic crock? Wasn't it English? She scanned the rows and was surprised to see exactly what she was looking for—there, on the top shelf. Dundee. Just as she remembered it. Maybe Snoot would like it too. Maybe Frouncy. A couple of bucks. Why not? She reached up for it. Someone else reached for it, too—a man's hand—Walker Owen's.

The jam stayed on the shelf. Claire had no idea how the next part began, but suddenly she and Walker were embracing, crushing one another tight, then breaking apart as if surprised at what they'd done.

"Look at you." She touched his cheek as if it were a miracle. He looked better with age, even kind of dangerous, with his boxer's nose and the deep smile lines creased into the skin around his eyes and mouth. And he still looked boyish too, his hair cowlicked in front, still sandy blond—still Walker, standing there in front of the rows of peanut butter. "Of all places . . . here. . . ."

"I took a chance, remembered you shopped on Fridays." He grinned, almost apologetically. "Hope you don't mind."

"Mind?" Claire prodded her wedding band with the tip of her thumb, put her hand in her pocket, felt herself blush. "Don't be silly." Had he forgiven her? "How are you?" She admonished herself not to flirt. "What have you been up to?" Why couldn't J have done something with his life? "Tell me everything." Her knees liquefied. "It's so good . . . to see you."

"Snoot called me." Walker seemed unsure of where to

begin. "I came up last night." He sounded like he was talking to a married woman. "Saw Frouncy this morning."

"Oh."

"She looked so *haunted*, I almost didn't recognize her, in bed without her teeth. Snoot says she's better?"

"Let's hope." Claire found herself caught up in Walker's face. Who did Walker remind her of? "It was touch-and-go for a few days, but she's improved. We'll know more soon." Himself. He reminded her of himself. "They don't know if she'll regain her speech or not."

"Snoot said. And you've been in to see her every day."

He was being so formal, so careful. "And *you* saw J."

"Yeah. Yesterday." A cautious pause. "He seemed okay."

Claire turned away and reached for the Dundee marmalade. "Still crazy for jam?"

Walker laughed. He was. His favorite. How did she remember? "After all these years. Thanks."

She put a jar in her shopping cart—and another. "Just in case." Then, searching his eyes, she saw those gray irises that turned smoky-blue in summer, and they reminded her what summers could be like—and hadn't. It spilled out. "It's been a disaster, Walker. A big mistake."

He bit his lip, nodded, brushed at his sandy hair, touched her arm. "Join the club." The tone had changed. "At least it doesn't show. On you. You're as beautiful as ever."

This time, she knew she blushed deeply. No man had told her she was beautiful in years, let alone in a supermarket. It felt so strange to hear it, to accept it as a compliment, so good, so overdue; she was determined to enjoy it, let it take her where it might. It was finally her turn.

They stood in the narrow aisle talking, laughing, trading questions for most of an hour. She forgot about the hospital, her grocery list, her kids, her husband. Walker was back, and he seemed as happy to see her as she was to see him.

"It didn't spoil you, law school, and all that." It occurred to her that while they were apart, they'd both had a chance to grow up. "And you never got married?" She wanted to know much more than she felt entitled to ask. Yet she felt bold—even brazen—and asked him to meet her the next day.

"Where?"

Alone, but not, definitely not, at the house. "Let's go on a picnic. The weather's supposed to be beautiful." Would he meet her?

Of course.

They'd drive up to Big Church, to Smooth Rock, their old picnic spot. Junior—who was Junior?—would be off hunting with Bud, up Mudchub Brook, in back of Fellows's on the other side of Dalton Pond.

"You'll come?" They'd be alone. Sure, sure, they'd wear orange so they wouldn't get shot. They'd catch up, talk, touch, maybe hold hands; it would be perfect. "I'll pack the marmalade," she said. "Both jars." And she realized that for the first time in a decade, the gloomy specter of Junior had vanished.

Dr. Sarnoff was standing by the unit desk when she got back from seeing Walker at the P and C. He wanted to apologize, he said, standing too close to her, reeking of mints. He asked her out to dinner.

He knew she was married—and so was he—but he had a reputation for ignoring convention. Sarnoff was a soft, white, clammy lecher, disgusting. He stared at her breasts as he spoke.

She said no, plain and unadorned. And if that wasn't clear enough, she told him she was going to be at Doodlebug's birthday party, a surprise she'd planned for that evening at six.

Sarnoff smirked. "So the guy in the P and C gets to go first, is that it?"

"Excuse me, Sam?" He'd seen her with Walker in the supermarket, had he? "What'd you say?"

Lewdness crossed his face. "What's he have that I don't have?"

Claire hesitated, then heard herself deliver an answer so unlike her, so unimaginable, that she decided the words must have formed themselves. "A *whopper*, Doc." She leaned down close to his oily forehead and held her hands a foot apart. "And he knows how to use it," she whispered, raising her eyebrows, flaring her nostrils, "like the *big* guys do."

Sarnoff crumpled, turned, and hurried down the hall, white coattails flapping behind him. Claire stared after him until he disappeared around a corner, then ran to find Jody, pulled her into a laundry closet, and collapsed in a bin of bedsheets, giggling so hard her cheeks ached, happy all over, delighted with the whole wide world.

Jody said she wasn't staying for the surprise party; after work she was leaving for the weekend, going over to New Hampshire to her boyfriend's cottage on Cummings Lake.

"You'd pass up Doodlebug for Bobby Dodds?" Claire teased. She'd met Bobby a few times at Jody's apartment and liked him, a good match for her carrot-topped friend. Claire often stayed over with Jody when they worked the late shift together, or on winter nights when the roads were too dangerous for the drive back to Dalton Pond. Claire had her own key, which Jody begged her to use whenever she wanted.

She liked Jody's place, a cozy ground-floor apartment in a big Victorian house. She was especially intrigued by the bedside photographs of Jody and the tall, bearded Bobby— mugging, riding a tandem bicycle, holding hands at a hospital party. They looked so attached, she thought, so easy with themselves, good friends—they cared for each other. The photos hinted at some connective undercurrent Claire had always wished for, and she studied them carefully, looking for clues to how it might happen.

"Doodlebug's more your type," Jody joked.

"I could eat him up," Claire insisted. Once in a while, a child came along she couldn't resist; invariably, they seemed to be the ones who never went home.

"I like your eye shadow," Jody remarked on her way out.

"Does it show that much?"

"It looks fabulous." Jody was all red hair, white skin, and freckles.

66

"I just thought I'd try it," Claire said, unable to hide the grin.

Jody nodded, all business. "It's about time you had someone to please."

"We're going on a picnic tomorrow. Sounds like high school, doesn't it?"

"You'll freeze!" Then: "Come to think of it, you probably won't. But seriously, what about J?"

"He'll be out hunting with Bud all day and half the night, drinking at Hubby's."

"Just be careful," Jody said.

Claire squeezed her friend's hand and, for a moment, wondered what on earth she meant.

Doodlebug loved his party. "We're going to New York City," he told Claire. "We're going to the Vampire State Building!"

"You'll be way up in the clouds!" She lofted him above the bed like a bird. "You'll be so high up, people on the sidewalk will look like little ants." Then his parents would take him for a bone marrow transplant.

"Like little teeny bugs." He giggled, pointing an arm almost as thin as the IV tubing taped to it. Then a worried face. "If I fell off, I could break my bones."

"You won't fall off," she told him. "I promise." Nobody was going to break anyone's bones. "Your mommy and daddy will keep you safe." She hugged his fragile frame. "They love you, Mr. Doodlebug." Claire closed her eyes, wishing for him and for herself, for love.

5

PICNIC

JUNIOR WAS in his wheelchair, dressed and waiting for Bud at half past five. It was cold in the kitchen, and as he sat in the dark he wished he'd made himself some coffee, eaten a doughnut, anything to settle his stomach. Instead, he lit a cigarette, then coughed so hard he couldn't smoke it; he wheeled himself across the room and stubbed out the butt in the sink.

He was tired. All night, he lay awake listening for something—or someone, he didn't know what—all night, the loaded Remington stood propped against the wall next to his bed. And now he was sweating and waiting again. A handful of ammo wrapped in a sock made a lump in his breast pocket, heavy against his heart.

Bud said he'd bring coffee and lunch. He promised there were "tracks all over," in back of Farley Fellows's barn. Bud had put a salt lick out there in May, said the Bambis were tame as lap cats.

Junior wheeled to the window and looked out, shivering, searching the valley for a sign of Bud's truck. He saw nothing but night. Frost etched the glass. Above him, Orion had slipped to the east of the sky. Claire could turn up the furnace when she got up—if she wanted to. She'd gone straight to bed last night, passed the door to his room without a word. Today was her day off—tomorrow, too. It was easy enough for her to do whatever she wanted. That was the problem, wasn't it?

Junior wheeled himself over to the cookstove, hoping to find some part of it still warm from last night's fire. But there was nothing left; the smooth cast-iron firebox was cool as polished marble. No doubt about it, Claire forgot to stoke it when she came home—late again.

Daddy had a lot of nerve inviting Walker Owen back. They'd slept out at the cabin last night, playing homo campers. Daddy'd probably show him off today, drag him around town, visiting, like he was something extra special. Let him. He could take Walker any place he wanted to, as long as he kept him away from Claire. That was the least he could do, wasn't it? Where the hell was Bud, anyhow?

Last year, hunting with Bud, Junior sat in a lawn chair by a brook and caught pneumonia. Bud was supposed to drive the deer to him, "Like an ambush." Then Bud got to trailing a buck in the opposite direction, followed him all the way around the mountain to Bob and Betty Ormsby's place, finally lost the trail—and Junior never saw horn one.

Bud was big on ambushes. Whenever they went hunting, he liked to talk about "tactics," like they were in the military. He asked Junior all sorts of questions about 'Nam, wanted to know about the juicy stuff. But Junior wouldn't talk about the sawed-off twelve-gauge side-by-side he used on night patrols, the straight razors and piano wire. That was his business. In 'Nam, he used whatever it took to keep him alive. He saw some unbelievable stuff over there—movie stuff—except it was real. He saw it *all,* and he never let it get to him. His tour in 'Nam accounted for some of the best years of his life—until the day he put his foot down wrong.

When he woke up in the hospital, he thought he was back in Vermont, thought his luck had run out, thought maybe the outcome of the Creamery Curve crash had been renegotiated. Then a redheaded nurse held his hand and set the record straight; his legs had been cut off six inches above the knees. Otherwise, he was dandy, not a scratch on him. And all he could think of was how proud of him Snoot would be,

70

now that he'd finally paid his dues.

They told him he'd be able to walk again, with plastic legs, told him he was lucky to be alive. He spent his twenty-second birthday in a VA rehab, then came home to find Loretta split for California and Claire willing to fuss over him. And he was lucky? Funny word for it. What about the pin-heads with the money and connections to find a way around the draft? Were they *un*lucky? Walker Owen and his pals? How would they have held up in a Quangnam Province ambush?

Off and on, for three years, Junior stared at ceiling cracks in the White River VA hospital—living in a bathrobe, watching TV, and eating from trays—months of therapy before he accepted his stumps. They outfitted him with artificial legs, but his skin wouldn't heal. They did more surgery, but he gave up, sick of infections, fearful of falling, of failing.

Claire babied him when he came home, sure she did. He let her. She felt sorry for him, she even married him—as if her suffocating pity could make him run up a mountain again. Sure, she finished college, finished nursing school, knew how to take his blood pressure and all that crap, but back then he didn't know if he wanted to go home, go crazy, die, or just hang out and maybe kill somebody with his bare hands, just for the hell of it.

The only thing he liked about the rehab center was lifting weights. He pumped iron for hours in front of a mirror, wore sleeveless T-shirts, oiled his muscles. Deltoid, pectoral, triceps, latissismus—he repeated their names like a checklist of the body parts they'd let him keep.

Then one day he got a letter in the mail, and he decided it was time to fish or cut bait: It was from Frouncy, penciled on the back of a log tally slip, and it surprised him:

Snoot won't say it, but I know for sertain he wants you home in the worst way. He feels bad about how it all ways went with you and him, and he wants you back in the house, like be for, but better. love, Mother.

• • •

Bud's headlights slashed at the treetops along the road below, then swept up the lane. Junior looked at his watch; they'd be in the woods around daylight, shivering with coffee and anticipation. Today would be the third year in a row Bud took Junior hunting on opening day.

His first invitation came right after Bud and Tot began sweet-talking him into selling the farm. He'd wondered, that first year, just how Bud pictured them up in the woods, all rocks and brush and jackstraw blowdowns. Maybe Bud figured he'd haul Junior up the mountain on his back—or did he think he could leave him in the truck with the heater on? When he showed up, that first morning, three years ago, Bud stood on the doorsill fiddling with his hat, unsure of how to load an amputee into a truck. He wouldn't ask either, that was for sure, so Junior kept him guessing as long as he could.

Bud knew better now. Now he drove in the driveway, circled around, and parked with the passenger door at the end of the ramp.

Junior closed the door behind him and coasted down the incline with the Remington across his lap. Diamond frost plated the ramp's wooden deck; it crackled with cold as he passed. He saw Bud turn the dome light on and rearrange the clutter on the seat, saw the sleeve of a red plaid jacket reaching to open the door, a hand with an Elks' Lodge ring on a finger as thick as a sausage.

"Ready for a big buck this year?" Bud asked, a pale pink shining through his backlit ears.

"You don't take and chase it around the other side of the mountain again," Junior said. He liked to needle Bud. "Goddamned right, I'm ready." He locked his wheels and reached up for the grab bar over the door. "I'm ready for anything. Any*thing* or any*body.*" He pulled himself into the cab and watched Bud look the other way while he settled his stumps under him. When the Remington was secure on the rack behind their heads, Bud started the truck and they began to move. They were going hunting, Junior thought, for the sport of it—going out to try and kill a large four-legged animal . . . for fun. He looked back at the house and tasted chalk in his throat.

They didn't talk much on the drive to Farley Fellows's. The truck rattled something awful, a piece of junk, to Junior's mind. It steered real loosey-goosey, wandered all over the road. Bud would no sooner haul it back to center than it would head for the other ditch. Gave Junior the willies. Bud talked out loud to it. "What'd you do that for, Buster?" Most people name their trucks for women. Not Bud. "Whoa, boy, come on, cut that out." Sometimes Junior thought Bud was talking to him, and once he almost told him to go fuck himself.

They swerved back and forth down the mountain and drove through the village past unlit houses, past the north shore of the pond. Junior stared straight ahead when they passed the Home where his mother slept, but he saw the light anyway, glaring so brightly it hurt his eyes.

They passed the abandoned bobbin mill, the iron bridge at Dalton Falls, then Hadlock's salvage yard. When he was a kid, he and his friends squeezed under the fence and stole the silver Vs from Cadillac hoods. Someplace around the house, he had a collection of them, mounted on a polished maple board; Caddy chevrons, twenty of them.

Heading east toward Quinntown, Junior thought the road seemed bumpier, twistier than he remembered it. He used to drive out here at ninety miles an hour—late nights, boozed up, radio tuned to an AM station all the way from Cincinnati. He looked for the break in the roadside trees and the narrow road to the gravel pit where he took Claire parking on Saturday nights, when she was still a high school sophomore and willing to learn anything he wanted to teach her. Claire and a few others, too, but never Loretta; he couldn't teach *her* anything—she knew it all. Goddamnedest two-room apartment over the laundromat in Catamount you've ever seen. King-sized bed, mirrors on the ceiling, deep shag zebra rugs, and a couple of pounds of drop-dead reefer in plastic bags in the freezer. Now she was in California or some place else she'd slipped off to.

Claire was different then, kept her mouth shut, knew

her place, a cheerleader, watched him star in football and basketball, saw him set state records in the sprints and hurdles. He drove a Mustang then, a 289, Hurst shifter and a three-quarter cam, traded it to some guy from—where was it, Contoocook?—traded it for the Chevy Nova he put into the trees on Creamery Curve, and Daddy acted like he owed somebody something because he didn't get hurt.

The other girls—he couldn't remember their faces or names. The other girls were northwoods tramps like everybody else.

Bud weaved down the middle of the road like he owned both lanes. Ahead, the sky was domed with fuzzy, refracted light from the direction of Fellows's barn. As they topped the crest of a hill, the barn and all its glare were suddenly visible.

"Frigging Stanley!" Bud pounded the steering wheel at the sight of a dozen cars and trucks bunched under the bright floodlights in the parking lot. Red-suited hunters, some familiar, some of them strangers, stood by their tailgates drinking coffee, milling around, talking, packing gear.

"Nice and private." Junior yawned.

"Sonsabitches." Bud pulled in sharply, turned the truck around, and started back for Dalton Pond. "Leave it to that mouthy Stanley Judd. I told him what I had up here, and he advertised it all over town."

"See the warden back there?"

"Where?" Bud jerked his head.

"Just yanking your chain." Junior snickered. "He'd love to catch your ass without a hunting license."

Bud waved him away. "Hazen don't dare touch me. I knew that little peckerhead when he was in grade school, stealing candy." The truck rattled over a washboard patch on the downhill grade to the village. "We'll hunt Big Church instead," he shouted over the din. "Far away from those dubs as we can get." Bud slurped at his coffee, sloshed it on his lap, and never noticed. "I like it better up there anyhow."

Turning south at the iron bridge, they started down the Jordan road, went a mile, and turned west on the Dunbar dead end. As they rumbled along, Junior watched his side of the narrow road for a fast-food shot: Bang-bang, chuck it in the back of the truck, and go home.

First signs of daylight came at the height of the land. Junior was sweating again, tasting that taste. He lifted himself in his seat, rearranged his stumps, and cracked open his window.

At the toe of Dunbar Gore, they forked west onto the one-lane track that led into Big Church territory. Bud liked it up there, rough country, up and down and thick and bony—a young man's kind of place to hunt. "Church is sermons, hymns, and ladies' hats," Bud said. *"Big* Church is the place you get religion."

I should have stayed home and kept an eye on her, Junior thought. He looked in the rearview mirror; behind them, dawn stained the horizon with watery milk, dull zinc all around it. Claire would be awake by now. Doing what? he wondered.

The truck wallowed over a water bar, lurched hard against a rock. Bud apologized to the truck.

He'd warned her, hadn't he? But she could be doing anything she wanted to, right now. How was a man supposed to stop her?

Bud started shouting and waving his hands over the noise of the truck. Here and there along the route, he'd gesture to where he'd killed this buck or that—eight-point, twelve-point, two hundred pounds—or show off where he'd tracked a wounded bear through a swamp for umpteen hours. War stories. He had a bunch of them, with all the words in perfect order from years of telling, over and over. And in every story, he turned out to be the hero.

They slowed down to a crawl for a flock of geese in the road at Darby Dunbar's place. "Watchgeese," Bud said. "Tear you to pieces, peck your eyes out if you don't be careful." He honked at the geese, but they wouldn't move until the last moment. He could have run over one and never known it.

Junior studied the house for a sign of Dunbar. No lights, no dogs, all he saw was a ribbon of woodsmoke pulled up out of the chimney. Dunbar was a hermit—at least that's what people called him. Some claimed he had a million dollars buried around the farm, but Junior never believed it, not from the looks of the place, all weathered and run-down. Out back of the barn the land dropped off to a hummocky pasture, boulders everywhere. There was an airplane out there, a Piper Cub, with trees grown up next to the windshield. A broken ladder was propped against the cockpit door; both wings were missing. Amputated. Bud said Dunbar bought the airplane for the motor, but he never got around to using it. While they were driving by, a cow was scratching itself against the propeller, moving it. Junior imagined the motor kicking over and what it would do to the cow. In 'Nam, he'd seen a water buffalo blown up into a tree, pieces of it hanging down from the branches like somebody's laundry, bleeding.

He was glad when they got going again. The place was weird, made him want to know what Dunbar really did all day, and why he lived alone.

Bud told a story about how he and Snap LeClair coon-hunted Dunbar's farm on summer nights. He pointed to a cornpiece where Snap's bluetick picked up scent and ran under a live electric fence. The choke-chain leash pulled against the wire, but Snap never saw it in the dark. He felt the shock run up his arm, cried out he'd had a heart attack. Bud laughed when he told how Snap was crumpled on the ground, holding his chest and crying. He thought it was funny.

The road past Dunbar's ended in a turnaround at the head of a big old beaver pond dammed across Crooked Brook's west branch. In high school, Junior and a bunch of his friends went out there on weekends and got drunk, broke bottles on the rocks and tipped the trash cans over—stupid stuff. Then a kid named Andy Fulton drove out there alone one night and shot himself. His girlfriend had just dumped him, or something like that. It was 1966, the year Junior graduated, and no one went to Big Church anymore; they said the place was haunted.

Bud drove around behind a couple of boarded-up cabins, then onto a logging road that skirted the shore of the dark brown water. Junior wondered if Bud would ask if he wanted to go fishing sometime—or was taking him hunting enough of a payoff?

Bud pointed to the cove where he hid his boat, told how he'd used a two-pound line to catch a bass "as long as your arm." Junior could see him hesitate when he said *your arm*, could see him wondering if it was okay to mention anything about Junior's body. He could imagine Bud saying to himself, "As long as your leg wouldn't be much of a fish."

As they approached the beaver dam, Bud stopped at a clearing and pointed out his window to the softwoods on the flank of Dunbar Mountain. "I'll head straight up through," he said, "straight up and over. Rugged country back in there." He wanted Junior to know he was headed into dangerous territory. "It's hellish going, spruce trees so thick they'll rip your clothes off. Worse'n barbed wire, any day." He'd never seen the silica grass in Quangngai, razor sharp and tangled up so thick you couldn't see the ground. In Quangngai, Junior walked point a hundred times before his luck ran out.

Bud drove another fifty yards and stopped at a washout. The overflow from the beaver pond had eroded the gravel from around a culvert, leaving a gully three feet deep and five or six feet wide. "This ought to be good right here," he said.

Junior studied the downstream landscape. Beside the truck, a big old sugar maple grew up out of the clay bank next to the water. The brook meandered through white alder bushes and cattails, straightened its course by a dead elm totem riddled with woodpecker holes, then zigzagged through a maze of boulders. Fifty yards downstream, the brook bed widened into a pool and then split, making an island of a huge smooth rock, shiny like the back of a whale.

Bud started talking tactics. Junior would sit against the base of the tree and wait for a shot. He pointed out that Junior could *control* the road for quite a ways in both directions, that he was in a good *tactical* position for anything that crossed his *perimeter.* What a laugh. Bud must have picked up his idea of army talk from the movies.

When Bud carried him over to the tree, it reminded

Junior of Snoot when he first came home: Snoot would do anything to avoid touching him, especially his stumps. Funny thing was, Junior didn't want Snoot touching him either. His daddy, or mother, or Claire, or anybody. Back then, he was ashamed of his body. He thought he wasn't worth much, so why should anybody else think any different? It took awhile for him to get that idea straightened out, but he still didn't like anybody touching his stumps. The way Bud carried him—hands stiff under his armpits, making sure he didn't drop him but at the same time making sure he didn't hold him in a way that might be misinterpreted—was exactly the same way Snoot did it, although Bud smelled different, stringent—too clean, maybe—and when his cheek brushed Junior's ear it was dry and smooth, like a woman's. It was spooky, compared with Snoot's brushy beard. But with Bud, up there in Big Church, Junior didn't really care. Just being outdoors with a loaded gun was good enough for him, even if it was with Bud. All he needed Bud for was to get him to the tree.

Bud put him down and brought him his canvas pillow, his sandwiches, ammo, and the Remington. He pointed at the features along the ridge—the hemlocks where the herd would yard up later in the winter, the oaks where they fed on acorns, a logged-off section where they fed on hardwood browse. It was almost like Bud owned it; every inch of Big Church seemed accounted for, all neat and clean in his mind.

"All set then, soldier?" he asked. "Need anything?" He would have loved it if Junior said, "Sir, no sir!" and saluted him.

Junior told him he guessed he'd be all right and looked up at the ridge. Claire could be in bed with Walker by now.

Bud said, great, if everything was set, he'd back up a hundred yards, hide his truck off the road in the bushes, and head for where the action was. The way he said it made Junior want to laugh. A few minutes later, he heard Bud thrashing through the woods, sounding like a crippled moose cow, paying no attention to where he stepped. In 'Nam, he wouldn't have lasted ten minutes.

After Bud was gone and the woods were quiet again,

Junior saw the ladder rungs nailed to the far side of the tree. Some other hunter, some other time, had made himself a hiding place up in the branches. Two-foot lengths of two-by-four were spiked for maybe thirty feet up the trunk. They led to a wide platform built into the intersection of three big limbs. Talk about tactical. Junior pulled himself around the tree and reached up to the bottom rung, testing it with a long, slow chin-up. It felt solid. He pulled himself up to the next rung and found a way to straddle the trunk without hurting his stumps. If he climbed slowly, it would be easy; it would be a cinch. He let himself down, strapped his rifle across his back, stuffed his gear in his jacket, and started up the tree.

It was turning into a beautiful November day. Yesterday's snow and cold were gone. From where he sat, he could see down the mountain to Dalton Pond and the thousands of acres of woodland beyond. All around him, the rolling web of branches looked so soft and rosy he'd swear he could dive into them from five miles up and they'd catch him soft as a pillow. The rippling water on the beaver pond sparkled brighter than stars.

After the last few nights' sleeplessness, he was content to stretch out on the platform and let the sun put him to sleep. A hundred deer could have stampeded by below, and he wouldn't have known it—or cared. Bud would be the hero today, and that was fine with him.

He woke up sweating and stripped down to his shirt sleeves, dozed off again, and had a dream about Claire; her face kept changing. She was trying to convince him he needed a new pair of Indian moccasins.

Around eleven-thirty he awoke again, flinching, this time, to the sound of a shot. The maple's stout branches and the clear New England sky held firm and reassured him. This was Vermont, deer season; he was home; everything was all right.

The shot came from the mountain above him. Hunting. Sport. Did Bud get lucky? That was what they were supposed to be out there for, wasn't it? But it bothered him—something was wrong about it—and he couldn't go back to sleep on account of thinking about what he'd seen bullets do, what bullets sometimes needed to do.

Maybe half an hour after the shot, he heard a vehicle approaching, creeping along, coming from the same direction he'd come from earlier. Now who? Had Stanley and his crowd got tired of Fellows's woodlot?

It was Claire's Subaru. "What the?" The car looked so small from above. He'd told her they'd be hunting back of Fellows's. Junior squinted at the windshield. How'd she know they'd changed their minds? The car came past the bushes where Bud's truck was hidden, kept coming closer—but wait, *two* people were inside? Junior tasted it again, strong as poison.

The car stopped directly under the tree at the washed-out culvert, the same place Bud had stopped four hours before. Junior put his hand over his mouth; he almost puked on the Subaru's hood.

Claire got out, then the other door opened. Looking down through a crack in the platform, Junior felt the tree trunk tremble. Claire and her passenger were wearing orange Day-Glo hunter's safety bibs—his bibs, on Claire and Walker Owen.

They went to the front of the car to inspect the road. Walker laughed and said they could take a run at it. Fucking idiot. Claire pretended to shove him into the water, like a kid; then she looked around and said something about a smooth rock still looking like it always did, and she pointed to the island in the brook bed.

Junior clutched at the rifle beside him on the platform. He tried to swallow and couldn't. It was un-fucking-believable. He squinted through the crack, face against the weathered boards. As long as he kept quiet, they'd never know he was there.

Claire pulled a picnic basket out of the trunk and led the way through the alders, along the brook to the big, smooth rock. When they were thirty yards away, Junior brought the rifle up to his shoulder slowly, leaned the barrel over the edge of the platform, and pressed his eye against the telescopic sight; the first thing he saw through the cross hairs was the back of Walker's head. *Field Tactics, Section 401: Contain entire unit before issuing signal to open fire.*

He squinted through a tunnel of light. The threads on Walker's jacket collar were suddenly stitched into the lens. Perfect. He heard how it would sound: "The way they were walking so close together made a hell of a day of it, lieutenant."

When they got to the rock, Claire hesitated for a minute before she jumped. She screeched when she did it, the way little girls do when they try things they're supposed to be afraid of. Was she for real or what? Once she was on the rock, she put the basket down and held her hand out to Walker. When she told him to jump, he gauged it wrong and slid off the rock into the brook, water up over his ankles. She laughed and helped him out, sat him down on the rock. They thought it was funny, said something Junior couldn't hear. He watched as she knelt down and slowly peeled off Walker's socks, wrung them out, and laid them in the sun to dry. He listened to them laugh again when she poured muddy water out of his shoes.

They opened the basket and began taking out food, a blanket, a bottle of wine. Junior's jaw ached. He caught himself grinding his teeth and reminded himself to blink, to breathe, to stop shaking. He loosened his grip on the Remington, tried to relax. The cross hairs wavered, then steadied and quartered a nose, an ear, an eyebrow. Walker was half turned toward him, facing Claire. The back of her head and Walker's face filled the lens, spread to the edges. Junior's finger traced the rim of the trigger. She'd make him sound bad, wouldn't she? Lie and bitch about everything.

Through the scope, they began to look like the people in 'Nam, the people Junior killed so many of, the people who'd killed so many of Junior's buddies and tried so many times to kill him. He couldn't understand the language over there, anymore than he could make out what these two were saying on the rock. It was easy to think of Walker and Claire as Cong—

same hair, skin, arteries, tissue, bone—they were Charlie, transformed through the ground glass lens to a catalogue of Charlie's body parts. Targets. Pick one, pick 'em all. Pick a piece of his wife. And Walker. Maybe that's how it should be, he thought. Hold the breath in? Squeeze?

He watched how Walker held his sandwich, drank from a paper cup, how he chewed and blinked and breathed. He saw bread crumbs on Walker's lips, saw him touch Claire's arm, saw her touch him twice in return; through the scope, it looked like they were three feet away.

He moved the cross hairs, looking for secrets, focusing on the bridge of Walker's nose, probing the hole in his ear. He became so absorbed in Walker, he realized he was licking his lips in unison with him, imitating his expressions, breathing the same breaths.

Half an hour passed. The sun beat through the branches in a perfect mimicry of August. A sweat pool gathered where his belly met the platform. He lay in it, soaked, unable to move. He watched them and he heard Claire laugh, a sound he hadn't heard for years.

They must have been there for an hour when Junior heard Bud's voice from the other side of the washout. He didn't turn to look, but he knew by the tone Bud was angry.

"What'd you go and park in the road for?" Bud must have wondered why Claire was having a picnic with Walker Owen, but he didn't mention it. He'd wait for that, mouth it all over tomorrow, at Tot's cantina.

Claire said she was sorry, she'd move the car as soon as they finished their picnic. Then she asked him why he wasn't hunting at Fellows's. She didn't ask where her husband was. The bitch.

Bud ignored her question, never mentioned the mob at the barn. He told her, even though the paper company owned the road, it was used by all sorts of people. They couldn't just block it off like they goddamn owned it.

Claire yelled back they could easily move the car if anyone came along.

Bud wouldn't let it go. "It's kind of late in the goddamned year for a picnic!" he shouted. "You ought to be wearing Day-Glo hats, too. You could get yourselves shot for a puke-poor deer. Besides," he told her, "it's illegal to build a fire up here without a company permit."

She said they hadn't built a fire. Goody Two-shoes.

Bud said okay, but if they got any funny ideas about building one, it was illegal.

Claire jumped off the rock and began walking through the boulders and brush to the car. She laughed at Bud and said he must be getting crabby in his old age; there wasn't a house for miles around, and the road was washed out anyway. She told him to relax.

Junior moved his head away from the scope and wiped at his eyes with one hand, holding the rifle unsteadily with the other; it seemed so heavy, now, and it wavered and tipped up between the branches. His clothes were soaked. His elbows were sore, and his shoulders ached, and he wondered what he was doing, wondered whatever happened to winning.

Was everything bullshit? He blinked his vision clear, steadied the rifle, and repositioned his eye against the scope. He found the rock, Walker's parka, Walker's hair, Walker's eyes. . . .

Walker was looking straight up at him. He was staring as though he'd caught sight of a long-extinct bird, staring into the rifle's bore as though it held a secret he was bound to learn.

Junior froze, hoping somehow it would all go away. It was so fucked up! There he was, leaning over the edge of a platform with his finger curled around the trigger of a high-powered rifle—and now Walker was goddamn smiling at him. Look at the sonofabitch! The smooth flesh on his throat below the upturned chin, the opened lips, the straight white teeth, the mashed-in nose, the cheeks, the eyes—staring up like a choirboy, smiling, quartered by cross hairs and bathed in a halo of light.

Junior took a breath. Held it, squeezed it into the chalk on his tongue.

He pulled the rifle to his side, rolled over on his back, and looked up into a wide blue heaven. If he'd known how to pray to that faceless, uncaring God, he would have prayed to be a child again, to understand the consequences of his actions, to be able to admit his terror when he signed up for 'Nam, to know what people wanted from him—or what he himself had to give. He wondered if there was any way to make it right with his mother before she died. Or with Claire, before she left. He asked himself if his father would ever, ever love him—and when he regained himself from the only answer he knew to be true, he ached to know what made a man like Walker understand himself, to know the difference between courage, fear, and desperation, to have the balls to stare an armed man down, smile at him, walk away, and screw his wife.

He heard splashing, probably Walker picking his way up the stream to the car. He imagined him standing next to Claire, waiting to leave, itching to tell her about who he'd seen. Bud finally quit talking, the fool, and they said their goodbyes. He heard the doors opening and pictured Walker and Claire climbing in. Then the doors slammed shut, and the pair of sounds rolled over the beaver pond together, echoing off the mountain in perfect unison.

Junior wondered when Bud would notice he wasn't sitting at the base of the tree—or would Bud forget him, go home alone, and invent another hero story to cover his flat-footed tracks? Junior wouldn't tell him what had happened with Walker, and he knew Bud wouldn't talk about any of it to him, either—he just wouldn't do that. They'd drive away as if nothing had happened, stupid with secrets, drink a couple of six-packs at Hubby's with the rest of the liars, and go home drunk at closing time.

Now that Walker and Claire were gone, the woods were quiet again. Junior was alone with Bud in Big Church. In a minute he'd call down, lean over the edge, and watch Bud's surprise. In a minute it would be back to normal. In just a minute.

Junior wiped his eyes again and rolled his head from side to side, searching the perfect autumn sky until he found a formation of feathery white clouds, off to the west. A little airplane was out there, flying so far away he couldn't hear its motor. He watched and wondered who was inside, what they were like, and where they were going—and he wished he could go with them, it didn't matter where.

He rocked over onto his elbows, pulled the Remington to his shoulder, and searched the pale horizon through the scope. When he found the plane, it was no more than a dot in the sky. At last it seemed to vanish, but then he found it again, and when he did he focused on it, held his breath, and squeezed the trigger.

So at last—at least—that part was finally done, however badly, however ill-timed. The plane flew on, away from the deafening roar in his ears, safe from the kick at his shoulder, away from him and all that he wanted, flew into the clouds and was gone.

6

SEVERANCE

FOR CLAIRE, the first day of hunting season began with the predawn sound of Bud's truck. She heard it turn around in the dooryard and stop at the end of the ramp, heard the kitchen door open and close and a fragment of conversation, Junior's voice, Junior's cough. Then the truck pulled away, and she listened to the rattling noises fade down the lane until she could hear no more, and when the house was still again she closed her eyes and put together a picture of Walker's face, hoarding the image through another two hours' unsuccessful attempt at sleep.

Her morning was an exercise in indecision. She tried on everything in her closet but couldn't remember what he'd liked; she even found a sweater he gave her the Christmas before he left, long since moth-eaten but greedily saved. She applied and removed eyeliner and lipstick and washed her hair twice. She braided it, combed it out, put it up in a French twist, combed it loose again, and left it parted in the middle as it always was, telling herself if she had arranged to meet him earlier, she wouldn't be wasting her time worrying about how she looked.

For the first time since she moved into the house, she found herself thinking about how it looked. Couldn't Snoot have stored his piles of treasures somewhere out behind the barn? Why had she waited so long to repaint the clapboards and window sash? The roof was a mess of rusty corrugated steel, with leaks in four or five places, big stains on the kitchen ceiling over the stove. It wasn't that she was ashamed of the place; the wrappings around things and people had never impressed her much. It was more a matter of not wanting Walker to feel like he was—well, rescuing her from poverty. She didn't want him to confuse the appearance of her home with her need to be free of the man with whom she shared it. After all, Walker was a lawyer now, probably used to a level of sophistication that made the place on Crooked Mountain look tacky. But then she consoled herself with something he'd reminded her of the day before at the P and C: he said that he'd never felt comfortable in New Haven, that he'd been saving for years so he could afford to come back to Vermont, and that, after all, his grandfather was a sidehill farmer in Windsor County when hers was teaching history at the university in Burlington.

She baked chocolate chip cookies and a batch of sourdough rolls for the Dundee marmalade. She lined the picnic basket with a red checkerboard tablecloth, added blue cotton napkins, cutlery, plates and cups, cold chicken sandwiches, and a thermos of tea. There were apples, bananas, and oranges—two of each—and sliced carrots. And celery, and olives, and a shaker of salt. And—risking the appearance of overdoing it—a bottle of Chablis.

The sun was near the top of its arc when she pulled on a sweater, went outside, and put the picnic basket in the back of her car. The sky was a bright china blue, the paddock dry and brown in the sun, silver still frosted the north wall shadows by the buildings. She went to the henhouse and fed the chickens, dropped a bale of hay down from the haymow, and dragged it through the paddock between the house and the barn, through thick, dead grass, heavy as the weight of Junior's warning.

At the fence line, she broke up the bale and tossed it over to the waiting heifers, all the while looking eastward across the pasture toward the Abenaki Ledges. The cleft rock face seemed to move in the static noonday light, shifting, tipping forward into the waving treetops at its base, and she felt a familiar tingle creep across her shoulders, leaving her puzzled, as it always did.

She looked below the ledges for smoke through the branch tops and saw none, searched the dark voids between tree trunks, and ran her eyes along the ragged stone wall. Finding no one, she squinted into the opening where the old road penetrated the woods; still no one. Then combing the landscape west to east for the second time, she suddenly found who she was looking for.

He stood at the edge of the woods by a clump of witch-broom spruce. She liked the offhand way he waved to her, as though their meeting was an everyday event. She raised her hand in return—a stiff little gesture—then bent down and climbed through the wire. A barb caught in her Levi's and scratched the inside of her thigh.

By the time she'd untangled herself, Walker was already halfway across the pasture, hurrying toward her with long-legged strides. She walked slowly toward him, resisting the temptation to hurry, holding his gaze every step of the way. He was grinning his old lanky grin. She had never seen his face so strong and sure, the dimple in his chin so captivating. He was happy to see her, she thought—and conspicuously unsure of what to do with his arms.

"How was the birthday party?" he asked, close enough to touch.

"It was good." But she wanted to talk about something else. "I was thinking about you, out there with Snoot in the cabin."

"I'd forgotten he was a gourmet cook," Walker joked. "I had no idea how much I missed him and the hemlocks—all of this." He swung his head toward the Ledges, then back to Claire.

She took it in. "Did he snore?"

"Only when he slept."

Claire laughed. "J left at five-thirty."

Walker nodded. "Oh." He looked as if he wanted to say

something more but wasn't sure if he should. "Good," he said. "You're sure they're at Fellows's?"

"Bud put out a salt lick in the spring, been taking them apples and clover all summer. He's been talking about it for months."

"So we should be okay."

Claire nodded yes, took his hand, and led him down the hill to her car. "We'll be fine," she said, crossing the thick grass by the paddock. "There's nothing to worry about."

It was sunny up in the hills of Big Church, and Smooth Rock was as warm as a stove top. Walker sat peeling a banana, toasting his paper-white toes in the sun. "There's enough food here to feed the Green Bay Packers for a week."

Claire sat across from him and watched him eat, ridiculous with pleasure. She hadn't talked and laughed with a man like Walker since—since forever, it seemed, and when she stopped now and then to remind herself she was married, she didn't care; it didn't matter. I need this, she told herself over and over again, I deserve it, and although she couldn't eat, she felt full, and warm, and understood.

Then Bud appeared, the big-eared loudmouth with the gray crew cut and the quaking jowls. Dressed up in red.

Claire felt tricked, then frightened, and finally, annoyingly, guilty. If Bud was there, Junior couldn't be far away. Why weren't they at Fellows's? The picnic seemed suddenly, stupidly, reckless. "We better get going," she whispered to Walker. "Let me take care of Bud first." But Bud kept yakking about parking in the road. Claire said nothing to encourage him further, nodding her head while she searched the circle of trees around them, looking for someone she prayed she wouldn't find.

When they were in the car, speeding away, and Walker told her what he'd seen, she thought she might not be able to hold onto the wheel.

"It was so weird."

Walker seemed too calm. Did he know what it meant?

"I didn't have time to be frightened—I'm more frightened now, talking about it, than I was when it was happening. Jesus. There was nothing I could do, no place to hide."

Claire squeezed his hand.

"So I just smiled—and hoped he wasn't going to pull the trigger."

"You're sure it was J?"

"I know it was."

"I saw ladder rungs on the tree," Claire said. "He still works out every day; he could have climbed it." It was a wonder he hadn't pulled the trigger. The Subaru hit a bump and bounced. Her shoulder touched Walker's and she savored the touch, a thousand bumps with him beside her, anything to avoid the inevitable confrontation.

She sped past Darby Dunbar's and began the long downhill section to the Jordan road. "I'm sorry I got us into this. J's been a skunk, but this is really going to get to him."

"I should have seen him when we drove in," Walker said. "Do you think he heard our conversation?"

Claire mentally retraced the topics they'd covered, fearful she'd divulged something awful about her marriage, a subject she'd tried to avoid as much as possible. "I just don't know. Whatever he heard or saw, he's going to—" She didn't know how to finish the thought.

At last, Walker looked worried. "We've got to give him some time to cool off."

"A lot of time." Another bump threw them against the Subaru's roof. She noticed Walker bracing himself against the dashboard and slowed down. The notion of speeding away from Junior was inextricably coupled with the question of where to go.

Walker must have been asking himself the same question. "You can't be in the house when he gets back."

"I'll stay with Mother, in town." The idea seemed instinctively right and yet wrong at the same time. Claire had lately come to see her mother as the kind of mother all daughters insist they will never be like. "I'll be all right."

"You sure?" Walker looked skeptical.

"I'm positive." She pulled the Subaru off the road and

stopped at the turnout by Staircase Falls. An hour before, she'd hoped they would spend all day together, allowed herself to think beyond it even, into the evening. Now she felt as though she'd ruined everything; going to Big Church was a dumb idea. She should have squared things with J, told him it was over, before she dove into this thing with Walker. Now she'd feel guilty in the bargain. She needed time to think, to have a long, final conversation with J on the telephone, and she needed to do that alone.

"We should go someplace." Walker touched her arm.

It was tempting, very tempting, but impossible until she'd told J what was going on. She shook her head no. "It'll be okay." But she couldn't go to her mother's. "Don't worry."

"You could come to the cabin. Snoot's a licensed chaperone."

She laughed. "I'll be careful." She would go to Jody's. "Promise me you'll be careful too?" Should she ask him to come with her?

"I've got Snoot guarding the door—not that Junior's too likely to crawl through the woods to the cabin."

"I'll see you tomorrow morning," she said. The worst would be over by then. "Coffee and doughnuts." And everyone in town would know what was going on. "Tot's, at nine?" She touched his hand, pulled him to her, and quickly kissed him.

"I'm still worried about you."

"Don't be," Claire said, grateful that he was. "I know how to handle him." But the words sounded fragile as they left her lips, and she wondered if she did, anymore. "I've just got to take care of first things first."

He got out of the car and waved. The last she saw of him, he was walking through the trees, straight and tall.

Claire drove without stopping to Jody's and spent the rest of the afternoon and far into the night trying to locate her husband, but no matter how many times she called the house, or Bud's or Stanley Judd's or Hubby's Tavern, there was no answer, or he hadn't been seen, or no one cared enough to find him; the drunks who answered the phone at Hubby's kept asking her for a date.

She was asleep when Junior pulled into Jody's driveway, still asleep when he jimmied the outside lock and opened the door to her bedroom. If she'd been awake, she would have heard him hesitate at the threshold and muffle a cough in his hand, seen his wide, squat silhouette blocking the doorway. She would have seen the cold white beam of his flashlight as it pierced the room, flicked into the corners, and skipped under the bed as if searching for rats. If she'd been awake and seen him shut the door behind him, if she'd watched him roll without a sound to her bedside—stripped naked in his wheelchair—she would have screamed.

But Claire saw none of that; she was deep in dreams between clean, fragrant sheets, beneath Jody's favorite hand-sewn quilt. She never saw the lengths of clothesline with the slipknot nooses, the roll of duct tape in her husband's hand, the pink hood of his penis budded up between his tapered thighs. She never saw him pause at her bedside and tug at himself, never smelled the bourbon soured on his breath, the stink of hate around him. Instead, she lay secure in sleep, on her back with her hands between her legs, her fingers pressing pleasure into dreams of Walker Owen.

She dreamed she was suffocating and woke up with a pillow pressed against her face. This is real. This is terror, she thought, as she fought to slide out from under a crushing weight, tried to breathe through the gagging mask of fabric jammed against her mouth.

Her shoulders were pinned to the mattress, arms tangled in heavy bedclothes, trapped at her sides. The pressure on her head was absolute, immense, and violent. She thrashed her feet, felt cold air on her calves and pumped her legs to free her upper body. No! She arched her back, flung her knees upward, kicked again against the invisible force, and struck nothing.

In unison with her desperately flailing legs, Claire's

mind flung bits of thought at her: How had he found her? She should have stayed with Walker. Just when things were turning around. Would they hear J upstairs? Would they call the police? An image from her childhood flashed by, the grisly sight of Roseanne deVeaux's bloated body washed up on the sandy beach at Robin's Point, on a sunny day in August, for everyone to see. Her face looked like a rotted pumpkin. She was a Catholic. Her father set fire to the church after the funeral. Nine years old and forever remembered as a Halloween fright, the first dead person Claire had ever seen. Her father's name was Howard.

A hand grabbed at her leg, took hold, and forced it outward. The pressure on the pillow lifted, and as she gulped for air, she felt an arm crooked roughly behind her knee, forcing it to her chest.

"No!" she gasped. The pillow clamped down again. He said he'd be at Mudchub Pond.

Cold air rushed between her parted legs. She kicked with her free foot, hit cold sweaty flesh, and kicked again. The pressure shifted, familiar now, in feel and shape. It was him, goddammit, it was *him*.

Her arms were loose. She shoved away the pillow and swung both hands, hit hardened muscle, clawed at skin. Then she felt the rope around her wrist and the pain in her shoulder as her arm was yanked outward—and held.

"No!" The pillow came down like a stone. A rope burned again. Now both arms were spread wide apart, away from her, tied tight against the bedposts.

He shifted his weight again, slid down on her, and pushed the pillow into her mouth. She felt the unmistakable bony points of Junior's stumps against her thighs.

"Bitch!" he hissed, prodding between her legs.

She twisted her torso and kicked with her free leg. He caught it; now he had both his arms locked around the backs of both her knees but no way to hold the pillow to her face. She shook it loose and screamed at him, "I'll kill you for this!"

He crushed his pelvis between her legs and steadied her face with a hand clamped over her mouth. Her knees were almost touching her ears. She heard the sound of tearing duct tape, and then her tongue touched the sticky, suffocating band of adhesive as it sealed her lips to her teeth, to her cheeks, all the way to her jawbone.

She heard her panicked breathing through her nostrils, her muffled protests, his coughing and grunting efforts to restrain her. And as she searched, wide-eyed into the darkness for the face of her husband—the wrong one, the lost cause, her failure in life—she realized that precisely what they'd avoided confronting for so many years had somehow made this night inevitable, and even as the idea seized her, its ironic truth was no consolation.

"You little whore." He pinned her legs to her shoulders and jabbed at her belly with his penis. "Turn my back and you're with him the first chance you get. Where'd you do it? The motel? The backseat?"

Claire exploded, incoherent behind her muzzle. It was none of his business anymore! She pulled at the ropes, pressing her rage at him.

"I could have wasted him, blown him away. Him and you—fish in a barrel." He rammed at her pubic bone. "You're lucky to be here, you know that?" He rammed her again. "Had a good time, didn't you?" He shoved his hands up under her nightgown and squeezed at her breasts. "Did he do it like *that*?" He pinched and twisted and coughed his sickness into her face. "Did you tell him you liked it, *bitch*?"

Claire flung her head from side to side, shouted, sobbing, through her stifling gag, "Stop!"

"Got what you always wanted, didn't you? Got you a rich little college boy's dick." He rutted at her again, sticky wet and spongy. "I should have shot it off."

Claire heard a roaring in her ears.

"I'll give you dick, bitch. That's what you want? I'll give you dick good."

She strained her legs against Junior's arms, felt them trapped, felt the vise of his biceps tighten against her knees, the vulnerability of her anatomy.

He ground himself against her, up and down, abrading

her. Then he stopped. "You told him I don't fuck you anymore, didn't you?" The air around Claire's head was plated with bourboned breath; spit splattered her face. "You told him wrong." He put a hand between her legs. "You're still my wife. . . ."

Claire buried her cheek in the mattress. She heard blood slamming through her veins, the sound of outrage. "Stupid." She wept. "Hateful and rotten. Ugly."

". . . a stuck-up bitch. You know that, don't you?" He squeezed her jaw as if to make her listen. "I'm going to teach you a lesson, see? Cheat on me, and you pay." He started moving against her again. "Teach you good." His breath came faster. "All your books and talk and high-and-mighty secrets."

She felt the wet thing slide up toward her navel, then recoil to her pubic bone, then up, and down again, up and down, up and down. He pushed at her breasts and coughed and called her *bitch* and humped her belly like a dog—and in the last few seconds of her ordeal, while he rutted and hissed and jerked and thrust, she felt a desperate sadness for them, for she knew the final severance had been made; that ten long years were forever lost in the gob of semen puddled on her belly.

In high school, when they did it first on a rainy night in the back of his car, she was stunned by the rude simplicity of the act, the quick and painful mechanics of it. No violins played, no heavens split open; it was over so fast, she was convinced she must have missed it. The next day in school he seemed distant, as though she'd disappointed him, but she was determined to find out how it really worked, how to solidify the bond begun that starless night, how not to disappoint him—and herself. By the time he left her for Loretta duBois, she was almost ready to believe her mother's veiled references to a necessary inconvenience. The notions of taking and surrender, giving and receiving, the adolescent context of pain and pleasure redefined, the act that love makes into something it isn't when love is absent—those notions remained mysterious until she met Walker.

• • •

Junior shuddered and groaned; she remembered exactly the hoarse, dying sound. She felt him release her, slump away, and collapse. She straightened her legs and pressed them together, turned her head to escape his stubbled jaw, stretched herself as far away from him as her bonds would allow.

Minutes passed; she listened to the stubborn drumming of her heartbeat while his heavy breathing slowed until it was replaced by the sound of his sobs.

Her cheek was hot and damp against the sheet. She twisted and lay on her side, her back toward him. When she pulled her legs up into a fetal position, his wasted fluid slid across her abdomen, to her hip.

"You bastard!" she shouted through the tape. She kicked through the dark with both feet, struck Junior's back, and sent him crashing to the floor.

He was still for a moment; then she felt him pulling himself up onto the bed, shoving his hand between her legs. "Kick a wounded vet?"

Claire rolled away from his leathery fingers, thrashing at the dark.

"Kick a vet? You crazy beaver!" he snarled. "Is that the way you show respect?" He tried to restrain her flailing legs; then her heel connected with his face and he seemed to fall away. His voice trembled. "Want to play rough, do you?"

She tensed for the counterattack. He sounded hurt, pathetic. "Fine by me, bitch." She heard him fumble for his wheelchair, his security. He found it and fell into it clumsily. "You practice awhile," he said, "and then we'll have at it. You and me, hornbug, hammer and tongs." He coughed his angry sputum into the dark. "You want to get mean—be my guest." He rolled away. " 'Cause I don't really give a shit." He coughed again, a spewing farewell. "We'll see who kicks who."

Was it over? Claire blinked and squinted at the harsh light glaring through the opened door. She saw Junior pause, bending inward with self-righteousness. Behind him, she could see Jody's living room curtains and, on the wall, the colored lithograph they bought together, at an auction in Kendall Center. It would never look the same to her again.

"You can take your Florence Nightingale and stuff it," Junior sneered. "I don't need it, understand? I can take care of myself. I don't need your looking down on me like I was helpless." He coughed and spit. "So fuck your pity."

The door jerked shut and the room fell dark. From the kitchen came the sound of slamming cupboards, the clink of a bottle, a pause, and then the crash of broken glass in the sink. More silence, the beginning of a new kind of terror. What if he came back? She began to shake uncontrollably, then heard the back door closing.

Claire pushed herself as close as she could to the head of the bed, and felt the ropes slacken. The bedposts were only inches away from her fingertips; the loops felt loose. She fumbled at one side, then at the other, panicked, feeling for clues as to how the knots were tied. Outside in the driveway, a motor turned over and started. Headlights splashed against the wall behind her, lit up the low, tapered bedposts and the hastily tied knots. She heard the van backing out the drive-way—turn—down Park Street—now fainter—now gone.

She leaned to one side and yanked the rope upward. Two more tries and she was able to slide the loops over the top. Her right hand was free, then her left. She peeled the tape away from her face and licked at the numbness around her mouth.

She dressed in a panic, left her coat, and ran out of the house. Mother's. Suddenly she was driving through the out-skirts of Jordan without knowing how she got into her car. The curves and dips and straightaways rushed toward her, adrenaline shaking her hands on the wheel. She'd say he was on a hunting trip. She braked for a curve and wondered if she would catch up to Junior or if he was waiting for her, parked in some dark lane along the road, ready to pounce. She sped on, away from terror, into confusion, weary with the reckon-ing of what it meant.

She passed the few cars she came upon, despite the curves and double yellow lines. She shouted at the top of her lungs as she flew around the corner at Creamery Curve,

"Sonofabitch!" and raced by the first cluster of houses in Dalton Pond at twice the posted limit. A bath, she told herself, shaking uncontrollably. A bath and a loaded shotgun next to the tub.

Dalton Pond was deep in sleep when Claire pulled up to her stepfather's store. Tot kept a few lights burning inside as a warning to thieves, but the porch lights were off and the door to the upstairs apartment had no buzzer. Claire knocked and called her mother's name. No answer. She knocked louder; still no reply. She pounded the door with both fists, looked over her shoulder at the dark street behind her—for Junior, imagining his hands around her throat.

A light went on upstairs. Claire rattled the latch and called for her mother in a stranger's voice.

Slow footsteps descended the stairs.

"Come on, come on!"

A maddening pause.

"Mom! Let me in!"

The deliberate metallic click of a lock released, and a tired face peered through the cracked-open door.

Even in the stuffy warmth of the living room, Claire couldn't stop shaking. She sat on the couch and clung to her astonished mother—and wept. She wept for terror and injury, for rage and vulnerability, for long, cold years and failed ambition. Nothing, it seemed, would ever stop her tears, certainly not her mother's baffled reassurances or Tot's bathrobed impatience; not even her own belief that the worst, at last, was over.

When she was finally calmed enough to let go of her mother, Laurie asked her if she'd been sick. "You've got a little rash around your mouth. Can I give you some lotion for it?"

Claire began weeping again—this time because she knew her mother didn't want to know. Laurie preferred to leave pain unaccounted for, as she'd left her brief marriage to Horton Flint. "It happened," was about all she was ever able to tell her daughter, so that Horton remained an aching mystery, an incompleted yearning in Claire's life.

99

"Oh, *Daddy*," Claire said aloud, to her own surprise. Had she suddenly brushed against the texture of an understanding?

"You had an argument with Junior?" Laurie ventured, ignoring Claire's plea to Horton. Laurie's tone was strictly quizzical, with a hint of accusation. She'd always refused to judge Junior. After all, he was a man, her daughter's husband.

"It's okay now, Mom." Claire's fingers tingled. She looked down at her hands and saw the raw red bands around her wrists. "It's over with." She knew she must learn to say that, again and again. "All done." She tugged at her sleeves and buried her hands in her cuffs of her sweater. If Laurie noticed she chose not to comment, but she was curious, in her way.

"Was it about selling the farm?"

"Not about selling the farm, Mom. Nothing to do with the farm," Claire whispered. "Nothing, Mom," and she couldn't help thinking it was no wonder her mother disappointed her so.

As she turned away from her mother, she felt the wet spot on her belly, tasted nausea rising, a return of panic. "I need a hot bath, Mom. I really need—" She choked on the word *need,* on the idea of deserving comfort.

"It's three in the morning—"

"Mom?"

Laurie helped Claire to her feet and led her to the bathroom. She seemed grateful for the shift away from the mess of emotion to neat practicality and busied herself finding washcloths and towels. She turned on the hot water and excused herself, then reappeared with a nightgown and a terrycloth robe. "Remember these?" She looked almost motherly as she offered the garments to Claire. "I'll make up the bed in your old room."

Claire nodded, watching her mother's lips move over her ill-fitting dentures, lips Horton Eagle-in-the-Wind had kissed.

"Sleep as late as you want," Laurie said. "Don't mind Tot. He'll be up early."

Claire felt herself sinking as she stared at her mother.

Had it really happened? "Thanks, Mom," sticky words on her lips.

Steam from the running bath warmed the room. Time seemed to have slowed to a crawl. Bubbles gathered at one end of the tub, mist covered the mirror. The light was too bright. Claire wondered how she would ever find the strength to get out of her clothes.

"Anything else, dear?" Laurie hadn't seen Claire naked since well before her puberty, and she made it clear she wanted to be gone before the first button was undone. "Claire?"

Claire shook her head, no. Time and water, sleep, rest—amnesia—being safe and alone in her childhood bedroom was all she could wish for now.

Her mother said good night. Claire closed the door and locked it. She unlocked it and locked it again, then took off her clothing, piece by loathsome piece, and sank down into warm, receiving water.

7

COMMON COURAGE

HE WATCHED until Claire's car was gone, then hiked up the path to the cabin, breathing hard with the pace he set for himself. In retrospect, the picnic was a mistake, but Walker wondered if he'd made a bigger mistake in allowing Claire to drop him off. What if she ran into Junior on the way to her mother's? What if she decided to stay home and force the confrontation?

He felt impatient with his in-between position; he was the new kid in town, no territorial rights, no local clout. Should he talk to her about getting a restraining order, an injunction against Junior? It might work. The grounds? He heard the judge deny the petition; there was no law against a man looking at his wife's boyfriend through a telescopic sight.

But he was more certain with each step that he should have stayed with her, protected her until they knew how Junior would behave. They should have left town, gone to Montreal, until she had a chance to talk to Junior on the phone—give him time to cool off. Or maybe she was right, it was better to have it out with Junior now and be done with it—but he should be there with her, just in case.

He was perspiring by the time he caught the scent of burning oak, then saw a trace of blue smoke lifting from the cabin chimney. A gutted buck hung from a tree by the brook.

Walker turned away from the tainted edges of the incision down the length of the whitetail's belly; a pair of sharp sticks spread the rib cage open. Today might as well have been the opening of a hunting season on human beings as well, he thought. He climbed the porch steps thinking about the Audettes' legendary marksmanship, how Junior could have picked them off, two bull's-eyes, one bullet each.

Snoot was sitting at the table cleaning a new rifle. He didn't look up when Walker came in. "One shot, from the porch," he said. "Dressed him out and drug him up here—whole shebang took fifteen minutes, from giddyap to whoa." He was proud of himself, of being in the right place at the right time. "Knew he'd come see me when he got ready. Put the spell on him, is what I done. 'Course, legal meat don't *taste* as good. . . ."

Walker delivered the expected praise quickly and then began to tell Snoot about the picnic. Snoot looked up when he came to the part about Bud. "Anybody else see you?"

"Just Bud, I guess. . . ."

"Goddamn him." Snoot turned suspicious. "Weren't he hunting with the boy?"

Walker hesitated. Should Snoot know everything? "Beats me." Getting Snoot involved, he decided, would escalate feelings all around. "We left as soon as we could."

Snoot bent over his rifle and polished it until it gleamed.

The afternoon crept into evening. Walker tried talking with Snoot about a legal strategy for stopping the development, but Snoot wasn't keen on the nuances of the law, and neither of them seemed able to concentrate. Walker couldn't do anything until the town offices opened on Monday anyway, so he gave it up, all the while wondering, worrying about Claire.

Snoot bragged about his buck and whittled a new handle for his ax. Walker complimented him where compliments were due, cooked supper, read a little, read some more, and closed the book, thinking about how they could have gone over to New Hampshire—taken separate rooms, if that would have made her comfortable. He finally went to bed when he heard Snoot snoring in his bunk.

Hours passed, and still he couldn't sleep. After the picnic, when he told Claire about Junior in the tree, she sped out of Big Church as if their lives depended on it. "He's irrational when it comes to you," she told him. "He's a maniac. Everything bad that's ever happened to him, he's blamed it on you or his father. Everything is everybody else's fault. He warned me, if I ever . . . saw you. . . ." But she wouldn't continue, despite Walker's urging.

Walker repeated the scene over and over again in his head: the rock, the tree, the rifle pointed at him, the wild drive down the mountain. In the sodden hours of the night, it came to him: He had to find her.

He searched the floor next to his mattress for the box of matches, found it, struck one, and looked at his watch: one-fifteen. He pulled on his clothes and climbed down the ladder still shoeless, a plan taking shape in his mind.

The fire in the stove was out. Snoot sawed away at the world's grandest woodpile, a leviathan under his blankets. Walker tiptoed to the bench by the door, feet curdled on the cold plank floor. He would do it, inappropriate as it might be.

He would? Yes, he would. Check on her, go down to the house—make sure she wasn't there—or, if she was, make sure she was all right; that was all. Just in case she hadn't gone to her mother's. If he heard or saw anything suspicious, he would—what? He sat down to pull on his socks and shoes. He would *intervene*, goddammit, do whatever he had to do. He stood up, pulled on his jacket, opened and closed the door to the porch. Crazy, the urgent geometry of this old triangle of theirs. Crazier still the notion that he could do anything about it but see his portion through. He tiptoed down the steps and ran.

If Junior was anything like he was in the old days, a few drinks turned him mean as a snake. There was a story about a night in a White River Junction bar, before Vietnam, when Junior and Jimmy Hebb got into a brawl, two of them against six railroad workers—and it came out a draw. Except Junior and Jimmy went back the next night and found one of the guys alone in the parking lot and whaled the shit out of him. When the guy was out cold, Junior dragged him out to the street and laid him face down with his open mouth against the edge of the curb. Then, the story goes, Junior kicked him in the back of the head. "Cleaned his clock," Junior bragged the next day at Tot's; he and Jimmy did a curb job on a dago, on a greaseball down at the Junction Bar B.Q. Bud sat at the counter shaking his head, proud surrogate papa. Claire swore it was all an exaggeration; Junior and Jimmy had made the whole thing up.

That was a long time ago. Maybe it happened, maybe it didn't—but it could have, and it could happen again. Walker ran. If he had to, he would find a curb for Junior's teeth; he would show no mercy for the cripple who would point a gun at him and Claire, who would mock a helpless Frouncy.

There was moon enough to race him along the woods road through the shadows, light enough at the edge of the trees to make the tarnished pasture grass a rolling sea. The distant house and barn floated like silver islands, ships adrift with phantom cargoes in their holds.

He stopped at the edge of the woods, out of breath, just in time to hear the sound of a vehicle, engine racing, the grinding of gears, tires spinning on gravel in front of the house. Headlights sliced the night, and the vehicle swung a tight half-circle, dove down the lane, and disappeared, leaving Walker blowing vapor into the cold dry air, heart hammering hard in his ears.

Walker leaned down, slid between the strands of wire, and loped across the pasture. Out in the open, washed in moonlight, the presumption of his venture struck him. But I don't care, he thought, even if Junior has me in the cross hairs. He could be hiding behind one of those pitch-black windows with an elephant gun, tickled as shit for a legal excuse to blow away this out-of-state trespasser storming his castle in the middle of the night.

Walker ran a zigzag pattern the rest of the way, head down, shoulders hunched, feeling a fusillade of lethal lead pecking holes in his body, feeling Claire's kiss on his dying lips, feeling alive.

When he reached the barn, he hid in the shadows, waited as he gathered his thoughts and his breath. With the barn between him and the house, he crept along the wall until he had a view of the driveway and the shed where Junior kept his van. Claire's car and the van were missing. He searched among the islands of dooryard junk, all the way out to the hulking profile of the Dodge Mahal at the edge of the hill, but the van and the Subaru were nowhere in sight. Maybe Junior never came home. Maybe the headlights Walker saw were from a hunter's car, someone lost and looking for a place to camp for the night.

With both vehicles gone, the house had to be empty—unless Bud brought Junior home, left the van in the parking lot at Hubby's. They'd been drinking, no doubt, and Bud wouldn't let Junior drive. Could be Bud just dropped him off, and Junior was watching every move from the house, itching to redeem himself. Not too likely. The point was, Claire's car wasn't there, so she must have gone to her mother's, like she said she would. That made sense, didn't it?

Walker thought it did, but as he retraced his steps to the back of the barn, he was still arguing with himself. Was Junior in the car that came and went in such a hurry? Was he out looking for her? A noise inside the barn interrupted his debate. Would Junior find Claire at her mother's? Cow noises, stomping in the muck. Junior would have to break in and crawl up the steps. Tot was known to keep a shotgun handy.

The air was cold, but Walker's shirt was soaked with sweat. A heifer bellowed in her stall, a frightened sound, the sound of shuffling hooves.

He walked out into the paddock beside the barn and slipped through the fence. When he was fifty feet away from the barn, he began jogging up the moonlit pasture slope toward the woods, wondering every frosty step of the way if he was one stride ahead of a bullet. He decided he would go to the moon, at least.

Once in the safety of the tree line, he stopped and

looked back at the house; it was rotting, he thought, even as he watched—wormwood, insidious with Junior's presence, a place never intended for Claire.

When Walker opened the door to the cabin, Snoot was sitting at the table paring his nails with a twelve-inch butcher knife. He sat shoeless and shirtless, with his baggy wool pants pulled over his long underwear. His suspenders hung slack to the floor. His hair was damp and matted into two asymmetrical Gothic towers, like a cockeyed pair of rhinoceros horns. He'd obviously been up for a while; the wood stove crackled with burning kindling, the coffeepot bubbled, and the lanterns were lit full wick. "Nobody home?" he asked, nodding westward to the farmhouse.

Walker gaped at him. "How'd you know where I went?"

"You couldn't tell?"

"Come on. Bullshit."

"Jeesum crow." Snoot was playing with him; now he'd make fun of him until he guessed. "You forgot everything I learnt you?" Snoot wagged his head. "Been downcountry too goddamned long, boy. City must of clogged your brain."

Walker looked around the room. Snoot's jacket hung by the door; his boots were by the stove in the middle of a damp spot on the floor. Walker bent down and felt wet leather. "You followed me?"

The cherub grinned. "Fast as I could. You was running like a hounded rabbit."

Walker felt embarrassed first, then stupid, then betrayed. "I never saw you."

"Seems though you didn't." Snoot laughed. "Never saw my hoofprints in the frost on the way back either, did you?"

"It was dark, goddammit."

"Ha!" Snoot thought that was funny. "Mine was a damned sight closer together than yours, and that's the truth. You was motivating!"

"I could outrun you in my sleep. But how'd I miss you?"

"Never heard the heifer in the barn?"

"Jesus. That was you?"

108

Snoot roared. "Hell, no! That was the heifer." He stabbed the knife into the table. "I treaded on her, not on purpose. Woke her up some, too."

"So you saw the whole performance?" Walker peeled off his coat and flung it in a corner, slipped out of his frost-soaked shoes, and sat down across from Snoot. "You creep." Dodging bullets, hiding in the shadows. He felt ridiculous. "Thanks a lot."

"No charge."

"Wise guy." But there was another issue involved in this game of sneaking around the woods. Walker was, after all, involved with Snoot's son and daughter-in-law, challenging their marriage. He was in love—did he dare think that?—yes, he did. He was still in love with Claire Tatro—Audette—and here he was sitting across the table with a father-in-law who'd watched him lurking around her house in the middle of the night. "It's not what you might think, Snoot." Maybe Snoot should know more about Junior in the tree.

But Snoot knew—didn't he?—not the specifics, maybe, but he knew enough to make further explanations unnecessary.

"He's bound to know about your little outing on the rock, and it won't set right, it won't at all. She ought to quit him quick as she can," he said, gouging at his yellowed thumbnail with the knife. "And we'll have to keep you put away where he can't travel to. He's not too likely to run that rickshaw through the woods—if you know what I mean." Snoot studied his thumb. "He'd probably like to shoot you."

"I'm sure it's crossed his mind—"

"But he won't, if I know him. And what you're after—she's worth the tussle."

Walker was grateful. "She's worth—" How could he explain?

"She oughtn't to have to live like that, him ugly all the time." Snoot went back to his surgery. The knife slipped. "Whoop."

"I'm meeting her again, this morning," Walker confessed, eyeing the bauble of blood, "at nine."

"Figured you would." Snoot sucked his thumb. "Now, you take her real daddy, Horton Flint—*that* man was a corker, and a lot like her. Thing of it is, life comes in different to them people. They hold it in, won't play no daylight on their troubles. Claire, she's got his blood, got a touch of his powers too, but she don't quite know it yet. Hate to see her drag around so glummy all these years."

"She always held her cards too close. . . ."

"She's put up with a raft of shit, done the best she could with the boy. Most of them, they'd of been long gone down the road." Snoot picked up the knife and whittled at the talon on the end of his left index finger. The truncated thumb next to it was cut off at the first knuckle; it had happened in a winter logging-camp accident. Snoot's account varied, depending on his audience, but in his best rendition, his hatchet got to drinking and cut too close while it was splitting kindling. Alone and gushing blood, miles from a doctor, he stopped the flow by cauterizing the stub against the top of a hot cast-iron stove. Then he threw the hatchet in the brook, and the thumb healed perfectly. It was almost cute, Walker thought, the thick little puppet darting about as if it were whole, a useful, cheery version of Junior's truculent stumps. "Didn't know if she'd ever come around to dump him," Snoot deadpanned, "till now."

"That's why you called me?"

Snoot's eyes popped open in a parody of innocence. " 'Twas not! Frounce was sick, and I figured you could cipher all those lawyer papers, put the kibosh on the development. 'Less the city's broke your book brain, too."

"We'll see about that." Walker grinned.

Snoot raised himself from his chair and went to the stove. "Even if you can't track worth a dead man's dink."

"Flunked tracking in college. What can I say?"

"Probably never saw Junior's van tread, either."

"Shit. That was *him?*"

"Tracks was starchy fresh. Probably headed for Stanley Judd's." Snoot sneezed and rocked the table. "Claire, I don't know. Probably went to her mother's."

"She said she would but I couldn't sleep, kept worrying maybe she hadn't."

"Well, there weren't nobody in the house, no smoke, no tracks on the ramp."

"Then everything should be okay," Walker said, but he didn't quite dare believe it. He and Claire had talked about driving to Sachem Lake in the morning. There was a little island on the lake with a chapel on it—for summer people, mostly—a steepled white Gothic miniature snuggled in the pines, rows of primitive pine pews inside, a beautiful stained glass window faced into the morning sun. They went there once, a dozen years past, the only time they'd been to church together. Canoeing out to it had been an eerie thrill, the drip of water from their raised canoe paddles, the haunting sounds of the chapel organ billowing across the lake and up into the mountains, musical fog.

Snoot went to the stove. "Have some coffee, Tutti Frutti."

Walker smiled at the nickname he hadn't heard for years. Snoot used it as a derogatory reference to Walker's education, a variation on Pinhead or Artsy Fartsy. Tutti Frutti was an envy-insult term, evoked when Walker used words Snoot didn't understand or when Walker second-guessed him, as he had with Snoot's pretense for getting him back to Dalton Pond.

"One of these days," Snoot said, Tutti Frutti playing in his voice, "I'm going to teach you how to track like Horton Flint."

"One of these days," Walker answered, "I'm going to teach you how to discuss a female's genitals in Latin."

They talked across the table until the dark emptied out of the woods, until the second day of hunting season began with the same bright promise as the first. By eight o'clock they saw blue sky through the window, saw the frost beginning to melt off the trees. Walker looked at his watch and wished for the hour to hurry. He couldn't stop thinking about Claire.

Snoot cooked breakfast and began a long tirade about

Bud Benoit. "Bud thinks he's the law."

Walker tried to listen, but Claire commanded most of his attention. Maybe she'd change her mind and tell him she couldn't see him.

Snoot was raving. Bud didn't care what people knew! Look at all the times he'd twisted the truth to make himself look good, jacked deer, took bribes, fished out of season, put town money in his pocket, beat up on people too sorry to defend themselves.

Walker decided he'd park across the street at Merton's Texaco.

Big-eared Bud had seen to it that Snoot lost his license. Bud wrote up traffic offenses to suit himself, lied to protect his friends—such as they were. And now he was stealing Snoot's land. Bud was long overdue to get his. He'd been asking for it too, too goddamned long. Snoot said he'd been holding an unplayed ace. "There's a story about him and a woman named Ruby Redd."

Claire would get in the car, and they'd drive to the lake, and all the gawkers at Tot's would know exactly what was going on.

"A stripper up to the Daintytown Follies."

"Stripper?" Walker knew about the Follies, a randy northwoods roadhouse at Colton's Crossing on the Canadian border. "So why not play hardball?" He heard himself talking like the kind of lawyer he'd never wanted to be. "Use the story to discredit Bud, put a taint on his part in the development."

" 'T'won't work." Snoot sounded convinced. "They ain't connected."

"So what was the story? What happened?" Now Walker was curious. "A stripper and Bud?"

"Let it set where it is, for now." Snoot crossed his arms, locking the story in. "Someday soon," he said, "we'll dust it off and use it good."

The first thing Walker saw when he drove into the village was Claire's Subaru parked next to Tot's store. Snoot was right about Claire, but where was Junior; what was he thinking? No sign of the van. What did Stanley Judd drive? Who, on this sunny morning, was looking for whom?

From his parking space across the street, Walker had a perfect view of the four tall windows in the upstairs apartment where Tot and Laurie lived. Claire had to be there. It was twenty to nine on a Sunday of his thirty-sixth year, and Walker felt like a teenager.

Tot's coffee-klatch crowd would love it. The plate-glass window at the end of the counter provided a good view of the red Wagoneer with the blue and white plates. It would take ten minutes for news of their meeting to spread around town.

"Climbed in his rig and off they went." Dalton Pond loved a scandal.

"Headed for tall timber."

No one was exempt from innuendo.

"Right under Tot's nose, and him and Junior business partners."

Walker studied the building's second floor; the two tall windows on the left were probably in the living room. No one came to look out from the curtains. Where was she? He looked away and waited.

Tot's parking lot was full. Several trucks had gutted deer lashed to their hoods, limp trophies on display. The coffee counter window drew him in again. He imagined the Worthington brothers, their clipped accents.

"Weren't he the hippie she kept house with, out in the boonies, by the Indian graves?"

He moved his car, pulled down Main Street a hundred yards to the front of the school, and waited. From where he sat, he could see the corner of Frouncy's room at the Home; he'd visit her again today, painful as it was for them both. There was a time when everyone in town took their troubles to Frouncy. She had a way of listening that made the speaker find the answers, a gracious way of holding up a mirror to the truth. It was she who led Walker to lead himself to law school, she who guided him to peace with being who he was, instead of the imitation redneck logger he imagined he could be. She never gave advice; she uncovered hidden confidence for everyone—except for her own Junior. How that must have pained her, yet she never stopped listening and offering the mirror. Now she had few visitors, and the mirror was forever broken.

Claire was halfway to his car before he saw her in his rearview mirror. His instinct was to jump out and embrace her, but something about the way she was walking kept him in the car. He leaned across the seat and opened the passenger-side door.

"Hi," she said quietly. Her glance ricocheted off his face and buried itself in the dashboard. "Sachem Lake's that way." She thumbed over her shoulder, without looking up.

"Claire?" Walker touched her hand. "Are you all right?"

"We better go, okay?" Her voice was flat and husky.

Walker turned the car around and drove past Tot's. To hell with them. They could gawk all they wanted.

A pickup truck with Massachusetts plates swerved out in front of them. The deer carcass tied across its hood broke loose and slid spread-eagled off the side of the left front fender. It hung suspended by a clothesline noosed around two slender ankles. The other two hooves skimmed the road, dragging shredded lengths of rope.

Claire put her hands to her face.

"Pigs," Walker said, pulling around the truck. Then he glanced over and saw the bracelets of raw skin around Claire's wrists. "Claire?" She was crying. He touched her hair where it fell against her coat. "Claire, what happened?"

She rocked her head side to side.

"Talk to me, Claire. Are you okay?"

She made a motion for him to keep driving, sobbing so hard she shook.

He drove slowly, with one arm around her, feeling the rise and fall of her grief. She huddled against him, her face in her hands. Several times she seemed to have composed herself, but when she began to speak, the weight of her words overwhelmed her resolve and she turned away, weeping again.

114

"Every time I close my eyes. . . ."

"I'm here, I'm with you," he told her. "You're safe. Take your time. It's okay now."

At the top of Little Squaw Mountain, he pulled into a roadside rest stop and drove behind a house-sized boulder. When he stopped, his car was hidden from the road, a safe retreat. To the east lay a view of Sachem Lake, spread out like a new moon creased into the autumn woods below. Chapel Island was a dark hole in the mirrored water, its white sliver of steeple poking through a crown of pines. A boat—a black dot—halved the distance between the island and the nearby shore. It sat immobile, anchored—drifting?—measuring unknown dimensions. Beyond the lake, a panoply of tired mountains dissolved into the horizon, earth and trees, stone and mist stitched into the hem of the sky.

She began circuitously, sometimes in reverse chronological order, first with her gratitude to Walker for being with her, then edging backward and inward, as if to fortify herself against the hard core of her story with the easy parts around the edges.

Walker sensed how it would end, then felt guilty about his dire assumptions. He had to let her talk it out. Maybe it wasn't as bad as he thought, but it occurred to him—and he chided himself for thinking it—if Junior were any less despicable, Claire might have stayed with him.

"I was asleep. I was dreaming about you. Jody was at the lake with Bobby." She hesitated, then continued. "I should have hidden my car"—she swallowed—"I never want to see him again."

Walker glanced down at her wrists. "He tied you up?"

"Like the deer on the truck." She dug in her pockets for a handkerchief and held it to her eyes. "Like a crufi . . . crucifixion." She choked up a laugh. "It's not funny."

"He's twisted," Walker heard himself saying, imagining her struggle. He wasn't sure he wanted to know what happened next, but then he realized he *did* want to know, if only so that he could know how much he despised the sonofabitch.

Claire continued. "I couldn't hit him, couldn't scratch."

Walker touched her wrist. "Rope?" He'd seen far worse signs of abuse in court—he'd made light of them in defense of his criminal clients—but to see the marks on Claire . . . there was suddenly no applicable doctrine of hallowed laws, no due process due, no right to counsel to anyone but Claire.

"I got loose, though, as soon as he left."

Walker closed his eyes—*the motherfucker*—shut out the unpardonable picture of Junior on top of Claire, stumps pointed into her. "He didn't . . . hurt you . . . after he tied you up?" Why was it so hard to say? "I should have stayed with you." He settled for that, held her tightly to him. "You don't have to talk about anything you don't want to."

Claire pulled away, held him at arm's length, and looked at him squarely. "Listen, Walker: He put a pillow over my head, tied me up, put duct tape over my mouth, and humped me." She paused, gathering herself. "Like a dog." Then she turned away, looking out the window, remembering. "He left his semen in my navel." She turned back to Walker. "I took three baths last night, another one this morning." She was speaking firmly now, in full control. "And you know what hurts? It's not the rope burns or the bruises, not the lumps on my face. It's not the physical that hurts. What hurts most is the betrayal, the *waste,* the stupid waste of trust and love and hope that things can get better. We were finished, Walker, our marriage was over years ago, but we got along, more or less—kind of numbed ourselves to it and went on with our separate lives. But we didn't hate each other—at least I never thought we did. Now he's shown me a side of him I'd never seen, and I'll never be able to think of him again without remembering what he did. It's horrible to know that about him, to know he's so sick." Tears spilled down her cheeks. "He said he hated me because I pitied him." She pulled herself into Walker's arms. "And I guess I did. He *was* pitiful."

Walker stroked her face. "That's not so bad, is it? He was in tough shape, back then. You wanted to help."

"But look what it led to."

"I shouldn't have left Dalton. . . ."

"Who could blame you?"

Walker thought about blame, about courage. He'd left because he'd been hurt, more than anything—that, and needing to feel he was doing something with his life. "I could have waited it out. I knew Junior wouldn't be easy."

"He's really . . . pathetic," she said.

"No more pity, remember?"

Claire laughed. "Am I thick or what?"

Then she began to talk—in splashes first, then waves, then torrents—until at last her voice was caught in a current ten years in the making. He held her, and he listened to a tide of words dismantled from a life of silence; they flooded the car, then spilled down the mountain and into the valley, a history being discarded, emptied into deep water below.

Walker convinced her they should drive back to the house and pick up her clothes. She could stay with her mother for a while, or stay with Jody—or, Walker hoped, stay with him. They'd find a house to rent, invite Snoot to live with them, bring Frouncy home and take care of her. That's what he hoped, but he knew enough to keep it simple. One step at a time.

Later, he couldn't convince her to file charges.

"All I want is a divorce," she said. "If I take him to court for what he did last night, it'll drag on for longer than I could bear. I want out, that's all. I need to get him behind me as fast as I can."

Except for what he admitted was an ugly desire for revenge, Walker had to agree she was probably right.

Junior's van was parked at the end of the ramp when they arrived at the house. Claire wanted to leave and come back later.

Walker disagreed. "He can't hurt you with me here. It'll never be easy, and it's better to get this over with as soon as possible." He stood by Claire protectively from the moment she got out of the car until they reached the door. Let Junior even look at her wrong! "No matter what he does or says"—

Walker felt himself going back and forth between the roles of counselor and bodyguard—"just get your stuff and ignore him." It would be a pleasure if Junior tried something. "Just leave him to me."

"No fighting, Walker. I'm serious."

"All I'm going to do is keep him away from you. Whatever it takes."

"We're here to pick up my clothes. Period. Okay?"

"Okay." Walker took a deep breath. Claire opened the door. They walked into an empty kitchen, to the sound of water running in the bathroom.

"The shower," Claire whispered. "He could be in there for hours."

"Hope he drowns."

"Walker." She led the way to her bedroom on tiptoe.

Walker followed and positioned himself between her door and the bathroom, two doors away. He watched her pull open dresser drawers, keep this, discard that—open the closet, pile the contents on the narrow bed, and fill two suitcases with clothes—but his attention was on the sound of running water.

The room she was leaving was sparsely furnished. It was clean but worn out: plaster was missing from parts of the ceiling, the window casings were skewed away from the buckled frames, the floor tilted into a corner. It was a room not unlike most of the rooms in the house, and as he considered it, he recalled his childhood reaction to rooms like this, remembered thinking they looked so much better than the clinically clean suburban boxes he lived in at home. Later, there was a period when even Snoot's house was too bourgeois; living in a rough-hewn cabin in the woods was all anyone should ever need. And then the apartment in New Haven with Nicole—walls filled with books and art—where, he teasingly complained, he was being forcibly housebroken. He reminded himself how they both must have known, when he left, that his trip north would add up to more than a visit.

Now he was watching Claire move out of—away from—a kind of house and a style of living she'd been part of for most of her life. He wondered what the next stop would look like—to her, to him. How would the coming convergence of their pasts convert to a future of rugs and furniture?

When she began to carry the first load of clothes out to the car, Walker's instinct was to help her, but the sound of splashing in the shower kept him where he was, on guard, itching for an excuse. . . .

"I'd help you, but—" He motioned to the bathroom.

Claire nodded and hurried out to the car on the first of half a dozen trips.

It was sad, he thought, watching; it took less than fifteen minutes for Claire to empty the house of everything she needed. There were still pots of house plants and other things too big to move in the Subaru; they'd send a truck for them later, a neutral party to cart away her dressers and tables, books and records, stereo and blanket chest. But now, in no time, she'd packed enough to close the door behind her forever.

"This is it." She said it from under a load of dresses on hangers. "We can go now," she whispered, halfway across the kitchen.

Walker watched her disappear through the door and began to follow. Two steps into the kitchen, he stopped. Snoot's Remington was propped against the wall. Walker picked it up, balanced it in his hands. "Not until he understands," he said, as he turned.

The bathroom was humid with steam. Junior's wheelchair blocked the door, but Walker moved it without a sound, moved it out into the hall, and left the door open, so that only he filled the space between the sink and the opaque shower curtain. He stood listening for a moment, then reached in and turned off the water.

A stillness followed, a protracted moment in which he felt the pattern shift. Claire and Junior and he were in motion; a new configuration was about to form in which Junior's portion would be enormously diminished.

Junior flung open the curtain. He was sitting in a folding aluminum lawn chair, pink skin boiled, hair matted to his skull. He was a water creature, a mutant amphibian, pitifully stranded, soaking wet. He glared up at Walker, saw the rifle, and lurched forward, unafraid. "What the fuck do you think you're doing?"

Walker moved a step backward, looked down at the desperate face, the furious torso, stole a glance at Junior's genitals. His rival, brother, enemy—opposite and yet—the same. "I want to talk to you." The Remington hung cold in his hand, its short barrel aimed at the floor. He wondered if it was loaded—as it surely was the day Junior pointed it at him. "She told me what happened."

"Get out of here!" Junior lunged from the shower, muscles taut. Now he was half suspended between his chair and the grab bar, splashing water on the floor. "Where's my wheels?" he shouted. "What'd you do with my wheels?"

Walker blocked the door; he pictured Claire, sitting out in the car, waiting for him, and prayed she wouldn't come in and find them there, bellowing at each other. "I'm warning you, motherfucker. You touch her again, and it'll be the last thing you ever do."

"My *wheels!*" Junior flopped to the slippery floor and scrabbled his way past Walker's legs, wet and panicky through the doorway, into the hall, grappling his way to security. "Sonofabitch, get out of my house!"

Walker moved aside to let him pass, and when their bodies touched the equation seemed different, all of a sudden, and vengeance seemed a hopeless remedy. What was he going to do, pull the trigger on Junior, kick him, stomp him, knee him in the back? He put the rifle in the corner of the shower and pulled the curtain shut, ashamed and sick to his stomach. He turned in time to see a maimed and naked body struggle up into the wheelchair, finally safe in its chariot, mobile again.

"Now get out!" Junior screamed, flesh abraded, splotchy red, a pointed finger shaking toward the kitchen door.

"Remember what I said. Stay away from her." Walker

passed him in the narrow hall, close enough to feel his furious helplessness, to smell shampoo—to choke him, tip him out of his chair, and slam the wheels down on his head. Walker passed him without doing any of that, without knowing how to express his own immense confusion.

8

FROUNCY STRUCK

FROUNCY WRUNG Snoot's hand and wept. She searched his face, then turned to Walker and tightened her tenacious grip, a plea for patience.

Walker lovey? Came to see her? Look at him. She reached across the bed and held his hand to her glistening cheek. A handsome man now, clean-shaved too, a handsome grown-up man.

She dared not speak. Her tongue was unpredictable, babbling insults, traitorous to her needs. "Take me home, Snoot, take me, please," was sabotaged, turned into nonsense. "Doxie!" she blurted out instead. Or, "In the cupboard!" Or, whatever the occasion, "Cherries!"

Snoot smoothed her hair.

If only she could tell him. She clung to his hand and closed her eyes.

What time was it? She liked it when her husband fed her, spooned her mashed potatoes and tapioca and told her what he did that day. Sometimes, she fell asleep while he told her stories, laughing at himself for the foolish things he'd done.

Junior came to see her.

Did he?

Her son was busy.

Busy.

Snoot never missed a day. Sometimes she'd awake to him reciting "The Cremation of Sam McGee." He made jokes with the nurses and sang off-key until Mrs. Thibodeau shushed him quiet. "This ain't a dance hall."

If only he would take her home to Crooked Mountain. "Doxie!" If only he could understand.

He listened as if he did.

And so did Dearie, bless her heart. Soft pillows and massages, sparing Frouncy's need to speak. Claire was the invisible visitor, the holding hands, the smiles and strokes. Claire's touch was medicine—not the drowsy white medicine the nurses gave her but courage, hope for words and home. It got so sleepy in the room.

Her days were spent mostly in bed—awake, asleep, or somewhere in between, where sedatives and failing hope mixed time around and spun it out in shapes at once familiar and unexpected. But there were places, whirlpools, inlets, islands in the murky flow, where Frouncy's eyes flashed bright with movement, full of sights and histories summoned forth.

Daddy notched a stick and stood it in the dooryard while the rain blew sideways hard and stole his hat when he stooped down to load the sow into the skiff and took the oars and rowed her clear across the forty-acre cornpiece where we couldn't see him any more and by and by he rowed back empty hard against the hurricane between the flying branches and the shingles tearing off the sheds and water up above the bottom pasture buckwheat lapping up the notches carved on Daddy's stick up to the tippy top and him afloat above the chopping block where chickens got the ax beside the barn he had to duck his head to row inside to put a twitch on Doxie but she balked and reared her hooves as stubborn as she was and him afraid he'd choke her trying to coax her out she weighed two thousand maybe more and Daddy in a rowboat couldn't move a horse so big he said he knew he couldn't do it so he left her in the stall for drowning and the skiff was pressed against the ceiling with the river rising so fast Daddy held his breath and swum out underwater through the barn door we could see him bob and catch a tree that floated by and Mother cried and lugged the furniture upstairs and us kids waving out the attic window felt the house a-tremble at the current while we watched our daddy swifted down the river that was wide as Abyssinia ocean water and him just part of all the bits of building rubbish guinea hens somebody's yellow hat and awful whirlpool snakes of floating chaff all getting smaller going got done gone there comes some more to take their place and mud lined on the seventh stair where Mother wrote a mark to show how high it came the day the water washed our daddy down to Tinkam Bridge and took him two full days to wade back home so he could bury Doxie.

The early morning sun poured in through Frouncy's windows, and she saw the light as time—or space, or water, dreams or history, sense or nonsense—a pearly medium that took her in and kept her for a while each day before it left her once again outside its opalescent veil. It warmed her and it eased the burden of the sounds and hands and faces, of the sheets and soap and voices separated from their good intentions. Holding hands with Snoot and Claire became her tie to present time; her other hours were spent waiting for the sunlight on the pond to wake and nourish her, to start the frightening, soothing, vivid, unrelenting recollections, the lulling, mulling push and pull.

Francine take your daddy's dinner bucket yes Mother and take a jug of onion broth yes Mother wait for him to eat and bring the jug back Francine yes Mother and don't forget his dinner bucket too yes yes Mother and mind you're careful of the oxen on the icy tote road yes'm don't get caught between a tree and Daddy's team I know I know the logs can break your legs to pieces quick as anything on slippery snow you'll hear him on the sidehill up above the ledges you can hear the chopping noise as soon's you cross the brook and yes Mother yes yes yes yes and then the hot jug and the steaming dinner pail and up the tote road through the hemlock tunnel eating snow cupped in blue woolen mittens licking icicles from branches hearing Daddy's chop and then a step and stop and chop again and in the road a cardinal as bright as crimson velvet chop again chop chop and then the creaking splitting sound and whoosh and whomp the mountain seems to shake and thunder when the tree comes down and no more chop to hear between the crunch of footsteps following the pair of hoof holes deepened in each side of Daddy's bootprints up the hill and no more chop just wind and snow and empty tracks that lead up past the ledges to the woodlot with the pretty prospect of the river just the empty quiet tracks that lead to Daddy with the tree caved in across his heart and blood-stained spittle frozen on his whiskers.

Sometimes the voices were familiar but out of focus— memories of night sounds from a distant room. They came in rolling waves, in tides that rose and ebbed around the light and dark inside the room. They came in patronizing, scolding, teasing, loving tones, with food and drink and pillows, wash-cloths, bedpans, liniments and combs, bright-colored pills in little paper cups. The walls, the ceiling, floor, and curtains, the white tile bathroom with the medicine smell—they came with all of those and meant her well, but all too often when they made their birdlike sounds they flew away, into the clouds, before she had a chance to hold them.

Snoot's voice rumbled in her ear like wagon wheels rolled down a summer road. She smelled the load of pitch-forked hay, the strong tobacco scent of Reginald, the hired man, driving the team to a lathery gloss. The sound rolled on, a steady pace, sped up, slowed down, and stopped—to water Doxie at a trough? Then the wheels began again among the sound of spoons and food and pigeons cooing back and forth above. Sometimes the wheels came close to Frouncy's face and slowed, as Doxie did with heavy freight against the traces, up the steep incline by Alton's pit. Sometimes the wheels-on-gravel hid themselves in bristly whiskers, brushing Frouncy's face before they rolled away. Sometimes she listened closer, trying to place the sound, certain she knew the road, the wagon, the team, the pasture mowed—expecting Daddy to appear and tell her what it was she heard, how much farther to the barn and Mother waiting supper in the lamplit kitchen.

Horton Eagle-in-the-Wind could make a virgin pregnant if she let him see inside her open mouth it only took a second quick and sneaky in a week or less she would be bulging out to here and Mother said the babies would be born with secrets they would keep forever magic Horton stopped the water coming down from Crooked Brook when Byron's sawmill wouldn't pay his wages all the other brooks were running full of snowmelt and a rainy spring except for Crooked Brook so Byron walked the pebbles all the way up to the source and couldn't find a puddle not a drop of water anywhere and heavy rainfall twice that week so he came back and paid the money all he owed and half a dollar extra for good measure sure enough the brook commenced to rush again and all the while the Indian never said a word and no one dared to ask him what on earth a man could do to stop a natural course of water some believed it was a trick but Mother knew of other things he'd done beyond the laws of humankind such as the poisoned cow he cured such as the miracle on Tinkam Bridge the day a cable broke and dropped a girder onto Leon Dooby's back they said it snapped his spine like kindling wood the bridge crew foreman sent a boy to run and fetch a block and tackle big enough to lift the girder fetch an undertaker for the dead man while they ate their noonday dinner silent underneath the east bank locust grove and never spoke when Horton came along and walked onto the bridge and moved the six-ton iron shroud off Leon breathed the sacred breath of life back into him a half an hour after he'd been dead and Horton tended him and helped him off the other end and turned down River Road bent over some but up on two feet walking so the men under the trees were in an awful state of shame by what they saw and come to find out later Leon Dooby's back was mended every place that Horton touched it with his hands.

• • •

Sometimes, Frouncy felt no more than a pulling toward the voices. Reminding her. A needing to do. What was it? She felt her body lifting, drawn to understanding like the ocean rises to the moon—but those tautened, tensile moments weren't enough to overcome inertia, and the voices came and went without accomplishment.

Mother told me never put a penny in your mouth it's dirty never let a boy she told me never let a boy she told me never let a boy I told her cross my heart I never would and into high school I believed her then the dances at the Grange Hall handsome black-haired Horton Eagle-in-the-Wind a statue by the door waiting to dart a look inside a virgin's open mouth and them all smiling at him with their lips sealed shut except for Pearle Lupien too young to know her teeth were parted and except for me with other ideas looking altogether else-where dancing box-step waltzes with Wendell Audette and every dance still less inclined to want to do what Mother told me wash your neck and knowing somehow she was wrong to be so glum on life and still in widow's black for Daddy keeping me from stories of the Rumney girl and wash your parts how Hester showed her titties for a nickel and the boys worked Saturdays so they could buy a peek and Hester only thirteen at the time as filled out full as any woman so I asked her could I see them she said what I said you know she said you show me yours and you can see mine so we went behind the barn and opened up our dresses come to find out hers weren't so much different than mine but how she stared and held my face and kissed me on the mouth and pressed her nipples onto mine and we were like a body with too many parts but hers and mine were different I could feel it and I never told about it until Mother said she heard that Hester Rumney was a dancer at the Follies up at Daintytown she showed her body every night for money and I said I saw it once for free and it was nothing in particular as if there wasn't anything could bother me because by then Wendell and I were doing every-thing there was to do and planning to get married soon's he got a little money put together not a pot to pee in not a windowsill to throw it over it was love I never doubted it so I told Mother everything and worried her half sick for being modern but I knew it was the only thing I wanted me and Wendell and it gave me courage just to have his keepsake locket hung around my neck and touched it every time he went away and stroked it late at night to give me pleasure him up logging in the woods and waiting to come back to me and Hester never knowing that her titties had another kind of worth that went along with love and having someone you could make a life with every day not just for minutes or for making money in a dancing barn but went along with love for always and forever.

"Claire asked me to stop and see you"—Lucian Webster from the bobbin mill stood over her, unfolding papers—"about the beneficiary for your pension plan. Turns out you forgot to sign the white space in the middle. You can still fill in Snoot's name."

Yes she would and give away the home place Walker there and Snooty there and Walker there and Lucian said to write her name and medicine and medical and out the window mousy water on the pond.

Lucian in a shiny suit, a silver pen, a green necktie patterned with flying flowers. Pippy little voice: "Can you sign this for me, Francine?"

Her sign: Francine Southworth Audette. "Doxie. Dox!" Frouncy's hand jerked to her nose; she kicked against her sheets, and a jumble of words bounced off Lucian's face.

"I know, I know. Let's try again. Can you hear me?"

"Doxie." Francine, not a horse. "Cherries!" Lord God. Snoot kissed her forehead.

"Dox." She loved him too.

The pen went in the pocket, and the buttons buttoned down the front of the jacket.

Frouncy wept.

"Ten years' credit on the plan"—the necktie bloomed into the room—"but no named beneficiary. There'll be some money due, when the time comes."

So much talking talking.

"It'll go into probate unless she names an individual."

"In the cupboard! Doxie!" Did he think she was two years old? She heard exactly what she meant. Why couldn't he?

Then Snoot's voice, booming, a mile overhead. "Leave her be, Lucian. She knows how to write her Christly name as good as gold. She'll do it when she's ready, and not a damn second sooner."

The window with the view of the pond needed washing. Mrs. Thibodeau should see to it.

"If she's incompetent, the probate court will—"

"Careful who you call incomsequent, mister boy."

Junior never was a little boy.

"This woman here was working sixteen hours a day before you learned to wipe your ass."

Up to Daintytown, they show it all.

"It's just that our plan requires certain—"

Walker talking, Walker talking, told the necktie thank you, but.

Snoot's voice booming: "How many million you going to make on this little deal?"

Out on the pond, a man with a pipe rowed a dory, a flag of smoke unfurled above his head.

Wilbur Judd still fishing for his supper.

"Company's folded, Snoot, you know that. They're not making a dime, just honoring their obligations to the folks who worked there."

"H'rassing Frounce. . . ."

Seventy dollars put your feet up here she said and doctor will be in to see you in a minute no no put your heels up on the metal rings she said and spread your legs so he can see and me too sick to leap up and get dressed and run away and leave the awful shame of opening the girl of myself up in front of strangers free to gape at parts of me I never saw in my whole life unfolding my insides and tearing out a crooked baby formed without a face without a hand he showed it to me held it up like ruined fruit and all my fault the doctor said for doing man's work heavy lugging me too opened up and hurt to wonder what he meant the picture of that slippery muscle dripping death in front of me I couldn't cry or move my lips or raise my hand to hold what should have been my own but never would and me disgraced and him there high and mighty with a snow-white towel drying off his evil hands and looking at his pocket watch for dinner knowing too much of my open wound to ever be entitled to enjoy crumb or ever be forgiven or looked straight-faced in the eye again and then a bill for seventy dollars which will set unpaid the day I die I swear he'll never see a cent.

"Don't the towel feel good? Let's dry our hair so's we don't catch cold."

"Dox." Die.

"There now. Don't that feel better? No running off to Boston while I fetch your bathrobe, 'kay?"

"Ummm." Walker had visited with Snoot.

"You want to use the commode? All right, dear. You set there. I'll be right back."

Snoot?

They did it in the parking lot for pay but not for him he promised I believed him Mother told me all I did was sleep for twenty days I couldn't move my body but to sip a little soup till Snoot got home and when he did I wanted to be ready for him bake a ham and make a deep-dish apple pie to give him something nice before I told him but I couldn't stand head woozy and the rusty ache kept sawing through me wouldn't go away he said he walked up from the highway knee deep through the blizzard caught me sleeping full-dressed on the davenport and me still crying when I should have been a comfort to him spending three weeks locked inside a cell for fighting with a traveling man that chewed his ear half off his head and now he was back home safe kneeling down beside me with the snow still melting off his shoulders while I cried and cried and told him what the doctor did Snoot squeezing on my hand to hold us both from sinking through the floor and both of us so sad it made me hate myself hate something in my body locked up tight and him tormented so he couldn't make it rise when it had always stood up voluntary every single time he ever asked and just as often of its own accord but now it was a useless thing and giving him an awful time and all the while I tried to make it better he was good as gold but like a brother not the same as man and wife but like a friend and when the weather warmed he worked up north he started staying over in the camps and having motor trouble with his rig he sent me money every time he got it and I figured he was going with somebody so I asked him straight out on his next stop home and he looked down ashamed and said it wasn't like I thought but he had been to see the dancing up at Daintytown but not to go with one of them that did it in the parking lot for pay but he was there because he couldn't understand what happened why his nature left him still too young a man to settle for a dry bed house he close to cried and ready to do anything to get it back and I said yes because I knew I wanted mine back too but I was curious of what they did at Daintytown the dancing was it dirty I'd heard tales of Hester Rumney but I couldn't quite believe it and he told me it was randy he supposed it was as rank as it could ever get but promised me the only part he wanted was a sign of manhood coming back to make him full again and I believed him and he went back to the Follies now and then but things got better even though I never did forget the ache and never told my mother all the things that happened to us all the complicated business with a woman and a man.

"Mrs. Audette, it's time we took our bath."

Snoot was gone? Her Walker lovey gone? What time was it? Did she do something bad? Did . . . ? "Doxie?"

"It's time we took our little bath and washed ourselves. Won't that be nice? We'll get our towel."

"Cherries!" Our towel.

"And get our robe and slippers."

"Ummm." Like back to being baby.

"Walk nice and careful—there we go. See how nice the water feels?"

"Doxie?"

"And we'll wash here . . . and here."

Two tramps pissing in the middle of the road and us in Wendell's Model B to sell a dozen geese four bits apiece for pillow feathers swapped two cord of maple limbwood for a quart of baby blue and painted up the crib the door the walls the floor and tracked our footprints everywhere it showed up on the bedsheets and the baby came and cried his lungs out with the colic all night long month after month and double earaches then the little teeth like needles on my dugs and Snoot won't touch the either of us sleeping grouchy in the back room jealous and apart from me and little Junior always holding onto me and biting crying monkey arms around my neck and choking me for want of everything and give and give and come to find out everything is never quite enough.

"How we doing, gaining on it?"

"Dox."

"All right, Doxie, take your time, set there as long as you like. I'll be right here having my cigarette."

"Ummm." Ashes.

"Christ, I hate this shift."

Junior called me names they use for animals and never told me what I did to put such poison in his heart and no way to undo it pulling frogs apart and drawn to witness any kind of pain and killing every autumn butcher time he waited for the hogs to die him always there to see the hole between the eyes the throat sliced open spilling red and then the running nowhere thrashing circles in the dust and Snoot would tell him dig a ditch beside the compost slide the guts in scold him for his staring at the pieces me beside him digging Kennebecs a bushel to a row and not a whisker on his chin he told me all I ever wanted was a slave to help me Jesus how the cold ground ached up hard between my legs he told me how he'd kill himself someday for spite to teach me what true suffering was to teach me good for never loving him for who he was and every day his words scabbed onto me and festered awful wouldn't heal and then and then and then and then I can't I won't remember can't remember anymore I can't I won't oh Jesus.

Junior?

9

FROZEN GROUND

WALKER LEFT the house feeling like he was about to vomit; his confrontation with Junior hadn't produced the tidy sense of resolution he'd wanted. It wasn't so neat, was it, hating somebody? It wasn't so easy to disregard an enemy's humanity.

"You talked to him?" Claire asked, as he climbed into the car.

"I turned off his shower."

Claire slumped down in her seat and closed her eyes. "What'd you say?" Was the weariness in her voice for Junior or for him?

"I told him I knew, and I warned him to stay away from you. That's all I said." The next part was more difficult to say: "I took his wheelchair away from him, put it out in the hall."

"Oh, Walker."

"I've never seen him vulnerable before." Walker shook off the image of Junior writhing on the slippery floor. "I mean, until a few minutes ago, it never occurred to me that he would ever have a reason to be afraid of me."

"We should have left when we saw his van. I shouldn't have pulled you into this."

"Of course you should have." If only there had been some satisfaction in warning Junior off. "He did a terrible thing. He's a rat."

Tears splashed down Claire's cheek into her lap. She seemed to be weighing something in her mind, pushing past the episode at Jody's. "I guess I did a terrible thing too," she finally said, "when I married him. Out of pity."

"It's not the same, Claire. You never meant to hurt him." But there it was—she'd identified the dilemma; there was no parity, no way to redeem one category of offense with another. "I took the Remington into the bathroom."

She shrugged: "That's nothing to be ashamed of."

Walker thought maybe it was, but he didn't argue. She was defending him against himself, and for an instant he wondered if she'd habitually done the same for Junior, insulating him from the self-awareness he'd never learned. "He was so goddamned helpless."

"Helpless to accept help."

She was right about that. "And it makes you feel guilty."

"Enough for a lifetime." She started the car. "Maybe two."

They spent the remainder of Sunday driving around in the hills with Milo Pippin, looking at houses for rent. Milo peddled real estate as indiscriminately as he chose his clothes each morning; his Sunday outfit included a salt-and-pepper leisure suit, plaid porkpie hat, and two-tone shoes with scratched brass buckles. His listings included a restaurant with gift shop attached, poultry farm, and four house trailers—all of which he insisted they "drive by, just in case," on the way to the houses he had for rent.

The first was next to a working sawmill and shared a bathroom with the crew. Claire politely declined before they got out of the car. The next was a two-family conversion on the outskirts of Catamount, with three Harleys parked in the downstairs hall. Milo insisted the new green carpet made the place a steal at half the rent, then snagged his toe in a tangle of shag and bumped his head on the walnut grain wallboard. Walker was relieved when Claire told Milo that avocado green made her sick to her stomach.

The next house they saw, on the Quinntown road,

looked promising; it was a freshly painted white, back from the highway, surrounded by trees, with no other houses in sight. Like the salesman he was, Milo had saved it for last.

"A doctor down to Hanover owns it." Milo found the keys to the front door, took off his hat, and patted down the few remaining strands at the edges of his balding dome. "Jenkins. Dr. Bradley Jenkins, over in Europe somewheres. Two years. Studying rats." As he spoke, Milo seemed to be studying Claire; he was patient but transparently curious to find out if Tot's married stepdaughter had all of a sudden decided to set up housekeeping with her old boyfriend—or who-knows-what? Unsure of Walker's status, Milo had directed his remarks to Claire exclusively ever since they got in the car. Little by little his questions were designed to unravel the mystery. "You looking for a lease or by the month?"

To Milo's surprise, Walker answered. "We'd like a year's lease," he said. "When we find what we want, we could move in right away."

The repeated use of the word *we* made the realtor readjust his hat dead center on his head. Claire squeezed Walker's hand and nodded at Milo, ratifying the decision.

"There'll be three or four of us," Walker added; a little extra intrigue would make Milo the center of attention at the coffee counter tomorrow morning.

"Oh," Milo managed. "That's okay. Fine." Then he flashed a big, bewildered smile, yellow socks and teeth blazing the way to the front hall.

The house was a partially restored colonial, furnished, clean and bright. There were paintings on the walls, a library full of books, and a ground-floor bedroom off the kitchen for Frouncy and Snoot. "Dandy garden spot out back," Milo said, "and a good prospect of the Catamount Heights. On a clear day, why, you can see all the way down to Canaan, see the radio towers perfect."

The upstairs was unfinished except for a cozy, slope-ceilinged bedroom and adjacent bath with a clawfoot tub. Walker took it all in, quickly, greedily: the wide painted floorboards, the miniature print wallpaper, maple dressers,

137

cut-glass lamps, the curtained dormer windows with a view of Crooked Mountain—and the bed, a four-poster, firm and wide with promise, plumped with pillows, decidedly too intimate to be seen in the presence of a third party. The bed alone outspoke all other objects in the room, yet Walker felt he couldn't look at it for more than a second with Milo lurking between him and Claire like a lost voyeur, still panting from the climb up the stairs.

"Well"—Milo moved into the hall—"want to go back down, then take a gander at the cellar? Brand new boiler and a pair of Maytags." He went down the stairs without waiting for an answer, giving Walker a moment alone with Claire.

"What do you think?" he whispered. Her skin looked smooth as satin in the dim afternoon light.

"It's good," she said, "and a little frightening, I guess." She glanced down at her wrists. "Things have happened so fast."

Walker felt her dilemma; it was partly his, too. After ten years apart, they'd seen each other for only three days. She'd just decided to leave her husband—and then the thing at Jody's; things *had* happened fast, and she needed some time to regain her balance. "We could put down a deposit," he said, "hold it for a while, move in when we're ready."

"Maybe in a couple of weeks . . . ?"

Walker pulled her to him, felt her arms wrapped tight around his waist. They stood at the top of the stairs, tempted, cautious. "Whenever. As soon as you're comfortable," he said. Behind her, the bed loomed large as Texas.

For a week, the weather held; then the thermometer dipped below zero for three days in a row before the snow began. Ice formed on Dalton Pond, and Merton's Texaco held its annual sale on antifreeze. The highway department's storage sheds were full of salt and sand; woodsmoke hung in the valleys. The last chevron of geese flew south; it was cold and dark by four, gunmetal gray on the horizon at dawn. Winter pushed down on the land like a frozen stone.

• • •

Walker awoke to the smell of burning Spam. Caught in that ambiguous instant between the end of sleep and consciousness, he wondered where he was. He knew he was sweating, cotton-mouthed, and lying on a lumpy, mildewed mattress. The air was thick with greasy smoke, but each of these sensations was tempered with a feeling of well-being, of optimism; something good was happening.

He opened his eyes, reached for his glasses, and slipped them on. Focus. Detail. Affirmation. A yard above his head, intricate colonies of cobwebs clung to the ceiling, delicate architectures decorated in dust. He ran his eyes down rows of calligraphic saw kerfs in the pine-planked ceiling, down the wall to the dusty windowpanes below. Snow lined the cross muntins in fluffy stripes. The cold mountain air, the cabin scent of mice and pine pitch, oak aflame in a cast-iron stove—he knew exactly where he was. No, it wasn't Nicole—how was it she seemed so indistinct so soon, so far away?—no city noises, no anxious ache, no whirring hair dryers and morning news. He'd been in Dalton Pond for a week and a half, put a deposit on a house, and seen Claire every day, every beautiful, blustery, snowy, northwind-howling day, and she was wonderful, and there was work to do—at last—on the Abenaki Ledges project; the day before, he'd been notified that the Act 250 applications had finally been filed in St. Johnsbury.

Below, he heard Snoot unlatch the door from outside, come in the cabin, and clomp across the floor to the stove. "Son of a hoor!" he whooped. "Burnt my meat!"

"Is that you, Dame Fonteyn?"

"Burnt my meat and out of coffee! Jeesum crow, you'd think the least a damn Canuck could do was cook a fatback slab of *cow*." A pan rattled and clanked; the hissing sound stopped.

"We'll send out for pizza," Walker said, as he swung his bare legs over the edge of the loft to the ladder. "Let me try room service."

"You scrawny little runt, put your britches on," Snoot called up to him. "If you was cooking, we'd need an amulance, and hope to crimus it got here quick."

They ate quickly and dumped the dishes in the crowded sink. A few more days and they'd scour the place thoroughly, for the last time. Walker had been surprised at how little Snoot resisted the idea of moving, then amazed on the morning he saw the first of Frouncy's belongings stacked in the back of the Wagoneer. Snoot carried them down from the house in cardboard boxes, five or six at a time: clothes, blankets, knickknacks, and tattered photo albums, everything she needed for the move to Jenkins's. "She's always wanted a place that sets near the road," he said one day. "Won't bother her a bit to live in a white-painted house. Put the comfort to her something scandalous."

Walker worried she'd never leave the Home. Every few days there seemed to be another setback, another loss in a losing battle.

They put on their coats and tramped through the falling snow, down the hill to the car. As usual, Snoot would spend part of the morning with Frouncy. Walker hadn't seen her in a few days and asked if he could go too.

Snoot hesitated. "You probably noticed, she's not always all that sharp . . . in the morning." But he agreed: they'd visit her after they stopped at Tot's for coffee. "Torments Bud every time I go in." Snoot grinned. "Tickles me to see him riled."

When they reached the road, Snoot stuffed a wad of Red Man in his mouth, gathered it in a lump inside his cheek, then offered the checkered pouch to Walker. "Chew?"

"No, thanks." He'd chewed when he worked in the woods with Snoot years before, but it was different then—he felt he had to; loggers chewed. Whether he liked it or not was never a question. "Maybe later."

Snoot worked his mouth around the tobacco, spat a brown spot into the snow. "Puts lead in your pencil."

"I'll pass." It was possible, finally, to say no to Snoot.

"You'll come back around to it, by and by. Man can't live in this poor backcountry without some form of contraband. We'll have you chewing before you leave."

140

"Leave?" Walker opened the driver's side door and sat inside, turned the key, and started the engine. "I just got here." He turned on the heater and joined Snoot in scraping the windshield.

"So you did," Snoot said. "So you did."

As he drove, Walker looked over at Snoot, at the way his hair brushed the ceiling, at the way he hunched forward on the seat, a bear in a cage too small. He held the dashboard with both cobby hands and breathed a wet, anxious fog against the glass, something conspicuously on his mind.

"Tore up my license, the floppy-eared bastard, lied bald-faced, and brown-nosed the judge—" Then Snoot stopped himself, waved away the sore subject of Bud Benoit, and rocked against the Wagoneer's door. "Not used to riding this side of the rig." He unrolled his window and stuck his face out into a cold rush of air.

As they approached the village, Walker tapped Snoot's half-acre back. "Warmed up yet?"

"Woke me up some. Can you smell it?" he crowed. "Perfect day for a murder."

"Glad you're in a good mood. Anybody special?"

"Jesus, Mary, and Joseph, yas! We'll start with Junior's pointy-headed lawyer, Beasel the weasel, then put the dun fork to the heap till we dig up Tot and Bud and—and maybe even Junior boy."

"For starters."

"Mis'able, ain't I?" Snoot motioned for Walker to park at the Texaco station. "But it 'furiates hell out of me, sometimes." He opened the door, untangled himself, and rose out of the car in a halo of steam. "Look at 'em swarm over there." He nodded across the street. "Common as shit and twice as nasty, come up from Taxachusetts, spend a thousand U.S. dollars to take home a hundred-pound spikehorn. Show the wormy little thing to their neighbors, brag on it all night, and then come time to dress it out, they dump it over the bank, horn, hide, and hoof, and leave it to rot." Snoot spat toward the cars by the edge of the road. "Ignorant, is what they are. Half a bubble shy of plumb."

141

Walker looked at Tot's big plate-glass window and burped up Spam grease. The window was at the end of the coffee counter, Gossip Central's lifeline to the street. He'd sat there comfortably, in the old days, trading tall tales, looking out at the passing parade, but the atmosphere changed after Junior came home, and Walker felt like unwanted company.

The few times he'd been in the place since his return seemed friendly enough. Some offered warm greetings; others ignored him as they always had. His renewed relationship with Claire and the move to Jenkins's were known to all. Punka Hurley was the only one to confront him face to face. They met one day at the nail bins in the hardware store in Jordan, and Punka wasted no time to get down to it. "First you take his woman off him," he said, "and now you're out to get hold of his land. What'd they teach you college boys down-country, anyways?"

"For starters," Walker shot back, "they teach us to get our facts half straight so we don't sound stupid when we accuse people of something they never did." He glared at Punka's mossy teeth. "If it's any of your *up* country business."

Otherwise, he almost dared to think he was allowed—or even envied—his good fortune. Every man in Dalton Pond had spent at least one cold winter's night dreaming of Claire Tatro.

News of his interest in the Ledges project spread quickly, too. The day after his first visit with the town clerk, he was stopped twice on the street by strangers; both encouraged him to do everything he could to stop "Tot's" project. One of them, a heavyset woman he thought might be Mrs. Pippin's sister, told him the Ledges debate was splitting the town in two. "You'll need broad shoulders," she told him, "because you'll be smack in the middle of it, taking the grief from both sides." Surprised, Walker thanked her and wondered what she meant.

"Look at how they've took and infested the place," Snoot said. "Try to find a Christly place to park, some bozo from Boston's got his Buick docked in slantwise acrost three spaces, head up his ass, no hope in sight."

142

Walker saw a few out-of-state cars, but Tot's parking lot was mostly crowded with pickup trucks, rear windows bristling with calculatingly arranged arrays of hunting rifles, fishing rods, and mason's levels.

Snoot stopped to wave to the driver of a decrepit flatbed truck. "Darby Dunbar's drove to town. Don't see *him* much down off Big Church." He put his hand on Walker's shoulder as they crossed the street. "Tot and them Massholes, the only thing they smell is the goddamned money."

A backhoe was digging inside a roped-off area, excavating a trench out from the corner of the store.

"Going to build an addition." Snoot made the shape of a building in the air in front of him. "Wants to double his business. Getting his footings in before deep frost." They watched the backhoe dump a bucketload of fresh brown dirt on the snow beside the ditch. "I can't see Tot digging up my land, no way."

"Maybe he won't," Walker said, although he still didn't know how Tot could be stopped. After two full days of looking at drawings and applications, reading minutes of the hearings, and listening to the town clerk talk about her Yorkshire terrier's prolapsed uterus, he hadn't found a thing; it looked as if Beasley Pruitt had done his homework thoroughly. Whatever chance Walker had would be in the Act 250 proceedings and the Wetlands Board reviews. There might well be some surprises in the next six months, despite Snoot's skepticism. "Just give me some time, Snoot. It's never over till the fat lady sings the last note."

Snoot was more interested in the town police car parked beside the trucks. "Goddamned Bud coughed up a hundred thousand, so they claim." He glowered at the blue light strapped to the roof of the Bronco. "Tot kicked in the rest, and he's acting like he's already made it back double. Give him a minute, he'd turn this place into Q'bec City."

The store's front porch was crowded with racks of red snow shovels, roof rakes, plastic sleds, chain-saw displays and snowblowers—all chained to the wall. Ten years before, the porch was bare but for summer's dogs and winter's snowdrifts. The old signs for maple sugar products, Dexter shoes, and Hires root beer were absent now, but the bulletin board—the same one Walker once used in his search for parts for the Dodge Mahal—was still three layers deep in thumbtacked notices. Next to it was a glass-front display case filled with colored snapshots of houses for sale, split-levels cloned in New Jersey; MARCIA DANFORTH REALTY above a photo of a perky blond yuppie in a tailored tweed blazer inviting everyone to invest in a piece of unspoiled Vermont.

Snoot spat on the porch floor, trod on his gob, and opened the door to the morning smells of Theodore Tatro's General Store. "Going to have me some java." Snoot winked at Walker. There was trouble to come. "Have me some satisfaction."

Walker decided he'd watch from a distance. "You go ahead," he said. "I'll be looking around." He glanced across the long lunch counter at Laurie. Yes, she was pretty enough to have been Claire's mother, but her face showed the burden of disappointment. Walker guessed she'd been much happier teaching school. She must have been beautiful, then. Now, coffeepot in hand, Laurie waited on people in the saddest sense of the word. It was common knowledge she felt nothing for Tot. She probably loved her daughter but refused to risk showing it. Claire was convinced Horton's departure had hurt her mother beyond repair. So if Laurie felt wary of Walker, a flatlander courting her married daughter, who could blame her?

She must have sensed Walker's stare; she looked up briefly, showed a flicker of recognition, then turned back to her customers. They were the original cast, the same perpetual regulars Walker hobnobbed with in the old days. Their necks were a little beefier now, their suspenders tighter against their backs, but still, even from behind, he knew them all: army sergeant Stanley Judd—Stan and Junior went to Vietnam together—Punka Hurley, the alchoholic mason, then Bobby Thornton, Pero Hanchet, Harley Blue, Stub McDermott, and Peach B. Pringle, the Agway salesman. Wayne and Woodard Worthington sat next to Peach; they were deservedly known as two of the best finish carpenters in the northeast kingdom. Walker worked for Wayne the summer he helped rebuild the teak and walnut curved staircase. Milo Pippin sat next to Woodard, and next to Milo sat Bud, an empty stool between them. Walker remembered there was usually at least one empty place next to Bud, wherever he sat.

Walker watched. Bud didn't turn his head when Snoot sat down, but it was unthinkable he didn't know—or smell—who was sitting next to him. Snoot was the kind of person whose mother was impossible to imagine. How could he have ever been small enough to have a mother?

Walker looked at a rack of postcards. There were cards with pictures of six-foot trout strapped to the hoods of cars, elk-horned rabbits, western-saddled kangaroos, and buffalo in high-topped sneakers, but the one he liked best showed a pig stretched out in midair, diving into a swimming pool. The pig was serious, pink, and sleek, the water turquoise blue. Fellow porkers in sunglasses lounged splendidly in deck chairs around the pool, ignoring the diver. Fine print on the back of the postcard credited the photograph to Hee-Haw Enterprises, Gatlinburg, Tennessee. Walker wondered how the Hee-Haw people trained the pig to dive.

He decided he'd send the pig to Robin and Sydney, his soon-to-be ex-law partners in New Haven: *Wish you were beautiful, the weather is here.* A corny follow-up to the letters he'd been sending to explain his decision to move north. He picked the card off the rack and took it to the cash register.

"That it this morning?" Tot asked. He was wearing bifocals, sixtyish now, delicate bones, shrewd as a fox—and studiously impartial to Walker. Did he know Walker was out to bust his chops? Did he care? Did he have so much pull he imagined Walker couldn't touch him? Tot's carroty hair was still alarmingly orange. Did he dye it?

"That's it," Walker said, hoping for a clue—even a negative one—but receiving none.

Tot rang up the sale, counted change from the cash drawer, mumbled, "Haveagoodday," and returned to penciling numbers on a clipboard, without once looking up. A busy, clever, ruthless little man. Walker wondered how hard he'd fight if he was backed into a corner, and he imagined himself as Tot's tormentor.

At the counter, Laurie was taking Snoot's order. He must have said something rude, because she suddenly blushed and hurried away to pour more coffee and tend to the grill. Walker felt sorry for her. Snoot laughed and elbowed Bud. The men at the counter turned in unison to see what the noise was about, grinned and nudged each other, and shook their heads. Bud stared straight ahead, sitting straight as a judge, determined to maintain what he must have supposed was his duty to dignify his badge.

Walker idled down an aisle of Ortho powders, tick spray, fishing gear, and guns. At the end of the aisle was the post office window, and the perennial Lillian Woodard. Lillian was a tiny spinster with shiny white hair pulled back in a bun, the kind of postmistress who made it her business to know everybody and everything that ever happened in Dalton Pond. "Lillian. You're looking well."

She beamed and wrung her hands, uneasy with compliments. She'd been kind to Walker when he was a hippie, despite her rock-ribbed Republican loyalties.

"Still got you chained to Uncle Sam?" he teased. She must have remembered his outspoken criticism of the war, his much-debated deferment for back problems.

"Forty-three years this August." Miss Lillian was proud of her service, proud of the flag she flew each day outside the post office door. "Isn't it a shame about Frouncy?" she asked. It was a skillfully designed piece of rhetoric; maybe Walker would bring her up to date. "They say she has some awful days."

Walker disappointed her. "She's coming along." A lie, but better than spreading the dismal truth.

Lillian rebounded gracefully. "You tell her hello from me, okay? And tell her we miss her at the Grange."

"You bet." Walker smiled, but he could see Lillian wanted more.

"Shall I hold your mail for you?" she asked from beneath a thin veneer of innocence, "or put it on the route to Jenkins's?"

"You can put it on the route," he said. "Starting Friday." Three days to go. "Claire's mail, Snoot's, and mine." Now Lillian had it from the horse's mouth. "And could I please have a postcard stamp?" Walker was comforted to know that as soon as he turned his back, she'd be sorely puzzled by the meaning of the diving pig.

Lillian handed him the stamp and motioned him to come closer. "Good luck stopping the you-know-what," she whispered, cutting a side glance at Tot. "Some people never know when to quit." She clamped her jaw tight around her words. "You'd think enough was enough, wouldn't you?"

Walker got to the lunch counter in time to see Snoot elbow a pitcher of milk onto Bud's lap.

Bud jumped up as if he'd sat on a tack. "*Now* look!" he cried, flicking at the white mess soaked across his crotch. "What the hell's wrong with you, anyway?"

Everyone at the counter turned to enjoy the ruckus; they nudged one another and giggled as Bud dabbed at the milk on his pants with little paper napkins, cursing under his breath. Wayne Worthington suggested a sentence of twenty years for Bud's foul language. Punka Hurley raised his coffee cup in a toast to Snoot, proposing that Snoot and Bud spend one night locked in the same cell, Bud without his badge and gun.

Snoot assumed an expression of pious innocence, hands lifted to his heart, pinkies raised in a parody of high-tea elegance. "Officer Benoit," he said, looking from Bud's blue uniform pants to his own greasy, dirty wool twills, "there's dairy splattered on my trousers!"

"Well, look at mine, you damn buffalo!" Bud's cantilevered ears were crimson; they seemed to be sticking out at least an inch beyond their usual span, and when he shook his head, they syncopated with the jiggle in his jowls.

Snoot feigned concern, then turned to the crowd. "I should judge the man could use some help tidying up." His grin spread like crabgrass under his beard. "Any one of you outlaws got a toothbrush handy?"

The room erupted. Toothbrush? Walker watched, dumbfounded, as ten grown men tumbled all over themselves in a chorus of howls and jeers and catcalls. "Toothbrush!" There was something about that word. *"Toothbrush!"* They wouldn't stop saying it. *"Pest* me with it!"

"Hawwwww!"

Bud jerked himself to attention, shaking with rage, all the color drained out of his ears. "I'll get you for this!" He was seething. "You overgrown woodchuck, I'll get you good!"

"Now, now," Snoot said, backing away. "There's witnesses."

Laurie edged around the end of the counter with a mop. Tot disappeared into the back room. Snoot bowed ceremoniously, slid a dollar bill under his plate, and escorted Walker through the door to the sound of applause.

"That pitcher was *full,* a six-pint creamer!" he exploded as soon as the door was shut behind them. "I could of kissed old sourpuss when she set it down betwixt us." He blew powdered sugar from his beard as he spoke. "Just a tink with the elbow, and over she went. You see Bud's face?"

"He was ripshit." But Walker still felt outside the excitement.

"Soaked his balls good." Snoot giggled like a schoolgirl. "Gawd!"

Walker looked back at the grinning faces watching from the window. "What was that toothbrush bit?"

"Ruby." Snoot hiccuped. "Ruby Redd, old warhorse stripper up to Daintytown, she—" More laughter overtook him.

Walker guided Snoot down the snowy sidewalk, away from Tot's, impatient to hear the rest of the story. "What, then? What'd Ruby do?"

"It was during the big burn in '71, ten thousand acres over to the Swanzey tract. She was dancing at the roadhouse up to Daintytown, and all the boys come in from the woods to goggle and grope and soak their throats. When she got done with the bumps and grinds, Bud poured on the charm and ponied up for a ten-dollar tumble." Snoot glanced over his shoulder and continued. "But he couldn't make it stand."

"Bud admitted that?"

"Hell, no. She's the one told the awful tale. Why, every hobnailed Romeo she ever entertained, first thing she'd do was tell him about the one that went before. I don't know but that she didn't do it on purpose either, bless her bosom. Must of kept them on their best behavior, anyways.

"Anyhow, Harley Blue, he was the next lucky lummox in line, so he heard it all, and he weren't never shy about working his gums, neither. The word got around town lightning quick, but nobody's ever dast speak of it in front of Bud—till now—how Chief Benoit was belly up to the world's finest banquet and couldn't lift his spoon."

Walker pictured a good-hearted matron in a red velour robe.

"Well, it irked *him* something wicked—he'd already paid her—and he was damned if he wasn't going to get his money's worth." Snoot reached down and packed a snowball for the punchline. "So he looked around the room for some form of remedy to his pitiful condition, spied the items on the washstand—and by the Jesus, swear to Mother Mary and all the saints, he went and told Ruby to pest his asshole with a *toothbrush!*"

They walked through the snow toward the Home, Snoot replaying the details of everything he did, from the time he sat down to the time he tipped over the pitcher. "Wish Frounce could have been there," he said, three—four—five times.

As they passed the church, two dark-suited men from Brady's Funeral Home were preparing for a noonday wake. "Now who?" Snoot asked, a catch in his voice. There was no comforting answer.

They walked faster, leaving the black hearse behind them. The playful conversation about Bud was over, leaving only the crunch of their boots on the snow. Walker looked across the road to the pond, felt the chill in the slate-gray water. They walked past the school, past the big white houses, past the little brick smokehouse next to the picket fence in front of the Convalescent Home.

Snoot pointed out Frouncy's window, to the right of the front door, facing south, facing water.

To her, Walker thought, looking across the narrow patch of snow between the road and the pond, the water must look hopeless.

10

DUE PROCESS

IT SNOWED all the way to St. Johnsbury. Walker drove the back roads from Jordan to Callaway, then followed the mountain road south, headlights useless in the midmorning whiteout. The trip took him twice as long as it had the day before, hampered as he was by poor visibility and only one lane plowed. A twenty-mile-an-hour pace was frustrating at first, but it gave him time to think; when he finally relaxed and accepted the storm, he imagined the snow to be a moving curtain around his car, a quiet, soft container of thoughts.

Claire wished him luck when he left, but it seemed, once again, too faint a gesture. Ever since his return to Dalton Pond, the blemished reputation of his profession hovered over them: shyster lawyers and their loopholes, comments on the exaltation of procedure, jokes about sharks, and the eclipse of common sense. He accepted the razzing from Snoot without question—it was part of the good-natured teasing they used to convey their affection for each other—but he wanted Claire to think of him differently, a white knight to the rescue, not a chiseler.

It had come up again when he and Claire went out to dinner the night before and Walker outlined his strategy for stopping the Ledges project. Aside from its immense impact on local services, there were wetlands to consider, aquifer recharge areas, deer yards, and Crooked Brook's east branch itself. For instance, could any of the property qualify as a fragile ecosystem or unique habitat for endangered species?

If it did, Claire wanted to know, would the courts close the project down completely or just put nets around the pools where the snail darters swam?

"That was nasty," he said, taken aback.

She apologized. "I'm playing devil's advocate," she said, and went on to ask some tough questions: How long would the fight go on, how much of the land would actually be saved once the battle was over, and how much would the legal proceedings cost?

He'd said he would do it for free, and she'd looked at him as though he were a child. He persisted; there was a good chance he could stall the permit process for at least a couple of years, but as he spoke he noticed she was idly brushing crumbs off the tablecloth, avoiding his eyes. He went on anyway; who could say how much of the land he might save? "Maybe half?"

She'd looked up at him, shaking her head: "So there'd still be a lodge, eighty acres developed, and thirty condos instead of sixty."

"Possibly. But—" Why was she stonewalling him? He talked about the economies of scale and diminishing returns. Maybe the project wasn't viable below a certain volume. And there was another angle he hadn't mentioned yet, "Toxic waste." The words echoed awkwardly across the dining room.

She stared at him.

He noticed the couple at the next table seemed to be enjoying the conversation; he lowered his voice. "Why not? Look, Snoot's been collecting junk cars and trucks for years," he argued, sotto voce. "He's probably spilled enough oil and acid around the place to justify a toxic dump review."

"Oh, Walker, come on."

"No, seriously." Why wouldn't she take him seriously? "And get this: Tot's bank would back out. Banks can be liable for cleanup costs." He told her of a case he'd taken two years to prosecute in Hartford. "The banks waved bye-bye. They'll drop him cold. Really. Nobody wants a lawsuit with the EPA."

"You're turning Snoot into some kind of criminal," she said. "He loves that land. It's been his life."

Walker took a deep breath. "But it's not *his* anymore. It's not Junior's either, or Tot's, or Bud's. It belongs to a paper entity organized under the legal obligations and privileges of the Abenaki Development Corporation. It's not personal. If there's toxic waste on the property, it's got to be cleaned up."

"They're going to comb a hundred and sixty acres for a few quarts of oil?"

"That's the hardball approach. We want to stop them, don't we?"

"I guess." Claire sounded discouraged, more with Walker than his plan. "But we want to live here too. Is it worth tearing the town apart? Everybody knows what you're up to, Walker, and the town's already choosing up sides."

"And a lot of them are choosing us," he said. "People care. They know about toxins and water resources. All those junked cars and trucks in the woods, in the yard, at the edges of the fields. There could be toxins all over the place." Walker felt himself free-falling into thin air. "We could be looking at an ecological disaster," he said, too late to open a parachute.

"Do you really believe that?" Claire asked, pained.

Ground zero was approaching quickly. "Professionally, I have to." His argument suddenly sounded stupid. "Look, it's an approach, a game. You take an extreme position to win a point. It's what the law allows."

Thump.

"But what about you?" She'd found the crumpled body. "What do you think, personally? What's your common sense tell you?"

When he was freshly delivered from law school, he would have said it didn't matter. Personal opinion had no place in the machinery of justice. The law was, by necessity, blind to the vagaries of personal opinion and so-called common sense; that's what made it work—such as it did.

But he wasn't fresh out of law school. His idealistic

instincts had been abused; he'd canceled his contract as a public defender in defense of his own common sense. Claire asked him the same questions he'd asked himself over and over again and never resolved.

"Personally," he said, "I'd have to admit it's overkill."

"Then how can you feel right about pursuing it?" Now she was kicking the corpse.

He hardly heard his own answer, but he knew it was filled with clichés like "The ends justify the means" and "Nothing's perfect," all of it telling him something about himself he didn't particularly like.

There was half a foot of snow on the ground when Walker pulled into the downtown St. Johnsbury parking lot. As he slogged through the alley and looked across Main Street the District Commission offices appeared empty at first, but then he saw lights in the upstairs windows, and as he approached the door he saw footprints packed in the snow at the storefront entrance.

Inside, he climbed the creaking set of stairs and found the receptionist with her bare feet up on a radiator, warming her toes. Without looking up, she asked about the roads, then waved him on to the formidable Mrs. Poissonbleu, doyenne of the archives in a powder-blue jumpsuit and matching perm.

"Back for more of it, are you?" She led the way past crooked rows of tatty file cabinets with the exaggerated confidence of someone who knows exactly where to find exactly what she's looking for. "Bernice must have filed it when you got done yesterday," she said. "Let's see. . . ." Walker noticed she wore a thin wedding band and wondered about her husband. Was Mr. Bluefish trained to keep things as neat and tidy at home as she did at work? "Here it is," she said, handing him a thick folder. At moments like these, she loved her job. "Abenaki Development Corporation. Would you care to use the table by the window again?"

The folder was two inches thick; half of it he'd already reviewed and copied. With a copy of *Vermont Statutes An-*

notated guiding him, he spent the rest of the day comparing the state's permit requirements to the information furnished in Abenaki's application. There were thirty-five pages of review instructions in the statutes, sections 6001 through 6089, half of it in fine print, covering everything from definitions to approvals to fees, acreage minimums, road specifications, natural habitats, growth impact, waivers, and appeals procedures. Outside, the snow blew sideways in the empty streets.

Abenaki's application consisted of some two dozen engineer's drawings and twenty-nine pages of Beasley Pruitt's badly typed narrative. Most of it marginally conformed to the state's demands; the summary enumerated the virtues of the four-season resort: "A jewel the whole community can be proud of"—Walker made a note to photocopy the final paragraph and tack it to Tot's bulletin board—"conceived in the spirit of our native American heritage, the Abenaki Ledges Lodge and Condominiums will continue the age-old tradition of living quietly with the land."

By five o'clock, another twelve inches of snow had fallen, and Walker decided to spend the night in St. Johnsbury. Mrs. Poissonbleu willing, he'd finish his notes and make copies of what he needed in the morning. He called Claire from the lobby of the Cascade Hotel.

"I'm glad you're not driving," she said. "The roads are awful, and the plowing is probably way behind schedule."

"The main drag hasn't been touched up here. Can you stay with Jody?"

"There'll be at least four of us there," she said, anticipating his concern. "The ER's already taken care of two crashes. Nobody should be out tonight. Especially you, pumpkin."

"I'll be right here, the designated drunk in the Sap Bucket Lounge," he joked, looking across the lobby at a paint-peeled ballroom filled with stacks of broken chairs. The Cascade had seen sunnier days. "This place is an exact replica of the Ritz."

"I miss you," she answered, through two counties of falling flakes.

Walker closed his eyes and pressed the phone to his ear. He knew they were thinking about the same thing: tomorrow night, they moved to Jenkins's. They were going to sleep together, live together—it seemed so natural to add the word—forever. Funny, how the decision had evolved.

It was almost archaic—Thomas Hardy, here we come—and so uncontemporarily sensible. Of course he'd wanted to jump on her bones the moment he saw her reaching for the Dundee marmalade, but she was a married woman; and then Junior pulled his nasty stunt, and of course she needed to wait and heal; whatever time it took was insignificant within the context of the fifteen years they'd known each other. When they were younger, the waiting would have been impossible—maybe because the outcome wasn't so critical; there was time enough then to make mistakes and start over. But time assumed a different value as he got older; it wasn't so expendable as it once had seemed, and he took increasingly greater pains to spend it wisely.

"Tomorrow," he said into the telephone. After supper in Jenkins's kitchen, they would say good night to Snoot and go upstairs.

"I'll be there." The dreamy texture of her voice aroused him.

"I thought about you a lot today," he said.

"I know." She sighed. "I think about you all the time too, you turkey"—taunting him. "Tell me about the applications." She sounded truly interested for a change, as if she loved him no matter what he did for a living. "Did you find anything useful?"

"Beasley's work looks thorough enough." Walker said. "I don't think there's anything he missed as far as the town's planning board regs are concerned. But there's something unconvincing about the engineer's drawings for Act Two-fifty. I swear, the brook is surveyed wrong. It looks nearly straight on the plans."

"Who surveyed it?"

"Ware Associates, out of Randolph."

"Billy Ware?" Claire repeated the name. "He's married

to Tot's sister, Aunt Franny. He's supposed to be my Uncle Billy, and he's a louse."

"He might be a lousy surveyor too." Was Claire finally going to be on his side? "Maybe he'll provide us with an angle."

"I wouldn't be surprised, the creep. He's been in trouble before. And dear Aunt Franny's got a heart of gold."

"I like this better all the time," Walker said. "Hey, you sure this doesn't conflict with what you've been ragging me about, being a slave to the letter of the law in spite of common sense?"

"All I meant was they shouldn't be mutually exclusive." She sounded amused.

"I know they shouldn't, but if we can nail Billy Ware for a bum survey?"

"Then nail him." Claire laughed at herself. "*He* deserves it."

Walker couldn't sleep; the radiators clanged and hissed all night, and every time he closed his eyes the pages of Abenaki's application lay open in front of him, demanding attention. He stared out the window and made mental lists of things he had to do: spend more time with the statutes, reconcile the surveys with the site, go to Montpelier to study the state wetlands application, when it came in, and look at the federal wetlands permit. Then there was the complicated issue of how to proceed, when—and if—he established a case.

It would take two or three months of cramming to prepare for Vermont's bar exam. Maybe he should begin studying for it right away; after all, someday soon he'd have to resume making a living. He got up and stood by the window, looking down at a fuzzy white streetscape. A snowplow went by and buried a parked car in its wake. It would be a long process: December, January, February, March, most of April, maybe even into May. With a few well-timed motions, Abenaki's proceedings could drag on at least that long.

But who would make the motions? Hiring someone else to do the legal work would be frustrating, put things beyond his control. He would have to check the board's rules on statutory parties and appearances. If fraud became an issue, he might interest an eager-beaver assistant attorney general in the case, but then it would be completely out of his hands, and a political football as well. It would be so easy if only Snoot's land were in Connecticut. But then Snoot wouldn't be Snoot, and Claire wouldn't be Claire, and the land wouldn't mean what it did.

What did it mean? Their perception of Vermont was different from his, more trusting and innocent, still shaped by a tradition that held the rights of an individual sacred.

Planning and zoning regulations—any kind of regulations—were anathema. He'd listened to enough scratchy tape recordings of the Dalton Pond Planning Board hearings.

"A man owns a piece of land, by the Jesus, then it's his and he can do what he wants with it, and nobody's got the right to tell him different."

"We can't tell folks that's lived here all their lives they can't sell off their land, that bunny rabbits is more important than jobs and people."

Snickering, the sound of applause. Good-old-boy consent.

"Shoot the bunnies!" Laughter, vengeance.

"Godamned dictators take and tell a man when to shit, how much, and what color."

"Lived here all his life."

The sound of a wolf-pack victory over the crybaby pinheads, down with the environment-elitists.

"Crank them dozers!" Junior's voice?

"What's good for Tot is good for the town. Right, Elwood?"

They hadn't seen the suffocating suburban sprawls he'd seen, couldn't conceive of the exponential impact of growth, and there was no way to convince them. He'd ostensibly come to Dalton Pond to retrieve Snoot's farm from developers; so far, he'd retrieved Claire from Junior, but his role as an agrarian savior seemed to have been diminished to a bit part by the same people he'd hoped would cast him as a hero.

He got back in bed and wrestled with the blankets.

Maybe he could interest one of the district commission directors or, better yet, the district coordinator. The tall skinny guy he'd seen talking with Mrs. Poissonbleu looked reasonable enough. Maybe he'd be able to sidetrack the proceedings. Or should Walker simply take the straight route, take the bar exams as soon as he dared, and hope he'd be licensed in time?

The room was too hot; the air was dry, smelled of mothballs and Lysol. Walker fell asleep befuddled with unanswered questions.

By noon on Friday, the sun was out, and everywhere the new-fallen snow sparkled headache-bright. Walker gathered his papers, thanked Mrs. Poissonbleu, and drove the winding roads back to Dalton Pond.

The drifts were three feet deep along the tote path to the cabin, but Snoot had apparently wallowed through a time or two since the storm, and Walker made the trip with ease. Snoot wasn't in the cabin, but the stove was still warm, and the boxes he'd left for packing were already filled and stacked by the door. There would be no note—Walker knew that—but the rows of waiting boxes said enough; Snoot was eager to leave.

Snoot knew why Walker went to St. Johnsbury, but he didn't believe in miracles, and he believed even less in the fair application of laws. Like many of his generation, he used a double standard when it came to the notion of regulating land: he could do whatever he wanted, but Tot and Junior and anyone else he disagreed with "should have the wood put to them." Furthermore, Snoot believed the law never worked for the workingman; the law was for "big shots and scoundrels. Look at how they twist and twirl it around their money-grubbing fingers!" Snoot tolerated Walker's efforts—seemed almost to pity his misguided belief that the courts could act fairly—but "getting the hell out" was Snoot's solution. "Later on," he told Walker one night, "we'll see about due process, all right, we'll see to the application of northwoods justice, workingman style."

• • •

Walker changed his clothes and followed the open brook from the cabin to the road, then backtracked upstream past the cabin, zigzagging from one S-curve to another. The snow was up to his knees most of the way, up to his waist in the drifts. By the time he reached the Ledges, his boots were soaked and his pant legs caked with ice, but the exercise was worth it.

Billy Ware's survey of Crooked Brook was bogus. Either he cribbed it from an erroneously drawn map, from a scale so small that the curves and oxbows didn't show, or he was grossly incompetent—or intentionally misleading. Walker strongly suspected the last; with waterway setback restrictions at a hundred feet, a straight brook bed was infinitely preferable. The route Ware Associates falsified would open up another dozen acres for development. If the discrepancy was intentional, Billy Ware would probably lose his license, and Abenaki would have to cut out eight or ten condos—unless they went back to the planning board and asked for higher density.

"Still a free country, ain't it?"

And at the moment, Claire was probably right when she argued that Abenaki would get every unit they wanted.

"What's good for Tot is good for the town."

Walker wanted to prove her wrong. Not because he needed to be right, necessarily, but because he needed her to understand there was a higher purpose to what he was trying to do. The law wasn't all cynical wheeling and dealing. Standing in snow up to his knees, he decided to begin studying for the Vermont bar exams.

He crossed the brook near the foot of the Ledges and looked up through the trees. The perspective was dizzying: sheer walls of granite rose vertically a hundred feet or more. He saw a raven circling above the boughs, heard its hoarse croaking *gawn* as it flew between boulders tipped out over the crest like giant teeth. He recalled sitting astride those boulders for hours, staring into an incomprehensible distance, meditating on the Abenaki spirits said to inhabit the great stone edifice, opening himself so they might inhabit him. And the spirits may indeed have toyed with him—at times he felt certain he was surrounded by powerful forces—but there was nothing he could grasp and hold, and he'd grown frustrated with sitting and trying and failing yet another time.

He brushed snow away from the top of a fallen log and unrolled Billy Ware's drawing. The blueprint showed dotted contour lines at two-foot intervals. Roads and buildings were arranged on each side of the fictitious un-Crooked Brook. A tight bunch of contour lines near the top of the drawing defined the location of the Ledges. The dark rectangle at the bottom of the Ledges represented the Lodge. Walker looked around and guessed at the distances; he concluded he was standing in the lobby.

He didn't talk about his plans while they were moving into Jenkins's. Claire was busy arranging things in drawers and closets, and Snoot spent most of the time before supper arranging the woodshed to his taste; he was resplitting some of the doctor's beechwood when Walker called him to the table.

"*You* cooked spaghetti?" Snoot asked, stirring the noodles on his plate with his thumb. "I never knew you had the Eye-talian."

"He's got all kinds of talent," Claire said, raising an eyebrow at Walker, winking luridly.

Walker felt the lump in his pants.

The conversation went from how to eat spaghetti to oil furnaces—Snoot said the house was making him sweat—to Snoot's plans for selling firewood. Inevitably, when they came to Frouncy, Walker knew the story of Billy Ware's fraud ought to wait.

"She'll like it here just dandy," Snoot insisted, flinging a noodle in the air with his fork. "All clean and proper. Doc says maybe two–three weeks. . . ." His fork poked at the plate, grew heavy, stuck to it.

Claire patted Snoot's arm. "I miss her too." Frouncy had become a missing person.

A long silence followed. Walker thought about how,

each time he saw her, she looked more haunted and hollow, more uncomfortable, more of a stranger. There was a time when she was the queen of Crooked Mountain. Now she had three meaningless words left to work with and a memory riddled with holes. It wasn't fair. He wanted to be angry, change the rules to the nasty game of getting old and dying, change the subject, change her back to what she'd been, but he didn't know how to begin.

Snoot squirmed. Looking for an escape, he once again retold the tale of Ruby Redd and Bud. "Old Bud, he got so riled up when I says the toothbrush word, why mister jeez, I thought it tacked his heart."

No one laughed, much as they wished they could.

Claire and Walker worked quickly together cleaning up after supper, washing the dishes—hurrying, it seemed: efficient, fussing, joking, nervous—seeing to Snoot's blankets and pillows and towels as if he were their precious child. Then, with no warning, everything that needed doing was done—all of it, to the last bit of wax paper wrapped around the last leftover dish on the top shelf of the unfamiliar refrigerator. The whole kitchen gleamed dumbly. Suddenly they were saying good night, clicking off the lights, adults playing house, Mommy and Daddy, Walker and Claire climbing the stairs as if it were the most natural thing in the world.

And it was. They fell on the bed together so quickly, so smoothly, so perfectly synchronized: ten years apart reduced to nothing. "The circle finally comes around," she whispered between kisses. Clothes fell to the floor. "Thanks for being patient."

"It was only fifteen days"—he paused—"seven hours, forty-two minutes, and thirty-nine seconds."

"Plus ten years."

"We'll make up for it."

"Promise?"

"I 'spect we'll prevail."

The language of skin prevailed. She pulled Walker to her, unafraid, as if there were no absences, no Junior, no horror, only the two of them, as it seemed they were always meant to be.

She shivered as he touched her, lips and tongue across the stations of the cross: from nipple to nipple, up to her chin, then slowly down between her breasts to her navel. "Like a miracle," was the last thing Walker heard her say before they tumbled into heaven.

He awoke in the middle of the night, to the sound of sleet on the windows, to the warm lightness of Claire's body on his. The dim bedside lamp was still burning. He watched her as she slept, still as stone. Tendrils of hair strayed to the edge of her pillow. Her left hand lay open beside her face, thin fingers curved, waving goodbye, hello. She slept on her side with one knee across his, an arm lightly folded against his chest. He copied her breathing, wrapped an arm around her, and cradled her breast. She stirred and drew closer into his warmth. When he twined his fingers into hers, she offered a velvety kiss, eyes still closed.

"Did I wake you?"

She kissed his fingers and pressed his hand to her cheek.

"Want to talk?" He was wide awake, buzzing. Billy Ware was a goner.

She opened one eye.

"Want to go back to sleep?"

"Sleep?" She slid an arm between them, reached down and touched him, held him. A sleepy yawn, a squeeze, another: *"He's* not asleep."

Walker nuzzled her ear with his lips, hiding a helpless smile in a thicket of her hair. "Insomnia," he said. He felt her grip tighten and kicked off the sheets.

They liked the new house. The weeks passed quickly, and they fell into a comfortable routine of work and play and long nights snug in the big four-poster. Snoot's woodpile grew enormous, Walker read the law, and Claire took care of her children. The Abenaki Development Corporation was rarely discussed; like the dresser full of Frouncy's clothes next to Snoot's bed, some things were better left alone.

The wetlands application was finally filed in Montpelier. Without telling Snoot or Claire where he was going, Walker spent an afternoon reviewing it; except for the falsified route of the brook, it seemed accurate and complete. Abenaki had done its homework, anticipated all the objections; they had hydrology studies, fish and game reports, and a biologist's review of the entire property. There were checklists of common plants: bladderwort, smartweed, sweet gale, frogbit, and hydrophyllum grasses; all were plentiful, all common enough, all expendable, however beautiful. There were no signs of *Gentiana crinita* or *Cypripedium parviflorum,* nor was there evidence of the fast-disappearing *Buteo lineatus,* the red-shouldered hawk. In short, no rare species were found and therefore no rare species endangered. Four-foot-diameter hemlock trees weren't mentioned in the inventory.

Walker telephoned a lawyer in Burlington who specialized in wetlands work. If he pursued it to the end, the best Walker could hope for was a delay in the project and action against the surveyor. Abenaki would admit there had been an error, hire another surveyor, and continue as it pleased— unless there were other grounds. Like what? Walker didn't mention toxic waste. Even he had given up on picking the fly shit out of the pepper.

Now it was a Sunday morning at the end of February. Flat on his back, Walker followed the tiny repeat apple pattern on the bedroom wallpaper, traced it across the sloping ceiling and down the wall, then back up again. The white spaces between the red dot figures formed a grid of avenues and thoroughfares—east and west, north and south—predictable and absolute. How many times had he traveled those endless orchards? How many times had his mind free-wheeled through that maze while his body was comforted by the woman beside him?

She stirred. "You alive?"

"Res ipsa loquitur," he croaked.

"*Res ipsa* what *quitur?*"

"A tort doctrine, 'The thing speaks for itself.' " Walker's brain was stuffed with legal jargon. For the past two months he'd spent six days a week studying for his exams, going to sleep and waking up in Latin. *"Res ipsa loquitur,"* he repeated, "it means—"

Claire yawned.

"Sorry."

She stroked his chest. "No, go on, go ahead."

"For example: If you're riding in an elevator, and it drops twenty stories, the rule of law says you would not have to prove negligence, in such a case. The main concept here is that a machine or instrumentality under someone else's control can be expected to operate within certain parameters of—"

"Walker?"

"Sorry." One more week and he'd be done with it, back to waking up in English. "I know I'm obsessed, but I want to pass this mother with room to spare." He'd already inquired into renting office space in Jordan, having a sign made, buying bookcases and furniture.

"You're still determined to go after Abenaki?"

"Claire. Why so stubborn? The case against Billy Ware is a piece of cake. I'm not going after them; they're abusing the laws of the state."

"Franny had to go back to see her oncologist."

"Franny?" Tot's sister was one of those women who adored their husbands, no matter what. "I'm sorry to hear it." She was a rosy, sweet woman, fond of Walker, dedicated to Claire—told her to hang on to Walker.

"She's got six months, maybe a year if she's lucky."

Walker thought of Frouncy, down to a hundred pounds and refusing to eat. "This aging stuff—there's got to be a better way."

Claire rolled over on her side and put her face so close to his she was out of focus. "It would break Franny's heart to spend her last days watching Billy on the losing end of a lawsuit."

There she went again. Captain Roadblock. "So you want me to drop it?"

"A lot of people do."

"A lot of people don't—most of my friends, anyway."

"Don't."

"I don't understand you sometimes, really."

"It's the town I'm thinking of, the people—and Franny."

"And to hell with the land."

"It's not either-or."

"Looks like it to me." Lately, he'd seen two kinds of bumper stickers around town; GIVE IT BACK TO THE INDIANS gave him courage, and SAVE THE LEDGES. People cared. Even Claire had one on her Subaru. But Tot was handing out another brand of bumper stickers—and buttons too—I AIN'T NO FLATLANDER was bracketed between crossed rifles, confederate style, and THE ONLY GOOD ABENAKI IS AN ABENAKI LEDGES LODGE. The town was split, innuendo was valued above fact, rumors mutated daily at Tot's coffee counter. During his no-contest divorce from Claire, Junior spread the story that Walker was starting an even bigger development of his own—two hundred and fifty units—implying that Walker's dedication to stopping Abenaki was in his own self-interest. Punka Hurley still repeated the story. Tot wouldn't speak to Claire. Laurie wouldn't even look her in the eye. Even Lillian had stopped being friendly.

Walker asked Claire if she doubted his motives; wasn't he trying to save a piece of Snoot's hard-working past, a piece of Abenaki history? "How come your heritage means more to me than to you?"

"What heritage?" She was elusive, willing to agree the site was worth saving, but at what price? Could Walker really save it all? Would the passion and hatred generated be worth a project of ten less condos?

He argued that her attitude seemed fatalistic.

"If I'd known my father," she said, "I might think differently. But look at me; I was brought up Yankee. Sure, I've got black hair and a tan all year, but no one taught me anything about my *heritage,* as you call it. No one seems to know much about it. So I don't feel like it's really mine. It's Daddy's—he's the guy they tell the spectacular stories about, and I'm damned if I'm going to fight for his people until he fights for me."

Walker held her and embarked on a long, lonely voyage across the wallpaper pattern on the ceiling. "Billy could be in big trouble," he finally said, faintly.

"He can wait."

Walker wished he could go back to sleep. "Abenaki's looking for approvals in May. Once the project passes, it's hard to revoke, especially if they've altered the evidence." He held her closer, hoping. "Which they'll do. Two days with a D-Eight, and you won't recognize the place."

She was silent for a while. He thought she'd gone back to sleep when she asked, "How about going after some other guy, a different slant?"

Walker looked up at the rows of tiny apples and followed a diagonal route across the ceiling until the lines blurred at the far side of the room. "I don't know if there is one," he said. "Like they say, it's a free country and all that jazz. They have their rights too." It made him feel weary.

It snowed and melted; the days got longer, and Frouncy suffered two more small strokes. One eye seemed to have closed permanently, and the other offered little more than a flat, dull flicker to her visitors, none of whom she now knew. Snoot moved the cardboard boxes of her belongings under his bed, taking them out and rearranging them after each visit, as if to exercise them, to keep some small part of her healthy.

Walker took the exams; there was a blizzard two days later; it melted and snowed again. On the nineteenth of April, he was admitted to the bar in the State of Vermont. He immediately completed plans to open an office, two sunny rooms with tall ceilings, upstairs over the savings bank in Jordan. His letterhead would read WALKER OWEN, ATTORNEY AT LAW, and after certification from the State Supreme Court he could add *Specializing in Environmental Matters.* He was determined to reassure Claire—and himself—that he was going to be one of

167

the good guys. Meanwhile, he was also determined Billy Ware's deception was at least going to cost him his surveyor's license.

Claire treated Walker to a celebration dinner at the Hotel Coolidge in White River Junction. She seemed wistfully proud of him that night, as if he'd accomplished a distasteful but necessary task, like the mercy killing of an aged family dog. She ordered champagne and raised a toast. "To us"—she reached over the candle and touched her glass to his—"and to your career."

"To us," he answered. "And thanks for the nod to the nasty villain, Jurisprudence. You might get to like it, if I live long enough to convince you. The law works both ways. It can be a good thing."

"*Res ipsa loquitur*, sweetheart," she said. "The thing speaks for itself."

11

CHAIN-SAW ARTIST

IT WAS FRIDAY, the sixth of May. After supper, Bud went out his back porch door and crossed the fifty feet of matted lawn to the prefab garage he used as a shop. He chose his steps carefully, avoiding the puddles. Someday soon—the money would be no problem—he'd build himself a flagstone walkway, or have it paved with asphalt or concrete, or hire Punka to lay out some masonry, antique brick in a basketweave pattern. Someday soon, he'd be able to buy anything he wanted.

For now, his feet sank into the top few inches of the final spring thaw, big bootprints in the muddy icing.

He paused outside the door to his shop and rubbed at the pains in his gut. "It's gas," Doc Shreve told him. "Cut down on the cabbage and soldier beans." The doc was a skinny transplanted flatlander, thought he knew everything. "Lose thirty pounds this summer, and you'll feel a lot better." Typical downcountry bullshit.

Summer was coming. Peepers blabbed in the ditches by the road, black flies were swarming, and from where he stood, rubbing his belly, Bud could see the hardwood flanks of Big Church country blushed with green. It was coming, and by the second week of May, the Board of Selectmen would open the roads to heavy trucking for another ten months, until next year's mud and the annual posting of the little white signs with the six-ton-limit warning. Like with all of those do-good committees and permits and approvals, those overgovernmented triplicate-copied boondoggles, all it took was the right person—like Tot Tatro—to find a way through it, get exactly what he wanted, and leave everybody smiling in the bargain.

Two weeks, and it would begin. Ragazzo Corporation had signed a contract with a penalty clause for finishing late; they had ten months to finish Phase One. The Abenaki Ledges Lodge would be substantially framed by the Fourth of July. Think of it. Bud couldn't wait to see a big yellow dozer crawl through Snoot's old kitchen, squash the buildings into splinters, and bury them in a gully for good, along with Snoot's acres of junk. Just think of it, clean as a whistle!

Tot knew his stuff, knew everybody who was anybody. He was the one who found Bobby Ragazzo, went down to White River and checked him out: good credit with the banks, heavy clout with the subs. Tot was calling the shots, and Ragazzo had better get used to it. Tot already had three logging crews chopping both sides of the brook to beat the band. Bud told him who to hire, of course—all donkey Frenchmen. They had six or seven hundred thousand feet of merchantable saw logs yarded up and ready to go. From Bud's you could hear their chain saws as early as six in the morning, hear the blat of the skidders until it got dark. Cross lots, it was less than a half mile up the hill to where they were working, damn near Bud's backyard. By the middle of last week, they had the place pretty well skinned out, from the edge of the pasture all the way to the foot of the Ledges. It took three days just to comb the site with a root rake rig, and bury the stumps in a hollow. Tot's architect figured there'd be about ninety acres opened up, a view from every lot and every guest room in the Lodge.

It was going to be easy with the brook straightened out; blast a little ledge, dig a hole, bring in the ready-mix, pour it, strip it, frame it up, side it over, roof it, glaze it, rock it, trim it out, sub it out, slap it up, open the doors, and rake in the money. Tot said you've got to spend money to make money, and he ought to know. Already, there were some big-time buyers snooping around. Abenaki Ledges Lodge. Even the

170

name tasted good on his tongue.

Bud unlocked the shop door, flipped the light switches on, and waited while the fluorescent tubes flickered and buzzed to full brightness. He was proud of his shop—the bench saws, planers, jointers, lathes, and drill presses, the numbered racks of shiny sharpened blades and bits—it was all kept immaculate, and it was all his. Bud spent most evenings and weekends out there, "just dubbin'," he told Pearle—if he offered any explanation at all. When the money started rolling in, he could see putting on an addition, maybe twice the size of what he had, maybe include a bay for working on antique cars, maybe a paint booth and a Bridgeport grinder, and definitely more space for the rabbits.

They looked up at him now, pink eyes blinking at the light. The cages took up half of one wall. Daphne and Brenda, Old Clyde, and his favorite, Pancho, the stud—what a character! Each had a separate little house of its own. Bud reached in the little doors and patted them with long, smooth strokes, clucking and cooing like he did every morning, like he did every night, or anytime he could during the day. In the summer he had a special cage for them outside, with wire mesh tough enough to keep out the coyotes and foxes. He brought them sliced carrots and romaine lettuce. Pancho liked chocolate chip cookies, the kind with the oversized chips. Pancho would sit on Bud's shoulder while he worked, tickle him with his whiskers. Brenda was as soft as anything Bud had ever touched. She was his Brenda bunny, wasn't she? All his, and no one else's.

Pearle wasn't fond of the rabbits, which was just as well, Bud thought. She stayed in the house, cleaning up, sitting around—he didn't know what she did with her time—watching TV, goofing off. Sometimes she'd bring him coffee between shows, lurk outside in the shadows while he sculpted on his wooden statues. The Wife was going on fifty-six, too goddamned old to be playing peekaboo, he told her. When she showed up all of a sudden like that—why, jiminy Jesus, it rattled him something awful. One night she scared him so he almost lopped the headdress off an Indian. Couple of nights later she was sneaking around, tripped over the shop-vac hose, struck a coffee can full of roofing nails, and splattered them all over the floor. Missed the rabbits, thank God. Cut her hand bad enough so she had to have stitches. Served her right, that's what he told her.

Pearle poured herself an inch of brandy and turned out the kitchen lights. She liked to sit at the table and think about things—no Bud, no TV—just herself and the dark. Her mother used to do the same thing when Pearle was growing up, before she had any idea why a woman might prefer to be alone instead of with her husband. Back then, she thought her mother was a little crazy, sitting in her overheated kitchen with the dripping faucet and the tilted floor. Then she married Bud and quickly understood that although waiting for something required courage, waiting for *nothing* was a heroic act of faith.

Bud put on his shop apron and began carving on the wooden Indian commissioned for the front porch of Tot's store. The addition was almost finished, and he wanted the Indian in time for the grand opening in June. Bud told him way back, as soon as he had an Indian-sized tree he'd get busy and carve up a chief. It wasn't until the middle of March that Tot hired Stub McDermott to dump the log off at Bud's shop—an eight-foot length of bull pine, four feet across, fresh off the stump and sticky sap all over. It was solid clear through and cut like butter. Bud used a come-along to winch it in the door, chained a pulley to a roof truss, and stood it up. Then he used his big chain saw to slab off the waste wood, switching to his half-pint Poulan to hog out the Indian's torso, rough out the arms and legs. You use them right, those little bitty chain saws, you could do just about anything. Up to Quebec, he'd seen a Frog build a five-room home with nothing but a two-pound hammer and one of these little Mini-Mights. Darby Dunbar, up to Big Church—he used his to butcher hogs.

• • •

With the money Pearle got when she sold her mother's place in Catamount, she'd wanted to buy a house with a cathedral ceiling. The extra height, she thought, would make for a special, churchy feeling—something she could hope up into every day, a special space to sanctify her life. And she wanted beams, big, hand-hewn, honey-colored, natural-wood beams, something to signify history, strength, and permanence.

They looked at a couple of houses with high ceilings and beams, but Bud said they all had problems—septic system gone flooey, faulty wiring, always something. So they ended up buying a prebuilt double-wide modular home on a two-acre lot wedged between Snoot's farm and Beasley Pruitt's. No beams, but Bud insisted the ceiling in her kitchen was cathedral. He said if it goes up in the middle, that's what it's called.

Now she looked up at it in the dark. She imagined it a hundred feet high and thought how wonderful she would feel standing next to someone she loved in a real cathedral, gazing up at the soaring stone arches, listening to music and the whispers of angels.

Bud bought his big chain saw wholesale from Tot; the little one he bought at Farley Fellows's Auction Barn, spotted it one night mixed in with a mess of northwoods white-trash rubbish on the back of French John's flatbed. Farley held it out until last because he knew it was the only thing worth a damn; if he auctioned it off first, the Frenchman might as well have driven straight to the dump with the rest of his culch and unloaded over the bank.

Bud paid twenty dollars, but before he bid, Farley asked French John did it run?

French John sputtered. Did it run? By the Jesus, he guessed to the Mother of Mercy it run, and he started it first pull, smoke and noise all over. Spooked the livestock, but he didn't care. He revved the engine, walked over to a dead elm stump alongside the paddock, and with everyone watching, he sawed out the likeness of a man's face. Took him ten minutes, and it looked pretty good—a hat, a mustache, and a pointy little beard.

Bud figured if French John could do it, it couldn't be too frigging tricky. So he bid on the saw, and he got it. Then he went home and sculpted a face every bit as good as the one at the paddock, sanded it smooth, and sealed it with Minwax walnut stain. Merton Judd traded him a new twelve-volt battery for it, kept it on top of the cigarette machine at the Texaco station, used it for his personal hat rack. Merton called Bud a chain-saw artist, but Bud was embarrassed with the "artist" label, even though he knew there was something special about how he felt when he was making things out of his head, out of nowhere. Like the feeling he got watching Pancho, Brenda, Clyde, and Daphne. Anyway, he didn't use the artist word. He said he was just another French-Canadian wood butcher looking for an Indian in a tree.

Pearle's birthday was a week away. Most of the time, Bud forgot it. He would have forgotten it every year, but she used to remind him; the reminder was likely to result in no more than a nod or a pat on the shoulder.

She sipped brandy from a bottle she bought for herself—more to delay the coming anniversary than to celebrate it. She liked a few brandies on the nights she spent alone in her kitchen; it helped her think, and it was good for her digestion. Vodka was a daytime drink. Bud hated the taste, so she kept it put away where he wouldn't have to look at it, took the empties to the dump herself on Tuesdays.

One time, during dessert, Pearle asked him if he ever wondered what Eskimos listened to on the radio. He left his fork sticking straight up out of his apple pie, went out to his shop, and didn't come back until midnight.

When she was seventeen years old and dreaming about getting married, she went to a Grange Hall social with her girlfriends and met a man from Quinntown named Horton Flint. He was older than Pearle, but he was the handsomest man she had ever seen, a full-blooded Indian. His grandfather was an Abenaki shaman as well as an English-educated orator who sat in the back of the Congregational Church on Sundays taking notes.

Horton spoke so seldomly that people around him lowered their voices, as if to provide extra room for his words. Pearle didn't mind his reticence; in fact she liked it, found it thrilling to imagine what he must have been thinking. In his silence she heard another language, as eloquent and subtle as she cared to make it, seeping from the fissures in his coal-black eyes.

She danced with him that night at the Grange and let him bring her home in his new Ford car. On the way, he pulled off into a cornfield, and they watched the moon and named the stars and did some things she'd heard about but never had the chance to try. She knew he could have had whatever he wanted that night, but he took her home before it happened, in a silence warm and wet with conspiracy.

It was after midnight when they pulled up to her mother's house on the Catamount Heights. Horton switched his headlights off, and she kissed him one last kiss good night and ran to the back door, stopping to wave goodbye—come back!—across the darkened yard. Then halfway through the unlit kitchen, she heard her mother's voice.

"Did you have a nice visit with Mr. Flint?" Her mother was sitting in the dark by the cookstove in her rocking chair.

Pearle answered "Yes," she was certain she did, but the sound of her reply was lost to the roar of a galloping heartbeat, and she fled to her room with the three-letter word grown enormous inside her.

Bud put down the chain saw and wondered what it would have been like if he had never fooled around with Pearle, if he had left her up there on the Catamount Heights until the next Horton Flint came along. Bud could have had a lot of women—Vi Milette, Harriet Hazelitt—plenty of good stock, ready for picking. Bud could have married into money. Instead he took on Pearle, like he was going to save her from all that gossip about her and the Indian, like he had to rescue her—Jesus!—her and her mother and that Christly run-down hill farm, barns caved in, heavy soil, wouldn't drain, pastures all grown up to alder bushes. How the wind howled off that mountain! And not enough hours in a day to ever put that place back to working order. Waste of time is what it was, but Mrs. Lupien, she had a way of making whatever you were doing, no matter how ignorant it might be—if it was for her, it was the right thing to do.

Pearle was nineteen when he met her, a good-looking girl and built generous, too. Her mother wanted her married off, wasn't shy about saying so either; easy setup. But there was something funny about Pearle, too. Sometimes she acted like she was floating away, like she was living in a storybook. On their wedding night, he took her to the Cascade in St. J, spent big money, ate, and danced, and here she acted like only half of her was there. She fussed about the place, the price of it all—swore she hated hotels, she'd be happier in a two-dollar tourist cabin. But Bud was out to show her a good time, and by the Jesus he gave it to her good that night—two, three times, goddammit—made sure she knew she was married to a white man. She moaned and groaned and carried on, loved every minute of it, no doubt about it. But when they got back home, it was altogether different, always something—female complaints, too tired, her mother might hear: typical bull-shit—and she wouldn't straighten out, no matter how much he hollered.

Pearle sipped at her brandy and ran her fingertips across the worn wood table top, searching for blemishes and crumbs. It was the same kitchen table she'd sat at as a child. The ladderback chairs ringed around it were half a set; her sister, Franny, had the other four, Franny who married the shyster Billy Ware and moved to Randolph when Pearle was only seven, leaving her little sister and mother alone in the windblown house on the mountain. Now Franny was doomed to die of the same wicked cancer that claimed their mother in '73. Pearle often thought of her sister and mother as the same person, sometimes forgetting whose face went with which name, sometimes thinking of all three of them crowded into a single grave, all victims of the same disease. She rubbed the oiled table top and tapped the wood. How pitiful; life slipped away so fast—and there wasn't another stick of furniture worth saving.

Bud started the little Poulan and began to remove a two-inch slab from behind the Indian's knees. Chips spurted out from beneath the saw and ricocheted off the floor. The slab came free, and Bud stood back surveying his work, revving the saw while he thought about his next cut. A thin blue haze of smoke drifted out the open door into the cool night air.

As always, the Indian would have a muscular upper body, wide shoulders, and narrow hips. Bud carved Indians according to the way he wished he himself were built. There was a time when it could have made a difference, but at sixty-two he wasn't sure it mattered anymore. He weighed two twenty-five, and the doc was right; too much of it was fatback. Arthritis bothered his hips and his knees, and a prostate big as a Kennebec spud had left him pissing on his shoes. Lately he'd found himself avoiding old people, detouring around the Home, driving out of his way to avoid the geezers sunning themselves on the porch. It scared him to think of himself over there, all alone, slumped in a piss-soaked rocker.

Pearle sniffed the brandy, ran her tongue around the sweet rim of her glass, and tasted Horton. He'd loved her; she never doubted it for a moment. He talked about getting married, even talked about setting a date. Then he got Laurie Pippin pregnant.

He couldn't help it; all the girls were after Horton, even the schoolteachers. Pearle hated Laurie after that, wished for her miscarriage, a fatal accident, anything to stop what had to happen.

But it happened. Laurie and Horton got married, and three months later Claire was born. They moved in with Laurie's mother on Main Street. Pearle would park across the road at night and watch for a glimpse of Horton through the windows, anything, a sign that he still loved her. Horton tried to stay faithful to Laurie, but everybody knew she wasn't right for him.

Bud decided he'd lag an eye bolt to the back of Tot's Indian so he could chain it to the porch wall, so some sonofabitch wouldn't sneak up in the middle of the night and steal it. That's what it was coming to in Dalton Pond. Sure, there were the rowdy families, but they usually kept it at home, never bothered anybody else. Take the Goodhues, on the dump road; they kept it at home, and they kept it comical. Big Betty, she beat up on Rex. The daughter, Wanda, *she* beat up on Rex, and Rex—you think he had the common sense to quit lugging home three six-packs every night? Hell, no, Rex enjoyed his little family get-togethers, but all he'd beat up on was the black and tan beagle. Then the beagle'd wait till Rex passed out and bite his nose.

Crime was everywhere now. Used to be you'd leave everything open—houses, cars, you name it. Lately, with all the flatlanders moving in, it was going downhill, wouldn't be long before the town was locked up tighter'n a cow's ass in fly time.

The problem was, too many people. There were places on the mountain where you used to hunt all day and never see another face. Lately, you had your picnic-basket and hiking-boot types. Pull a trigger and you were apt to bag a party of Massholes watching tweety birds and eating bean sprout sandwiches. It was definitely getting out of hand.

Bud drilled a pilot hole, put a steel bar through the eye of an eye bolt, and turned it into the pine. He liked the feel of the threads cutting into wood fiber, the progressive resistance with each revolution, the tight squeak at the end when the bolt was in up to its shank. He could have turned it farther— torqued on the bar and bent the eye open—but he didn't. It was his decision, stopping when he did, and it made him feel good to know he knew when enough was enough.

But then, sometimes enough *wasn't* enough. Take Snoot Audette. What was his problem, anyway? No manners, no common standard of decency. Why was it just because some people lived like pigs, they treated other people like they were pigs, too? Sloppy mess of hair all over. Laughed too much. Too damned big was what he was, didn't know how to act in front of normal people. Didn't care to, either; *toothbrush.* Look at him, living in Quinntown with his boy's ex-wife and her reconditioned hippie boyfriend, all in a pig pile. What a zoo! You'd think at least the woman'd have more sense than that. You'd think. . . . Jesus, what a waste, pretty little vixen living with a gimp in that run-down dump for all those years . . . Big chimney fire at Snoot's in '77. Four o'clock in the morning, cold as hell. Get the fire put out, the boys go home. Bud hangs around, watching for smolder. She's shivering in her nightie. Bending over next to her, he offers to relight the stove. He smells the bed smell on her, realizes he's forgotten what it's like. It's been that long. Her hair brushes his face. Silky black. White frost on the ground outside, and he can't hold the matches still. Where in hell was Snoot anyway, running around with his Daintytown dollies?

Pearle saw it like it happened yesterday, her first secret weekend with Horton in Plattsburgh, New York.

Laurie was sick, and Claire was still an infant, but the world outside Room 22 didn't matter.

They never got out of bed. It was like old times, before Horton had to get married. Or was it even better? He told her he loved her more than ever, that he thought about her all the time. She believed him, and it made his marriage to Laurie seem insignificant. That weekend in Plattsburgh, he convinced her to go ahead and marry Bud. It would make things easier, he said: it would make them equally free.

She worried about his job—the explosions, the machinery, the flying rocks—but it left him plenty of mobility; his work took him everywhere, from the Adirondacks to Maine, wherever new highways or dams or building projects needed the skills of a dynamite jockey. After work each day, his time was his own. He could see her whenever she could get to him.

So she married Bud and dreamed about Horton. They

met on weekends near his projects, rented cheap rooms, pulled the blinds, and ate their meals in bed. Pearle told Bud she was visiting Franny on Lake Bomoseen. He didn't care who she visited. The meetings continued without anyone knowing, month after month, until Horton disappeared—quit his job, left everything he owned to Laurie, and vanished. Baby Claire was two. Laurie went back to teaching school and hired a lawyer to track down Horton, found him in the woods in Maine; she divorced him by mail. Pearle waited to see what would happen next, wedded to her secret. Three or four times a year, she'd look up from what she was doing and find him standing next to her. Was she dreaming, or was he really there? She learned to ignore the distinction.

God damn Snoot Audette. Bud put down his tools, whispered goodbye to the rabbits, and left the shop by the rear door, closing it quietly. He had half an hour before full dark. Pearle would never know he was gone. If she brought him a coffee, he'd tell her he stepped outside for a minute to water a tree. She'd believe anything.

Straight up the hill through the woods, it was only a ten-minute walk to the raggedy fence around Audette's barnyard. The sales agreement allowed Snoot to keep his livestock there until the fifteenth of May, when he'd have to find them new pasture. Snoot came by in the afternoons to feed his heifers, but otherwise the place was deserted, the buildings stripped. Junior was living high and wide in a waterfront Dalton Pond condo with his high school floozie from California, Loretta the junkie, needle tracks all over her arms. The farm was empty, all done, an eyesore, waiting for the dozers. All done except for one little piece of even-up work, long overdue.

Bud climbed the hill; gas pains had worked up into his chest, and he stopped to catch his breath at the base of an outcropping ledge. A mound of corn snow lay melting in the shadows. He stood in it and smoothed out a patch with his boot, mixed mud into the coarse white kernels. Snoot never should have spilled the milk on him; it was a stupid stunt. And to bring up the dirty lies about him and Ruby! But Snoot had to, didn't he? Snoot the coot, big dumb galoot. And after what Bud had done for Junior, cutting him in on the Abenaki deal! Jesus. Whatever happened to gratitude? And the rest of them—they still looked at him funny at the coffee counter. No respect. Months, now, and he was still taking abuse. Bud hated the idea of people laughing at him. Officer Toothbrush. Snoot's fault. It rankled wicked bad.

Horton took her big-band dancing at the Cascade in St. Johnsbury. They'd dance until they got too hot, then go upstairs and drink apricot brandy or Canadian whiskey smuggled down from the border in the back of his truck. She learned to drink on nights like that, clean hotel sheets and Horton Flint stretched out like polished mahogany beside her. He rarely spoke, but how he communicated with his eyes! She made a game of languorous offerings—an arm, a breast, a bathroom door ajar while she bathed—and luxuriated in his focus. It seemed he never took his eyes away, was blind to everything but her, Indian X rays tracing every contour of her body. Sometimes she wondered if those nights were the only real parts of her life, if all her years with Bud were no more than a ten-cent movie.

Bud stopped at the edge of the woods and looked across Snoot's paddock. Just what he thought: three fat yearling heifers up to their ankles in shit and nobody around. He climbed through the barbed wire and called to them. "Hey, boss, hey, girls!" They stared and chewed. "Hey, boss, boss, boss. C'mon, c'mon." Bud walked up the slope and into the open barn. "Hey, boss, c'mon!" He felt his way around in the dark, switched on the lights, and found a barrel of grain. He put some in a bucket and banged on it; they came at a trot.

They were Holsteins, yearlings, close to five feet tall, gluttons for sweet feed and naturally curious. He put the bucket down and stepped aside to watch them compete. They immediately knocked it over and pawed at the grain in the chaff on the floor. Bud watched them and soon picked out the one with four white stockings and a map of Florida on her flank. "Hey, Disneyland, hey, you. Want some? Want some?" He picked up the bucket and put it on top of a stanchion. "Wait here, bossy, I'll be right back."

The cow stared after him as Bud climbed up a ladder and through a hatch to the hayloft above. She jumped back when three bales fell to the floor in front of her. Then Bud climbed down the ladder and began his preparations.

The idea was to arrange the bales like steps—like the victory platform at the Olympics on TV—two bales on the bottom, end to end, and one on the top, in the middle. The idea was to make Miss Florida comfortable, make her put her front feet up on the steps, so that her hind feet would still be on the floor while her head was almost touching the ceiling. Kind of like a dog, begging.

Bud stuffed a length of rope in his coat pocket and went to the grain barrel to refill the bucket. The cows watched him, curious and hungry.

Hunched over against the cobwebbed ceiling, he stood on the top bale and offered the bucket, first tipping it down, then raising it upward. "Beg, bossy, beg." They stared and shuffled at the strange sight, smelling the grain, wondering, salivating, hungry, edging closer. "Beg. C'mon, now. Sit. That's a girl."

Bud wished he had a camera, had a picture of the way she stood up with her front feet on the hay bales, eating out of a bucket slung between the ceiling joists with baling twine. He wished he had a photograph of the noose tied to the joists, the thick rope slipknot looped twice around her neck. The other two heifers—he wished he had a picture of the way they pawed and snuffed at the grain he sprinkled all over the hay-bale steps. One bale was already busted open when he left. The other two were beginning to sag, and the grain was settling down between the spreading sheaves.

As he climbed the fence, Bud heard Miss Florida wheezing. Her friends thought the victory steps were tasty. They seemed to like their hay spiced up with Blue Seal feed. Bud began to pick his way through the woods until he found the path, then ran down the hill to his shop and a chocolate chip cookie for Pancho.

Eleven-thirty. Johnny Carson. The sound of Bud's shop door closing. Pearle flicked off the TV, finished her brandy with an audible swallow, stood up, turned on the lights, and walked a crooked line down the hall to the bedroom, yawning.

He was in the kitchen now, locking the back door—cursing at the way it stuck. She heard him turn out the lights and bump into the chair she'd left between the table and the refrigerator. Then he came down the hall and went into the bathroom without a word. In a few minutes, he'd come out smelling like mouthwash, wearing his locomotive print pajamas.

She changed into her nightgown, put on the pink organza housecoat Franny gave her, and got into her bed with one of Bud's hunting magazines. He liked her to read to him before he went to sleep, and she didn't mind. It was, after all, the only time he ever listened to her without interrupting.

He came out of the bathroom and got into his bed without speaking. She opened to an illustration of a bighorn sheep at the edge of a cliff and began to read the accompanying story.

It begins with a description of a midnight drive through a mountain pass in the middle of a thunderstorm. Three hunters, Bob, Ed, and Russ, are lost on their way to a remote hunting cabin. They get lost. Bob is kind of grouchy about it, but Ed is the comedian and calms him down. Then they see the twinkling lights of a ranchhouse in the distance. The rancher greets them warmly, insists they spend the night, and sends them off the next morning with detailed instructions to their cabin and some good tips on where to find game.

Pearle reads slowly—the thunderstorm, the mountain pass, the hunters' names, the smell of coffee at sunrise—and as she reads she pauses now and then to look across at her husband, lying on his back with his eyes closed, listening—maybe not listening—awake, asleep, it doesn't matter; this is

183

her time. She'll read to the end, her voice clear and steady long after he begins to snore, and she'll feel the space between their beds increase until at last she will be far enough away to imagine never coming back.

Bud hears her reading and feels the weight of his chest pressing in on him. He wonders, for the millionth time, what it feels like to have a heart attack, for he is terrified he will die of massive coronary insult like his father did, lurching forward into his soup bowl at the dinner table, stone dead, purple—gone. It scares Bud every time he thinks about it, and he wonders, at times like these, if he deserves better, if doing something better or different in his life might bring him to a peaceful end.

12

EAGLE IN THE WIND

ON A LOW PALISADE along the Trafton exit to the Maine Turn-pike, four men worked at dismantling rock. It was the sixth of May, a sunny Friday, midafternoon, and the murky scent of low-tide salt marsh wafted in from the coast.

Drilling deep into granite since seven that morning, the workers would end the day with the *whoomp* of yet another explosion, reducing the last of the cliff to its final incarnation of manageable pieces, loading the leftovers into the dented iron holds of hulking trucks, driving them away to a nearby gully, which, once filled, might become the site of a sweater outlet, Jiffy Stop, or lobster restaurant, Down East style.

The air around the drilling site was clouded with pul-verized geology, roaring with the sound of diesel-powered air compressors. The clattering of carborundum teeth on stone and the pounding chatter of the air-track drilling rigs seemed to vibrate up from the center of the planet. Four men against one hundred thousand cubic yards of igneous rock—and they were winning, overwhelming nature with technology. The work was dangerous, dirty, and deafening, a world apart from the shiny commuter traffic detouring by below.

Kneeling in the middle of a grid of holes laid out on four-foot centers, Horton Flint shut out the dust and noise and calculated his daughter's age. If he remembered correctly,

Claire was born in 1952. Hadn't he met Pearle just after the war, in '48, Laurie in '49 or '50? So '52 would be about right, which would make her around thirty years old. Horton wiped his hands on his pants and stared at the two-inch diameter cavity in the ledge between his knees. Hard to believe a life could pass so fast and end with open circles. He straightened his back, reached into the cardboard box beside him, and began to pack the hole.

First, he dropped in a sausage of Du Pont Anfo primer, a plastic-wrapped gel, crude oil and fertilizer. It came implanted with a choice of detonating caps and a pair of wires for a tail. Burn it, crush it, drop it twenty stories—the only way to detonate the Anfo was with electric current. He liked the stuff. Nobody used nitro anymore—dangerous, headache inducing—he hadn't seen it on a job since the early seventies, up in Machiasport. Before she married the Audette boy.

With the primer at the bottom of the hole, he funneled in a charge of bulk product, the dry orange Anfo pellets, checking the amount with a calibrated tamping stick; for this hole, he would fill four feet of product before he sank his second deck of primer with its factory-shunted caps and wires joining the first pair up out of the hole. Greg the kid, the laborer, would seal the deck with peastone later; blasters like Horton didn't tamp.

With thirty years of drilling and blasting work behind him, Horton planned his shots by experience and instinct. Formally calculating numbers of pounds of delay by millisecond-rated caps and lift capacity was something he learned and forgot about decades ago. Now he could almost feel in the stone what he needed to do to control the size of the rubble, the direction and sequence of the lift, and the intensity of the fly. With cable mats and a two-foot grid, he'd lifted ledge six inches away from a Casco pottery shop and never rattled a cup. The lady who owned the place kissed him. Horton Flint was known as the best powder monkey in northern New England. Trafton Corporation knew it and paid him accordingly, went out of its way to keep the old white-haired Indian happy.

As Horton moved from hole to hole, he mulled over the

snatches of news he'd heard over the years from this or that one who knew someone in Dalton Pond. She grew up a quiet child. All those times he almost went to see her—but didn't. She was good to the people around her. It seemed that the longer he put off visiting her, the harder it would be for her to accept him. And she was a beauty. By now, she probably didn't want to see him anyway. He pictured her with long black braided hair, like his mother's. He could have gone to the wedding or watched from across the street when they came out of the church. They said she married him out of sympathy—Snoot's boy; couldn't be all bad—and yet Horton had no mental picture of him, only rumors of a kid who lost his legs before he found his soul.

The drillers were finished. The long line of holes Horton had marked out for them were ready for packing. They pulled their drills, shut down the air tracks, and switched off the bellowing compressors.

Horton looked up at the shocking silence, saw the drillers a hundred yards off, their dust-creased faces turned toward him, looking for the gesture of dismissal that would mean another day was done—shower, beer, wife, supper, quiet, sleep. A hard-working crew. They deserved so much more than they'd ever get. He waved them home, lingering on the shapes of their tired bodies as they climbed down the ledges: good drillers, good men. If it weren't for them, he wouldn't have known.

He heard about it a week ago during lunch, during the thirty-minute midday pause when the noise shut down and the sweetened coffee and sandwiches reminded a man of the comfort waiting in the world outside. He heard it mixed in with the occasional gossip of coming jobs: which of their competitors was bidding on what, speculations on how far away from home they would have to travel to the next job—Portland? Burlington? Millinocket? Then he heard the words Dalton Pond, and the conversation was suddenly more than typical noonday gossip.

They said they saw it posted in the office: Ragazzo Corporation was soliciting bids on drilling and blasting work in Dalton Pond, Vermont. They'd seen the specs and drawings, a stack of them, this thick. Abenaki Ledges Lodge, a three-story hotel at the base of the cliff Horton called Pompasook, at the root of the Tooth of the Earth.

They watched Horton when they said "Abenaki," but they knew better than to try to bring him into a conversation about himself or his heritage. So they talked about hoping Trafton didn't get the job. It would be a pain in the ass, a six-hour drive; it would mean staying in a motel a week at a clip, alone and away from their families. Greg the kid liked the idea; a new town meant meeting new girls, trophy wenches waiting for him, maybe even in Dalton Pond. He hoped Trafton won the bid. The drillers told him to wise up, stop acting pussy-crazed; Dalton Pond was on the other side of Hick Dick City, East Bumfuck, man, Nowheresville. As usual, Horton listened without comment.

Two days later, Horton's drillers talked about another job in Bangor—closer, coming up for sure. They said the big shots in the office decided to forget the Dalton Pond proposal. Too far away, they said. Who wanted to fiddlefuck around all over New England when there was plenty of good rock needed moving ten–twenty minutes from home? Bangor would be dandy, right, chief? Right. God's country. Maine. Horton moved his head in a slow circular pattern—not up-and-down, yes; not side-to-side, no—the kind of answer they knew to expect of him when his opinion was asked about anything other than work on the job.

The drillers were gone, and in the next two hours Horton and Greg decked and tamped the remaining holes. Horton then strung the web of skinny red and blue wires to the shooting box, sounded the siren, charged the condenser, and waited for the green light to come on. He let Greg push the button, watched his neck muscles tense at the moment of detonation, smiled as the boy searched the sky for random birdies whistling his way.

Wind caught the sudden puff of dust and blew it inland.

Horton crossed his arms and surveyed the mound of rubble. It was a good shoot. A deep, sharp thump followed by a symmetrical rise of liberated bedrock, an instantaneously leavened loaf of bread, risen miraculously from a quaking table top. No rambling roses, no sneaky Petes, no flying nuns—the pieces stayed together like a family, all in one, yet separated, split apart by forces beyond its control.

Horton nodded his satisfaction to Greg. A good kid. Except for the cleanup, the hauling away, the job was done. The Trafton exit from the Maine Turnpike was about to have two lanes instead of one.

Greg left at a trot, eager, unbreakable, accelerating into life after work on the wings of a self-appointed hero.

Horton walked slowly to his faded-blue four-door Cadillac, rusted and dented and covered with dust. He looked back at the pile of rubble he'd made—one of thousands, all of them different, all of them the same. The sum of which was . . . what?

He got in his car and drove into downtown Trafton. Up Bridge Street, at the iron works yard, he turned across the tracks to the Trafton Corporation office.

It was payday. He parked, found a notepad and pencil in his glove box, and wrote out a brief letter of resignation, effective immediately. He folded it twice and wrote the company president's name on the flap. Inside the office, he nodded to the payroll clerk, picked up his check, and handed his note to the president's secretary on his way out the door.

Forty minutes later, he was at the front steps of his little house trailer in the white pine woods above MacLean Lake.

Horton lived alone. Over the years, a number of women kept him company there in the woods, women who cared for him and told him they loved him—but in one way or another, they all seemed to need something from him that he was unable to give, needed some link to a part of his heart they said they couldn't locate, the private preserve he'd staked out long ago as his and his alone.

His women were talkers, and they all began by telling

him how much his silence excited them, how mysterious he was, how protected they felt, how good it was to be listened to. But after a while—sometimes it was as little as a month, sometimes as much as a year—they told him they needed to hear his voice, they were starved for conversation and the sharing of ideas, they needed to talk about things. When he didn't comply—he truly felt he didn't know how—they became unsure of themselves and grew to resent his reticence. They went to flea markets and collected cartoon animal salt and pepper shakers, plastic cuckoo clocks, and commemorative plates. They filled his trailer with flowered tablecloths, printed napkins, lamps, and doilies on the sofa—poodle ashtrays, loungers, bookshelves: *pets*—until he was immobilized with the weight of their possessions, suffocating with the stuff of permanence. It seemed to him that each of these female possessions was another bar in a cage designed to quiet him, another link in the shackles of his freedom, choking him into the kind of silence that hurt: hurt him because he couldn't speak, hurt his women because they couldn't hear what they wanted him to say.

"Selfish," they said; "Too wrapped up in yourself," they shouted over their collections of precious painted platters. "Why don't you say something, medicine man, say a word, make a noise, yell at me if you want to. Anything!"

Silence drove them away, in tears, frustrated, packed into cars with their loads of pitiful rummage. He'd watch them disappear through the pines, and he'd feel his throat loosen as soon as they were out of his sight. Within minutes, his tiny rooms would suddenly expand to enormous dimensions, light and mobile and noisy with possibility.

By the time his hair turned white, he gave up the ongoing company of women, despite their considerable comforts and unceasing attraction to him. He asked himself if his decision was based on wisdom, frustration, or fatigue, and although he didn't know the answer, he knew the wind in the pines and the loons on the lake had at last become company enough.

• • •

Horton left the trailer door open to the evening air. Inside, the two small rooms were spare and neat, stripped bare of ornaments. He ate a simple dinner of rice and beans, washed up, and began to assemble his things for the trip.

By dark, the old blue Cadillac was packed—for a week, for a year, or for the rest of his life. It was all the same, wasn't it? He would leave the trailer unlocked. If there was something inside someone wanted, it would be theirs for the taking. He would have everything with him he needed.

Horton took one last look at his possessions before he closed the car's trunk: At the back of the compartment were a dozen big cardboard boxes with the Anfo logo stenciled in red block letters across their tops; packed in front of the cartons were a toolbox, blankets, pillow, mess kit, a canvas duffel full of clothes, a few cherished mementos from his grandfather in a braided leather bag, and a snakeskin pouch stuffed with hundred-dollar bills. Horton had never trusted banks.

Wrapped in a towel inside the duffel was a polished wood box containing two framed photos—one of Pearle Lupien at age eighteen in a long white dress, a beautiful woman; the other of a two-year-old girl with a solemn face, patting a dog with a big wooden spoon. The faces in both photos were the last things he looked at before he closed his eyes each night, and they were the first things he unpacked wherever he went, moistening the glass with his breath, polishing it with his sleeve.

Travel light. Leave no traces. How did the rest go?

Travel fast, leave no regrets.

Horton slammed the trunk shut.

He drove on roads of blackest satin. A phantom company of forest, swamp, and mountain galloped along beside him through the darkened window glass, now bright, now dimmed in the half-lit towns of Liberty, Palermo, and South China, extinguished in the phosphorous glare of Augusta, then quickened back to life in the trees and water, moss and rock of the patinated hinterlands.

He drove to melodies of wind sounds whispered to the

191

wide underbelly of the speeding two-ton Cadillac, to the sighing, singing witnesses to speed and winding highway, confed-
erates in the traveling Kingdom of the Night.

Under the perfect creamy circle of a rising moon, he
crossed Maine's sleeping western flank, the buoyant lakes and
rivers, sandy sloughs and sad mill towns, sped over the rapid-
ridden Androscoggin at Auburn—Norway, Harrison, Frye-
burg—across the invisible border to New Hampshire and into
the hustle of Conway's mercantile frenzy.

Due west of the car parks and poison-lit plazas, at last
the road climbed into the sanctified preserve of the White
Mountain National Forest, climbed upward against the crashing, downstream flow of a thundering brook awash with
melted snow.

At the highest point of the Kancamagus Highway, Horton stopped at the side of the road, got out, and walked a half
mile into the woods. There was a place his people knew, a
place with the powers of Pompasook, one of the few. He found
the clearing at the top of the rockslide, an open space between
the trees with a single, flat-topped boulder in the center, a
podium, an altar, and an anchor to his past. He climbed onto
it and sat cross-legged, stretching his arms out to the silent
peaks around him.

Time passed; rock merged with blood. The pulp of flesh
and sap and spirit quickened to a common pulse. Out over the
valleys, he followed the rolling shoulders of a dozen silver-
dark horizons as if he were riding the contours, caressing the
peaks, plunging into the dark wet caves, stroking the valleys;
up and down he slid and flew and hung in perfect symmetry
above the loving body of the living mountains.

The moon edged westward; somewhere in the distance,
a fox gave cry. Horton answered. Knowing filled the void
between. He heard the sound of icy water falling to the
oceans. Wind chased the clouds to where the path to One
Creation both began and ended. He rubbed the air between his
palms, inhaled the night, and entered.

• • •

At 2:00 A.M., in Quinntown, just past a sign pointing to Dalton Pond, he stopped for gas. The all-night service station was built on the edge of a field he'd worked in as a boy, cutting hay with a scythe for a dollar a day. The farmer's name was— Pickering? That sounded right. And there was a daughter, Luvie. She was—she was one of them—stranded on the farm, exiled from hope, from love. Her father caught them half undressed in the cow barn, shouted, "Goddamned heathen," and ran for his shotgun. Luvie Pickering, hungry, long-boned, blond albino. He remembered how she kissed until his lips bled. Would they know each other now? Was she faded parchment, pale and wide, all the tension sprung away? Would there be the slightest recoil of recognition? And if there was, what good was it now?

The attendant counted out change. Horton nodded, then turned and pointed to where the Pickering farmhouse lay in his memory, hidden by the dark, long gone, perhaps—or was he mistaken? Was it never there at all? Was his finger pointing at an old man's need to reconfirm himself? He dropped his hand. The attendant looked at him as if he were about to ask him what he wanted, then apparently thought better of it, shrugged his shoulders, and walked back inside to a jangling radio.

An old, dented Cadillac eases by Tot's store; it is the color of night mist, coasting on cushions of somnolent air. Through the village and up the Crooked Brook road it glides without effort, confidence and purpose in the deep, quiet thrum of its powerful engine. It pulls off the road at the Staircase Falls; the lights are turned off, the engine is silent. A door clicks open and tumbles shut; the driver crosses the road and starts up a path by a stone wall, into the forest.

Half a mile up the trail, Horton saw through the trees in front of him a broad expanse of night sky where there should have been a thickness of branches, saw unexpected moonlight where there should have been shadows. He slowed his pace—what happened here?—then stopped in disbelief when he came to a brush pile at the edge of an enormous clearing.

Where a forest had towered since the time of his ancestors' ancestors, not a single tree was left standing. The earth was ripped and torn in jagged furrows all the way up the slope to Pompasook's startled gleam.

The clearing stretched from where he stood to the pasture fence to the west, up to the Ledges, and over the horizon to the east. The hemlocks he remembered had vanished; even the stumps were gone. And hadn't there been a little cabin somewhere along the banks of Crooked Brook? He searched the featureless wasteland for a point of reference. Where *was* the brook?

An incongruous shadow cutting across the furrows told him: Crooked Brook's never-failing East Branch had been straightened. Who would do this? Crooked Brook had been confined to a trench, a ragged gutter, straight as a string. He heard it scuppling in its muddy, bloody bridal bed, the sound of angry water.

He picked his way through a pile of severed branches and walked into the wasteland, every inch of it foreign and suddenly hateful. Except for Pompasook's Tooth, he would have been lost. He walked through a spastic tangle of feeder roots ripped out of the soil. A numbness crept up his legs, held him away from the earth that had received his fathers, that had given them life. He stumbled on slivers of shredded saplings, stepped across upturned rocks and pulverized tree parts crushed into the corduroyed mud.

Horton stopped when he came to the base of the Ledges. Clouds crossed the moon, sure signs that a storm was making itself ready. The great rock wall above him seemed to rumble, ready to burst and bury the awful desecration at its feet. Horton watched and waited; clouds passed, returned, passed. Granite swayed; Horton swayed with it; then they both stood still.

As a boy, he was brought to Pompasook by his grandfather, Eagle-in-the-Wind, and was shown it was a place of great power, where the possibility of conversations between the

Abenaki and the Great Ones was enhanced by the unique configuration of earth and sky, rock, wind, and forest. He was awed by the gap-toothed shaman's stories of warriors, magic, and spirits within the cliffs—and he was frightened by his grandfather's necklace, giant bear claws strung like beads to each side of a silver cross.

The claws, he was instructed, were symbols of strength and unity. The bear ruled the forest without abusing his might. The bear was huge, but the point of each sharp claw was judiciously small. Five claws on each side of the cross represented God's five fingers, workers in the service of Creation.

The heart of the cross, his grandfather explained, was the white man's connection to Creation, his symbol for empathy, his bridge to compassion. This part was good too, worthy of study and application. The outstretched arms of the cross, however, were to be understood by a careful reading of Genesis and interpreted as "reaching," the right to dominion, the right to exploit all of Creation for the purpose of man's needs alone. In that belief, he warned gravely, the white man's cross would lead unwary followers away from union and oneness with nature, confusing the idea of exploitation with the intuitive wisdom of stewardship. There was no entitlement to dominion, he lectured; all of nature was knit together in a unity of Creation, and to behave toward it otherwise was to ensure its destruction.

Horton stood with his back to the Tooth of the Earth, looked at the leveled battlefield, at the moonstruck detritus of nature upended, and saw the painful contradiction of his own life—drilling and blasting away at the face of the earth as if peeling away its skin might reveal the ultimate truth of the Creator's purpose. Was it a quest for dominion that had led him to work every day? Or was it the need to test himself against difficulty? And if it was the need to test himself, where did that need come from, and why had he applied it as he had?

He bent down and picked up a rock from the rubble at the base of the cliff; he sniffed it, licked it, weighed it, rubbed it with his thumb—and instinctively calculated what he would have to do to move a mountain's worth. He dropped the rock, dismissed his thought, and heard them both fall with a thump at his feet. But the other question wouldn't go away. Where did the need come from?

His grandfather had been a great and wise man, yet he sat through the liturgy each Sunday in a church built to the glorification of Christ. A white man's church, a house of dominion. How did his grandfather reconcile the teachings of Genesis with the oneness of Creation? Did he himself need something from the church that the old ways no longer provided him?

Horton left the Ledges behind him and picked his way through the upturned soil to the deep-shadowed ruts of a skid road leading to the Audette farmhouse. He knew the place well. Four generations of Snoot Audette's family had worked the land and always given back more than they took. Horton had seen Snoot's grandfather planting apple saplings in his eightieth year, trimming the sugar bush, replenishing roots. Snoot's people knew what it meant, and yet look at what they'd allowed to be done. It made no sense, and yet—in this world of dollars and haste—it did.

The ruts led him to a giant bulldozer parked in the dooryard between the house and the barn. A tarpaulin was spread across the seat; its fuel tanks, hood, and ignition panel were padlocked against theft and mischief. Horton walked around it, shoulders even with the tops of the tracks, the crest of the root rake blade above his head. He yanked at a branch stuck between a track and an idler, then left it stuck there, cantilevered, a springy, lone survivor.

He circled the bulldozer twice; it was, in fact, an innocent miracle of machinery, a perfect tool for the men who operated it, no different from the rigs that stripped the sites on his drilling and blasting jobs—except this one stripped land in the shadow of Pompasook. He kicked it. Stupid. He must leave it behind him. Soon enough, it would be moved to the next grove of trees, to the next disorderly brook. He resisted the impulse to kick it again and walked away, toward the house.

It was deserted, picked over, abandoned; the window sash were missing, the doors hung open—or were gone altogether—sold or stolen, for salvage, for pig fence, for somebody's kindling wood. Tattered curtains flew back and forth in the soft night breeze, sad flights, on wings of ruin.

Horton began to retrace his steps up the hill when he heard a sound from inside the barn. Not a man sound, he thought; more the sound of an animal, or animals, the sound of hooves—and something else he couldn't quite place. He went to the corner of the building and put his ear against a weathered board. Cattle. Oddly restless. He opened the gate to the paddock, walked along the wall and around a corner to an open door; he peered in, waiting, as his eyes adjusted to the dark.

A pair of heifers bolted at the sight of his shadow. Horton stared after the sound of their retreat, searching out the bold white markings. "Whoa." He thought he saw them, then he wasn't sure. "Okay, okay," he whispered. It was too dark to see back into the corners of the barn, but he heard them breathing—two of them—wary, skittish, rubbing raspy flanks against a post. He turned to go.

As he did, he thought he saw something else, but it made no sense. Beyond a post to his left, he thought he saw . . . it looked like patches of light, floating, disconnected shapes. What thing was this? A few steps closer, he realized he was looking straight into the black and white belly of a hanging cow.

From the feel of the mud at the edges, he knew the bootprints were no more than a few hours old. Despite the growing clumps of clouds, the moon was bright enough to show each step; one set of tracks came up through the middle of the paddock and into the barn, another set left the barn and recrossed the same wet ground; they hesitated before crossing a sag in the fence by the trees: the same tracks, the same man—a heavy man.

Horton crossed the fence and started into the woods, bending down every few steps to feel for indentations in the earth. He watched for openings in the spiky understory, calculated the route a man would take around overhead branches, or the detour he'd choose to avoid a dense thicket. He confirmed his guesses with each discovery of another crescent-heel imprint, a snapped twig, or the pulpy, crushed fibers of a trodden-on log.

When the path was so dark he couldn't see the ground, he crawled from print to print, sniffing at the earth, following the scent of barn muck left in the tracks.

At a ledge outcropping, he found a patch of snow, dull white in the half-dark, topped with a melting imprint of the wide-soled boots with the cross-block tread.

He continued down the hill through the woods. Now he was on a path, and it was easy to spot the close-spaced prints going up the hill, the long strides coming down. The distance between the downhill tracks increased, started running. The heels of the boots left deep semicircle divots in the path. Someone was ashamed of what he'd done.

Horton thought back to the men he remembered from the area. True, that was years ago, and there were undoubtedly plenty of newcomers Horton didn't know in Dalton Pond, but there was one of his acquaintance who could easily fit those craven boots, who could hang a cow and run away scared.

The woods ended abruptly at a lawn behind a garage. On the other side of the garage was a house, then a road. Horton waited in the trees and watched. Any sign of dogs? He threw a stick over the garage and heard it clatter across the roof of a vehicle, snick on the gravel driveway: no growls, no startled yelps. Another stick: still nothing, no dogs. Instead, he heard a symphony of insects, nightbirds, peepers, and trickling water. Peaceful, quiet. Balanced. The way it was meant to be.

Walk. He stepped out of the woods, briefly followed the tracks to the back door of the garage—then, satisfied with the evidence imprinted in the mud at his feet, he edged along the dark side of the building toward the house. In the driveway, he saw two vehicles: an old truck and a four-wheel-drive

Bronco with a domed police light centered on the roof. His hunch was right, then: now Bud hung cows, still a big man in town. And her? How had she managed to survive a life with him?

A light shone from a room at the rear of the house. Horton appraised the fifty feet of open space between the garage and house and imagined himself on the opposite side. In the next breath, he was across the lawn and hidden behind two lilac bushes beside the illuminated window. He paused and listened to himself. What was the purpose of this continued curiosity?

To see her.

Would she resurrect the uprooted trees, bring back to life the hanging heifer?

No.

Would she explain why individual need was in such conflict with common necessity?

He decided she would not; his curiosity was vain and reckless; he admitted he was only hoping for a glimpse of someone who had made him happy many years before.

He remembered the day after Pearle married Bud. Bud ran into Horton in the village, pulled him aside with a friendly, public wink, and when he knew no one else could hear, he threatened to personally castrate Horton if he ever saw him within a mile of Pearle again. He also told him he should stay out of Dalton Pond. "It's dangerous here," he said. "People get themselves in some terrible accidents. Especially foreigners."

Horton remembered watching the words spew out of Bud's mouth and thinking of the arrangements he and Pearle had made to meet that next weekend. He'd left Bud's threatenings without a word, gone straight to a phone booth, and made reservations at the best hotel in Albany, for three nights instead of one, paid extra for a king-sized bed.

Moving to the edge of the window, he looked into the room. A woman in a bathrobe sat with her back to him at a kitchen table, balancing a glass between her fingers. She sat the way a person sits when sleep won't come, slumped inward, staring, concentrating on nothing and everything at once. She sat in the kind of room Horton had feared all his life, the kind of room a woman spins around a man, a web.

He took it all in: the swagged lace curtains, rows of family photographs, stacks of china, dangling cups, and constellations of decorative trivets. He saw the framed needlepoint projects, hooked rugs, pots of ivy, and painted ceramic knickknacks on the windowsills—and it looked uncomfortably familiar.

She lifted the last of her drink to her lips, rose from the chair, and put the glass in the sink. When she turned to reach up and switch off the overhead light, he saw her face. For one brief second, he saw the softened features of the only woman who never tried to put her things around him, a woman he'd always imagined living without the smothering possessions of domesticity.

Hello, Pearle.

He saw that she'd changed—of course she had—but the lines on her handsome face and the thickening beneath her robe were nothing compared with the desperate clutter of junk in her kitchen. She never would have done that, never.

The kitchen light went out and another went on before she walked down the hall. Then it, too, was dimmed, and the house was dark.

Did she sleep in the same bed with the hangman?

Did she ever think about their weekends in Albany?

What would it be like—now?

He left the window, crossed the backyard, and walked into the shadows behind the garage. He stared at the sunken footprints by the door. It occurred to him that maybe the stuff Pearle collected around her was a form of insulation from Bud, trapping him out instead of in. False testimony of false contentment; misleading, perhaps, but how else to survive a fool?

Horton tried the garage door; it was locked. He took a knife from his pocket and knelt down beside the knob. A minute passed, and the latch clicked open. He went in, closed the door behind him, and struck a match. Four rabbits stared at him, blinking, chewing.

It took most of an hour to do what he did: finding the block and tackle, the rope, sawing grooves in the sides of the carved feather headdress, fixing the noose—working by matchlight—stopping to listen for Bud.

When he was finally satisfied with his work, he patted the rabbits, relocked the door from the inside, and retraced his route through the woods to the barn and the hanging cow. From the barn, he hiked up through the pasture and across the clear-cut until he found the tote road leading to his car.

The rain began before sunrise. Horton was thirty-five miles from Dalton Pond, in a little motel on the outskirts of Lawford, New Hampshire. From the faint trace of salt in the air outside his open window, Horton guessed it was the start of a long, heavy storm, a hurricane, blowing in from the Atlantic.

Sleep eluded him. He lay tossing under a rough, thin blanket, and wondered if he should arrange to see Pearle, how he would find his daughter and introduce himself.

I am your father.

Could he explain his absence? Would they remember him? Hate him? Would Claire understand that the combination of being in love with the police chief's wife and a woefully mismatched marriage to Laurie made an Abenaki's future in Dalton Pond impossible? Could he ever explain to his grandfather what he'd seen at the Tooth of the Earth?

He fell asleep still asking questions, then woke to the sound of rain on the roof. He sat on the edge of the bed and thought about the night before: the first thing to cross his mind was a match-lit image of a wooden Indian, hanging from the trusses in Bigfoot's garage.

13

MUDDY WATER

EVEN THE coming hurricane didn't stop the Saturday auction at Fellows's. Snoot told Walker he was in the market for seed potatoes and pepper plants. Claire had drawn Saturday rounds at the hospital, and Walker decided to catch up on some reading at his new office; his first two clients walked in the door before the walls were painted, and he was already pressed to keep up. He'd work until Claire's shift was over; then they'd drive back to Fellows's, pick up Snoot, and take him up to the farm to feed the heifers, Dolly, Polly, and Pomona.

"Weatherman calls for heavy showers." Snoot scoffed as he climbed out of Walker's car at the Auction Barn. "You'll see some showers on your way back home from Jordy. Ground's about soaked in all the water she wants. Brooks'll be up past Toby's touch hole."

It rained all day. The wind drove hard from the east, carrying the raindrops sideways, battering the windows. A flood watch was called for the northern part of the state and over into New Hampshire. Walker and Claire left Jordan early, and on their way home they passed dozens of uprooted trees and cars abandoned to flooded sections of the road.

Walker parked next to a cattle truck in Fellows's lot and ran a zigzag pattern through the puddles to an open door. The barn was almost empty, but the sound of water hammering on the metal roof filled the space with the roar of a thousand voices.

At the far end of the barn, a dozen damp people sat transfixed as Farley Fellows overwhelmed the racket on the roof with a hypnotizing patter of his own. "Ten-ten-ten, gimme ten? Whodagimme, whodagimme, half a twennydollabill?"

Snoot was sitting on the bottom bench of the arena bleachers, nodding to the singsong repetition of Fellows's voice. He had a clutch of bags around him, some of them tied tight around the root ball of an apple sapling, others overflowing with the wilted shoots of starter plants. When Snoot saw him, he stood up slowly, joint by joint, rubbed his back, and began assembling his collection.

"Would of bought us an umbrella, if Farley'd put one up." He nodded to the open door. "Brooks up, are they?"

"You should see the brook by the iron bridge." Walker shook his head. "Over the roadbed."

As if to dispute him, Farley cranked up his spiel. "Twennydolla, twennydolla, whodagimme twennydolla, *twenny*dolla—Now folks, this clever little mechanism is in good working order—Twennydolla, *twenny*dolla, whodagimme. . . ."

A flash of lightning was followed closely by a rolling clap of thunder; Farley faltered. Walker picked up the remaining plants and followed Snoot down the length of the barn.

"Twenny*five*, quadda of a hunnadolla, quadda of a hunnadolla, twenty*fi*—Lots of life left in this old girl—Yessum! Thankyou! Yessum! Thutty, thutty, *thutty*dolla, whodagimme *thutty*dolla . . . ?"

Another crack of lightning and an immediate rumble above the barn roof, rain coming down now thick enough to swim in. Walker shouted and gestured; he would bring the car up to the door.

It wasn't until he was in the car, with the windshield wipers flapping fast, that he realized Snoot had followed him, slogging through the puddles at a casual pace.

"Damp enough?" Snoot asked Claire as he loomed into

the backseat, steam rising from his soggy clothes.

The car windows were fogged with vapor despite the defroster and constant wipings. Walker drove slowly with his headlights on; at times, he could see fifty feet ahead, at other times, much less. There was something almost sinister about the rain, the amount of it, the intensity, so wantonly brutal and unnecessary.

Ahead, he saw the side railings of First Bridge over Crooked Brook, then he heard the water under the car and realized what it meant: somewhere above them, the brook had crested over into the road. "Must be coming down past Beasley's like crazy," Claire said.

"Measley's," Snoot snapped.

Walker saw Claire reach behind her and pat Snoot's arm. "Beasley could have webbed feet by now," she joked.

Snoot pulled away from her hand. "Mud and muck all over the Christly highway." His voice held a warning; the sound of cracking knuckles segued into a roll of fractured thunder. "Hurricane's tore out half the county."

Walker wiped at the windshield and held his breath; he glanced in the rearview mirror. Snoot was glowering, rocking from side to side.

Ahead, just past Second Bridge, the full width of the roadway was coffee brown, a riffling sheet of muddy water racing toward them. It split at the bridge, half a river to each side ditch, before spilling back onto the road below.

Snoot pushed his own dam against the back of Walker's seat and cursed the rain. It came down in a fusillade, a billion silver bullets ricocheting off the dirty wash. Surrounded by water, below and above, Walker drove through the cut in the Ledges; now, the rough rock walls were like the sides of a deep canal—except the sloped sluiceway was thick with liquid topsoil.

A hundred yards farther up the road they came to Third Bridge and the turnout by the Staircase Falls. Snoot stuck his head out the right side window, bumped Walker's shoulder, and growled, "Cut the motor."

Walker pulled off the road and stopped. Snoot climbed

out and slammed the door. Claire rolled down her window to a head-on view of the East Branch thundering out of the woods.

It had eaten a channel ten feet deep into the earth where the tote path had been, and swallowed the stone wall beside it. The ancient brook bed had vanished, its course unimaginable now. In place of its mossy cobbles and drowsy ferns, a roaring brown torrent of chocolaty mud puked undigested scraps of landscape out into the middle of the road.

Snoot stood in the bruising rain and stared. His fists were clenched at his sides, rivulets streaming from his hair, water everywhere around him. A bolt of lightning lit the sky above him, followed by a jumble of thunder. When Snoot finally got back in the car, his jaw stuck out square as a chimney block. "Those sonsabitches," he said. "Those greedy sonsabitches."

Walker thought about trading his precious law books for a gun. He started the car. As he was about to pull out into the road, he saw the running lights, then the wide chrome grille and a WIDE LOAD sign across the bumper of a trailer truck coming down the narrow road. He rolled down his window for a better view and felt the car tip to the left as Snoot shifted his weight and rolled down his window, too.

It came at them slowly, a train without the customary clamor of clanking iron and hissing combustion. Whatever sounds it made were drowned in the tumult of the East Branch rampage. The driver? A ghostly blur behind steamed glass, if indeed there was a driver. The truck, train, ship, caravan, parade—it could have been a mirage, for all Walker knew. God *damn* Billy Ware.

Lights brightened and focused. Sculpted metal fenders flexed and gleamed—tall blood-red flanks appeared, ribbed, louvered, pin-striped hood, a mighty fortress: RAGAZZO in bold white letters high up on the door. Mud flaps awash—tires bulging, glistening black and big as Ferris wheels—it kept coming, huge, unstoppable.

Chained to the low-boy trailer in back of the cab was a gigantic yellow bulldozer outfitted with a billboard-sized blade. A row of shiny foot-long teeth were bolted to the bottom edge. Walker knew how it worked; he'd seen the deep furrows left in the wake of a root rake's pass. And he knew where this one had been.

Not only had those teeth polished themselves bright in ninety acres of willing woods dirt along the banks of Crooked Brook, those teeth had chewed up a cabin and swallowed it whole, mixed hallowed dirt and bricks and nails with painted shards and sacred bones and known nothing of their differences, let alone their affiliations.

He and Snoot had watched it, the Saturday before, from the top of the Ledges, watched it pillage and plunder and straighten the brook to conform to Billy Ware's fiction. He went home angry that day, angry at Claire for being a compromising coward, even angrier at himself for becoming one too. "I should have—you should have—" They argued late into the night.

"But poor Franny—"

"Tough. What about the land?" Why didn't Claire get it? "Once it's gone, it's gone forever."

They went to sleep still arguing; he had dreams of a D-8 running amok. He woke up and did the best he could to explain his dream to Claire, but he didn't tell her he was going after Ware Associates, whether she liked it or not.

The truck and its trailer passed within an arm's length of the car—a solemn *whissshhh* the only signal of its passing—and then the red taillights blurred and faded down the mountain and all of it disappeared into a forest of rain, washed away with the uprooted soil of Snoot's great-grandfather's farm, washed away with the memories of the forgotten Abenakis.

They sat without speaking, three of them paralyzed with the realization of what the storm was doing, of how powerless they were to stop it; they sat gathering courage, as if renewing resolutions. The windows were still open to the rain, but it seemed wrong to close them, to hide from the storm, when all of nature around them was being so helplessly punished.

Claire traced a drawing in the film of vapor on the inside of the windshield, a stick figure of a girl with five stick fingers at the ends of each stick arm. The girl's head was a circle with dots for eyes and a crescent frown.

Snoot began to drum his fingers on the back of Walker's seat.

Walker watched Claire draw.

Finally, Snoot spoke. "I suppose them heifers have got to have some hay."

Walker drove up the hill. The lane to the farm was awash with twin freshets filling the parallel wheel ruts in a series of miniature rapids. He put the Wagoneer in four-wheel drive and splashed up the slope. At the top, the Dodge Mahal seemed to shrink away from them, cringing in the storm. He drove slowly through the mud. Ahead, the view of the Ledges was lost behind a heavy veil of rain. As they approached the windowless house, a gust of wind pried loose a section of sheet-metal roofing and curled it back. Walker hoped he was the only one who saw the flapping tin, hoped no one else noticed the jagged stump of broken bricks which had once been Frouncy's cookstove chimney. Behind the house, he thought he saw—and then refused to see again—a dark delta of silt, oozing out of the amputated woods and down the pasture slope, like blood.

He parked next to the barn, pointing the car away from the things no one wanted to see.

Snoot unloaded himself from the backseat and slammed the door. They watched him through the watery arcs of the wiper blades as he sloshed through the downpour to feed his heifers. His footprints were flooded with water as soon as he left them, a growing chain of miniature lakes curving around the corner of the barn and out of sight.

The rain came on in windy waves, hemorrhaging, inexhaustible, indecent amounts of it, pounding the car, rocking it; thunder rumbled over Big Church.

"This has to be one of the worst days of his life," Claire said.

Walker knew what she meant, but he was in no hurry to agree with her about anything. He wiped all the fog from his window before he spoke. "It didn't have to happen." Did he sound accusative? "It never should have gone this far."

"Please." A plea. "Don't blame me, Walker."

"I don't. I blame myself. I should have found a way around your Uncle Billy." Walker waved his hands at the rain. "To tell the truth, I guess I do. I blame you too."

"If I'd known this would happen—"

Walker interrupted her. "Can I ask you something?"

She nodded, yes, of course.

He spoke quickly. "From the very first time the subject came up, you've made it clear you didn't want me meddling with the project—as if I'd embarrass you or something. I should leave it alone. I love you, so it's okay if you tease me about the legal profession—it's okay because there's a lot of bullshit going on that ought to be set straight—but what I was proposing wasn't bullshit. It was a matter of exposing an act of plain and simple fraud, and yet you resisted me. You know what I'm talking about?"

She looked down at her muddy shoes, then out the window. "Go on."

"You've been so resistant, which seems odd, if you ask me, considering your father and Snoot, and I was just wondering. . . ." The thing that had lurked in the dark corners of his mind for months was finally about to see daylight. "I was just wondering if—if there was something else involved."

Claire drew another stick figure on the window. "Like what?" The straight white part in her ebony hair seemed to divide the back of her head in half.

"Like Junior." Why was it that the hardest question was always the last one asked? "Were you trying to—you know—protect him again?"

"That's ridiculous." She rubbed out the drawing. "Why would I?"

Thunder shook the air around the car. "I don't know."

Was he being ridiculous? "Conditioned reflex?"

"What?"

The rumbling stopped, but the rain kept on. "I said, maybe it was a conditioned reflex." Now he sounded shrill, but he didn't care. "Maybe you were in the habit of protecting him for so long, you didn't know how to stop?"

Claire cut him off. "I thought you'd give me more credit than that."

"It was a question."

"Well, it's a dumb one." She moved away from him and rolled down her window, ignoring the rain splashing in on her. "Maybe you should think about *your* motives, while you're in the mood for analysis."

"Maybe I have." Maybe the trees would still be growing along Crooked Brook.

"And?"

"And nothing. I wanted to do it for Snoot. And for the land, and the trees, and the Abenakis. The place has a history." Walker suddenly felt lonely. "For you too, or so I thought."

She ignored the challenge. "And?"

"And what?" Was she bluffing him? "What?"

"Think about it."

She was right; there was something else. She knew him better than he thought she did. "Okay, I guess I wanted to get back at Junior for what he did to you, too." There was still something else. "And for pointing the gun at me." More. "And I wanted to do something . . . for the town, for the Abenakis, something worthwhile, so I wouldn't feel like a goddamned tourist all my life, something lasting. I guess I wanted to be a hero."

She rolled up her window and slid across the seat to him. "Listen, Walker. I love you for who you are. You don't have to save us poor Injuns and hillbillies from ourselves, dazzle us with your legal skills," she said, "but it's not the kind of victory I need right now. You and I have a life to build. The past is over with; this is our home. Junior's an angry, lonely man, his own worst enemy. There are no Abenakis left. Well, hardly any." She touched Walker's face. "You couldn't protect

210

them if you wanted to—and believe me, I don't want to even think about Junior, let alone protect him. So enough of this revenge and retribution stuff. Tot and Bud have a long way to go before they ruin our lives. Who knows? They may fall flat on their faces; the whole thing could go belly up, go bankrupt, catch on fire. Look at the partners, for crying out loud. What a combination."

She turned the wipers on, then off, clearing a brief arch of light on the foggy glass.

"Mom says Tot wants to buy out Junior's share. He'll do it, too. When Loretta heard J was rich, she couldn't get back east quick enough, and unless she's found religion or something, they're going to put a lot of money up their noses in a hurry. She'll bleed him dry. From what I hear, it's a wonder they haven't killed one another already, fighting over money. It's bad soap opera, Walker, and they can have it. You and I, we've got something real."

Walker sighed. She was right, she was right, she was *right*. And she was wrong. Someday he'd bring her Billy Ware's revoked license, like it or not. "You'd make a good lawyer, you know that?" He slid his hand down between her and the seat. "And you've got a beautiful butt."

The downpour continued. They sat talking and necking in the car for another ten minutes, when Walker suddenly wondered if Snoot hadn't been gone too long. "I'll check," he said. "Don't go away." Halfway to the corner, a gust of wind knocked him off-balance and he fell face down in the mud. He picked himself up, found a clean patch of sleeve to wipe his glasses on, and looked back toward the car. At first he couldn't see it through the rain. When he did he realized he was, oddly, immensely happy at that moment, in spite of—because of—he didn't know what, but he felt lighter and looser than he had in a long time. Then he turned and saw Snoot.

Halfway down the paddock slope, Snoot stood with his back to the barn, a moving granite statue. He had a makeshift harness roped around his shoulders. Leaning downhill at a precarious angle, he was dragging Pomona behind him, pulling her toward the fence line, inch by inch. The smooth trough left behind them was slick as a toboggan run. Her belly was swollen, her legs stuck up stiffly in the rain, four white stockings pointed at the sky. Thunder rolled over a distant mountain, barely audible over the sound of everlasting rain.

The storm passed around midnight, rumbling northward toward Quebec, where it would dump itself onto the flat clay plains spreading south from the St. Lawrence River. Now it was almost daybreak; Snoot couldn't sleep.

Walker and Claire were still in bed when he left the house. He eased out the kitchen door, sat on the steps, and laced up his boots. The flagstone walk was damp with night mist; blackened dew covered the grass. Birds called from the hedgerows, summoning strength for a new day. Snoot looked up the hillside across the road, saw the first pale splash of light spill onto the crest of the Catamount Heights, and thought about bringing Frouncy home.

He walked westward along the road to Dalton Pond, stopping by habit at every bridge and culvert to listen to water rushing under the road. The brooks were receding, abandoning stranded mats of flood chaff high in the bushes along their beaten banks, but they couldn't hold his attention, and he left each of them quickly, impatient with the endless sound of water, itchy with himself.

The smell of water was everywhere. He passed the empty auction barn, then a stretch of soggy fields, and, soon, the scattering of houses east of the village. A dog barked as he went by Eddie Aubergine's trailer; Snoot growled at it, and it slunk away.

Dawn unfolded into daylight. In the village, two big maples lay uprooted next to the school, branches crushing the playground fence. Two days with a chain saw, Snoot calculated—five cords, split and stacked.

The water in Dalton Pond was a foot above usual, and the gorge below the iron bridge was crisscrossed with logs and pulsing with foam. Snoot passed it without stopping; he'd seen worse. Christly '38 was ten times worse—talk about a storm—

and besides, he was looking for someone.

He walked up Main Street pushing a long shadow in front of him. A few cars went by, then a truck approached and passed; somebody waved. Who in hell? Blue Chevrolet ton dump, spanking new. Punka Hurley traded up again. A bright star of early sunlight twinkled across the polished windshield. Won the bid for the chimbley work, did he? News of the Ledges Lodge bid winners and losers was updated daily at Tot's coffee counter. Snoot flopped a halfhearted wave at the truck. Leave it to Punka to piss it away before he'd laid a single brick.

A van drove by, headed west toward the Crooked Brook road: Junior's van, with a woman driving, and here it was barely a quarter past daylight. No sign of him since deer season, and now they claimed Tot'd bought him out; him and his floozy was leaving town. So be it. The van disappeared around the corner, leaving an empty hole at the end of Main Street.

More cars, more trucks went by, some with out-of-state plates. Bunch of vultures looking for a meal. Snoot walked to Tot's store, up the worn granite steps, and in the double doors, first customer of the day.

The bright overhead lights cast a leatherette sheen on the trouser-polished stools at the counter. What should have been green took on a sickish yellow tint, brown turned to olive. Snoot suddenly felt queasy; it was too goddamned warm inside, smelled like last year's ashtray soot—like it always did—but worse, this morning.

He unbuttoned his coat and sat at the counter by the plate-glass window. At the other end, Laurie was pouring boiling water into the top of a big coffee urn. Snoot watched her reaching up, frail arms shaking with the weight of the pot. Tot would work her till she dropped. She stood on tiptoes, in scuffed white waitress shoes; the knotted veins in her calves looked painful. Snoot leaned over the counter for a better look, then settled back onto his stool and tried to picture Claire's legs next to Laurie's—mother, daughter—not the same. Would they be some day? Hard to imagine. Unclear why. And Frouncy's—no, no, no—and on to Ruby's, pink high-heel shoes up on the stage at the Daintytown Follies. Whoa, boy, crimus, come on back. He shook the images away.

Still facing the coffee urn, Laurie put down the pot and rubbed at her swollen hands. Snoot guessed she weighed less than a hundred pounds. Didn't Tot feed the woman? When she turned and saw Snoot watching her, she nodded an ambiguous greeting, gestured that the coffee would be ready soon, and hurried to the kitchen in back of the store. She probably thought she didn't deserve to rest, on account of how Tot took her in. Snoot thanked her with a wave and a smile, bowed like a diplomat waiting for an appointment.

They came in ones and twos and sat shoulder to shoulder, the length of the counter, garrulous with tales of washed-out bridges, roofs blown off, and mighty trees across the road. They would drink five hundred cups of coffee before all the stories were told, and Snoot would overhear countless versions of the same tired statistics, weather theories, who-got-hit-worst, and, "Gawd-weren't-it-awful-up-to-my-place." Tot sat in the middle of it, poker-faced, carrot-topped, hoarding information, counting his money, never once looking Snoot's way.

Snoot listened to the noise and lifted his cup to each greeting, but he didn't join the fracas either. Instead, he kept watch out the window, drank his coffee, and waited.

He was surprised, as he waited, that no one told the story of the East Branch breach and the foot of silt on the Crooked Brook road. Hadn't anyone been by there yet? Or didn't they want to talk about it in Snoot's presence? He decided he appreciated the consideration—if that's what it was. It was a good crowd, always used him decent. Whatever it was, he was determined to sit on his stool by the window until someone walked in the door who looked as if he knew something about a hanging heifer.

Bud drove his Bronco into the parking lot around nine-thirty and bucked to a stop. When he got out—mud all over his shoes—he left the motor running and the dome light flashing.

Someone snickered. "Bud's come into some business this morning."

"Super trooper."

The few who bothered to look quickly dismissed the embarrassing spectacle of Police Chief Benoit on official duty.

"Dickless Tracy." Laughter, groans. Blue streaks blipped across the wall behind the counter.

Bud's grand entrance went wasted. His dramatic pause at the door—his fiddling with the knobs on his portable dispatch radio, his painfully tucked-in gut and deliberate strut to the far end of the counter—all went unrecognized except for Snoot, who leaned back on his stool to watch.

Bud appeared to notice no one; he seemed dedicated to the importance of looking important. First he was busy ordering something to go, then he was busy waiting for someone to ask him what was going on.

Snoot stared. Bud must have felt it; he fidgeted with his hat while Laurie fumbled with the lid on his coffee cup. Sweat glistened between the bristles of his close-cropped temples; his gut sagged out over his belt like an unwanted pregnancy.

Snoot followed him out to the Bronco. Bud might have sensed someone behind him, but he didn't turn to see who it was until he had his hand on the door.

"Busy?" Snoot asked. He stood close enough to inspect a dried yellow crescent of shaving cream beside Bud's ear.

Bud turned halfway around and stopped. His gaze glanced off the porch, to a parked car, to an unspecified view of something down the street. "Quite a storm," he said, swallowing. "Lot of cleanup going on."

"East Branch run some, didn't she?" Snoot moved his face closer to Bud's. He'd get to the business about Pomona later.

Bud studied the Texaco sign across the street. "Lot of water."

"Seems even a horse's ass would save some dirt to push around. Make pretty lawns and such. But I suppose the money ain't in dirt these days, is it?"

Bud flinched, still refusing to look at Snoot. "How're

you going to stop it from raining?" Now he was shaking his jowls at a puddle between his feet. "Hurricanes, they do a lot of damage."

Snoot felt another storm coming. "Hurricanes has hit that Christly mountain since Methuselah's goat was a kid! Never bothered that brook bed *once* and never would, if a bunch of Eye-talians hadn't tore it all to hell."

A tractor-trailer truck roared by close to the curb, splashing water on Bud's muddy shoes. He seemed not to notice. "It's approved by the state."

"Look at me," Snoot said, inches from Bud's nose.

Bud ignored him, tugged at his gun belt instead. "I said it's approved, and I got business to tend to."

He was turning to get in his car and drive away—with the blue light flashing for no goddamned reason at all—when Snoot grabbed his arm.

"Approved to look like Billy Ware's wet dream?" Snoot felt the sting of adrenaline rising and couldn't stop—didn't *want* to stop. "Flush good growing dirt off the mountain?"

Bud opened the door.

"How come you won't look at me, Buddy Benoy?" Snoot yanked Bud's arm off the door handle and spun him around. "I'm asking you something, hangman!"

Bud went limp in Snoot's grip. He looked confused, like a man uncertain of where he was—or who he was. The pink drained away from his ears. The tough cop part of him had dissolved; the little boy sagged and surrendered. Then, as quickly as he'd faded, he recovered—almost.

"I don't know what you're talking about."

Snoot whispered, "You sonofabitch." He squeezed Bud's arms like rotten fruit, lifted him off his feet, and shoved him into the Bronco. "You'd best be going, Buddy boy, before I wrap a rope around *you.*" He slammed the door on Bud's ankle, opened it, and dumped the limp foot inside, then slammed the door again.

Bud drove off, weaving down the street.

Snoot looked up at the store window, at the shocked expressions on a dozen faces. No smiles this time, no toothbrush tales. They could think what they wanted. And mind their own business. Snoot turned and splashed through a deep puddle, headed home.

It went a long way back, and it still hurt. It went back to the hulk of a boy in a one-room schoolhouse, to the clown, the dunce—*Hose Nose, stinky Wendell Audette*—one, two, then three years behind his grade: a head taller than everyone else, including Miss Simpson, teased by the girls and, every day, humiliated by Buddy B, baffled by spelling and long division while Buddy filled his desk with gold stars and Linda Ackerly let him take her behind the outhouse after school, put his hands up her petticoats, and stroke her pussy.

It went back to the day Snoot climbed out the schoolhouse window while everyone watched, cut home through the sunny April woods, and told his mother he was through with it; he wanted to work. He'd run away to Canada if she ever made him sit useless through another day locked up in a hateful classroom, the butt of Buddy B's jokes. It hurt.

His father lay on the tattered davenport and nodded his approval. "He's man enough." His father's cough, the shredded lungs, the smoke rings hovering over the chain-smoked Luckies. "We need the—*hccchh, hccchh, hccchh*—the wages." It went back to the hurting sound of his father's dying voice.

And it went back to cold and being poor. His first week's paycheck went to buy his father's funeral. Bud was off somewhere with his mommy and daddy on Lake Champlain, while Snoot shoveled dirt on the cheap brown casket. It rained that day, and as the dirt turned to mud, and the clouds scowled black, Snoot fought off a picture of Bud in white sneakers, driving a speedboat full tilt, skimming over sparkling water with his hand barely touching the throttle.

It went back to the first jobs working sixty-hour weeks in the winter woods, thirty-five below, fifteen years old and running a double team of oxen, earning enough to finally buy a secondhand truck, while Bud flitted through high school and a year of college up in Burlington, working summers at a soda fountain, dishwater turning his fingers white as a girl's.

217

And it never stopped hurting. On Bud's first day as the Dalton Pond cop, he stopped Snoot for driving an overloaded truck. It was loaded the same as every other truck that came down off the mountain that year, but it was Snoot's. Bud wanted fifty dollars cash, wrote fancy words on his policeman's pad, made a show of his shiny uniform next to Snoot's greasy wool baggies. "Better smarten up, Hose Nose." Say that again? *"Hose Nose."* Snoot's fist was in Bud's face as quick as a bobcat's paw, cold-cocked him, so he took off and hid out over the Q'bec line. He spent two weeks in the House when he came back, but it was worth it. Bud's nose still black and blue in the courtroom, playing on the judge's sympathy.

And worse: harassment, hassles, chickenshit offenses, day-late inspections, misspelled registrations, burnt-out turn signal bulbs—Bud rode him ragged every chance he got.

And Snoot got back every chance he got: drilled holes in the bottom of Bud's bass boat, flattened his tires at night, mixed sugar in his lawn-mower gas—but it was never quite the same, and nowhere near enough.

It went way back, and it never quit. As Bud's belly grew bigger year by year, so did Snoot's file in Montpelier, until it was finally stuffed with enough of Bud's trumped-up complaints and court indictments to take Snoot off the road for good.

Snoot walked eastward, homeward into the rising sun. It would be a good day, a drying-out day, and at last the fight with Bud was finally private—no rules, no files, no judges and jails, just one on one. Snoot liked it that way. How could Bud complain about Ruby Redd's story or the door slammed on his ankle? He was probably grateful to think he'd settled up so quickly for Pomona, traded even, and nobody the wiser. How could Bud complain about much of anything from now on? The tide had turned; sure, it went way back, but from now on Snoot had the feeling it was going to go his way.

14

GOING OVER, COMING BACK

IT WAS Monday morning, two days after the hurricane. Claire had just finished giving Doodlebug a bath when she was called to the nurses' desk telephone; it was Mrs. Thibodeau, from the Home. Her voice sounded hesitant and pinched. She was sorry to be the one to deliver the news. Claire knew what was coming: Frouncy had died in her sleep.

Claire heard the words she'd been prepared to hear for weeks, but they refused to coalesce into meaning. She'd rehearsed her response, done a part of her grieving, and adjusted to the inevitable conclusion of Frouncy's fragile course, but she hadn't imagined it would feel so irrevocable when, finally, it came. "In her sleep?" Her question was one of the many little redundant confirmations required to seal the truth to unwanted circumstance.

"She went over peaceful," Mrs. Thibodeau said. "I thought I should call you first."

"Yes. Thank you," Claire answered. She looked at her watch. Where was Snoot?

Mrs. Thibodeau echoed her thoughts. "You'll tell him?"

"I'll tell him," Claire said. He would be finishing up at his woodpile.

"Before he gets here, if you can. They're sending her over to Quig's any minute now. You know Snoot. . . ."

Claire began to dial Walker's office, but then she remembered he'd gone to White River for the day to take depositions for one of his clients. She hung up the phone wishing she'd spent more time with Frouncy the night before. Now it was time to find Snoot. She knew exactly what she had to do, but her mind seemed to work in slow motion.

First, tell Jody what had happened and ask Jody to cover for her.

Next, get in the car and drive home to Quinntown. Snoot shouldn't be alone if he hears the news elsewhere.

She drove. Arrangements were already being made; Frouncy's body would be taken to Quig Brady's mortuary, to remain there pending further instructions from the family. Dear Frouncy. She drove faster. She thought of Junior at Creamery Curve, wondered if he'd allow himself to feel his mother's passing or push it away as he'd learned to do with everything else that threatened to touch his heart.

She was half a mile west of the auction barn when she spotted Snoot walking toward her along the side of the road. Claire knew his schedule; he'd been splitting firewood since dawn, and now he was on his daily two-mile stroll into town, perfectly timed for the coffee-and-gossip ritual at Tot's, followed by his visit with Frouncy, ever hopeful.

He saw her approaching and raised both hands to shoulder height, greeting her, squeezing invisible oranges in the air. She waved and pulled into a barway, dreading what had to follow.

He bent down at her open window, unwitting widower, happy as ever to see her, grinning a yard wide. Snoot was born with two extra pairs of molars, top and bottom, and they gave his smile an added dimension Claire had always found appealing. But how could she smile back today? Feeling duplicitous, she tried anyway. "Hi, Snoot."

"Skipping work again?" he teased. "I should judge you picked a perfect day for it, and no shame taking the rest of the week off, too."

"Snoot—" How did she begin?

220

He saw it. The smile melted. "What?" He knew. "What's going on?"

"It's Frouncy." Claire reached out the window and touched his chest, felt the tip of his beard on the back of her hand, nodding recognition.

"Last night," he mumbled.

"In her sleep," Claire whispered. "Peacefully."

"Figures," Snoot said, standing up, looking behind him. "She woke me up, going over." He bent back down to the car window and worked his mouth into painful shapes. "That's what it was. I didn't want to believe it." He stood up again, slowly. Now his suspender belt clips were level with Claire's face. "Frouncy, going over." He turned and walked across the field, into the woods.

Snoot didn't come home that night. Walker worried about him, but Claire insisted he'd be all right; he'd be back when he was ready.

Lying in bed in the dark, Walker talked about Frouncy; she'd been the one true wizard in his life. "She made me feel like I could do anything I wanted to, and at the same time I knew she wouldn't be disappointed if I did absolutely nothing. She made me feel good about myself—in a way my mother never did. Funny, but as I think back on it, I can't remember a thing she said, specifically. She just gave me room to be me, for better or for worse. And she was right; after all, what more can anyone be than themselves?"

Claire said she knew what he meant; she'd felt the same liberating permission from Frouncy too, but as Walker spoke, lying next to her, warm and reassuring, Claire wondered where Junior had come from. What mischievous conspiracy of genes had thrown them together as mother and son?

She went to sleep dreaming of Frouncy alive and whole, of Frouncy enjoying herself, as she always had; the dream ended with a sense of peaceful resolution, with Frouncy floating down a river, waving, white geese in her hair.

Late in the night, Claire dreamed Walker was in pain. The dream was so vivid, she awoke—to the dream made real.

221

Walker was curled inward beside her, restless and sobbing. She gathered him in, stroked his hair, felt the dampness on his cheek. She held him like that for hours, a mutual vigil for Frouncy, Claire, and the only man she'd ever known with strength enough to weep for someone he loved.

Two days passed, then a third, and still no Snoot. Walker wanted to go look for him. Where, he wasn't sure. Claire pleaded patience. Snoot needed time. Frouncy's funeral service could wait. Frouncy wouldn't mind. And besides, Claire needed time to reconstruct a picture of life without her.

Punka Hurley called Claire at the hospital on the fourth day. He said he'd been fishing, up at the cascades on Little Squaw Mountain, and surprised Snoot at one of Great Dominion's abandoned logging camps; Snoot was holed up in the cookshack tending a smoky stove; there was a deer hide tacked to the door. "Yeah, he looked okay. A little bug-bit and sooty," Punka said, "and he weren't none too happy to see me, either. Said she snared the deer with barbed wire."

Snoot came home to Quinntown during supper on the seventh night, filthy and gaunt, but there was a lightness to him as he paced around the kitchen, a friendly familiarity, as if he'd been gone since lunch.

Walker set a place for him at the table. Snoot sat down gratefully. "Had room to think in the woods," he said, "and I can tell you this, no ifs, ands, or buts: Frounce was the best big-bosomed redheaded woman ever put on God's green earth"—he spoke to the ceiling—"and that's the truth of it. She's on the other side, now"—he pointed his charcoaled fingers out the window—"but she's free of all her troubles. She can be her own self again, altogether better." He nodded his head matter-of-factly, agreeing with himself. "Won't be long, I might be going over myself."

Claire stood behind him, picking pieces of ferns and bark out of his tangled hair. "You'll have to bathe before they let you in."

"Took care of that last year," he parried. "Besides

which, Frounce wouldn't know me, clean." Snoot was glad to be home; whatever he'd resolved during his week alone had been good for him. "I'm too mean to die, anyways," he added. The tribute to Frouncy was over. "Right now, I've got to have a glass of milk."

After supper they lingered at the kitchen table, and Snoot began to discuss what he wanted for Frouncy's funeral: no preacher and no Bible talk—he had a thorough list. He wanted a brief memorial service, and he wanted Vernon Hall, a retired farmer, to conduct it. Vernon was Frouncy's distant cousin, a man of great economy in all things, especially in the expenditure of words; he wouldn't ramble, and he wouldn't carry on in tones like some of those damn fools did every time they got within ten feet of a pulpit. Snoot wanted no reception at the end of the service, and he wanted Claire to find him a suit, a gesture to Walker, perhaps, who now wore a coat and tie to work every day. Snoot also said he wanted Frouncy to be cremated.

"By and by, they'll take and develop the cemeteries too, build on top of the graves." He insisted that her ashes be delivered directly to him. No one argued. He'd spent the week roaming the woods to figure it all out and find a place where she'd be safe and happy, and he was ready to see her home.

Claire made arrangements for a Thursday night service. Most of her time in the remaining few days was spent on Snoot's clothes. She finally found a size 56 houndstooth-check wool suit in a thrift store in Jordan and spent an evening sewing on buttons and letting out cuffs.

Snoot complained anyway. "Makes me itch worse'n the crabs," he groused, scratching at his crotch. "Necktie gives me the gas." But Claire knew better; she caught him looking at himself in the mirror over his shoulder, shooting his cuffs like a riverboat gambler. She cut his hair, trimmed his beard, and shamed him into using the bathtub, but finding him proper shoes was impossible—no one carried size fourteen, triple-E—

so he wore his better pair of logging boots, polished for the first time ever and tied with new black laces.

The service began at seven sharp in the chilly white Congregational church. Claire sat in the front pew, wedged between Walker and Snoot, her men, her family, each adding to the strength she must have to accept Frouncy's final absence without self-pity. There was still family enough; they would go on. After the service, Claire would realize she never once thought to turn around and look for Junior.

Shoes scraped the floor. Whispers. Coughs. Behind them, a hundred people sat upright on hard, pine benches, waiting for Vernon Hall to begin. The room grew quiet. Claire touched Snoot's hand.

"Most of us in this room have been tending land since we were old enough to hold a hoe." Vernon spoke without notes; a black and white ribbon of mourning was tied around the sleeve of his white dress shirt, above the elbow of his left arm. "And we can be proud of it, too. Because we're fortunate. There's no work anywhere in the world puts us so close to where we come from—or to where we're going. Oh, you can thank your storekeepers and bankers and doctors and soldiers for all that they may do for you, but not one of those occupations can compare with what it means to work with your hands and heart in the soil, planting in the season of promise, growing in the season of strength, harvesting in the season of preparation, and resting in the season of reward."

Vernon paused and rested his ice-blue eyes on Snoot, then glanced quickly on Claire and Walker, nodding his respects.

"Our friend—our loved one—Frouncy has earned her season of reward. God bless her. Every grain of God's green earth she ever touched was left the better for it. You've seen it, so have I. She tended life in all she did, planting and growing and harvesting the seeds of hard work, humor, honesty— she knew about the things that keep us next to nature. Where we belong. She knew that we were meant to be custodians of nature's bounty, put on earth to husband nature's needs as well as to profit from her generosity."

Claire looked up at the high white ceiling, to images of garlands, faded ribbons commemorating Frouncy's Grange Hall achievements with fruits and flowers, vegetables and antique breeds of poultry, lambs and rams and Hampshire sows, proud rows of blue and red citations draped from the window casings in Frouncy's room above a mosaic of photographs— her family, long-gone barns and oxen, windrows of new-mown hay on rounded hillsides, blossoming orchards sepiaed with age, patterns of Frouncy's life with Snoot on Crooked Mountain—her witnesses.

Vernon continued. "We have something to learn by Frouncy's example, and remember how she met seasons of good times *and* adversity without a moment's hesitation. The droughts and floods and abundances of her life were all parts of the eternal cycle."

The pine pew creaked as Snoot shifted and muttered. "I promised Frounce I'd never let anyone cut a stick of her hemlock woods." He folded Claire's fingers into the warm loaves of his hands.

Vernon looked as if he'd heard Snoot. "Frouncy never broke a promise in her life."

Claire felt Snoot wince.

Vernon added: "And she was the most forgiving woman I ever knew. She was forgiveness itself."

Claire squeezed Snoot's hand as she recalled Frouncy's defense of the old-growth hemlock. Whenever money was scarce, which was often enough, the topic would emerge. As saw logs, the trees were worth more than Snoot earned in a year. He'd chopped down many a woodlot for a fraction of what his own would yield, but Frouncy insisted—and he always agreed, despite the temptation—that the grove below the Ledges was too old, too precious, too much a part of their lives to be traded for money. "What would Horton's grampa think?" Frouncy would ask. "Him and all those Indian ha'nts up there without a patch of shade?"

Vernon finished quickly. "Our obligation and our privilege to pay tribute to Frouncy won't stop when we leave this

225

place tonight. Myself, I plan to set out six new sugar maple trees in Frouncy's memory, dig down deep into the soil and spread their roots out wide. I intend to fertilize and mulch and prune and care for them as long as I live, and every time I look at them, every time I see their buds in the spring of the year, their blaze of glory in the fall, when I see their branches spreading out to the sun, their trunks growing stout and strong—I'll remember Frouncy. And I'll be," Vernon's face twisted, "the richest man in the world."

There was a murmur of amens, and Claire felt the weight of love for Frouncy pressing forward from the crowded seats behind her. There was no neat finality here, none of the abstract churchy reassurances she'd heard too often but never trusted. Instead there was an awkwardness: a shuffling, rustling surge of life continuing to search and feel for workable answers—exactly what Frouncy Audette had done all her life.

"If anyone needs a ride up to Catamount . . ." Vernon said.

Claire felt Walker's warmth beside her, felt secure and unafraid. It was over, but it wasn't; it would never be, none of it, and that was the comforting part.

Vernon thumped Snoot twice across the shoulders, hugged Claire, and then got busy, his features still wrenched. "Bernard, you'll get the lights and set the thermostat back?"

Claire stood and turned to face the back of the room; half the town was there, it seemed, and not one had ever carried a grudge against Frouncy. The Hurleys, Judds, Harley Blue's family—three generations—the Thorntons, Pringles, Worthingtons, even Darby Dunbar in a brown plaid suit. They shuffled and stretched, fumbled with coats, polished eyeglasses, and made awkward bits of sad conversation. Lillian Woodard craned her neck and smiled, patting at the bulb of her perfect white bun. Tot and Laurie nodded from the back row and ducked out the door, as if embarrassed to be seen caring.

Walker pawed at his cheeks with the cuff of his coat. Snoot shook himself, as if emerging from a long hibernation, then took Claire in his arms, great woolly-mastodon bones draped over her until she felt she'd all but vanished. On tiptoes now, she found her head was buried below the ragged outcrop of his beard. He smelled like an attic, like an old opened chest of drawers, like the history of hard work and scrimping. Her hands navigated the wide circumference of his back, pressing promises, reassurances of life against death.

A few approached Snoot and offered variations on the ever-inadequate "Sorry" and "She's better off, now." Snoot accepted it all without comment, clutching Claire's arm, eager to be out the door and into twilight, into air.

"She made the best darn pickles."

Some mentioned the project. "Pouring concrete, are they?"

"Never seen so many damn trucks up that-a-way."

Claire felt Snoot flinch when Darby said, "Lucky Frounce never saw what they done to her woods."

They went home from the service in Walker's car. At the curve past the gravel pit, Claire saw a line of cars, stopped in the eastbound lane ahead of them. Around the corner, out of sight, something must have been blocking the road.

"I wonder what?" Walker said, as he pulled to a stop behind a pickup truck.

"Flatlanders," Snoot grumbled, disinterested. "Maybe moose."

"I'll run up and see," Claire offered. It was a short walk to the curve.

"Be careful," Walker called after her.

Claire hurried along the shoulder of the road past bumper-to-bumper cars and trucks, all a blur to her, all anonymous metal and rubber; she'd never been able to tell one from another.

She stopped at the curve and stood with a group of people, watching; a big maple lay across the road, roots torn from the soil next to the roadside fence. Men had come from their pickup trucks with axes, lopping off branches, joking, a willing atmosphere. Now a chain saw started: noise, blue smoke, a limb fell, another, more helpers, a pile of wood grew at the side of the road. A few minutes more, and the work would be done.

Claire walked back to the car along the yellow center-line, head down past the waiting vehicles, thinking of Frouncy. Frouncy would have been up there clearing the branches from the road herself, teasing the men about their inadequate wood-cutting skills, borrowing somebody's ax, heaving to. *Dear Francine. . . .*

For reasons she would never be able to piece together, Claire looked up from her walking reverie at the exact moment she reached Junior's van.

Loretta was behind the wheel, staring at her, pupils dilated out to the edges of her pale green eyes. Junior sat beside her, in a cowboy hat, watching—no, transfixed—a stranger behind mirrored sunglasses. Claire felt no connection to the past between them.

Stoned, Claire decided. She nodded, and they nodded back, in unison, like wooden puppets. Out of their gourds. A quick glimpse into the overloaded back of the van told Claire the rumors were true: they were leaving town, bound for California. Tot bought out Junior's share—at a discount, no doubt—and now the money would see them to Los Angeles, where they would live, and quarrel, and hurt one another until the money was gone. And then what? What was there to say, "Have a nice life"?

Junior suddenly leaned over and pulled himself to the driver's window, his face a mask, his shoulders crushing Loretta to the back of her seat.

"Saw you at the funeral." A calm voice, slurred.

"Oh." So he was there, she thought, surprised. Good. At least he felt something for someone. "Guess I missed you."

"We're headed," he said. "Sick of this place."

Claire nodded and noticed he had lost a front tooth. She said nothing, felt less than nothing, no response to a man she'd spent ten years with.

"There's one thing," Junior continued in a monotone. Loretta tried to push him away from her, but he ignored her.

"It's not because you won, okay? You see what I mean? I'm leaving because I *want* to, not because I'm running. You understand?"

"Sure," Claire said, watching Loretta squirm under Junior's weight. "I understand." Then she heard Walker's voice behind her.

"Understand what?" he asked, his arm around her like a shield. "What's going on?" He must have seen the van and hurried to it when he saw her stopped in the road.

Now Junior's voice had an edge to it. "We're headed," he said, "but not because you won. Remember that."

Claire felt Walker's muscles tense, pulling her away from the van, back to the car. She was glad to go. When she looked back, Junior was leaning out the window, calling after them.

"You didn't win nothing. It wasn't like that. Nobody won, okay?"

Walker hugged her to him and they quickened their pace, leaving the tired voice behind.

"The hell we didn't." Walker laughed, lifting her off her feet. "We won it all."

Claire found herself watching Snoot carefully for the next few days, more curious than concerned. He seemed so accepting, so surprisingly calm. How did he make the transition work? How did someone shed a lifetime of companionship so easily? Would it be that easy for Walker and her?

One morning when Snoot was out at his woodpile, she opened the door to his room. There was a small cardboard box on an undisturbed pillow beside Snoot's rumpled blankets; a framed photograph leaned against it, Frouncy sitting in a fancy gig behind an Appaloosa pony. A pocketknife lay on top of the box, a Buck—Claire recognized the worn turquoise handle, the eagle insignia—the only gift Junior ever gave his father. She backed out of the room on tiptoe.

The first Sunday after the service, Walker left early for a day of trout fishing. Claire spent the morning in a wicker rocker on the screened porch with a book. The air was alive with lilac blossoms, songbird sounds, and thrumming insects—a perfect day. Claire dozed off after fifty pages, then awoke to the clockwork *thwack* of Snoot's splitting maul echoing into the hills.

She was making sandwiches when Snoot came into the kitchen at noon.

"Good day for it," he said, and went into his room. When he emerged a few minutes later, he was dressed in the same clothes he wore to Frouncy's service—minus the necktie—and he was carrying the cardboard box.

There was an awkward standoff at the table; Claire thought he looked as if he wanted to speak, but couldn't. She didn't press; the silence spoke for itself. He stuffed a sandwich in his coat pocket and waved to indicate he was leaving. She hugged him. He patted the box and walked across the road into the woods, up the long north slope of the Catamount Heights in his size 56 Sunday suit.

Around two that afternoon, Claire left her book and went into the kitchen to make a cup of coffee. For the past two hours, she'd been thinking more about the mystery of Snoot than the mystery novel she was reading. Despite his rumpled, shambling appearance, Snoot was oddly methodical and meticulous about certain things. She'd seen that side of him for years, in the way he repaired machinery, planted his star-shaped gardens, and arranged his woodpiles, every log lined up in perfect order. And now he was organizing the part of his life that had to do with Frouncy. In the two weeks since her death, he'd arranged each day around the task of seeing Frouncy off, almost as though he needed it done with, neat and clean, in order to make way for yet another chapter in his life.

Claire took the kettle off the stove and poured coffee into a blue and white cup. She stirred in a teaspoon of sugar and looked out the window, across the road, up at the mountainside harboring Snoot—and Frouncy.

Claire's reverie stopped when she noticed a dusty blue

sedan parked in the driveway next to her Subaru, where Walker usually parked. It was a Cadillac with Maine license plates, no one in it—maybe somebody lost. All kinds of strangers stopped by since they'd moved near the road: traveling salesmen, Watchtower missionaries—it could be anyone—but how long had they been there, and why hadn't she noticed before?

Claire crossed the room to the door and looked at her watch: Walker could be back at dark or, if he'd caught his limit, any time now. She sipped her coffee and straightened a picture frame on the wall beside the window, listening for footsteps on the porch; not a sound. She looked out the window again. The car was empty, and there was no one on the flagstone walk, no one anywhere in sight.

A tingle ran down between her shoulders, but she ignored it, opened the door, and stepped out onto a vacant porch. The sun was high and hot, and the mosquitoes were hungry. There was no place between the back of the cars and the edge of the road for a person to hide, no trees, no bushes—and no reason to hide.

"Hello?" she asked. A blue jay screeched back at her from the big box elder tree by the woodpile. "Can I help you?" she asked, louder. The bird flew to the top of an oak by the road. She walked to the driveway and circled her Subaru, then the Cadillac, and felt foolish. What would she do if she caught someone hiding behind a car?

She walked across the lawn to look around the corner of the house. But why would anyone go back there? No path, no stepping stones, no indication of any other entrance to the house but the flagstone walk to the porch—and the open front door. Mosquitoes were getting in the house. Her sleeveless blouse was no protection against the bugs; she crossed her bare arms, cupped each elbow in the opposite palm, and rubbed herself as she walked up onto the porch. Enough of this. She was bitten and slightly annoyed at Walker for not being home. The Cadillac could have been there for hours without her noticing it, she supposed. It could belong to a friend of Walker's, a client maybe, someone he went fishing with, someone he forgot to mention when he left this morning. She closed the door behind her, wondering where she'd left her coffee cup.

He is sitting still as stone, symmetrical, small, and straight-backed, in a chair against the far wall of the kitchen. His elegant brown hands lie opened upward in his lap. A thick mantle of snowy hair is parted in the middle and pulled back behind his head; his angular cheekbones seem to squeeze firelight from the anthracite depths of his eyes. He stares at her, and she is unafraid. There is only one person in the world she would have him be, and although she has always pictured him younger, larger, and darker, she knows at once he is her father.

"Daddy?" Her voice filled the room, although it was only a whisper. "It's you?"

He nodded and closed his eyes, hiding the light.

"Your car. . . ." How funny: her father, the shaman's grandson, wielder of magic, driving a Cadillac.

He nodded again and got up from his chair. She noticed his palms were still opened forward, as if they were sensors, supplementing what his eyes and ears already knew. He took a few steps toward her and stopped, offering himself, making no demands.

So old and smooth and small, she thought. He's spent his life. Away. She crossed the room and put her arms around him, pulled him to her: stranger, father, myth, all of those, but bone and blood and sinew too—an impossible combination, three decades of an abstract, ethereal figure made suddenly physical.

It seemed so odd: his body was small compared to Walker's, tiny next to Snoot's. Weren't daddies the biggest and strongest of all? She realized she had never held a man like this, other than Snoot or a lover. A father embracing a daughter—a man embracing a woman—she had never thought about the differences or similarities. The embrace was physically the same, but the feeling was meant to be different—wasn't it?

She closed her eyes and felt his heartbeat on her chest. She breathed in his aroma, night scent from the woods on Crooked Mountain. A father should be . . . she had no choice. A father was . . . she gave it up. A father was . . . what a father was. She held him closer, and the embrace took on a meaning of its own.

When they released each other and stood at arm's length—absorbing, reciprocal, knowing, timid, bold—she imagined herself a newborn in his trust, and she was frightened.

"I've always wondered," she ventured. "I've got a photo, but that's all I had to go on. . . ."

He looked as if unbearable pain prevented him from speaking.

"Please sit down, please," she said. "I was just having coffee. I'll make you some too. Do you want some cookies to go with it? Here, take this chair, it's comfortable, Daddy."

Daddy.

She wanted them to renew themselves in each other immediately, but it wasn't easy; Horton was consistently tongue-tied, whether from shyness or habit she didn't know, but she quickly found the best way to communicate with him was to ask questions he could answer with a nod: yes or no.

"Are you still living in Maine?"

Yes. Or was it no?

It wasn't clear. Try another question. "Still in the blasting business?"

Yes. Or maybe.

"Retired?" Was he married?

Yes. Or maybe no.

"Can you stay with us? We've got room. You can stay as long as you like. I'd love for us to catch up, for you to get to know Walker." She'd explain everything. "And you must have known Snoot? He lives with us too."

For the first time, Horton unfolded a trace of a smile.

Claire continued. "I was married to Snoot's son, Junior?

He's a vet, handicapped. Vietnam. Anyway, Snoot and Frouncy gave him the farm on Crooked Mountain."

Horton nodded.

"Then he sold the place, and I—we got divorced, and—" Claire decided she owed no one, not even her father, an explanation of what had happened to her marriage. "And my old boyfriend from years ago, Walker Owen; he came along." She heard herself laugh, a plea for approval, tossing her opened hands to the room. "And here we are."

Horton seemed to approve.

Claire locked her fingers together. "Except Frouncy just died." It almost seemed like a trade: Frouncy passing over, Horton coming back. "And they've bulldozed the hemlock woods all the way to the Ledges."

The light in Horton's eyes flickered. He turned away from Claire and walked to the window, looked out at the incongruous Cadillac, then up to the swelling slopes of the Catamount Heights.

Watching him, she imagined she saw the mountain through a transparency of his body, the same insistent pulse of life connecting him to rocks and trees and everything that lived among them. His hair hung halfway down his back; he stood motionless, her father, merged into the rocks and trees beyond.

"I'm sorry," she finally said, and for the first time since the Ledges Lodge development began, she realized how truly sorry she was. The sale of the farm and the stripping of land had been upsetting, but Franny was dying and land got sold and houses got built every day of the year. It wasn't unnatural. Trees would grow back. Snoot was a logger, wasn't he? The brook would heal. People had to have a place to live; tradesmen and carpenters had to have jobs.

Horton's silence was provocative, forcing her to say exactly what needed to be said for both of them.

"Walker tried to stop it." Now it was more complicated than ever.

Horton turned to her, curious.

"But it was . . . you know. Walker wants to go on with

it." She felt guilty for having discouraged him. "Aunt Franny's sick, and her husband. . . . Did you know Billy Ware?" It wasn't the right time to go into all of that. "Mom still lives in Dalton, still married to Tot. Mom's okay, a little thin, maybe. You want some sugar in your coffee?"

Over the course of an hour, Claire coaxed few words out of her father, but she learned he'd been in Vermont for a couple of weeks, that he was planning to stay "a little," but it was unclear where he was staying or how he was spending his time, except "in the woods." He indicated he would like to come back for a longer visit and meet Walker, but she couldn't pin him down to a date. Then Walker burst into the room with a creel full of trout and a face full of questions.

"Walker! This is Daddy, this is Horton Flint," Claire said, pulling her father across the room. "And this is Walker, Daddy. Walker Owen." She nodded her head to wish it all perfect and added, "He's a lawyer."

"I'm glad to meet you," Walker said, looking stunned. "I've always heard . . ."

Horton looked astonished—and pleased, Claire thought—the way she wanted him to feel. She needed it to work both ways, all ways; she wanted a loving mother and father, and sisters and brothers, too; she wanted, at last, to be crushed by her own true, enormously loving family.

Horton stepped forward and pressed Walker's hands between his own. He held them as though he were encoding them with secrets too precious to be spilled into the random casualties of spoken words. To Claire, it seemed he was approving her through Walker and vice versa. She held her breath, unable to swallow past the pressure of her heart against her throat. Then the umbilicus between the two men slowly parted, and the need for wishing fell away. Horton nodded to Walker, and Walker grinned back, glistening bright with consecration. Claire exhaled, past empty, drained. It was done: the father, the lover, and she were in the same room.

• • •

They sat at the table: Claire next to Walker, across from her father. She studied him with the same intensity she'd studied herself in a mirror, looking for and finding herself in his bones and teeth and hair. Certain expressions—the tilt of his head when he listened, the way he lifted his hands in search of a word—were undeniably an imitation of her; but of course it was quite the opposite.

He remembered it all, he said, as if he'd never left. He came back to "prepare himself." He wanted to be near the Tooth of the Earth where "Grandfather was born." Bud, Tot and Laurie, and his past in Dalton Pond were "nothing. There is another way," he said, and he had come back to follow it. Then, as quickly as he'd appeared, he was gone.

When Snoot returned late that afternoon, he called Claire and Walker out to his woodpile. "I'm back in the business," he said, cheerfully. "Frounce and me, we had a little powwow up on the Heights." He raised an arm to the horizon. "There's a cliff up there, topped off by a big bull pine. That's where I buried Junior's Buck. You can look right down on my chop block, here, or gaze off every which way on the compass. Dandy prospect. Sun all day. Breeze comes up through the balsams sweet as candy." Snoot's nostrils flared. "See that dip and the pointy pine tree to the right of that cloud that looks like a three-legged hedgehog?" His finger waved a circle around the distant mountaintop. "That's where the spring is. Cold clear water from a white quartz vein. Ginseng up there, ginger root too. Deer signs all over." He grinned. "And that's where Frounce is now."

Later, as Snoot listened to Claire's account of Horton's visit, his sly-fox grin grew huge. "Mister clean-jump Jesus!" He was delighted. "They've had the radish now." Claire asked what he meant, but he wouldn't say. The more he heard, the more he nodded and paced the room, grinning. "Mister Jesus, Joseph and Mary, Katie bar the door!"

15

LOVE A DUCK

It rained most of June; the lawn seemed to need mowing every other day, and the basement smelled like mildew. The bugs were ferocious. Weeds thrived in the gardens, Walker's car needed fixing, and trout were rising in his absence—big ones, he was sure—waiting for him in sun-dappled pools. He was busier than he'd ever been in Connecticut, too much to do and not enough time, a growing list of clients at his new office, and two nights a week volunteered to help draft a zoning ordinance for Quinntown. He took all this as a good sign, as living fully in the place he loved, but he missed Frouncy, even as she had been at the end.

Snoot convinced him to take an extra day off for the Fourth of July holiday weekend. "You've been bulling and jamming seven days a week, mister boy. Time you did some walking around in the woods with Uncle Snoot."

"You haven't been around much lately yourself," Walker said.

Snoot brushed off the accusation. "Besides, I want to show you something."

Walker was happy to take the extra day off. They left after breakfast, hiked up the road to Fellows's, then up and over the ridge behind the auction barn. Down in the sag on the other side, they followed the brook from Mudchub Pond due west, until it merged with Crooked Brook. A few hundred yards down Crooked Brook, Snoot swung north, up a steep trail that brought them out at the top of the Ledges. He'd built a crude stone bunker between two huge boulders at the edge of the cliff. It was there, he explained, that he'd been spending his time, watching the work below.

"Why?" Walker asked. "Why watch the bastards?"

"Reasons, that's why." Snoot crouched behind the wall and motioned Walker to join him at the peek holes between the rocks.

"Why torture yourself?"

"It ain't all torture anymore," Snoot said. "You wait and see for yourself."

Below, the site was humming with workmen and machinery, stacked with materials, raucous with sound. Mud was everywhere; some of it, beyond the building site, was tinted with the first signs of recovery, green patches on the coffee-colored crust.

At the base of the Ledges, close enough to drop a rock on, the foundation walls of the Lodge imitated a miniature grid of city blocks. The middle of its south side thrust out to the view like the bow of a ship; it was aimed at two Port-a-san toilets, yellow buoys on a wave of mud.

Walker looked down on the canopy of a bulldozer winching a ready-mix truck through the muck. The clumsy procession was aimed toward an earthen ramp at the southeast corner of the foundation, but first it had to wallow through one of the filled-in meanderings of Crooked Brook. Billy Ware's rationale was convincing; the old Crooked Brook was inconvenient. A ghostly dark discoloration was the only clue to its original route; its inefficient serpentines had been bulldozed in, smoothed over, disciplined by a big D-8. Now it ran string-straight through the property—muddy, raw, and wrong—cutting under the caved-in banks, sabotaging the arbitrary, making plans of its own.

"Jesus, Snoot, this is awful." Walker was glad he hadn't let Claire talk him out of pursuing Billy Ware. A suit was now pending, and it looked promising. Since Horton's appearance, even Claire was enthusiastic, despite what it might do to Franny.

Leaning closer into the peek hole, Walker searched for the place where the cabin had been but found no reference points to work from; all the landmarks were gone. The curve in the brook, the little falls, the trees, the old logging road—the land itself was gone. Ragazzo had revised geological history. How could Snoot sit there and watch such a pitiful substitute?

More noise rose from below. Cables tautened, and a duet of whining diesels in search of traction echoed up the steep stone cliffs. The wallowing ready-mix truck finally made it through the crossing and moved ahead to firm ground without the bulldozer's help; water flooded into the wide ruts left in its wake.

Snoot nudged Walker's arm and pointed to the concrete forms by the ramp. They were the tallest and most intricately braced of all the formwork on the site—maybe sixteen feet high from the footings to the top—empty receptacles about to be filled with tons of liquid concrete.

The ready-mix truck turned around and backed up to the top of the ramp, high enough for a gravity pour down into the forms. The driver had just finished assembling the chute when Walker noticed Snoot was watching the scene through a pair of military-surplus binoculars.

"Where'd you get those?" he asked. Snoot's big bulbous nose looked like a piece of overripe fruit between the shiny barrels. "You look like the Supreme Allied Commander."

Snoot ignored him.

"Where *did* you get them?" Walker asked again.

"Auction." Snoot pawed at him impatiently. "Now shhh!"

"Shhh yourself," Walker mimicked, as the first wave of concrete slid down the chute into the forms. "They'll never hear us over all that racket." Snoot was definitely losing it.

"Shhhhhh, goddammit!" Snoot repeated, eyes pressed deep into the binoculars. "This ought to be dick-dipped dandy."

The forms were almost full when the bottoms split

open. From the bunker on the Ledges, it looked like slow motion: concrete gushing out like a spreading stain of spilled oatmeal. The men by the truck gestured helplessly at the molten tide. Others ran over to watch the puddle swell. The drum on the ready-mix truck stopped turning. Engines were shut off, hammering stopped. When everything on the site had come to a halt, Snoot put down his glasses and sat back against a boulder.

"Slicker'n a trout," he allowed modestly. "This old woodchuck ain't beat yet."

"You?"

Snoot raised an eyebrow to a cautious pitch. "Helps even it out. . . ."

Walker'd remembered Snoot's speech about north-woods justice. "But, how did you—?"

Snoot looked at him, making up his mind, apparently, to tell the whole story. "Form ties. Keep the forms from spreading." Snoot stretched an imaginary rope between his hands. "Wicked pull on a form tie at the bottom of a pour. 'Specially on big tall pours like that one there." He waved at the formwork. "The whole shebang's held together with nothing but goddamned form ties."

"So?" Walker suspected he already knew the answer.

"So if a fella was to take a fine-tooth hacksaw and nibble three quarters through a dozen ties way down at the bottom next to the footing, see—"

Walker saw. "That's where you were last night?"

Snoot shrugged.

"You turkey."

"Fell in a ditch, too," he said, rubbing at a scrape on his hand. "Black-cat dark, she was, and that's the truth of it."

"Snoot. . . ." How to put it to this stubborn galoot? "Snoot, they'll bust your chops for good if they catch you."

"Haven't yet, though, have they? See that fella in the white hard hat? He's the foreman, big boss man, tells everybody what to do. Thinks he's smart." Snoot spat out over the bunker wall and waited for the sailing gob to drop a hundred feet to mud. "Shit stinks, smoke rises, payday's on Friday."

Walker laughed. "What?"

"That's about the limit to White Hat's smarts. Every afternoon, him and his sidekick—see that scrawny little puke in the green baseball jacket?—every day at quitting time, they wait around until everybody else has went home. 'Course they don't know I'm still here."

The green baseball jacket looked like the one Walker wore in high school. He squinted at the kid Snoot called a scrawny puke, looking for a hitchhiker, but at that angle and distance he couldn't be sure. "And?"

"How they load it on. White Hat's took home enough lumber and nails and ce-ment blocks in the back of his pickup to build a Hollywood whorehouse. Too busy thieving to notice his layout stakes has been moved, too greedy to notice his column pads don't line up straight. Main thing he's watching out for is a full load after quitting time. He's six moves behind me and still don't know he's even in the game."

Walker shook his head; he should have known Snoot was up to something. "What kind of a game are we talking about, Grizz?"

Snoot liked the bad boy role. "Dirty doings, like they deserve." Snoot the guerrilla. "Ragazzo's already three–four weeks behind . . ."

"Snoot, listen—"

". . . and more than a few dollars short since Uncle Snoot come on the job with his little bag of goodies."

"Snoot, look." Walker was about to plead for reason, patience, moderation, legal channels. "You can't—"

"Damn you!" Snoot grabbed Walker's arm. "Who says I can't!" A ring of white showed all the way around his irises. "Look what they done to my goddamned land!"

"I know, I know, but—"

It was true. What was Snoot's crime compared to what had happened to the land below? Was a deed to a piece of land a license to destroy it? The development never should have happened, but there were ways to stop it, and there were *ways.*

"You just can't do it like that." Claire would agree,

wouldn't she? "They'd love to catch you down there some night with a hacksaw."

Snoot sighed and drew his hand away. "Truth of it is, I had more in mind than a bitty old hacksaw. Maybe I shouldn't have brung you up here, but I was kind of hoping you'd help me."

Walker winced at the request. It was rare that Snoot asked for his help outright, and his answer could only be equivocal at best. "I'll help you, Snoot—but not like this. I can't."

A long silence passed. Snoot said nothing. Below, the noisy commotion of trucks and hammers resumed. Walker had a lump in his throat; he watched a raven soar above the Ledges in perfect unison with the wind. He wondered where it nested—if it had nested there on the Ledges before the ruination began—what the destruction meant to a bird. A shift in the wind swept the raven to the west. A hoarse croak: *Gaawwn.* Snoot waved the bird away, stood up, and walked toward the head of the trail. "Like somebody else I know," he muttered, "comes and goes as he goddamned well pleases."

Three long days passed before they spoke more than a few words to each other. Walker tried to engage Snoot but was rebuffed every time. There was no fun in the house, and Walker felt like a traitor, wished he could loosen up his notions of propriety. Then early on Saturday evening, Snoot broke the impasse with an invitation. "Tonight's Ruby Redd's last tango up to Daintytown."

"You going?" At least Snoot was talking.

"Maybe." Snoot looked slightly embarrassed. "Thought maybe I'd have a look-see," he said, and Walker could almost hear him begging Frouncy to forgive him.

"Long drive up there, is it?" Walker asked, looking for a topic to expand upon. Or did Snoot only want his blessings?

"You could come, if you wanted, I suppose."

"Me?" Walker felt a weight sliding away. "Maybe I will." Of course he would. "As long as I don't have to look at the girls," he deadpanned. "I'm too young for anything raunchy."

• • •

The Daintytown Follies Club was in a converted dairy barn on a lonely stretch of gravel road three miles south of the Canadian border. The night was July hot and humid, perfect for the corn that grew up to the edges of the parking lot, hot enough to make anyone want to take their clothes off. Walker wore a John Deere tractor cap; Snoot had a fifth of Black Velvet stowed away in his overalls. They'd come to put their friendship back together, to talk on the long drive up and back, and to see the notorious Ruby.

A half moon hung beyond the outline of a silo, a henhouse tilted out from one end of the barn. In the distance, Walker heard a coyote sing a warbled song. He followed Snoot to the door, where a fat man leaning on a crutch collected five dollars a head. Snoot insisted on paying. The chilly weather between them had finally thawed; Daintytown was Snoot's offering, his peace pipe—adolescent and awkward, perhaps, but eagerly accepted.

Inside, the barn opened up to a smoky, cavernous room. At one end was a bar; at the other end, four feet off the floor, was a stage. Snoot pointed to the curtained wall at the back of the platform. "That's where they change their outfits." He draped an arm around Walker. "This poor little Brandi's going on first. Course, her real name's Susan. I knowed her sister, Cloris, from way back when. She weren't no box of chocolates, neither. Worked at the bobbin mill down to the pond, tended a pup lathe till she up and took religion. Hitched up with the Bible thumpers, run off to South Amafrica, or some goddamned place full of jigaboos and snakes." Snoot pulled out his pocket watch and held it at arm's length, squinting. "Five minutes, you can see for yourself." He nudged Walker toward the stage. "Slip over there now, and we'll have us a place up front. Not too close, mind you. Old Brandi's rank enough to gag a maggot."

Walker did as he was told—anything to avoid breaking the spell—but he felt awkward and out of place, chagrined to think of himself as a horny gawker, a sexist pig, a dirty old man at thirty-five.

A hush fell over the men behind him as a needle found its groove and a scratchy record began to play. He guessed he was ready for Brandi, but he hadn't expected the overhead lights, the bare bulbs in rows on wires draped across the stage like winter vines. He understood the smoky room, the raucous knots of voices—nervous, like him—but he was surprised at the color of his hands as he held to the edge of the stage, at the unsettling brightness of cold blue flesh—his own and, soon, the dancer's.

The curtain parted and the music started and stopped as if by mistake, then started again with a scratch and a buzz. Brandi walked out under the lights, pigeon-toed in panties and pasties, still in conversation with someone behind the curtain. Then she turned and stared into the rafters, high above the audience, focusing on something far away. She nodded her head to the music and twitched her shoulders. The rhythm seemed to ripple along her spine and spread to her hips. She began to move, slightly off the beat. Thirty seconds into her act she tossed off what little she wore and dared every eye in the room not to look.

How odd it was, Walker thought, how bizarre to be watching a woman doing what she was doing. She was as skinny as a boy. Her arms and legs were sticks. Little bumps for breasts, pale fuzz between her legs, and not the slightest acknowledgment to artifice in her sad imitation of dancing.

The crowd was cheering. Someone yelled, "Put it back on!" They laughed, but Brandi's expression never changed. Walker rehearsed his apologies to Claire. "It was embarrassing," he would tell her later. "It was lonely, almost grotesque."

The crowd cheered louder, and Brandi started to dance faster, taunting, defiant, hitching to the record's rhythms, almost making the music work.

Snoot's elbow, then his sour-sweet breath. "Cloris don't look nothing like her. Big rack of horns and a nose like a pig." He burped. "I'm going to get me a gin-fizz toddy."

"I'll go with you."

"Like hell you will." Snoot was offended. "Have a good time, Tutti. Enjoy the show."

Walker watched Brandi dance a repetitious pattern from one corner of the stage to the other, back and forth, a box-step waltz. Her lips formed little words he couldn't hear. Now and then she frowned, the way he imagined Claire might if she'd forgotten something in the grocery store.

At the end of her act, Brandi lowered herself to the floor, lay on her back with her feet toward the crowd, and lifted her hips from the stage. The men whistled and cheered and clapped their hands as she imitated an unmistakable motion. Walker couldn't see her face, but she had a Band-Aid on her ankle and a rash—red bumps—along the inside of her thigh. The bare, hard light raked down on her without a trace of compassion. Walker looked up into the rafters and waited for the music to stop.

Snoot was back beside him, bathed in alcohol and sweat. Together, they watched Brandi edge her way back to the curtain and disappear with a stiff little wave, blowing baby kisses at the howling, cheering, jeering men.

"Little meat and potatoes wouldn't hurt her none." Snoot blew his nose into his palm and rubbed it on his pant leg.

"Some dancer," Walker said, nostalgic for the days when he and Snoot agreed on everything, when the terms of their friendship required no more than a sunny afternoon and a fence to mend.

Snoot snorted. "Next record comes on, and by the Jesus you're going to see what 'eye sweet's' all about."

Walker nodded and looked across the room, searching the faces waiting for Ruby's act to begin, searching for a clue to what constituted their kinship—with one another and, lately, with him. The old myth of the northwoods hero suffered in a place like this. Had he never seen the flaw so clearly before? Had it always been there? How close were they able to get to a woman, naked or otherwise, in a real conversation, nonobjectified? Were their wives and girlfriends waiting at home? Was it okay with them? Claire had seemed a little irked when he and Snoot left, said, "Have a good time, *boys.*" He couldn't blame her, but he'd had no time to explain Snoot's sudden invitation.

Cigar smoke hung in low blue clouds across the stage. Another record began, the curtain parted, and Ruby Redd appeared in a dazzling blue robe and red high-heeled shoes.

The men stomped and bellowed, the plywood stage quivered, the barn timbers shook with the tribute. Walker stared. It was true: she was still beautiful, a powdered, picture-book queen smiling down on her subjects. The tilt of her shoulders was playful, flirtatious. Waves of ruby-red hair shimmered about her head like imitation silk, topped with a bright rhinestone crown. She was big but graceful as a swan, and old enough, Walker guessed, to be Brandi's mother.

Ruby winked at her lovers and moved into the music, gluing her hips to the syrupy beat. Walker smiled.

Snoot pawed the stage, murmuring, "Jesus, God bless her!"

Ruby danced to the front of the stage, to within a few feet of Walker, and untied the robe at her waist. Rocking into the rhythm, she slid one end of the sash halfway out of its loops—then stopped and winked at Snoot as though he were a baby. The crowd howled, delirious. Snoot was a hero; his forehead glistened with pride.

The sash came off—in time—and the robe fell open—slightly. Little by little the tempo increased and Ruby made the fabric glide and swirl in flowing patterns designed to show and hide and show and hide exactly what she wanted her hobnailed worshipers to see, and not see—and think they saw—an artist at work.

Between outbursts of thunderous approval—when she pulled her robe up to her waist from behind, when she shimmied her glorious breasts in time to the rollicking beat—the barn was so quiet with watching and wonder that the music and tap of her backless shoes was the only sound left in the universe.

The tempo increased and every ounce of flesh and bone in the barn was hers, every fiber pulled taut as she drew their bodies into hers. She moved faster and faster now; she was snapping her red lacquered nails like a metronome, bruising the beat with every bounce of her body, pumping the room with her grace and her fire, pulsing with life—when she fell.

Walker gasped.

Snoot reached to her, groaning, his palms opened upward. Every man in the barn became her father, her widower, her orphan.

She had dropped to her knees, then fallen over backward with one leg twisted beneath her. Her robe slipped from her shoulders, lay strewn in a puddle beside her. One shoe stood empty, off on its own, pointed away from her foot; she lay perfectly still.

The lights glared, undaunted, and the music played on, calling her back to a crowd now gone silent, to cheers turned to vapor, to two hundred frozen grins broken in half.

A policeman jumped onto the platform and knelt down beside her, rearranging her robe. From somewhere far off, Brandi screamed. They carried Ruby offstage through the break in the curtains. Walker saw the rhinestone crown catch on the ragged folds. It clung to the coarse cloth long enough to pierce him with a sudden streak of silver light before it fell.

The road back to Dalton Pond came at them gently, rolling curves and dips and rises. It seemed they drove for miles without the glow of a farmhouse window, without the lights of a passing car. At the top of Little Squaw Mountain, Snoot broke the silence.

"Cat got your tongue?"

"I've been thinking." How would he put it? "About the fragile contract. Separating life from death. About a lot of stuff. . . ."

Snoot's voice was hoarse. "For instance, how could Ruby take and have a heart attack?"

Walker nodded. "And it made me think about you and the Lodge, what you're doing up there. Why."

Snoot sounded suspicious. "I know, I know. It don't set right with you and that's that, now that Tutti Frutti's read the law. Bygones is bygones—and now, here, Ruby's gone bygone too."

"I've changed my mind."

"What?"

"I want to help you."

"How?"

"Up on the mountain."

"Love a duck!"

"And I want to feel like we're doing it for Frouncy."

"Rest her."

"And Claire, whether she likes it or not."

"Mother Mary and Joseph!" Snoot bounced on the seat.

"And Ruby. In the spirit of survival. We'll do it together, however you say, reckless, rowdy, and right. Or wrong, I don't give a shit, but let's do it, before it's too late."

Now it was late on a Friday afternoon, close to quitting at the Ledges Lodge; Snoot and Walker were on the way to their third mission after Walker's Daintytown conversion.

Snoot rolled through the tangle of woods like a freight train; Walker had to trot to keep up. In the old days, they'd have stopped to talk about why lightning had chosen to strike a particular tree, stopped to examine the ground below an owl's nest, speculate on what they'd been eating by the leftover bones. In the old days, there was always time to talk and wonder, there was always time. But something had happened.

Whatever it was, Walker was convinced it was the only course available to him. Claire didn't object to what they were doing either, just wanted them to be careful. Walker told her he liked to imagine each act of sabotage reduced Junior's debt to her. She didn't buy it, but the idea pleased him anyway. Or he could think of it as compensation for Frouncy and Snoot and ninety acres of a plundered ecosystem. It sounded better that way. He formulated a ready defense of his behavior, convincing an imaginary judge that he and Snoot were acting on behalf of the laws of nature, defending decency and common sense. He and Snoot were in it together, partners, and he had to admit it felt a hell of a lot better than looking for spilled battery acid.

The pattern of their dirty work was subtle; everything they did could be blamed on one of Ragazzo's careless employees or one of the many subcontractors' plausible incompetence—nails removed, bolts loosened, chimneys clogged with "leftover" bricks, a gob of concrete accidentally spilled into a septic line. They drilled pinholes in a water main the night before it was buried. Walker spent two hours one night with a propane torch up under a crawl space, melting solder out of a series of sweated copper joints. His handiwork wouldn't be noticed until the heat was turned up high on the first cold night of winter.

But the project had progressed despite the missing Lally columns, hidden leaks, and tumors. The wags at Tot's swore the roof would be on by Labor Day. Snoot loved to hear them talk, especially Tot, the official spokesman, font of wisdom. If and when the building ever opened, it would be a sagging, racking mess, backed up and flooded in no time, and no one would ever know exactly how or why the problems began.

Some of the sabotage was discovered. When a pressure test uncovered a leak in a disconnected coupling, it was blamed on shoddy workmanship. A deflected girder was traced to a column missing from the center of the span. The consensus at the coffee counter blamed Ragazzo for hiring boneheads and buying cheap foreign-made junk. Snoot went to Tot's every morning for an updated report and played the innocent customer, dipping doughnuts in his coffee by the window.

Walker was out of breath by the time he and Snoot reached the top of the Ledges; Snoot seemed unaffected by the climb he made two or three times a day. Walker resolved to spend less time behind his desk.

They lay on their bellies, looking through the peek holes in the bunker wall, watching the men finish another day's work. The last section of the floor joists and plywood decking was finally being nailed into place. Now and then, the white-hatted foreman waved his arms at the carpenters, but they seemed to ignore him. Maybe they too knew he was a thief.

Walker had watched the men enough to be able to identify most of them. A few lived in the area—Punka Hurley and his tenders were working on the chimneys—but most were imported labor from outside, and Walker and Snoot assigned them names: Harley (for his mode of transportation), Gramps, Big Boy, Slim, and Red were the hardest workers; White Hat, Dub, and Tink did the least; and one of the carpenters' helpers—Baseball—was indeed the hitchhiker Walker picked up on I-91. He still wore the green jacket, still looked too thin to hold a hammer. Walker wanted the kid to think the foreman was an asshole, wanted him to know something was wrong each time he loaded the truck.

Snoot put down his binoculars and scratched his beard. "Can't make it look on purpose," he said, "but what if them walls was laid out wrong?" Below, the foreman was on his knees beside an open set of working drawings, marking lines on parallel sills and plates.

Snoot explained what White Hat was doing: each line and X he drew located a stud, jack stud, cripple, corner post, or intersection with an inside wall. His measurements would include the exact widths and locations of all doors and windows, too. On Monday, the carpenters would spread the sills and plates apart on the deck, end-nail the studs between them—like rungs between the stringers of a ladder—then tip the walls up into place. Every vertical stick in the building would be nailed according to White Hat's layout templates.

By quitting time, there was a couple of hundred lineal feet of wall marked out and ready for fabrication. Walker and Snoot watched White Hat load six sheets of plywood into his truck before he left the site. "Loaded light, tonight," Snoot grumbled. "Must have strained his yellow-bellied back."

When the truck had disappeared down the hill, dust swirling after it, Walker was ready to go to work. It was after five o'clock, with more than four hours until dark, but the plan was too tempting to put off. "So," he said. "Do we start our shift now, or do we come back with a flashlight?"

Snoot hesitated. "Never day-shifted before, did we? But then, this little enterprise shouldn't take too long to finagle."

They climbed down the trail at the west end of the Ledges. "We'll need an eraser," Walker said. "Something to remove the marks."

Snoot shook his head. "No erasing, it'll show. We'll use fresh lumber, set it right alongside what he just done, and imitate his chicken scratches. But us Canucks"—he tapped his forehead—"we'll stretch and shrink as we go, ever so little. Inch or two here and there will do us dandy, throw the whole kit and kaboodle off. Hide his layout and he'll never know what happened. Old Red and Slim'll never let him forget it, either."

They'd never been on the building site at ground level during daylight, and although the prospect didn't compare to the view from the top of the Ledges, it was still spectacular. It seemed ironic that ruining ninety acres of ancient trees and fertile soil should be rewarded by such beautiful scenery. "They need a good strong mirror," Walker said, "to see what they've done—from out there. This view of theirs just confirms their slash-and-burn mentality."

Tot already had Marcia Danforth marketing the place. She'd written a memorable Abenaki Ledges Lodge sales brochure. *Revel in a blend of traditional appeal and modern convenience.* Snoot brought one home from the store. *Experience the joys of Vermonting,* it read. *Vermont: a state of mind.* The brochure invited the discriminating buyer to *experience our amenities package.* The clear-cut view was definitely part of an amenities package experience. And Crooked Brook was simply an unspoken nuisance, to be straightened and crossed with a culvert when necessary.

They dragged fresh sills and plates from the lumber pile and laid them out next to the patterns on the deck. Walker found a pencil in an open job box, and using a piece of plywood for a straightedge he duplicated White Hat's work. Snoot coached him as they moved along on their hands and knees. "See how he made his Xs?" Walker's counterfeit was perfect. "Don't move it too far, now, just a few inches at a time."

"Wait till them sons-a-hoors try to fit their four-foot windows in a hole three inches shy."

When they finished the revised layout, they began carrying the originals into the woods to the west of the Ledges, covering them with leaves and duff. From start to finish, the job took no more than half an hour, and while it seemed foolproof and well worth risking in daylight, Walker caught himself watching the access road to the south. What they were doing felt right, and yet it was wrong—and it was right. One conclusion surrendered to the other. Through it all, a sticky pull of conscience dogged him—as if he were being watched and judged and found wanting.

Snoot was beside him on his third trip to the woods. Walker was carrying two sixteen-foot lengths of two-by-six on his shoulder; Snoot was carrying four. They were halfway between the building and the trees when Walker looked up at the top of the Ledges and saw a person—a person who didn't want to be seen. "Somebody's up there," he whispered to Snoot.

"Up top?" Snoot sounded unconcerned. "Sure he is." He kept walking without looking up.

"Near the bunker," Walker said. "Between two boulders, watching us."

He pictured an avalanche of rocks in midair, hurtling toward them, then a picture of Bud, holding out two pairs of handcuffs, a sneer on his face.

"C'mon, Snoot!" Walker wanted to run to cover, still twenty yards away. The planks across his shoulder sprang up and down in clumsy arcs as he hurried toward the trees.

"Kinda ghosty was he?" Casual Snoot.

"What?" Walker called back, tripping, then regaining his balance. Snoot was taking his time, all right, the pigheaded Yankee. "Come on!"

The woods were now only a few steps away. Cool, shaded earth, thick branches, shelter, a place to hide.

Walker dumped the two-by-sixes on the ground and

stood with a thick oak branch between him and the Ledges. Snoot ambled up to the tree and yawned, ignoring the heavy load of lumber he carried. "Nice and coolish in the woods," he said, looking up into the thick foliage. "A coolish day."

"You're too much, Snoot."

"Eagle scare you?" He yawned again and showed his extra set of molars, top and bottom, rows of perfect ivory, white on pink.

"Eagle? That was Horton?" Walker felt the hairs stand up on the back of his neck.

Snoot looked smug. "Horton Eagle-in-the-Wind, flying around. I see him all the time. Signs of him, anyhow." With a dainty sidestep, Snoot dropped his load of lumber, shed it, in a perfect row next to Walker's. "We ain't the only ones don't like what's going on."

"Claire thought he was back in Maine," Walker said, moving from behind the tree and peering up through the leaves. "She hasn't seen him for weeks." Claire talked with her father several times after he first appeared, but he was elusive, even with her, and unpredictable in his visits. She left work late one night and found him sitting in her locked car. She got up early one morning and discovered him standing in the kitchen, pouring coffee, two plates of eggs and toast on the table. One time he met her in the superette in Catamount and pushed her grocery cart around as if it were a baby carriage. He had a way of reassuring her he'd be back soon, but she confessed she never could remember what he said to convince her.

Despite it all, she said she finally felt completed, and knew much better who she was, but she was disappointed that she saw him so seldom and that her mother refused to talk to him. "Stay away from him," Laurie told Claire. "He's never been reliable, and he never will be." Claire told Walker she felt closer to Horton in a week than she had to her mother any time in her life.

"What's Horton got in mind?" Walker asked.

"Dunno," Snoot said. "Whatever 'tis, he'll do it on his

own. If he sets his mind to it, he could"—Snoot laughed and held out his hands like a magician—"he could do anything."

They finished their work and left the Ledges. On the way home, Walker hoped to see Horton on the trail or to see his Cadillac parked in Fellows's lot. When he saw neither, he asked Snoot, "How'd he get up there, anyway?"

Snoot shrugged. "Flew. Crept, crawled, swam, tunneled like a mole through the mountain." He laughed. "Walked over from Little Squaw Mountain on his ears—"

"Come on, goddammit!"

"I don't know how he got there, boy, and there's no man living on God's green earth could say without lying his teeth out, neither." Snoot acted as though he wasn't interested in the answer anyway, no matter what it was. He seemed defensive, almost grouchy. At first, Walker was puzzled by Snoot's reaction; then he understood: Eagle-in-the-Wind had upstaged him.

They walked along the Quinntown road without speaking. Snoot kicked at a beer can on the shoulder. "Anybody ain't man enough to wing their empties in the woods ought'n to be allowed to drink and drive in the first place."

"How *did* he get up there?" Walker persisted.

Snoot was sick of the question. "He didn't need to *get* there, Tutti. He just *was*. Him and you and me and Raggedyatso-fatso, we all get up there one way or another, stand there posing this and that, like a bunch of kid goats playing king of the mountain. Eagle, he's different, I got to admit, especially up there."

"Well, no wonder. I mean, it's really his."

"Like hell it is, Tutti. Nobody owns a goddamned mountain. Eagle knows that, and so should you."

That night, as Claire and he undressed for bed, Walker told her about the afternoon and the unexpected sighting of Horton. She stopped midway down the buttons on her blouse, waiting for more news of her father, but there was nothing more Walker could tell her, except what he'd seen and Snoot's

254

odd reaction. He stripped off his shirt and wondered aloud if Snoot was jealous of Horton, if he was afraid Horton would outdo him.

"All this sneaking around is so seductive," he said, "I'm not sure if I'm rationalizing it for the sake of the adventure— and being in it with Snoot—or if I really believe it's justifiable. But I like it."

"Did seeing Daddy raise the ante?"

"It made me wonder about how far it will go. If he's in it—and if some of those stories about him are even halfway true—"

"He must have meant for you to see him," she said. "He wanted to tell you something."

Walker took her hands and put them on his shoulders. When he felt her fingers on his neck, he began undoing the rest of her buttons. "Like what?" he asked. Claire wore nothing under her blouse.

"I think he wants you to know he knows what you're doing, that's all. And that he approves."

"Do you?" Walker parted the front of her blouse and nudged her to him, felt the warmth of her breasts against his skin.

"I'm glad you're doing what you're doing," she said into the bones that covered his heart. "And so is he."

"He told you that?"

She paused. "He wants us to be together. For a long time."

Walker held her tight and closed his eyes. Horton wanted them to get married, is what she almost said.

"He's happy for us. He respects you, what you tried to do to protect the land. He's grateful you know what caring for it means." Eyelashes brushed against his nipple. "He's one of the last to understand the powers his grandfather had." She pulled back and held him at arm's length, her blouse wide open. "I've seen him use them."

The amber lamplight on her skin was unfair competition for the conversation. "How?" He wanted to believe her, but the proof of metaphysics always seemed more a matter of trust and faith than science.

She squeezed his shoulders, stared at him, and lowered her voice. "He moves things, Walker. He can make himself disappear." She took a deep breath. "I've seen him do it."

"Where?" Why was she being coy? "What? When?"

"They aren't just stories, Walker." She pulled him to her, backed up, and tipped him over on top of her, onto the bed. "There are things he can do that would astound you."

16

EQUITY

It was close to midnight on the second Sabbath of July, warm and humid at the foot of the Ledges. Walker stood watch as Snoot picked at a lock on the basement-level service door. Snoot cursed and jimmied; the steel door shook in its frame. Walker held his breath, watching the shadows; then something clicked, and the door swung free. When he tried to lock the door behind them from inside, Walker found the thumb turn wouldn't turn the deadbolt. Snoot must have crushed a tumbler pin; the bolt was stuck. Until it was noticed, they'd have free access to the building.

Walker hung on to Snoot's shirttail and followed him down a dark corridor, past a stair, to the mechanical room. Once inside a second door, they switched on their flashlights, played them against the walls, and found what they were looking for.

At the far end of the concrete vault, a pair of four-hundred-amp service panels were bolted side by side to the wall. Above each, a shower of cables hung down like spaghetti, hundreds of black and white plastic-coated wires waiting to be stripped and lugged to their respective circuit breakers. Each wire was tagged: "lobby north," "lobby south," "well pump," "east hall 1," "compressor subpanel," "refrigeration unit A"—and on and on—all perfectly organized.

Snoot touched one of the wires and smiled. "Never did like electric."

Walker untied a tag and exchanged it with another. "No wonder. It wasn't even invented until you were—what—thirty?"

Snoot imitated the sound of flatulence and picked out a tag from the jumble above the panel. "They'll wonder why the water well pump keeps tripping the goddamned breaker, won't they?"

In half an hour, they'd switched the tags on every cable. Circuits requiring fifty amps were slated for twenty, and vice versa. It would take days to reformat the grid.

Walker worked fast, cold sweat running down his ribs inside his shirt. This was the real thing: sabotage. They were inside enemy territory. The door was unlocked. There was no other way out. If someone came along, they were trapped. If only he could vanish now, disappear at will, and reappear instantaneously at home, the way Claire insisted she saw Horton do one day after they'd driven up to see what was going on at the Ledges.

"The visit was physically painful," she'd said, "all that erosion, all that emptiness, the stupid plywood lodge plunked down in the dirt beneath the Tooth." Horton had been furious, but he didn't speak, as usual, just took one long look and motioned for her to turn her car around and leave. On the way down the mountain, he asked to be left off, said he needed to be alone.

"He got out. He was standing by a stone wall, and he nodded—that little motion he does with his eyes?—and then he was gone, I swear." Claire wanted Walker to believe her. "I got out of the car and looked for him behind the wall, called to him, looked everywhere, but he was gone."

A few days had passed since Walker heard the story, and he still didn't know what to think of it; he only wished he could do what Horton was reported to have done. Leave the explanation to someone else.

He finished the last of the tagging and motioned Snoot to the door. They turned off their flashlights and walked past the open stairway in the dark. Walker felt an ambiguous pride in their mischief; on the bright side, it would be another serious setback for Abenaki, but some poor electrician would probably get fired for it, too.

Snoot was in front of him. He pushed open the jimmied door, crossed the threshold, and stopped. Walker bumped into him, then froze in disbelief as a voice called out, "So it's *you!*"

Snoot swung and connected. Walker watched him move in for a second punch, slick as grease, no sign of the arthritis that dogged him on rainy mornings. He dipped like a dancing bear. Another sound of impact, bone on bone; a body hung in the air for a moment, then fell in a lump at Snoot's feet. Walker stared. White Hat was down for the count.

At Tot's the next morning, Snoot learned White Hat's name. Whether Rudy Gastingneaux was guarding the place against vandals or simply stealing more building materials was Rudy's secret; the gossip gallery had ideas of its own.

"Rudy's taking a few days' vacation."

"Truck T-boned him, hit-and-run, Ford stake body, Jim Boyce seen it, damned Q'bec plates, he said they was."

"Ruint Jim's day."

"Rudy's some, too."

"Found him flat-ass on the road by Poole's Pea Patch, over to Kendall."

"Stopped his pocket watch, seven minutes to midnight."

"Black-and-blued him wicked bad. Busted his jaw."

"Lost him some dentine."

"Don't remember nothing."

"Don't want to."

"Ain't it something," Snoot said to the boys, "the way them Frenchmen team their vehicles? Dangereuse out there."

And then back to the ongoing rumors about Ragazzo: the Lodge was two months behind schedule, walls had been torn down and reframed because none of the doors and windows fit, the water and sewage systems were plagued with leaks and backups. Half the roof trusses had to be removed and redesigned. An inspector found some of the stamped metal connector plates had slits in them—factory defects—almost as if they'd been sawed partway through, he told the carpenters.

The old folks in town said the land had a curse on it. Darby Dunbar told Lillian Woodard that once the graves of the Abenakis had been disturbed, their spirits would never rest. Two plumbing subs had been fired, and the coffee-counter quarterbacks blamed the rest of the troubles on Rudy Gastingneaux. Rudy was rumored to be building a laundromat in Catamount with materials from the site. Bud was supposed to nail him, they said, but he accepted part-ownership of the laundromat instead. Bud's carved Indian disappeared from Tot's porch. Some said Tot burned it to get back at Bud; some said it was stolen by irate Native Americans; some said Junior took it with him to California.

Snoot sat through the old stories all morning, waiting for more about Rudy, but none were forthcoming; White Hat's difficulties apparently didn't arouse much sympathy.

That night, Snoot, Walker, and Claire sat around the kitchen table, rehashing the run-in with Rudy. "That'll be the end of it," Walker insisted.

Claire agreed: the expeditions had to stop. She'd heard Ragazzo was hiring Bud as a full-time night watchman.

Snoot looked disgusted. "Just quit it?" He pushed himself back from the edge of the table.

Walker tried to reassure him. "We'll think of something else," he said. "There's only so much we can do up there, anyway." Maybe it was better the cloak-and-dagger stuff was over before somebody got busted.

"Go ahead, then, suit yourself." Snoot's voice deepened. "Do what you want, by the Jesus." The stump of his amputated thumb was twitching. "*I* ain't done yet."

"Rudy knows who hit him."

Snoot turned his chair around, showed his back to the table, and shook his head. "Rudy's got too much to hide to point his sticky fingers at me. Rudy don't mean dinky dip."

"What about Bud?"

"Haw!"

Walker glanced at Claire for support. "All we've got to do is change directions." There it was again. His so-called reason versus Snoot's spontaneity. Was he talking about changing directions or a rationale for chickening out? "T'll try some sticky legal bullshit—a court injunction—put the spotlight on Billy Ware's case, get the newspapers involved."

Snoot had heard it all before. He sat large and silent with his back to the table. The X of his suspenders warned, *Keep out.* "Bud don't matter since he hung Pomona."

"But they'll put it together," Walker said, reluctant to bolster yet another argument in favor of caution. "The trail, the bunker, the obvious motivation. They'd love to—"

"Bud ain't worth cowflop. He's done the last of his p'lice business with me, and he goddamn knows it, too." Snoot began cracking his knuckles, a sound like the snapping of kindling wood; with one finger he was rebuking Bud, with another, Tot, then Rudy, then his son. With the next? Was he warning himself against losing Walker?

"Going to bed," Snoot said abruptly, got up, and closed the door to his room.

Claire had been quiet during the conversation, quiet even for Claire. Since her father's return, she no longer argued in favor of leaving the development alone. Sometimes Walker felt she wished he were doing more to stop it than even he was willing to do.

They went upstairs.

"You don't have to be Snoot, you know," she said, undressing.

"I know. But he's—"

"Your hero?"

"I guess he was, in the old days anyway. This time around, it's not so simple." He kissed her behind the ear. "I don't think of him as bigger than life anymore." He paused. "It sounds funny, but it's because I've finally realized he needs me. Before, I always felt it was only me needing him. There was no equation, no equity. Now, there is. People need to be needed. I need to be needed."

"So do I," Claire said. "We all do."

He holds her. Cool sheets, warm skin. Shoes *thunk* to the carpet one by one. Socks, pants, and shirt follow, sighing, to the floor. Somewhere hidden in the room, a cricket lends its chorus to the creaking of the bed. Night light turns amber, sweeter, brighter—brilliant. Gone. Time wobbles, the cricket sings.

The next morning, Snoot sat cold as ice through breakfast, unyielding to Claire's hand on his shoulder as she passed his chair. Walker tried to thaw him out, but failed, and soon found himself thinking how contented he would be living in a little house up in the hills alone with Claire, lots of books, a dog, and a view of the pond. He found himself thinking about how nice it would be to grow old with the woman he loved.

The morning passed slowly. Snoot chopped wood, Claire went to work, and Walker stayed home to finish composing the final pages of a brief against a landfill application in Canaan. It was messy: jobs were at stake, alternatives were too costly, passions were heated—he'd received his first piece of hate mail: *Butt out, you pinhedded bloodsukker.* Stopping the landfill was an unpopular position, but the site was over an aquifer recharge area, and even the manufacturers agreed vinyl liners were unreliable after thirty years. Luckily, recent case law supported the growing body of evidence: Landfill leachates had to be retreated before coming in contact with groundwater. More expense, more taxes, more illegal dumping. Taking out the trash was getting complicated. Garbage, plastic, PCBs, poison—he was watching the death of his good-life northwoods myth.

At noon, Walker went out to ask Snoot if he wanted some lunch. As he turned the corner of the house, he saw Snoot swing at a chunk of stovewood. The maul landed, and the chunk exploded; two halves flew twenty feet to each side of the chopping block, and the tip of the maul wedged itself deep in the block. Snoot swatted the handle, but the maul was stuck fast, so he lifted it up over his head—the maul and the two-foot-circumference chopping block—arched it high above him, and thudded it to the ground.

"Hi, Tutti." The chopping block was in two pieces; the maul was loose. Snoot was smiling, his clothes dark with sweat.

"Want some lunch? Claire left us tuna salad. There's Coke and iced tea—"

"Sounds dandy," Snoot said. "And it'll give me a minute to explain my idea. Been communing all forenoon with Frounce." He nodded to the Catamount Heights. "I know, I know, you're a good Tutti boy, but if I ain't convinced you inside of ten seconds, I won't say nothing about it ever again."

Sticky with heat, they drove across the river to New Hampshire on a hot tar road. Snoot's plan was outrageous: "Them buck teeth boulders at the lip of the Ledges was always meant to topple. How I pushed on them pebbles when I was a boy." He clenched his fists and spread his elbows. "Played Samson, me and Frenchy Tibb. Didn't have no house jacks then, though, did we?"

He'd proposed nothing less than to roll a boulder onto the roof of the Lodge. Frouncy and he had decided it was the best thing to do. Walker agreed to help, astounded at the extent to which his need to keep the northwoods myth alive was able to corrupt his judgment.

"They moved the damn church, didn't they, chimbleys and all?" Walker lived in town when the Dalton Pond Congregational was moved half a mile down Main Street. "Shouldn't be no problem a-tall. This time we do some business, by the Jesus!" Snoot pounded the dashboard to emphasize the landing impact of a bus-sized boulder.

Walker thought about a variety of applicable felony and misdemeanor charges. "If they can't take a joke, to hell with them, right?"

"Bankrupp the bastards, pound 'em silly."

For the rest of the afternoon, they drove around to salvage yards and junk shops in New Hampshire, looking for house jacks; Snoot wanted three, twenty-ton capacity each.

At Walker's suggestion, they bought the jacks singly—one from the greasy heap behind Merritt's Shell station in Lawford, another from a perspiring Frenchwoman "Junktique" vendor on Route 29, near Littleton, and the last from a run-down farm on the dump road, south of Tinkamtown, where the arthritic farmer refused their help as he pulled the jack out from under a flattened shed.

"Held up good till the damn corn snow tipped her ass over teakettle end of April." His white beard was striped brown with tobacco juice. "Hard to believe it on a stinker like today," he said, wiping his face with his sleeve. "You fellas got some heavy jacking to do, then, do ya?"

Walker winked at Snoot. "Some."

As Snoot described it, the mechanics of moving a mega-ton block of granite sounded simple. They'd wedge the jacks horizontally between the back of the boulder and the vertical rock face behind it, then crank away, turning the screws a quarter revolution at a time with a stout steel handle, like turning a capstan, on its side. When the jacks were extended their full six-inch throw, they'd back them off, add a six-inch shim behind them—a squarish block of stone would do—and crank again. Since the space between the rock face and the back of the boulders was less than a yard wide, it would take only two or three sequences to send the boulders over the edge. Then, "with any luck a-tall," the falling stone would hit the wide shelf that ran across the Ledges about a third of the way down and bounce onto the Lodge roof, through the Lodge roof, through the floors below, and into the earth, stuck, like Snoot's splitting maul in the chop block.

"Talk about a ruckus." Snoot rocked the car with his gestures as he speculated on the sound of the boulder hitting the building. "Like a hundred-weight anvil on a truckload of eggs."

He went back over each step of the operation, laboring

over the mechanical particulars of tension, compression, and leverage.

Walker listened. Snoot's brand of engineering was an optimistic mixture of magic and intuition. It even sounded reasonable occasionally, but Walker couldn't help but ask himself, what if the boulders didn't bounce right? He didn't ask Snoot. What if somebody got killed? He pictured Baseball sleeping off a drunk in the empty building, flat as a pancake under the wreckage. A boulder through the roof wasn't going to stop the project anyway, he reasoned—but there he was again, inventing reasons for holding back. He told himself to shut up and act—for Snoot and Frouncy's sake, for Claire and Horton, for the memories of an uprooted forest. Hell: for himself.

They are driving home with their loot in the trunk of Walker's car, speeding through Pike Depot, a wide spot in the road next to the Connecticut River. A voice on the radio insists there is a lot of money to be made in ballroom dancing.

"God, it's hot." Walker leaned his head out the window, into the rush of slightly cooler air.

"Wouldn't be thirsty for some groceries, would you?" Snoot motioned to a sign on the right, BEER, GAS, CIGS, MILK.

Walker pulled over and stopped by a dented ice machine next to the door. "I'll keep an eye out for cops."

Snoot thought he was joking. "Haw!" He slammed the door, stuck his head back in through through the window, and grinned. "Don't move an inch. This here's on me." Then he turned and waded into the dingy little store, great hairy angel in a heaven of his own imagination. He belonged between the mossy capstones of a medieval castle turret. Walker pictured him loading a catapult with rubber chickens, pouring hot chocolate over the crumbling castle walls, cackling.

"King Eddies and a couple of racks of hydraulic," Snoot announced, rummaging through the paper bag in his lap. "Celebrate our shopping campaign." He popped the tops off two cans of Bud, handed one to Walker, lit a cigar, and proposed a toast: "To big-hearted women and mother's milk. God love 'em to pieces." He raised the red and white can and splashed beer on the dented dashboard. "And mercy, Percy, on us poor boys. Don't ever let us do without."

Walker lit his own cigar and pulled out onto the highway with spray on his glasses and a dribble of foam down his chin. It was hot in the car, but the sun would soon set, and the rushing air felt good as they gathered speed. Snoot fiddled with the radio, sang, "Hinky dinky tong-tong," and opened a third can of beer.

As they topped a hill on the outskirts of Quinntown, Walker saw the humps of Crooked Mountain in the distance. Curtains of dark clouds hung over the peaks. He watched the heavy blue fabric shredded open with the ragged capillary signature of summer lightning. He tipped up his can in salute; cool liquid soothed his throat. "To doing what you gotta do," he said. "To courage."

"Heat lightning," Snoot pronounced. "Dry storm coming, from the looks of it." Cigar smoke unfurled out the windows and caught in the wind, pungent banners of their campaign.

They made small talk, drank, and smoked; dark clouds hastened evening into dusk. The road seemed merciful and welcoming. They drove home to Quinntown like cowboys, like outlaws, in a brave evocation of a self-made myth.

They ate sparsely and quickly. Snoot washed the dishes while Walker explained the plan to Claire. She wasn't impressed. Snoot tried a bribe. "Soon's we get back, we're going to take you out for a midnight ride in Walker's lemma-zine, ramble up to Little Squaw Mountain, and gaze out over Sachem Lake. Drink us a bottle of strawberry brandy." His proposition hung in the air like an unclaimed consolation prize at a third-rate bingo hall. He backed off. "Or some such type of celebration party."

"Anyway, it's going to rain," Claire said. "I don't want you guys getting hurt." She glanced a question mark at Walker. "Or hurting somebody else."

266

"'T'won't rain," Snoot insisted. "Nobody's going to get hurt. Heat lightning's all it is."

"It'll be okay," Walker whispered into her hair. "We'll be careful."

"I wish Daddy were going with you," she said.

"Now *that* would be something," Snoot quipped, jiggling the door latch, itching to leave.

"Somebody said they've ordered five hundred trees to plant up there in the fall. After cutting them all down. Why are people so stupid?"

It was finally dark. Walker drove alone to Fellows's parking lot and hid the jacks in the bushes behind a light pole. Then he drove back to the house, left the car in the driveway, and prepared to set out on foot with Snoot.

Claire stood at the door as they left. "I want to be with you," she whispered to Walker, "for a long time. Be careful."

Thunder boomed like battlefield cannons over Crooked Mountain. He kissed her. "It's a deal."

They hid in the trees alongside the road when cars passed by, but otherwise the trek to Fellows's was uneventful. Walker followed Snoot's lumbering shadow along the edge of the two-lane blacktop, not quite matching footsteps, dumb with deference to an idea he knew was unsuited for debate. You did it, or you didn't. Action versus endless argument. He decided he would ask Claire to marry him.

Snoot carried two of the forged-iron jacks; Walker carried one and the steel rod used to turn them.

"You get used to it," Snoot said, lurching out of the branchy shadows with a house jack in each hand. "I've drawed worse loads than this." He tipped his chin to the pouch of Red Man in his breast pocket. "Chew?"

Walker grimaced on cue, swung his forty-pound jack to his shoulder, and fell in behind Snoot.

They pointed their flashlights downward, dim disks on the trail just ahead of their feet. Each time a strobe of lightning flashed, Walker saw himself plunged into a photograph, a quick step into a vacuum of light. Then it would be dark again, and he'd watch the lingering afterimage fade—Snoot's torso stepping over a rock, tree branches racked in unexpected shapes, a stretch of mud, a log, a root: fading, faded, gone.

They climbed slowly, despite the now-familiar terrain. Sometimes Walker heard Snoot stop. He'd look up and stop too, holding the gap between them. Then a foot would clunk against something dark, and he'd be moving again, waiting for the surprise of the next bright image.

The temperature dropped as they climbed. A wind tossed the treetops, bringing with it a brief splattering of rain—the same refreshing wet tattoo that beat on Walker's teen-aged face one distant summer afternoon.

Frouncy drives the flatbed farm truck, creeping steadily along the windrows while he, the helper, follows on foot. He gathers the waiting bales, one slung from each hand and bumping against his knees as he hurries. Twine cuts another lifeline across his palm—northcountry stigmata—and he likes it. He reaches the back of the truck and heaves the heavy bundles high into the air. Stubble scratches his forearms, chaff sticks to the sweat on his upturned face, seeds of timothy prickle his sunburned neck. It smells like goodness itself.

Snoot catches the bales and knits them into a towering temple. He blocks out the sun with his hugeness. Rain falls— big drops—but only enough to beat down the dust, and then the sky is clear again. Snoot laughs at the passing clouds; his hay won't be ruined, his barn will be full. Walker hurries after another bale, looking up at the sky, to be certain.

Within fifty feet of the top of the Ledges, a flash of brilliant incandescence singed the air; a withering punch of thunder sledgehammered it home. Walker ducked at the impact, imagining angry shamans, scorched flesh, a headline in the *Jordan Journal:* LIGHTNING CLAIMS TWO.

Dark again, and windy. He was cautious of his footing, wary of the edge. Iron clanked on stone as Snoot stripped himself of his freight. A flashlight beam darted into the empty bunker, across the boulders to each side. At last. He dropped his jack next to Snoot's. His legs trembled from the climb. Snoot was singing: "Wooga wooga whoa, got me some wimmens down in O-hi-o."

With the next flash of lightning, Walker saw the Lodge roof below. It looked closer in the sudden glare, and pathetically vulnerable. Was Bud walking his rounds? Sitting in his car? Playing solitaire in the Lodge?

Snoot moved quickly, ignoring Walker's attempts to help him position the jacks. "Now," he rasped, "we got us some cranking to do." He knelt down and began taking up slack.

"We should check the building first," Walker said. "Somebody could be inside."

"What?" Snoot sounded stung. "How we supposed to do that without them knowing we're up here? Anyways, ain't nobody down there."

"You hope," Walker said. "I'll go down, and don't worry, I'll make sure no one sees me."

"Go down?" Snoot stood up and crossed his arms. "Bud catches your lawyering ass, and that's all she wrote."

"We drop a bus on somebody's head, and that's all she wrote, too. This is big time, Snoot."

"It'd serve 'em right."

"Bullshit. I'm going." Lightning lit the mountainside, and for one phosphorescent moment, Snoot's face was cast in irreducible opposites. Walker saw him as part of a black-and-white universe, every atom made of pure light or its absence, every nuance resolved, no space between right and wrong. The forged-iron implements beside him, the boulders, and the sky were all flattened and simplified, stripped of hue, color and tone, and moral ambiguity. Snoot's startled face looked hairless and smooth as a baby's, unguarded and afraid—that was it: he was afraid too! Snoot wasn't a god or a hero. He was him. He was Walker. The charged field of static between the two men had refused to recognize the convenient, fabled archetype; Snoot the immortal, Snoot the giant, was finally— just Snoot. Walker stared; he'd seen a photograph he would never forget.

Thunder followed like an exclamation point. "We can't risk killing somebody."

"You going against me again, Tutti Frutti?" Snoot stuck his flashlight in Walker's face.

"It's not a matter of going against you." He squinted into the blinding glare. "It's being sure the building's empty before we bomb it."

Snoot flicked off his flashlight. "Being sure," he mocked.

Walker pointed his light in Snoot's face, then toward the trail that led down around the end of the Ledges. "It'll take me twenty minutes to check the place out. Either I do that or the deal's off. Period."

"It's all the same to me." Snoot acted hurt. "Take me twenty frigging minutes to work my strength up anyways." He slapped the boulder. "I'll try not to bounce it off your noggin while you're down there snooping around."

"Thanks a lot, Grizz." Lightning zapped overhead. "You're all heart." Walker started down the trail.

He stopped and hid at the base of the Ledges to watch and listen in the dark—for Bud on his rounds, lights, vehicles, radios, guard dogs, voices, anything and everything—he would stay alert and keen. But the night was quiet except for the soughing wind and his heart thumping in the back of his mouth.

Between lightning flashes, he raced across a hundred feet of vacant landscape to the service door. So far, so good. Ah ha! The door was still open. He slipped inside, stopped, and listened.

Now up the stairs, feeling stealthy but out of place, a schizoid tourist/adolescent/commando/attorney/flatlander. Dummy. He hurried down the hall to the two-story foyer, the dining hall, kitchen, and lounge—big rooms, empty and familiar—one sweep across the floor with the flashlight and on to the next.

One flight up the east stair tower, he hurried down the corridor; a regular rhythm of wall studs lined each side, but all of the guest rooms and closets and baths were still without sheetrock and easily visible. There was nowhere for anyone to hide—not even him.

The top floor was similarly unfinished, all of it open to rapid inspection. Walker calculated he'd been in the building less than ten minutes when a zigzag of lightning lit up the night; it was followed by a sharp crunch of thunder, not a boulder on the roof. Thunder was nothing but cold air colliding with warm air a mile above, harmless. But did Snoot really know what he was doing?

Walker tiptoed quickly down the west stair tower, all the way down to the service entry hall. Once again, he stopped and listened. Quiet. There was one more place to check: the basements and mechanical room, the darkest dead-end traps in the building.

But they too were empty, which made for a hundred percent. They could drop Big Bertha without worrying about manslaughter charges. He turned off his flashlight, closed the boiler room door behind him, and started for the service door.

It was wide open, and, God almighty, someone was standing in it, filling most of the frame. There was enough backlight from outside to make out the silhouette, and the man was big—too big to be Rudy, or Baseball, heavy around the middle—and it was impossible to tell which way he was facing, in or out. He might have had something in his hands, a flashlight or a gun, or he might have had nothing; it was too dark to see details, but there he was, five yards away, and looking a lot like Officer Benoit.

Walker waited, statue still, tingling. A fox barked in the distance. Something rattled, tinny, brittle. Another bark, a screech, an insistent rattling, a thump. The doorway was suddenly empty. Walker took a deep breath and ran.

17

RECKONING

HORTON HAD PACKED, tamped, and wired the last section of the fissure when he heard them coming up the trail—first the singing and the familiar signature of Snoot's footsteps through the trees, then the other sound, lighter and quicker—Claire's husband-to-be.

They were good men, both of them. It had been interesting to watch them over the last few weeks, but once again, their timing was an inconvenience. It made working doubly difficult when they were around, especially tonight; Horton had no time left for distractions.

He was behind a boulder, on an outcrop above them, when they reached the bunker. With the next flash of lightning, he saw what they carried and immediately guessed how the jacks would be used. Snoot was ingenious, in his heavy-handed way, and admirably stubborn. The jacks might work or they might not; by the time the night was over, it wouldn't make any difference.

Horton watched and listened. Snoot argued with Walker, but the boy had good sense and the courage to insist. Whether he was wise enough to conduct himself safely was another question. Better to watch him. Better to take no chances. Horton gathered himself for the descent.

He was but another shadow in a thickness of spruce

when Walker arrived at the foot of the Ledges. He watched him pause and search the surroundings for danger—seeing but not quite seeing—watched him run like a rabbit to the service door, and he wished him luck. Let him go, he thought, and be the braver for it. Let him see for himself and learn to manage fear.

The building would be empty; Horton had searched it an hour before for the same reasons Walker insisted upon— and he knew Bud Benoit was still in his Bronco, hidden nearby in a grove of hemlocks at the edge of the cut. Bud sat there at night lately, listening to Red Sox games, snoozing, making his hourly rounds, missing everything under his nose. He would miss Walker too, unless the boy did something foolish.

Now Eagle-in-the-Wind was in the hemlocks; the Bronco was ten feet in front of him, a stretch of raw dirt and the Lodge beyond. He waited, resting on a stump, tired; it had been a strenuous night—packing, tamping, stringing wire, the last of many long days of preparation.

He'd always known the fissure was there, but he never dreamed he'd put it to such use. Two yards back, and parallel to the face of the cliff, it followed a natural seam. And it was deep; last week, he'd plumbed a lead weight on a fishline down to more than fifty feet into the center of Pompasook's Tooth. A thousand winter thaws had seeped in, frozen, and expanded, wedging the rift wider and deeper, making ready.

But would it be tight enough to hold a charge? Would a lateral fissure halfway down bleed the load sideways and blow out a dud? What hidden patterns of geo-architecture was he dealing with? What secrets slept behind the curtain?

For now, he had no choice but to trust the seam was deep, wide, and tight. If it lay as he believed it did—as all his experience and instinct told him it should—the face slab would hinge out away from the mountain, and fall in one piece, like a slice of bread falls from a loaf. The top of the slice, where Snoot's stones were bunkered between the great boulders, would arc out as far as the prow of the dining room. As they fell, some of the boulders would tumble off and drop under the wake of the monolith, buried forever beneath a fittingly familiar blanket; others might fly all the way to the brook. Flung far enough into the night, some might never return to earth.

But all of that was mostly a matter of mechanics, predictable physics, cause and effect. Seven hundred pounds of Anfo explosives in the right configuration could lift the side off any mountain. He knew exactly how to make it happen, and he had proceeded accordingly.

It was the other issues, the eternal inquiry into the rights of dominion, stewardship, and the suppositions of a unified Creation—these troubled him still. He'd failed them all, he knew he had. He'd spent his life knowing only the questions, unable to find a way to live the answers as it seemed his fathers had. He'd spent his working days energetically blowing things apart because he was good at it, surprised at himself for not hating the falsehood of how he conducted his life. There was so little of his heritage in how he lived. He'd always avoided the gathering in, the putting together, the building up of life, because the life he was born to live was no longer viable, and it was impossible to communicate the loneliness of being the only one left.

And so it had come to this night of reckoning, this final gesture. He would leave this place the only gift he had to give.

In the distance, the sound of a hoot owl became its own echo; again, *hoot*, again, *hoot*, again. Closer by, the brook scuppled its reluctant course, laying out a blueprint for revision.

Horton attended the darkness and listened to the sounds as signals of change, replacement, and renewal; each cricket, each peeper, seemed linked to the voices in him, all of them destined to sing a single song.

A brightness in the distance: he looked up in time to see a flare of light in an upstairs window of the Lodge, then another—the reflected beam of a flashlight searching the rooms. It was to be expected; Claire's Walker hadn't yet learned to see in the dark.

Bud struggled out of the Bronco, moving like a man

unsure of what he'd seen, afraid of himself, terrified of death. Lightning hissed across the landscape. His ears glowed pink. An angry admonition of thunder followed the lightning; Bud strapped on his gun belt, cursing and trembling.

The profile of Horton's shadow merged with the trunk of a maple tree. He watched Bud creep across the burial ground, an old man walking into uncertainty, badly worn and tired.

Downwind, Horton smelled it before he saw it, then made his way around to the back where the stench fell off to the brook below. The steep incline behind the portable toilet was littered with construction scraps and garbage from workers' lunches. Horton found an empty soda can and climbed back up the bank; a handful of pebbles dropped inside made it rattle. The cry of a fox would get Big Ears' attention. *Errrrrrck!* Then a rattle. Add another fox crying, *Errrrrrk! Erk!* The scream of a wild spirit caught in a trap.

Bud came around the corner of the building balanced on his toes, legs wide apart, with his pistol drawn, searching the dark. "All right! Who's out there?" Did he expect a fox to answer?

Errrrrrck! Horton crouched behind the Port-a-san and pounded on the fiberglass panels as if someone were inside. *Rattle, rattle!* Then he waited. Even upwind, the thing stunk of sickness. Long overdue to be pumped out and perfumed, gallons of excrement stewed in a holding tank under the seat. He gagged at the idea of what the air must be like inside, wondered how anyone could go into a place like that when the woods were fifty yards away.

Bud crept closer, gripping his gun with both hands. Lightning lit up the Ledges behind him. Thunder boomed. Bud ducked at the impact and ran the last few steps, pursued, out of breath.

Horton thumped again.

Bud kicked at the door with his boot. "Okay, you. Come out slow and don't try nothing funny."

Now Eagle-in-the-Wind was behind him.

Bud rocked the Port-a-san with another, braver kick. "I'm done waiting on you!" The voice of a worried man.

Silence in the Port-a-san.

With his service revolver in one hand, Bud took a flashlight out of his pocket, snapped it on, and held it between his legs. The beam of light shook a blurred ellipse across the Port-a-san logo. Bud reached for the handle, paused for a moment, and yanked the door open. "Gotcha!"

Horton caught the stink of the air inside as he drove his head into the small of Bud's back. He saw the flashlight fall to the ground, saw the beam brighten white on a cigarette butt. Next came the heavy sound of flesh collapsing against the rear wall, then a splash and a groan and a frightened voice: "Wait! *Please!*"

A fox screamed. The door slammed shut and locked tight. Horton pushed; the Port-a-san teetered on the edge of the embankment, rotated its center of gravity, and toppled backward, into night air. With a terrible thumping inside, it sloshed end over end down the garbage-strewn slope and landed upside down, stuck fast in the muddy water of Crooked Brook.

Horton left Bud and hurried away to find Walker, following his innocent trail up the side of the Ledges. By the time they reached the top, Horton was ahead of him. A few stars were visible; it was cooler, a welcome change. The dry storm had blown by; now it dragged streamers of feathery clouds in its wake, full speed across a quarter moon.

It had become a great effort, the running and hiding, the watching and waiting. If Snoot and Walker would only finish their little business with the boulder, Horton could attend to his and be done. He was tired; there were tasks ahead that would demand his energies. He found his resting place behind a boulder, settled in, and waited.

Snoot was hunched over one of the jacks, straining to turn it. "Goddamned *son* of a bitch!"

Walker approached him, full of his tale.

"Can't spin a thread!"

"Bud almost had me." Proud of his escape.

Snoot ignored the implications, yanked himself upright, and held out the jack handle. "I'd like to wrap this piece of junk around his jiggly old jowls."

Walker lifted his flashlight; Snoot had bullied the thick steel rod into the shape of a capital J. "Go easy on it, Snoot. Bud's prowling around."

"Worthless piece a . . ." Snoot threw the bar over his shoulder. "Didn't I warn you not to traipse around down there?" The bar ricocheted off the top of the bunker and dropped over the edge. One long second later, Horton heard it clatter against the Lodge roof, heard Walker say "Shhh!" and continue his story.

"He was in the door, blocking it, then something distracted him, perfect timing. Sounded like a fox."

"So it did. Kinda screechy." Snoot swung around and kicked at the stone. "Samson hisself couldn't budge them cinders." He stomped on the jacks at his feet. "Usless as a mule's tit, not that anyone around here gives a good goddamn."

"Not true," Walker said. "But we ought to boogie. Bud's on our case."

He was being predictably sensible, Horton thought, a good partner for the unpredictable Snoot, a good partner for Claire. He watched Walker pacing along the narrow shelf to the east of the bunker when he saw him stopped suddenly still, pointing his flashlight at his feet, bent over. Horton lost sight of him but knew what Walker found: the detonating wires to one of the charges had been impossible to hide along the bare rock face.

Snoot seemed not to notice—or gave that impression— it was difficult to tell in the dim light. Walker stood up quickly and hurried back to the bunker, where he picked up one of the jacks.

"Why don't you grab those babies and we'll shag on home."

"Christly made in *Jap*-pan." Snoot picked up his jacks and clanged them together. "Bud can stick it where the sun don't shine."

"We can try it some other time." Walker ushered him to the head of the trail, leaving the cliff top with an urgent glance over his shoulder, one last searching look. "Who knows what we'll find, next time." His voice returned to the trees in front of him.

Snoot's words bounced back, louder. "That weren't a fox, Tutti. . . ." Then his voice was gone, too.

Horton climbed upslope through the brush to the little cave where he'd hidden the shoot box. He lit a match: the discarded wire spools, empty Anfo bags, and a few leftover caps would stay where they were. Someone would find the meager cache and call it evidence, just as they would call three trees a forest.

He lifted the shoot box out of the cave and carried it carefully down through the tangle of rocks and brush to the edge of the palisades. Red and blue relay wires trailed behind him, tugging at snags, coming loose, following.

He climbed to the top of the highest boulder, shivering in the current of cold air coursing down the mountainside. He sat cross-legged and waited for his heart to ease itself into the pulse of Pompasook. The moon listened and approved.

It was a time for clarity, time to prepare for understanding and acceptance. He would undertake the burial of two pasts, one sacred and ancient, the other momentary and profane—both hammered into the same dark grave. He must be confident of his decision: Time would be fair to Truth; beyond the smoke and thunder and falling stone, the one and only true eternal spirit would prevail.

With the shoot box clasped tight to his chest, Horton looked out over a panorama of fertile valleys, gentle hills, and mirrored water. He lingered on the swollen mountains, eager forests, waving grasses, and imagined the extravagance of creatures sleeping, mating, hunting, dying through the perennial promise of the seasons, through ice and steam beneath a sky all-seeing, all-forgiving, and ingenious—everlasting. Horton looked into the Source, the Godhead—Creation itself, beyond possession—annealed the sight to his soul forever, and closed his eyes.

The wing nuts tightened over the wires, the condenser was charged. Light from a green bulb brightened his chin. He heard the murmur from the Great Place and prepared to enter for the final time.

Fingers did the bidding of the brain; the circuit closed. Horton Eagle-in-the-Wind rose to the stars astride the best shoot of his life.

Sitting at her kitchen table in the dark, Pearle felt the tremors, then heard the tidal wave of thunder washing down the mountain, and knew it must have come from the Ledges, the place that Horton had always called Pompasook.

Yawning, she rose and switched on the overhead light. Bud was supposed to have been up there on watchman's duty tonight. He'd talked about it being a dangerous place, about suspicious things he'd seen and heard, but Bud was always talking like that, always wanting to look like a hero.

Still, Bud was up there; she pictured him asleep. Then she pictured him awakened by the roar of whatever it was. Then she pictured him hurt, pinned under a tree perhaps, groaning. Then dead, blood on his face. She sighed; each picture looked so much the same. So empty. So pointless.

God forgive her, but it was time. It was *time,* she told herself, and she put into motion a series of actions she'd rehearsed so often over the years that she knew them by heart. Within ten minutes she had the prepacked suitcase out from its hiding place in the storage closet, her money belt on, her savings passbook and the Trailways bus schedules secure in her purse. Before she left, she watered the pot of ivy over the kitchen sink.

Bud's old truck would get her to White River in time for the 4:00 A.M. express to Albany. From there, a web of bus routes stretched across the country in a pattern intricate enough to lose anyone who wanted anonymity as much as she did.

She backed out the driveway and turned. Calm with

280

curiosity, she started up the mountain for one last look at Bud Benoit.

The truck rattled and groaned up Snoot's old driveway and across the flat where the house once stood. All the buildings and fences, orchards and stone walls were leveled, part of Bud's dumb idea of revenge, part of his childish fear of anyone who spoke his mind openly without fishing for something in return.

She wrestled the pickup up the hill across the old pasture, bouncing across the dirt track where the old hemlocks had grown. Her headlights crossed the windshield of Bud's Bronco, parked in a grove: it was empty, or he was lying down on the seat, out of sight. She got out to look, to find a picture, any picture; it didn't matter which.

The Bronco was empty, but there, beyond it, at the base of the Ledges, she saw a strange shape, something frighteningly unfamiliar and wrong, and its oddness immediately confirmed her conviction that it was time to go away and never come back. She stepped closer and squinted; the Ledges had fallen on top of the Lodge. Some stairs were the only thing left standing.

As if in a dream, Pearle circled the enormous pile of smoking rubble looking for a sign of Bud, rather than for Bud himself. She wanted to find a little token, a patch, a piece of him—not the blustering bullying whole—just a remnant, small enough to discard, to flick away from her, to feel the act of willful separation for the first and final time.

She walked the perimeter once, and half around again. What a nice going-away present, she thought, so neatly crushed, so perfectly packaged. She stood and measured her size against the enormity of what had been done—what could be done—and felt as tall and strong as she'd ever felt in her life.

Every dozen steps or so, she'd stop and look up at the Ledges, imagining the whole thing tipping over in slow motion, imagining a young and wiry Horton Flint—how else could she remember him?—blowing the cliff to kingdom come without a moment's fear. Horton Eagle-in-the-Wind,

281

soul of the wind; the wind itself, blowing away.

She turned and continued walking to a narrow space between the rock pile and the edge of an embankment leading down to the brook. There was a Port-a-san lodged in the mud below, a stink around it, horrible. As she hurried by, her shoe dislodged a stone, which rolled down the bank and clicked against the plastic shell. Bud's muffled voice surprised her.

"Who's there? Get me out of here, goddammit. *Please!* There's been an explosion, maybe an earthquake!"

Pearle nodded; a "please" from Bud was one for the books, but someone else would have to write it in. Her book was closed.

"Somebody? Help!"

Chief Bud Benoit would have to read himself to sleep from now on. Pearle kicked another rock over the edge, then set loose a little landslide of pebbles and rubbish, walking away as it clattered down the bank.

She drove down the hill through the pastures where Snoot had grazed his cattle. If only they could have been friends all these years; Snoot and Frouncy had always been neighborly enough. But Bud wouldn't allow her even Frouncy. If only Horton had come back—in person. If only.

She slowed down to a crawl past the flat part of the hill where Snoot and Frouncy and Junior had lived, all of it buried and gone and soon to be forgotten.

But then it wasn't all gone. At the edge of the hill, before she started down the lane through the trees, Pearle spotted something in the grass, a glint of moonlight sparkling on a shiny surface, a tiny piece of a brilliant star. She stopped and poked around until she found it, an angel, wings folded back, sculpted by the rushing wind. She picked it up and polished it on her sleeve. All the way to White River, she admired its beauty, and she decided it was meant to travel with her, to Albany, to New Orleans, to Santa Fe, to anywhere, a talisman at last, her very own.

They were a half mile east of the Ledges when suddenly the trail moved under Walker's feet, a jolt and a back-and-forth motion, as if bedrock had liquefied, the whole earth set to jiggling. He stopped in his tracks when he felt it, not so much to balance himself as to prepare for the sound, which he'd tried to imagine ever since they left the top.

As the tremors rippled up through his boot soles, he realized that his and Snoot's efforts had been no more than a naive prelude to the cataclysm under way. The impulsive decision to rush out and buy the house jacks, the giddy anticipation of rolling a boulder over the edge, seemed far away and frivolous now—and yet those feeble gestures were necessary, part of what it meant to care for the mountain, part of what gave them at least a tiny share in Horton's success.

From the beginning, Walker had sensed Horton's presence. Ever since the day he'd seen him looking down from the cliff above, he'd felt him watching, and tonight it was almost palpable. Maybe it was the noises he'd heard as he went down the Ledges to the Lodge, and the same, coming back up. It was nothing he could pinpoint, but there was something protective and surefooted around him, he would swear to it.

And what about Bud? Was it simple circumstance that distracted him from the doorway at the critical moment? Snoot knew the cry of a real fox from an imitation—as usual, he probably knew more than he was telling—and he didn't argue when Walker wanted to leave so abruptly. It made sense; Horton needed them out of there. The uncovered wire was his only mistake.

Or was it?

Snoot must have felt the tremors too. Walker found him turned around on the trail, looking back toward the Ledges, straining to hear what would presently follow.

Walker snapped off his flashlight, and as he did the concussion began. The first buds of explosion flowered into a hundred blossoms more. It seemed to grow up out of the mountain's core, gathering breadth and width as it grew and flourished in the freedom of a cool, dark night. The sky flashed red, leaves trembled in the trees; the atmosphere recoiled, hurt with the punishing sound of matter expanded and reconfigured, of energy unleashed—of redemption.

As he would remember it later, there was a pause before the second part, a moment after the bombardment stopped— when a return to silence seemed possible—a long moment, in which he dared picture a free-falling megastone, half of Rhode Island, imagined it arching through space, falling closer and closer.

The earth shook as it struck, shook only once, this time, leveled off, and held firm. Then the sound followed: compared to the first rolling boom of a gathering, additive blooming of thunder, the sound of impact was more finite and crunchy, a meteoric *splat.* Walker thought it sounded gorgeous.

"By the Jesus!" Snoot pushed past him, headed back to the Ledges. Walker followed, running wildly; he soon caught up and elbowed past on an uphill stretch, both of them laughing, gasping, grunting with pleasure, the beams of their flashlights flailing crazily at the trail.

They sloshed along the brook and finally came out of the woods at the foot of the Ledges. When they stopped, it was eerily quiet; moonlight fell like dusty pollen on the cockeyed landscape. Slabs of stone, taller than a man, were strewn everywhere, a patchwork blanket half an acre square. Where, an hour before, Walker had seen and touched and walked in a three-story building, only the west stair tower was left standing; the rest made a low hump in the middle of the blanket, faint token to the flattened mess below. Around the edges of the fallen stone, stacks of building material and a few job trailers stood lonely as abandoned cattle.

Snoot broke the silence: "Un-frigging-believable."

"Gone. Just *gone!* And look." Walker pointed upward to the Ledges. They looked taller, cleaner; a new face glistened and smoked in the moonlight. The boulders at the top, the bunker, the shelf they had stood on just minutes before were no longer there, the red and blue wires. . . . Where was Horton now? Walker shivered when he tried to speak his name.

"And, Jesus, what about Bud?"

Snoot laughed. "He's all right."

"How the hell would you know?" Sometimes Snoot was an arrogant pain in the ass.

284

"See for yourself." Snoot skirted the puzzle of broken slabs and stopped at the embankment in front of where the dining room once stood. Billy Ware's brook bed ran along the bottom of the slope. Snoot pointed at the water.

Walker saw the Port-a-san upside down in the mud. A car-sized boulder had been flung to within six feet of its upstream side. It made a dam in the brook; a new channel was being cut, to the east, making its way to the old, crooked serpentine.

"You still in there, Officer Bee-noit?" Snoot shouted, poking an elbow at Walker.

A thumping from inside the Port-a-san, then a muffled voice. "So there *is* someone there. Why'd you go? What are you waiting for? Get me out of here. This is an emergency!"

Snoot shrugged his shoulders to Walker, a question mark across his grin. "Time to shit or get off the pot, ain't it, Bud?"

Walker started down the bank.

Snoot grabbed his arm and pulled him back. "He's right to home. Let him fester."

Walker resisted—enough was enough—but then Bud was booming, a full-throated bellowing through the walls of the upended toilet. "I'll give you money, Audette, I swear"—*thump, slosh*—"I'll buy you all the cows you want." A pause: "Okay, then, *please!* Goddammit."

"Give the money to Baseball in the morning," Snoot shouted. "He'll be here early"—Snoot glanced behind him at the shorn stair tower—"looking for a job, same as you."

Now the voice was belligerent. "I won't forget this, Snoot Audette."

"I'm sure you won't." Snoot turned to go. "Just like I won't forget Pomona."

Walker led the way home, confident of the trail despite his dimming flashlight. Leaving Bud bothered him; he promised himself he'd go back to the site first thing in the morning to make sure someone had come to the rescue.

But the idea of the Ledges flung over the Lodge like a

lumpy rug, like a giant mosaic of six-foot-thick slabs, so suggestive of fury, so absolute and final that no amount of insurance payments, no bonding or buy-outs, would ever put the project back together again—it all seemed too miraculous, pure Eagle-in-the-Wind at work.

Walker would go back to the site many times, no matter what; he'd take Claire and show her what happened, and they'd stand in innocent wonder with the rest of the inevitable crowd, to speculate and guess and gawk, and he'd pinch himself, over and over again, to be sure what he saw was real.

By the time they crossed the field behind Fellows's barn, the flashlight batteries had failed altogether. They left them and the jacks hidden in the bushes beside the road and began the last leg home, side by side along the dark blacktop.

At the top of the little hill, west of the house, Walker saw the light from the upstairs bedroom window, a fuzzy yellow beacon in the distance. He touched Snoot's arm and pulled him to a stop. "It was better, Horton doing it."

"How'd you know he done it?" Snoot asked, playing dumb. "Could have been lightning."

"Gimme a break. You know it wasn't lightning." Walker swatted Snoot's arm. "Horton was the only one who could have engineered it, the only one who had it right."

Snoot was quiet. He rummaged in his pocket, then waved the scent of Red Man under Walker's nose. "Chew?"

"Nah." A few paces in silence. "Oh, well." Walker took a pinch and stuffed it inside his cheek. "Too bad about the jacks, and all the other stuff that didn't work."

Snoot went a dozen steps before he answered: "Like you said, it was better him doing it"—two more steps—"Tutti boy."

Walker stopped in the middle of the road and grabbed Snoot's sleeve. It was time to get something clarified between them, time to declare himself now and for all seasons, instead of waiting for that illusion of a perfect moment; it was time to settle up. He reached around Snoot's sweaty back and embraced him with both arms, squeezing himself and his mentor and hero into a single viable person. "I'm glad I'm not your *boy,"* he said, "because if I was, we'd probably never have been friends."

"Thought about that a few times myself, I suppose," Snoot answered, looking up at the horizon to the south. "See how pretty the moon plays on the Catamount Heights?"

Walker climbed the stairs two at a time, tipsy with excitement and tobacco juice, eager to talk. The light in the bedroom was muted and warm, like a summer sky half an hour after sunset. Claire was asleep in a silky white nightgown, bedcovers drawn down to her waist; a bearclaw necklace was draped across her bosom.

She woke to his touch. *"Walker!"* She hugged him long and hard. "It was on my pillow when I came upstairs," she said, touching the necklace. Her fingertips traced the shape of a silver rood at the center. "It was spread out in a perfect circle, like a display in a museum."

Walker sat close to her, studying the intricate work on the necklace. He'd heard all the stories; tonight he believed them. "Horton."

"But I never saw him, never heard a thing. I was reading in the living room until eleven, then came up to bed—and there it was."

"And you slept?"

"After a while. What time is it, anyway? I woke up a few times—once, to an incredible roll of thunder—are you okay?"

"It's late, and I'm fine, and you heard it, all right." The story would take awhile to unravel, even longer to put back together. "There was lots of thunder."

"And Snoot?"

"Good. Fine. We didn't do it, by the way. Snoot bent the jack handle into a pretzel—but it doesn't matter." Walker touched the necklace tentatively. "We didn't need to." Where could he begin? "The lightning was unbelievable. You could feel electrons buzzing through the air. And Horton was there. He was everywhere—even came to see you." He glanced at the necklace, the bear claws and cross.

"I think it's his goodbye present."

Walker heard the curtains twitching by the open windows. What had Snoot said about Horton? He's where he wants to be. He just *is*. "Maybe it is. It's the way he'd do it, isn't it?" Walker fingered the tip of a bear claw. "He's passed it on."

"Why wouldn't he talk to me?"

Walker hesitated. "Why would he start now? He probably thinks the necklace will tell you everything you need to know."

"I've worn it ever since I got in bed, and all I could think about was flying. Everything was flying around the room. I thought about the hospital, and it was flying."

Walker laughed. "Did you see me flying?"

Claire laughed. "No, but I saw Daddy flying up and down Pompasook's Tooth. Big hunks of it were flying. And then you were here." She pulled Walker onto the bed next to her. "Thank goodness."

"You want to hear one hell of a story?"

"Tell me."

He began, including every detail he could remember—the climbing up and down, arguing with Snoot, searching the building, Bud's silhouette, the fox, the wires, and on and on, up to the incredible sight of the Lodge crushed and buried—and as he spoke he felt a sad satisfaction gathering, something lost, something gained. He choked on the telling of what must have been Horton's patient presence, swallowed hard against an unpayable debt. "He was there, I swear, the whole time, waiting and watching us fooling around, knowing what he had to do. I feel like I owe him something, but I don't know what, or how to find him, or what I'd say to him if we ever met again."

Claire knew they would never meet again, just as she knew there was no way to ever know him if they did. Perhaps there was no way to ever know another human being—except to try, and hope, and endure.

She took the necklace off, put it on the dresser, and slipped out of her nightgown. In bed next to Walker, she listened to him talk, his voice rising and falling, sadly, happily—a good man; even her father had said so. She held him and listened to a story of thunder and lightning, retribution and redemption, until a pale glow seeped across the flank of Crooked Mountain, easing light into the valley.